The Way Home

The Angel Island Titles

THE INN AT ANGEL ISLAND

THE WEDDING PROMISE

A WANDERING HEART

THE WAY HOME

The Cape Light Titles

CAPE LIGHT

HOME SONG

A GATHERING PLACE

A NEW LEAF

A CHRISTMAS PROMISE

THE CHRISTMAS ANGEL

A CHRISTMAS TO REMEMBER

A CHRISTMAS VISITOR

A CHRISTMAS STAR

A WISH FOR CHRISTMAS

ON CHRISTMAS EVE

CHRISTMAS TREASURES

A SEASON OF ANGELS

Thomas Kinkade's Angel Island

The Way Home

KATHERINE SPENCER

BERKLEY BOOKS, NEW YORK

THE BERKLEY PUBLISHING GROUP
Published by the Penguin Group
Penguin Group (USA) Inc.
375 Hudson Street, New York, New York 10014, USA

USA / Canada / UK / Ireland / Australia / New Zealand / India / South Africa / China

Penguin Books Ltd., Registered Offices: 80 Strand, London WC2R 0RL, England
For more information about the Penguin Group, visit penguin.com.

This book is an original publication of The Berkley Publishing Group.

Library of Congress Cataloging-in-Publication Data

Spencer, Katherine, (date–)
The Way Home : Thomas Kinkade's Angel Island / Katherine Spencer. — First Edition.
pages cm
ISBN 978-0-425-25289-5
1. Cape Light (Imaginary place)—Fiction. 2. Angels—Fiction. 3. Christian fiction.
I. Kinkade, Thomas, 1958–2012. II. Title.
PS3553.A489115W39 2013
813'.54—dc23
2012045917

FIRST EDITION: April 2013

PRINTED IN THE UNITED STATES OF AMERICA

10 9 8 7 6 5 4 3 2 1

Cover image: *Hometown Pride* copyright © 2006 Thomas Kinkade.
Text design by Tiffany Estreicher.

To Thomas Kinkade,
whose talent has brought joy,
hope and inspiration to so many

Dear Friends,

It's always a pleasure for me to return to the Inn at Angel Island and to share the stories of the island's many visitors and catch up on the lives of the two women who run the elegant, hospitable bed-and-breakfast—Liza Martin and Claire North.

Liza has been managing the inn for more than a year now, and this summer she begins to see the seeds of her hard work bursting into bloom. The inn is flourishing, the rooms are filled, and the guests are delighting in the many pleasures of summer.

Liza knows she would never have come this far without the steadfast aid of Claire North, her cook, housekeeper, assistant, and everything in between. Claire's wisdom and quiet strength (and her legendary cooking) have been a touchstone for Liza and so many others.

But this summer, unshakable Claire is set off-balance by an unexpected visitor—twenty-year-old Jamie Carter. When they met at a shelter in Boston ten years ago, Jamie was a troubled boy, badly in need of care. Claire's heart went out to him and she even made plans to be his foster parent until a family emergency forced her return to Angel Island, and forced their separation as well.

Now a young man, wandering without goals or direction, Jamie is in even greater need of her guidance. Claire believes that God has brought them together again for a reason. But will God show Claire the way to help Jamie make a new start and head toward a brighter future? And will she have the strength and the faith necessary to face the possibility of failure?

Avery Bishop has also come to Angel Island to make a fresh start and find a new home. She's opening a restaurant called Café Peregrine. A talented chef, Avery is determined to succeed entirely on her own. Still reeling from a painful breakup with her fiancé and former business partner, Avery is determined to fly solo this summer in every way.

No wonder she's wary of Mike Rossi, the handsome owner of The Lazy Tuna—a popular eatery down the street. Mike is not only her main competition, but a charming, teasing distraction. Is he a rival she needs to avoid, or the sturdy hand who will guide her through the season's rough waters?

From the day Liza's Aunt Elizabeth opened the inn, she thought of it as a home away from home—a place where visitors would feel as welcomed as family. On Angel Island, where the cliffs that look like angel wings spread out across the blue sky, offering shelter and protection, it is easy to remember that God can help each one of us find a place to call home.

I hope you enjoy this visit to Angel Island, and may you always find the way home.

Katherine Spencer

Chapter One

"I guess I'll head out to the garden and catch up with the weeds now that we have the guest rooms under control." Claire North carried a large bucket filled with cleaning supplies into the spacious kitchen of the Inn at Angel Island, then stowed it in the broom closet near the pantry.

She and Liza Martin, the inn's owner, had made quick work of cleaning the second floor, most of which had been occupied over the weekend. Their guests had left in a flurry of farewells and compliments after one of the inn's legendary breakfasts. The kitchen was still in disarray, nowhere near Claire's standards, but she decided to tackle that job after lunch, when it would be too hot to work outdoors. It was only the first week in June, but spring was unusually warm this year, especially for New England.

Everything in the garden seemed to be blooming at once. While Claire gazed out the kitchen window, wondering where she should start—the vegetable patch or the flowers?—Liza filled two glasses with cold water and handed her one.

"Don't work too hard out there. I can do the flower beds later when I get back from town. I meant to weed them all weekend, but there wasn't a second to spare. We'll have a full house next weekend, too, and there's also a guest checking in today."

Liza kept track of reservations on her laptop and now had the computer open on the kitchen table. She gazed at the screen. "Bookings have definitely picked up this year. And we're just past Memorial Day."

Though the inn was open year-round, summer was their busiest season. Memorial Day was the start, the opening gun to a hectic sprint toward September and Labor Day Weekend. Summer passed so quickly. In the blink of an eye, Claire felt as she grew older. Why did the months and years seem to go by so swiftly as you aged? To children, the long blue and gold days of summer seemed endless. She often wished she could still experience the season that way.

Claire took a sip of water. It tasted so refreshing after her morning's work. "The warm weather must be bringing people out to the shore early this year, don't you think?"

"Partly," Liza agreed. "But we have to give ourselves some credit. Guests who were pleased with their stay are telling all their friends. And that review in the *Boston Globe* a few weeks ago was definitely a boost. We got a lot of calls from that one. We're starting off with a ton of reservations. And that's not even counting that big wedding rehearsal in July." Liza looked up from the computer. "We're going to be very, *very* busy."

"I'm sure we can handle it. I'll do more cooking in advance," Claire told her friend. "It's always a relief to have some extra loaves of bread or some chowder in the freezer. It does my heart good to see the rooms filled and a big crowd around the table in the morning.

Just the way it was when your aunt Elizabeth was here. I know she's looking on and feeling happy. And very proud." Liza had inherited the inn from her aunt Elizabeth almost a year and a half ago—a gift she shared with her brother, Peter. Their first plan had been to sell the property. But once Liza returned to the island, a magical place where she had spent many summers growing up, she decided to give up her city life and stay on to reopen the inn.

The inn had not entertained guests during the last two years of Elizabeth Dunne's life, and the beautiful Victorian was neglected and in a terrible state of disrepair when Liza took it over. Renovating the place and reviving the business had been a daunting job, with plenty of bumps and setbacks along the way. But Claire always knew that if Liza stuck with it, there would come a day when she'd be able to sit back and see the inn bloom again in full glory, a bona fide success. Now it seemed that day had come.

Liza snapped the laptop closed and smiled. "I think about Aunt Elizabeth a lot, too. I know she would be happy to see how well we're doing. I also think we're going to need some more help around here. I don't want to be burnt out by the Fourth of July. I'd like to hire someone soon, so they get to know the routine before we hit the high season."

"That shouldn't be too hard. Maybe a college student looking for some summer work?"

Liza had started jotting down a list of errands, but glanced up briefly. "Possibly. But we need someone who's responsible and polite. And patient."

Claire had to agree. Guests could be demanding. A good innkeeper had to learn the fine art of holding one's tongue. The customer was always right. Even when they were wrong.

". . . and someone who's willing to go the extra mile to make guests feel comfortable . . . and act happy to do it," Liza added. "You and I make it look easy, but we both know it isn't always. I would have trouble trying to list all the things we do in one day."

Claire knew that was true. She found that it was usually best not to think too much about the details of a long, complicated task, like getting the inn ready for guests or planting a big garden. It was far better to just dig in to the work than talk and fret about it. What was that old saying? A job begun is half done.

"Yes, a pleasant disposition and a willingness to work hard would be part of the job," Claire said. "But I have a feeling that just the right person will come along. These things have a way of working out."

"That's what you always say." Liza's smile was indulgent.

Claire returned her smile and shrugged. "It's usually true. Don't you think?"

Though she and Liza were alike in many ways, there were marked differences, too. When they first met, Liza had balked and even argued with Claire's perspective, which was based on her strong, calm faith and one of her favorite Bible verses: "Cast your burdens on the Lord. He will sustain you." By now, Claire could see that Liza not only accepted her view, she sometimes drew strength from it as well.

But before Liza could reply, they both heard the brass knocker rapping on the front door. Liza rose quickly from her chair. "I'll get it. It might be Daniel."

Daniel Merritt, Liza's boyfriend, was a master carpenter and all-round fix-it expert. He had practically renovated the inn by hand and dropped by almost daily to make random repairs, or to just visit with Liza. But Daniel usually came to the kitchen door, strolling in and pouring himself a cup of coffee, in his casual, charming way.

Claire doubted it was Daniel knocking so formally.

A moment later, Claire's hunch was confirmed. She did not hear Daniel's deep, distinctive voice but that of a young woman.

She went out to the hall to see if it was anyone she knew.

Liza stood by the front door with a young lady Claire did not recognize. Petite, with long brown wavy hair that was gathered at the back of her head in a messy bun, she wore huge sunglasses that hid half her face. She tugged on the handle of a large rolling suitcase, a big wicker bag slung over one shoulder. She looked hot and harried, though it wasn't even noon.

Liza turned to introduce them. "Claire, this is Avery Bishop. She'll be staying with us this week. Avery, this is Claire North, our cook, housekeeper, and everything in between."

Claire met Avery halfway down the long center hall. "Welcome, Avery. Let me help you with that," she said smoothly, taking the suitcase. She rolled it to the bottom step and turned back to their new guest with a smile. "Your room is ready. Do you have any more luggage?"

"A few small things, out in my car. I'll bring them in later. I know check-in time isn't until two. I just wanted to drop off my stuff. I can't stay. I have an appointment in a little while on the other side of the island," she added, checking her watch.

The watch had a large face and looked very utilitarian, Claire noticed, a sharp contrast to Avery's feminine, petite build. But she did look fit, her slim, toned arms revealed by a dark blue tank top. She looked as though she worked out a lot in a gym. Or maybe even did some sort of challenging, physical work.

"Would you like a cold drink before you head off? Some lemonade or iced tea?" Liza offered.

Avery hesitated a moment. "That sounds good. How long do you think it will take me to drive up to the north side of the island, where the ferry from Newburyport comes in?"

"About ten minutes. We don't have much traffic here," Liza answered with a smile.

"Then I would like some tea, if it's not too much trouble. I've been rushing all morning."

A few minutes later, the three women sat together on the inn's wide, shady porch, facing a spectacular ocean view. Avery had removed her glasses and looked up at Claire with stunning blue eyes. Eyes the same color as the sea, Claire thought. Avery smiled and murmured a thank-you as she took her glass of tea.

Claire had also brought a plate of bite-sized cranberry oat squares, left over from breakfast, and set them on a wicker table beside Avery.

"Mmm, these are great. They look healthy, too." After a few testing bites, Avery stared down at the rest of the cookie, as if analyzing its ingredients. "I'd love the recipe."

"I'd be happy to give it to you. Do you like to bake?" Claire sat back in a wicker chair next to her.

"You might say that. Cooking and baking are my life. I went to culinary school then studied in Switzerland and France for about two years. I've had a few jobs at restaurants in Boston, too. But now I'm just about to open my own place. Here on Angel Island."

Liza leaned forward, her eyes bright with interest. "How exciting! Did you find a spot?"

Avery nodded, loose strands of hair framing her pretty face. "Yes, it's a great location, right near the ferry station and the new beach. We're opening this weekend."

"Wow, that's soon," Liza said. "Are you ready?"

"I am . . . I hope," Avery replied. Her tremulous smile was an endearing mixture of excitement and nerves.

Liza laughed and patted her arm. "Take it from me, you're never really ready. But you'll figure it out as you go along. I didn't know a thing about running an inn when I took over here. Luckily, I had a wonderful teacher," she added, meeting Claire's steady gaze. "But it sounds as if you already have plenty of experience."

"I have worked in a lot of kitchens. I was a partner at the last place, the Tulip Café . . ." Avery seemed about to say more, then suddenly looked down and picked up her glass. "It didn't work out. But that was for the best. I'm sort of a perfectionist, I guess, the type of person who's happier doing things my own way than always having to compromise."

"A true artistic spirit," Claire observed with a mild smile. Avery did look like her own person; no slave to fashion in baggy, khaki shorts and flat, leather sandals. Her face was bare of makeup and didn't need any, Claire thought. She had a beautiful peachy complexion. Dangling silver earrings with blue beads brought out the color of her eyes. She was very pretty, though she didn't seem to realize it.

"What's the name of your restaurant?" Liza asked.

"Café Peregrine. I named it for the peregrine falcon that migrates to this part of New England every year. It seemed to strike the right note for me."

"Very pretty . . . and memorable," Claire agreed. "What type of food will you serve?"

"I'd call it New American cuisine, with touches of French and Asian influence. A lot of fish, of course. We'll have about thirty seats," she added. "That's small enough for me to change the menu every day, depending on what I find in the market. I want to mainly serve local seafood and produce. There'll also be a selection of fine wines and some fabulous desserts."

"That sounds lovely." Claire imagined the restaurant much like the small, sophisticated cafés in Boston.

"I can't think of any place like that in Cape Light," Liza said. "And none right here on the island."

"I'm glad to hear that. I wasn't able to find any competition in that niche either, though I don't know the area that well. There are a few comparable restaurants in Newburyport, but I have the water view and the beachy setting going for me. I've been staying in Newburyport the past few weeks," she explained. "But I wanted to be on the island now that I'm opening. I haven't had to time to look for a cottage or an apartment yet."

"It will be hard finding anything this time of year," Liza said honestly. "We can work out a discount if you would like a long-term stay here."

"Would you? That would be great. One less thing to worry about."

Liza smiled at her. "Check that off your list, then. We'll figure it out when you have a chance."

Avery finished the rest of her tea, then quickly redid her hairdo, pushing some loose strands back in the bun. She rose and grabbed her handbag, gracing Liza and Claire with a big smile.

She looked much calmer and more refreshed than she had when she arrived. Claire felt satisfied to see that. Claire considered it the very purpose of this inn—to provide a rest stop in peoples' lives, a welcoming place to renew and restore. Even for the few minutes it took to sip a glass of iced tea.

Avery glanced back at her watch. "Thanks again. You've both been so sweet. I'd better head off. I'm meeting an electrician at the café, and I don't want to stand him up."

The women said good-bye, and Avery headed off to her car, a small white SUV, parked in the drive at the side of the inn. She waved as she pulled out and turned onto the main road.

"Opening a new restaurant all on her own . . . Pretty brave, if you ask me," Liza said. "And she's so young."

"Yes, she is." Claire guessed Avery to be her in late twenties, at most. "But she seems very independent. I wonder if there's some way we can help her."

"I was wondering about that, too. We can recommend her café to guests and keep a copy of the menu on hand. But maybe there's something more we can do. Let's think about it."

* * *

As Avery drove north on one of the island's two main roads, she gazed out at the passing ocean view. She could have picked a lot of places to open her café. She had wanted to find a town outside of Boston, a destination that drew summer tourists, but not one that was too crowded, too expensive, or too built up.

She had been sitting in her dentist's office, paging through a magazine, when she saw an article about Angel Island and how the north side of the island had been improved to encourage more visitors, with a new beachfront, a boat slip, and a public park. There was a new ferry service from Newburyport that ran throughout the day and evening. Photographs showed the new ferry station house and an old-fashioned wooden boardwalk nearby that ran parallel to a short road with a few quaint-looking shops.

Avery was struck by a chill of inspiration; gooseflesh popped up on her arms. This was it. Angel Island. An opportunity to get in on the ground floor in brand-new summer destination. She had heard of Cape Light and had even stayed over in Newburyport once or twice, on weekend escapes out of Boston. She had heard of Angel Island but had never seen it.

She drove out to Cape Light the next day and then across the land bridge to the island. She told herself she just wanted to explore, especially the area featured in the article. It was a cold gray day in January, and the place looked nothing like the magazine photos. But Avery still felt sold on the idea of starting a business there.

As she walked down the boardwalk, there wasn't a soul in sight and a stiff, cold wind off the ocean made her huddle in her down coat. She easily found the row of old buildings on Ferry Street, all of them closed up tight for the winter. A sign posted on a shuttered window read FOR RENT OR LEASE right above a phone number. Avery peered in the spaces between the boards that covered the windows and could see it was a deserted ice cream parlor.

It was sort of a wreck inside. It would take time and money to transform the shop into the image she had in mind for her café. But once the freezers and the glass-topped counter where the ice cream was served were pulled out, it appeared to be spacious enough to fit the number of seats she wanted.

Peering in another window, she saw that the shop had a commercial kitchen in back, modest in size but large enough. Out front, there would be enough table space, she thought. She loved the location, and felt something deep in her bones, telling her that this was the spot.

Five months later, Avery still felt sure she had made the right choice. She parked in front then gazed at the blue-gray awning with its artful black script—*Café Peregrine.* In the window, another eye-catching but tasteful sign: JOIN US FOR OUR GRAND OPENING—THIS COMING WEEKEND. CALL FOR RESERVATIONS.

It was still hard to believe, but she had pulled it all together just in time for the summer season. It was all hers: lock, stock, and barrel, and she was very proud. And scared.

The boardwalk and beachfront were quiet today, but the area had been bustling with visitors over the weekend. Though Avery had been preparing the café for almost four months, she hadn't yet met all the other shopkeepers on the street. Most of the other businesses had just reopened for Memorial Day, barely a week ago.

Her closest neighbor was Sunshine Sundries, which sold everything a person could possibly need for a day by the sea—sunblock, beach balls, rubber shoes, cold drinks, and boogie boards. Avery thought the row of giant, inflatable water toys set up outside the store every day was a little messy looking. But the shop closed at five, and the owners did bring them in every evening. You couldn't worry about every little thing.

The next store on the street was Angel Island Anglers, a bait and tackle shop with a big display of fishing rods in the window and a handwritten painted sign that boasted NIGHT CRAWLERS, MEALIES, AND RED WIGGLERS. Avery didn't know what that meant and didn't want to know.

Surprisingly, there was no real competition for her café in sight. Just one lone eatery at the far end of the row, the Lazy Tuna. A FAMILY RESTAURANT. SOMETHING FOR EVERYBODY, one of the many signs there read.

Avery wasn't sure why, but even the name the Lazy Tuna annoyed her. How can a tuna be lazy? Was there such a thing as an industrious, motivated tuna? The whole idea of it was just . . . ridiculous.

Lazy or not, the Tuna was her only competition for miles.

And not much, she thought. She hadn't been able to sneak in and check the place out yet, but she was willing to bet the menu was just as tired and uninspired as the weathered signs, CIRCA 1960.

CASUAL DINING—LUNCH, DINNER, SNACKS & ICE CREAM. REAL HOME COOKING, FROM OUR TABLE TO YOURS. Translation: burgers, hot dogs, gluey chowder, and fries. It was no threat at all to the Peregrine. Her café would attract diners looking for more sophisticated fare, those sailing over from Newburyport on a pleasant ferry ride, just as the sun dipped below the horizon. She had advertised the grand opening in local newspapers, playing up the romance of a beachfront, gourmet dinner. She still had a lot to do this week to prepare for the opening; the Lazy Tuna wasn't worth worrying about.

Avery let herself into the café. It was hot inside, and she threw open a row of tall French doors she had installed in front, in place of the plate-glass window. She planned to keep them open most nights and set up outside tables under the awning. Which was why she needed someone to install the ceiling fans along with the light fixtures today. And check some other little glitches with the circuit breakers.

Avery had plenty to do while she waited. She hauled three large drawstring sacks of freshly washed linens out of her SUV and began to put them away in the new storage closet that stood near the entrance to the kitchen.

The table linens, purple and marigold yellow, gave bold touches of color to an otherwise spare decor. The wood floors were sanded and bleached white, with white wainscoting halfway up the walls. Above that, the walls were painted a soft blue-gray.

Black-and-white photos that captured local landscapes were hung in boxy, gallery-style frames—the various faces of the sea, bright days and stormy; a flock of terns skittering through the foam at the ocean's edge; the waving tall grass in the marshes; the Cape Light lighthouse at dusk; and the legendary Angel Island cliffs, a site Avery had yet to visit.

When it came time to buy furniture, Avery had found just the right number of white wooden tables and chairs at an auction, from a café that had gone out of business. She did feel lucky finding the bargain but felt bad for the previous owners. She didn't even want to imagine her efforts coming to that sorry fate.

She was happy with her choices. The decorating set just the mood she was looking for, relaxed and uncluttered, a beachy atmosphere but still neat and sophisticated. It was different from most restaurants in the area, and the food would be, too.

She heard someone at the door and turned to see the electrician.

"Hello? Anybody home?" he called out.

"Be right with you," Avery called back. She slipped a few more napkins onto the middle shelf then turned to meet him.

But just as she walked away, the new closet—bursting at the seams—began to sway and tilt toward her. Avery gasped and reached out to push it back. The tall, heavy unit was leaning so much that linens began to fall out. A few landed on her head, and she couldn't see. She didn't dare let go and hastily shook them off, like a wet dog coming in from the rain. "Help! This stupid thing is falling down on me!"

The electrician was already on his way and suddenly, right behind her, so close she could feel his strong chest against the back of her shoulders. He stuck out his arms, much longer and stronger than her own, and pushed on the closet.

Avery felt surrounded by him. She felt his breath on her bare neck and against her cheek. She dared a split-second glance over her shoulder. He was intent on his task but caught her gaze for a moment. He had dark eyes, chocolate brown, and dark hair to match. He was so close she smelled his aftershave and saw a shadow of beard on his cheeks.

She quickly turned and looked straight ahead. He was attractive, *very* attractive, and she felt something arc between them.

Suddenly the closet was in place again, and he stepped back. Avery took a moment to compose herself before she turned to face him. It had all happened so fast. In the blink of an eye. She wondered now if she had imagined it.

But when she finally looked up at him, she knew she hadn't imagined it. She couldn't quite believe what she was feeling. She was still reeling from a painful breakup. Ever since, men either seemed annoying or simply invisible. Somehow, in barely five seconds, this unknown rescuer had jumped up on her radar screen.

"Thank you," she said quickly. "I didn't realize the cabinet was so wobbly. I shouldn't have packed so much in."

Avery knelt to gather the fallen linens. He stooped over to help, giving her another jolt when their hands touched by accident.

"Close call. You were nearly buried alive in a pile of purple tablecloths. What a way to go." He handed her a napkin, and she nearly dropped it, too busy studying the dimple in his chin.

She stood up, holding the napkins in both hands. "Don't worry, I would have clawed my way out. I'm opening this weekend. That is, if you can hang the ceiling fixtures and figure out why the mixer keeps tripping the circuit breakers in the kitchen."

He looked amused at her request. "I'd be happy to try. But my expertise with wiring doesn't stretch much beyond lightbulbs."

Avery was puzzled. "You're not Done-Right Electric?"

He shook his head, looking even more amused at her confusion. "I'm the Lazy Tuna. Down at the end of the street? I've seen you coming and going here for a while. Sorry it took so long to say hello. Mike Rossi," he added, extending his hand.

This was the Lazy Tuna guy? She wasn't sure what she had expected, but it was nothing like this man—so fit and attractive. So close to her own age.

"Avery Bishop. Nice to meet you." She took his hand and quickly shook it. His grip was firm and strong but restrained, as if he were mindful not to crush her smaller hand in his own. "Thanks for saving me from the purple tablecloths."

"No problem. The shopkeepers around here have to stick together. We're a small but hardy bunch."

She heard his New England accent clearly in that remark but, for some reason, it seemed more charming to her than usual.

"I'm beginning to see that." The little commercial strip was out of the mainstream. She imagined that the shopkeepers did need to look out for each other.

Mike gazed around with interest. "You've done a lot. I can't even remember what it looked like in here before. Nice job."

"Thank you. I didn't have a lot of money to renovate, but I think it turned out well."

"Very well. Very . . . upmarket." She sensed an ironic, teasing edge to his compliment but couldn't quite put her finger on it.

Maybe I'm imagining that since his place is so different. Maybe he really does like it, she told herself, trying to give him the benefit of the doubt.

"I'm hoping to make my café a little different from most of the restaurants in the area," Avery said honestly. A little classier, she really meant.

"I can see that. What will the menu be—French food?" he asked. "Café Peregrine, that sounds French to me."

"The peregrine falcon migrates to this area every summer. I read about it. That's where I got the name," she explained.

"Oh . . . oh, right. I forgot," he added. "So the menu isn't French?"

He was curious about her food, wasn't he? Of course, that's why he was here, to size up the competition. *Well, I was curious about his place, too,* she realized. *I'm sure he can see we're not even in the same ballpark.*

Avery smiled patiently. "It's more New American, with some French and Asian touches. It's sort of eclectic, hard to categorize."

"Sounds interesting."

"Oh, it will be," she promised.

She put the crumpled napkins on a tabletop and began to fold them. They were soiled now and needed to be washed again, but she needed something to do. Whenever a guy like him said "French food" or "sounds interesting," it sounded like a subtle putdown. Not even that subtle, actually.

But Mike's smile and the teasing light in his eyes were so disarming, she couldn't be sure. Was he laughing at her, the newbie on the block with the arty photographs and purple tablecloths?

Quite possibly, but not in a mean way. Maybe he was just a down-to-earth, meat-and-potatoes guy who didn't do sauces. She had met plenty like Mike Rossi before.

"Are you running this place all by yourself?" he asked.

"I am. Owner, manager, and chef, all rolled into one."

He looked surprised. "That's an adult portion, if you'll excuse the pun. Where did you work before?"

Avery was used to this, other people in the business—especially men—doubting she could run a kitchen and the front of the house, as the dining area was called. She wasn't sure if it was because of her age, or because she was a woman, or some combination of the two.

"I was in a partnership in Boston, a little café in Cambridge, near Davis Square."

He looked impressed. "Nice location. I bet you did a good business there."

"Oh, we did. We were filled every night. For a while." With Avery's cooking and Paul's good looks and charm, the Tulip Café was always crowded. They had been so happy at first, riding a jubilant wave of success and rave reviews. Avery had never known anything more exhilarating than doing the work she loved best, side by side with the man she loved. The man she had hoped to marry.

But Paul had never loved her the way she loved him. Or maybe he started off believing he did, but all the success and attractive women vying for his attention had turned his head, and made him forget his commitment.

It was painful to think about those days, a mixture of happy and sad memories. Avery tried not to think about it at all.

She suddenly realized that Mike was staring at her curiously. "So how did you end up out here?"

Avery shrugged. "My partner and I had some differences. He was turning the place into a singles scene, and I wanted a real restaurant, a quiet spot with some culinary quality."

That part was true, too, though it was not the entire story. But she had not spent years at a prestigious cooking school and two more in Europe, only to run a kitchen at a place where the food was just a footnote to Happy Hour and the martini of the day.

She spared Mike Rossi the details.

"I decided to go off on my own. It was all for the best," she concluded, before he could ask more questions about that phase of her life. "I saw an article about Angel Island and how the waterfront near the ferry was being developed. So I came out and looked around. It seemed like a good opportunity, the right place to start something new."

Mike nodded, looking impressed. "That it is. Are you always so decisive?"

Impulsive, some people might say. But she liked his interpretation better.

"I can be . . . at times." *When I'm not flip-flopping, fretting, and driving myself crazy,* she added silently. "How long have you been here?"

"A long time. My dad opened the Tuna when I was a kid. I used to help him practically every summer when I was growing up. I took it over a few years ago, when he passed away."

His restaurant had been in the family. Avery found that interesting. So she couldn't hold him accountable for the name, could she? Though she doubted he had any objection to it.

Something in his expression had softened when he spoke about his father. Avery sensed he had admired his father and missed him. She had lost her own father recently and missed him very much. She was sure that if Ned Bishop had lived to see her launch out on her own, he would have been her biggest fan and cheerleader.

Fortunately, her mother had been very supportive, even loaning Avery some of her retirement savings for start-up money when various bankers kept turning down her loan applications.

Because Paul had called her a partner in the Tulip Café, she had never asked for a formal agreement. She had trusted him with her heart and soul—and all the business arrangements. They were going to be married. Drawing up a business contract just didn't seem necessary. She never dreamed she would end up leaving *their* restaurant empty-handed. She was grateful that her father had not seen that episode of her life.

When all was said and done, she was left with a diamond engagement ring. Paul had insisted on buying her a large round stone in a flashy setting, though it wasn't really Avery's style. But the money she received from the sale did help her start again, so that was one thing he had done for her.

Mike's deep laugh broke into her wandering thoughts. "—sometimes I think I've been running the Tuna too long. But here I am, another summer on the boardwalk. Guess I'll quit when I'm either too old to stand in front of a stove, or it's not fun anymore."

"That seems like a good approach," Avery said, though it was far from her own. She loved food, loved cooking, and loved feeding people. She was excited about the idea of running her own restaurant. But Avery wasn't sure if she would really call it fun. She took cooking seriously. Maybe too seriously.

It sounded as if Mike also ran the kitchen and the front of the house at the Tuna. And though it would seem only natural for two cooks to talk about food, something warned her off venturing in that direction. She was fairly certain they did not speak the same language when it came to menus, and decided to avoid the subject all together.

Avery was about to ask some polite questions about the island and summer visitors when she noticed that the real electrician had arrived.

Saved by the circuit breakers, she thought as a red truck that read DONE-RIGHT on the side pulled up in front of the café. No confusion about it this time.

A gray-haired man in jeans and a tan work shirt hopped out, opened the back of the truck, and took out at metal toolbox.

"Here's your electrical expert," Mike said. "Hope he gets everything straightened out for you by the weekend."

"I do, too. But rain or shine, lights on or off, we'll be open for business on Friday night."

She glanced at him and realized that her voice had taken on a tone she hadn't really intended. As if she were tossing a gauntlet of some kind. She hadn't really meant to sound so . . . challenging.

Then again, maybe I did, Avery realized. He had been perfectly friendly but they were still competitors, fishing in the same pool for their daily catch of customers. She couldn't let a few charming smiles and those warm, dark eyes make her forget it.

Mike smiled, looking amused and not at all offended. "That's the spirit. No guts, no glory, Avery," he added, as if they were already old friends . . . or familiar adversaries. "Good luck this weekend. If you need anything, just holler."

"Thanks." She smiled and nodded, though she doubted she would be hollering for Mike Rossi anytime soon. Under all that niceness, she had also sensed a certain "men are better at this business" attitude she knew all too well. And he was too attractive. She didn't want or need that either right now.

As the electrician walked up the path, Mike wished her luck again and walked out. She felt relieved to see him go and hoped she didn't run into him too much. Though their restaurants were so close, he might be unavoidable.

Well, you don't have to be so chatty next time, she chided herself. Mike Rossi was fun to talk with but . . . something about the Lazy Tuna guy just got under her skin.

Chapter Two

At this time of year, it took a keen eye to distinguish between the green tufts of leaves that were supposed to be there and the weeds that were not. About two weeks ago, Claire had cleared and hoed the patch of land she used for her vegetable garden and laid neat rows of small plants and seeds—tomatoes, lettuce, squash, string beans, carrots, strawberries, even a few rows of corn.

But the various sprouts could only be distinguished by her small, hand-lettered signs stuck in the ground on wooden stakes. Everything looked about the same size and color, and weeding was a tricky business. Sometimes the persistent invaders weaseled their way right into the middle of a useful plant, hiding there, hoping to escape her knowing gaze and gloved but nimble fingers.

Claire knelt in the soil, wearing knee pads over her baggy tan garden pants and a large floppy hat to block the sun. Gardening was so much like life. It took patience and slow, persistent effort, weeding away the distractions in order for the fruit to grow and flourish. That was your reward in the long hot days of summer to come, juicy ripe strawberries, plump red tomatoes, cantaloupe as sweet as sugar . . .

But Claire was not a long-suffering gardener, toiling unhappily just for the end results. She was as happy working in the dirt as she was in her spotless kitchen. She loved the scent of the damp, dark earth, the digging and yanking, the clipping and shaping. It was not work to her at all.

Despite her light shirt and hat, she still felt the heat as the day wore on and the sun rose higher. Liza had left for town and would not be back anytime soon. Claire thought she would stay outside until she felt too hot and hungry. She had been working over an hour and was making good progress. If she could weed half the garden today, she would do the rest tomorrow.

Totally immersed in her task, she didn't hear the footsteps on the gravel drive that continued all the way across the lawn behind the inn. She didn't realize anyone was there until a long shadow stretched across the rows of green plants, and someone called her name.

"Claire? Is that you?"

Claire sat back and turned so fast that her hat slipped off her head and fell on the ground.

She stared up at a young man who took a step closer. The sun was in her eyes and she could barely see his face, though she did see—or maybe just sensed—that he was smiling. She shaded her eyes with her hand but still didn't recognize him.

Though something in his voice did sound familiar. And something in the way he stood—his head titled to one side—and his shy, wary smile struck a distant chord of recognition.

"Miss Claire? Don't you remember me?"

Miss Claire . . . only one person in the world had ever called her that. Then she realized who he was and his words stabbed her heart, a painful but amazing stab that sent her rocking back on her heels.

"It's me, Jamie. Jamie Carter," he said quietly.

"Jamie? . . . Dear Lord in heaven . . . Is it really you?"

A silly question to ask, once she heard it out loud. She realized that when he just grinned and nodded in reply. She could never forget Jamie. Not to her dying day.

But she could hardly believe it was true, that Jamie Carter stood there on the lawn behind the inn. Claire wondered if she was imagining this. Maybe she had just been out in the sun too long.

She hurried to stand and stumbled a bit, her legs stiff and weak at the same time. He gently grabbed her arm, steadying her.

Claire tilted her head back and stared into his face, deep into his dark eyes. Heaven help her . . . it *was* Jamie. There was no mistaking it.

"It's really you. I can't believe it . . ."

Jamie didn't answer. He just laughed. An unmistakable sound that echoed like a bell in her heart and memories.

Claire smiled back then suddenly couldn't get a deep breath. She pressed her hand to her chest. Her knees felt weak as water, and the green surroundings began to blur.

"I'd better sit down . . . I'm a little dizzy," she admitted.

Jamie took her arm and led her to a chair in the shade. "Geez, I'm sorry. I shouldn't have snuck up on you like that. *That was stupid,*" he admonished himself in a heavy Boston accent.

He poured her a glass of water from the pitcher on the table and handed it down to her. "I didn't mean to scare you."

She was not scared. But she was shocked. Down to her bones. She remembered this boy every night in her prayers and had often asked God to reunite them someday. But she never expected her prayers would be answered today. Not in this way.

Claire alternated sips of water with glances at her unexpected visitor. He sat across from her, leaning forward in his seat, his hands on his knees. He looked anxious, waiting to see if she was all right.

"I can't believe it . . . after all these years," she said finally. "I looked high and low for you . . . How did you find me?"

"I saw an article about this place in the newspaper a few weeks ago. They printed your name and your picture. And your recipe for clam chowder. You told me you'd never give that out to anyone."

Claire laughed, though she was blinking back tears. "I did say that. But everything changes . . . Last time I saw you, you were a little boy. Now you're all grown up, a young man."

Jamie nodded, looking self-conscious. "Yeah, I am. No denying it."

There was no denying it. An image of Jamie as she had last seen him, a lanky, dark-haired ten-year-old, flashed before her eyes. He had changed a lot over the years, tall and lean, over six feet now, she would guess. But there was something in him that still seemed scared. And he still looked hungry.

She reached across the table and patted his forearm, just to make sure once more he wasn't a hallucination brought on by too much sun.

"May twenty-second," she said, announcing his birthday. "I thought of you that day. You were twenty years old. But I couldn't picture you any differently than when I knew you at Crosby Street."

Crosby Street Center was the soup kitchen and respite center where Claire had met Jamie. A visiting preacher had given a sermon at the church in Cape Light, where Claire had attended her whole life. Claire had been deeply moved by the minister's description of the neighborhood in Boston where he had organized volunteers to help those in need.

The huge, renovated warehouse was a haven for the neighborhood, offering food, clothing, and after-school care for children, or help finding work and navigating the city's support system for adults.

Claire had felt a call deep in her soul. She wanted to do what she could to help people less fortunate, to let God's love for the world work through her. Soon after hearing the Boston minister's talk, she'd left Angel Island to take a job at Crosby Street, putting her talents to good use in the big commercial kitchen. She had worked there for about two years, not a long time. But a phase of her life that was deep in meaning and memories.

"You remembered my birthday. That's nice." Jamie's deep voice, familiar and unfamiliar at the same time, broke into her thoughts.

"Of course I remember. I remember all about you. So much." Claire's voice cracked with emotion. She pressed her hand against her mouth. She didn't want to cry. After all, he was the one who had been hurt.

She could barely look at him, remembering what she had done.

"I'm so sorry, Jamie. I know you never understood why I had to go. I tried to find you. I came back to Boston to look for you. I went to your old neighborhood, your old school. I just wanted to know what had happened to you. If you'd grown up all right and finished high school. If you had gotten a good start in life," she added quietly.

If you had managed to avoid so many of the dark paths that surrounded you—trouble with the law, drugs and alcohol, she really meant.

"I just wanted to tell you that I was sorry," she confessed. "I know that I hurt you, that I disappointed you. I was brokenhearted to have to leave you. But I had a duty here. My father was so sick. He was all alone. There was no else to help him."

She had explained it all to him, way back when, and even put it all in a letter. But she was never sure how much of it a ten-year-old boy could understand.

Claire was crying freely now. There was no hiding it. She took out a tissue and wiped her eyes. Jamie rose from his chair. He leaned down and put his arm around her, patting her back a little awkwardly.

"Don't cry, Claire . . . Hey, we don't have to talk about that. I just wanted to see you, say hello. No big deal. Okay?"

She looked up at him and forced a smile. "Okay. I'm so happy to see you. I'm so thankful. What a gift. What a gift from God."

She stood up and Jamie hugged her. He was tall now. The top of her head just reached his shoulders. But his body was still rail thin. She could feel his bones under his loose T-shirt. The boy had always needed a good meal. Some things just didn't change.

Feeling composed again, she stepped back and looked up at him. "You must have had a long trip today. Can I fix you a bite to eat?"

Jamie laughed. "I was wondering how long it would take for you to ask me that. I was thinking, like, ten minutes."

"What has it been?"

He checked his watch. "You beat me by three."

"Good. I'm pleased to hear that, and I will take it to mean you would like some lunch. I haven't had any yet either. We'll have a bite out here and catch up."

Jamie followed her into the kitchen and watched her make two large sandwiches with roast chicken, lettuce, and tomato on freshly baked bread. Claire brought out some homemade coleslaw and pickles, adding them to the tray that Jamie volunteered to carry.

"These are super-sour, but crisp. The kind you like."

They were soon sitting outside again, enjoying their food and catching up on their time apart. Claire had so many questions to ask, she didn't know where to start. She did realize he might be sensitive about some of her inquiries. His early years had not been easy, and she had a feeling his life had not gotten much better after she left.

"Tell me about yourself. What are you doing these days?"

"Nothing special." He shrugged, talking around a mouthful of sandwich. "I've had all kinds of jobs after school."

"So you finished high school?"

He nodded and wiped his mouth. "Yeah, I made it. Last two years in an alternative school. Graduation was like . . . like getting out of prison," he said with a laugh. "I started at a community college. But I had to quit and take a full-time job. It wasn't working out."

Of course he would have to work. He didn't have anyone to support him. She wondered what had happened to his father, in and out of jail. And when he was out, prone to drinking and disappearing for weeks on end. Which was a good thing for Jamie, in a way. When his father was around, Jamie would bear the brunt of his angry, drunken moods.

The timing had been so unfair. When Claire had finally figured out just how dreadful Jamie's home life was, she began to investigate the processes of fostering and adoption. It wasn't even a week after that when she was called back to Angel Island to care for father. Once she left Boston, those plans had to be set aside. Was he ever taken out of that home?

Claire nodded, focusing on their conversation. "It's hard to juggle school and a job."

At least he'd finished high school. That was something.

Jamie was quite intelligent. She had no doubt that he could get through college and find some career path—if he had the means, the motivation, and the self-esteem it took to even aspire to such a thing. If only she had been able to help him when he was younger . . . But she didn't want to dwell on that. The past was past. Perhaps there was some way she could still help him.

"You've got your high school diploma. That's a big achievement right there. You're very young. You have time to go further with your education if you want to. You have plenty of time."

"Yeah, I want to go back. Someday. I needed to help my grandmother. She can't work anymore. She was just getting by. She was always there for me, you know?" He took another bite of his sandwich, his expression serious again.

Sally Carter, Jamie's grandmother, had been the only halfway stable influence in his life. Halfway, because she suffered health problems and could neither provide for Jamie nor control him. She shared the house with Jamie and his father. Claire hoped she had tried to protect her grandson.

"Do you still live with her?"

He shook his head. "I moved out a while ago. Now I share a place in South Boston with some guys. I'm sort of couch surfing 'til I can find a new job. It's not much, but it's a place to crash until I get my act together, find something better."

Claire nodded. South Boston neighborhoods could be rough. She couldn't tell from his tone if the place was a disaster or just a typical twenty-something apartment. In either case, Jamie seemed fine with it.

"What sort of work are you looking for?"

He shrugged again. "Oh, just about anything with decent hours and half-decent pay. I've had all kinds of jobs, working in warehouses, food stores, factories. I did some work as a house painter and a janitor in an office building. I even drove a taxi. The money was good, but I didn't like sitting all day," he said making a face. "I need to keep moving. It makes the day go faster."

Claire smiled. Jamie had been an active, almost hyperactive, kid. Did he still have that restless energy?

"I might try waiting tables again," he continued. "The tips can be good, especially in the summer if you work in some vacation place. Like, out on Cape Cod or up in Maine."

"It's hard work but not a bad way to earn money. As a summer job," she added, hoping that he also had some larger ambitions for himself. Then she caught herself. She hadn't seen him for what—more than ten years? Was she already judging his choices and plans? Was she about to start giving him advice on how to improve his life? There had been a time when she had earned the right to guide him, advise him, even correct him. But she had forfeited that right long ago. She had no business offering up any kind of advice now. All she could do now was sit and listen, get to know him again, as an adult. Accept who he was without judging but offering all the affection she had saved in her heart. Anything more would be worse than presumptuous—and might even chase him right out the door.

"Claire, I'm back. I got that plant food you wanted at the hardware store. Do you need it out here?" Liza came out of the kitchen door and first looked at Claire and then Jamie. "Oh, I'm sorry. I didn't know you had company."

"Liza, this is a dear friend, Jamie Carter. We haven't seen each other in ten years. But he saw that article in the *Globe* and came all the way out here to surprise me."

Liza seemed surprised by the story but managed a smile.

"Nice to meet you, Jamie." She sat at the table next to Claire and poured herself some water. "Do you live in Boston?"

"Yup. Always. That's where I met Claire."

"When I worked at the Crosby Street Center. I think I told you about that," Claire said to Liza.

"Yes . . . I remember.."

Claire had told Liza about her work at the center. But not about her special relationship with Jamie, how she had planned to become his foster parent or adopt him. It was hard to remember now how close she had come to calling him her son.

"Jamie and I were friends, special friends," Claire tried to explain.

"We're just catching up. It's been so long." She smiled at Jamie. "I still have a lot of questions I want to ask you."

"My life is pretty boring. Just working at dumb jobs and hanging with my friends. What about you, Claire? Have you been working here a long time?"

"Ever since my father died. First for Liza's aunt Elizabeth and now for Liza. The inn was run down for a while. I was more of a companion and housekeeper to Elizabeth toward the end than an innkeeper. But Liza whipped the place back into shape in no time. She's done a fine job."

"I wouldn't say 'in no time,'" Liza corrected her with a laugh. "The place is still a work in progress. But we are doing better and better. We should have a very busy summer."

"I like old houses. This one is really cool. You always told me about the island," Jamie said to Claire. "I used to try to imagine what it looked like, mainly when I was falling asleep at night. I know it sounds weird, but it's just like I imagined it."

Claire was touched by his admission. She had forgotten how much she used to talk about the place she called home. Building it up to some magical land in a little boy's mind. But if any place could live up to such lavish description, it was this island.

"You haven't even been on the beach yet. Let's go down for a walk," she said, rising from her chair. "I'll just bring all this inside and grab my sun hat—"

Liza quickly rose and shooed Claire away from the dirty dishes. "I'll clean up here. Don't worry."

Jamie stood up and glanced at his watch. "I guess I have time for a walk. My train doesn't leave for about two hours. All I need to do is call a taxi."

"Oh, no reason for a taxi. I can run you into town," Claire told him. "I'll just get my hat. It's in the kitchen."

Claire went inside and Liza soon followed. Liza put some dishes in the sink and stepped over to her, her voice low. "Would you like Jamie to stay over tonight? We can have dinner together and you can really catch up."

Claire was surprised and pleased by Liza's offer. She had been so busy asking Jamie questions, she hadn't even thought that far.

"Thank you, Liza. I'll ask him. I hope he will stay."

A short time later, Claire was walking along the shoreline with Jamie, trying to keep up with his strides. They had left their shoes at the bottom of the long flight of wooden steps that led down to the beach, and Claire had rolled up the bottom of her pants.

The tide was rushing in, and the waves tumbled one on top of the other with hardly a break between them. The midday sun beat down steadily, but Claire hardly felt the heat. The salty spray cooled them, and ocean foam soaked her pants almost to her knees. Claire didn't mind it. She didn't think Jamie minded either.

"I'm glad we came down here. I hardly get a chance to walk the beach in the summer. We're so busy most days at the inn."

"Really? If I lived here, I'd be swimming every day. This beach is awesome. Maybe I can find a job near the beach this summer. I think I'll go up to Cape Cod. There must be lots of summer jobs up there."

"There probably are," Claire agreed, though she suspected most of those positions were filled by now. Most hotels and restaurants hired summer help by Memorial Day. But she didn't want to dampen his spirits or seem critical. And he might find a job up there. Who could say?

She saw him glance at his watch and remembered Liza's invitation. "Jamie, you're welcome to stay over for the night if you like. Liza asked me to invite you."

He looked up and smiled. "Really? Sure, I can hang out a little longer. I don't have anything going on tonight. Do you do all the cooking here?" he added.

She nearly laughed. "Yes, I do. But I'm not going to tell you what I'm making for dinner. It will be a surprise."

"Okay. I can handle that. I'm sure it will be something good, surprise or not."

They talked a little more on the way back, and walked along in silence a while, too.

You never know what God has planned for you when you wake up in the morning, Claire thought as they started back up the stairs. Seeing Jamie Carter today was the last thing she had ever expected. She still felt a jolt of surprise every time she looked at him. Yet, talking to him seemed like the most natural thing in the world. They still shared some sort of bond, she thought, some special connection. That had not faded entirely, even after all these years.

Claire clung to that heartening thought as she began to climb the long flight of wooden steps. Maybe she could still help him in some way. Maybe God, in His wisdom and mercy, was giving her a second chance, sending him here. She truly hoped so.

AVERY Bishop had called the inn while Claire was on the beach and told Liza she wouldn't be back in time for dinner. She had too much work at her restaurant.

Claire prepared a simple meal for just the three of them. Not gourmet fare but an old recipe that she knew was one of Jamie's favorites—meatloaf with gravy, mashed potatoes, and string beans.

She had been glad to find she also had all the ingredients on hand to make his favorite dessert—strawberry shortcake.

After dinner, Liza went into her office to catch up on phone calls. Jamie helped Claire clean the kitchen and then joined her out on the porch. While she worked on her knitting, he opened a book, a paperback thriller he found in the inn's small library.

The book didn't hold his interest very long, she noticed. He had never liked reading very much. She remembered coaching him, word by word sometimes, on his reading assignments.

He walked around the porch and gazed up at the sky. It was a clear night, and a multitude of stars dappled the inky black sky.

"Wow . . . so many stars out here. You can't see any in the city."

"There's no moon tonight. That makes them even brighter," Claire said.

"Do you know the names of any constellations?"

"Oh, just the basics. The Big Dipper and Orion and such." The constellations every child learns about from a parent or grandparent. Maybe on a camping trip, or just some ordinary summer night. But he had missed those typical childhood moments. She remembered how Jamie would often be the very last child to be picked up at the center by his father or grandmother. She doubted there was any talk about stars on the way home. Some nights, he would wander out into the darkness all alone and a little piece of her heart would go with him.

"How do astronomers even know what they're looking at? How do they name all the stars and find them?" He wasn't really asking her to explain, she realized, just wondering out loud.

"That's a good question. It must be difficult, even with all their special telescopes." She sat quietly, pushing the yarn along the needles, adding one stitch and then the next.

After a moment she said, "I tried to find you." The thought

popped into her head and was voiced aloud before she even knew what she was saying. "After my father died. I tried very hard. I went back to Crosby Street and asked everyone who knew you. I went to your old school and your old neighborhood. I even hired a private detective," she added. "He couldn't find you either."

Jamie walked over to her chair and looked down at her. "I left Boston for a little while. With my dad. He took me to live in New Jersey. Then he got in trouble again and I went back to Boston to live with my aunt . . . It's okay, Claire. We don't have to talk about all that stuff."

Claire wanted to talk about it. She wanted him to understand that she had not forgotten him, even though it must have seemed that way.

"I want you to know that I tried. I really did," she said again. "But sometimes that's not enough."

She couldn't help but think how different his life might be now if she hadn't been forced to leave the city without him. Or if she had been able to find him after her father died.

Jamie shrugged and flopped down in the chair next to hers. He picked up the book again but didn't open it. "Who knows? I try not to get hung up on stuff like that, sad things you can't change. It only brings you down."

Claire nodded. She understood what he was trying to say. You couldn't live in the past or dwell on what might have been.

"I didn't get it when I was a kid, but I understand now why you had to come back," he said. "I'm not mad about that."

Claire had written him a long letter and gave it to him the day she had to go. She had explained to him the reason she was leaving. She knew from the look on his face, he hadn't heard half of what she was telling him. She had always hoped that later, in a quieter moment, the letter had helped him understand. But he didn't mention the letter, so she didn't either.

"Thank you, Jamie. Your forgiveness means a lot to me," she said honestly. She hoped with all her heart it was true.

She put down her knitting and turned to him. "I am so very happy that you found me. I know it can never be the way it was when you were a boy. But I hope we can start over and be good friends again."

"Yeah, well . . . sure. I guess, I thought we kind of still are friends . . . or I wouldn't have come out here."

"I hadn't thought about it that way," she admitted with a smile. From the outside, it seemed as if she was the one who had been doing all the helping. But she knew then, and she knew now, her bond with Jamie, his affection and trust, had brightened her life and made it richer in so many ways. He had helped her back then more than he would ever know.

Today, they had been given a second chance, the type that doesn't come along very often. Claire prayed that she would not squander it. Or let it slip from her grasp.

Tonight, she would fall asleep offering prayer upon prayer of pure gratitude.

Chapter Three

Avery had not returned to the inn Monday night until eleven. Claire had been in the kitchen, preparing things for breakfast. She heard Avery come in and go straight up to her room.

But here she was at half past seven Tuesday morning, the first one up, except for Claire herself, who always rose at six whether or not she had work to do. She liked to start her day when the world was quiet and still. It helped her feel centered and peaceful.

Avery came into the kitchen where Claire stood before the stove, waving a metal spatula like a symphony conductor, as she orchestrated a meal of French toast, bacon, and a salad of orange slices and strawberries.

"Breakfast is almost ready. It'll be just another minute or two. Help yourself to coffee," Claire told her, nodding at the big coffeemaker on the far side of the counter.

Avery filled a mug to the brim. "This smells good. Dark roast, just the way I like it," she murmured. "A little cinnamony," she noted between sips.

"I add a dash or two," Claire confessed. She turned the bacon strips with a pair of tongs. The scent was enticing, sure to lure Jamie from his room, she had no doubt.

She checked the first wave of slices, golden on both sides and nicely puffed. She slid them from the pan and set the platter on the table.

"You can start, if you like. More to come," she promised.

"That looks delicious. But I have to run." Avery had finished the coffee and refilled the mug. "The staff is coming in to finish the setup, and we're going to do some training."

Claire dipped more bread slices in the batter and set them on the hot skillet. "Sounds like a full day. Have you found good help?"

"I think I have. It's hard to know in this business until the heat is on . . . if you'll excuse the pun," Avery added with a grin. "But everyone is experienced and excited about the grand opening."

"How many have you hired?"

"Two waitresses, a kitchen helper, and a busboy. I wanted to find a seating hostess, someone who could manage the floor. But I can't afford it right now. I guess I'll be running in and out of the kitchen for a while. I need to see what's going on in the front of the house when we start off anyway."

Claire turned back to the toast and flipped the slices. "The grand opening is still set for this weekend?"

"Kicking off Friday night. I know today's only Tuesday, but that's not much time." Avery checked her watch. "I have to run. I need to make some calls. I'm still missing a few deliveries."

Claire understood Avery's urgency but didn't think she should race off with only coffee in her stomach. Breakfast was the most important meal of the day. "At least take a little something with you," she said, offering the young woman a yogurt and a banana.

Avery thanked her and stashed the food in her big purse. Claire wondered if she would ever find it. "I probably won't be back for dinner again. No need to wait for me."

Claire had expected that. "You have a good day. A productive one, too." She watched Avery rush out the kitchen door as if someone were chasing her.

Liza came into the kitchen just as Avery left. She walked over to the coffeemaker and filled her mug. "Was that Avery? Leaving already?"

"She has a lot to do today. She's training the staff. She's hired four people so far."

"That sounds about right for a restaurant of that size." Liza picked up the *Cape Light Messenger*, which sat folded on the table. "Our ad won't appear until tomorrow. I hope we get a good response."

"Are there many other ads today?"

Liza kept her gaze on the newspaper as she answered. "I haven't gotten to the classified section yet. I'm stuck in the news articles. Did you know there was a Garden Tour in Newburyport last Sunday? Guess we missed it."

"That would have been enjoyable. Might have even given us a few ideas for the property, but we weren't free last Sunday," Claire reminded her as she brought the food to the table.

"Maybe once we find a good helper, we can take turns sneaking away and having some fun, doing what all the tourists do when they come here," Liza said, still scanning the paper.

"Maybe we could." Claire shifted in her seat and took a sip of coffee. She listened for sounds from the second floor. All quiet on that front. Jamie was not up yet, though she expected that with the scent of bacon filling the inn, he would be down shortly.

"There's something I'd like to ask you, Liza, if you have a minute to talk. It's just an idea, and I won't be the least offended if you don't—"

Liza looked up from the newspaper and closed it on the table. "You think we should offer the job at the inn to Jamie."

Claire couldn't tell if Liza was in favor of this idea or not. But at least the notion had crossed her mind, too.

"I do. He's worked as a waiter and also as a janitor. That's relevant to the job here, don't you think? And he's very good with people," she added. "Very smart and catches on quickly. I'm sure he'll be happy to do whatever is asked of him."

It would be a good opportunity for him, too, she thought. It sounded as if he didn't even have a decent place to live. He would get free room and board working at the inn and be able to build some savings over the summer. Maybe even enough to go back to school.

But she held her tongue. She didn't want to overwhelm Liza with all her thoughts on the subject, which had spun through her head for hours. Liza had taken a slice of French toast and was fixing it on her plate while she listened. Claire could tell she was trying not to smile.

"Sounds like you've thought this out pretty thoroughly."

"Yes, I have. I thought about it a lot last night, before I fell asleep. I prayed about it. And when I woke up this morning, it seemed clear to me. Hiring Jamie will help us—and help him."

It seemed the perfect solution, an ideal way to keep Jamie close, help him get back on his feet, and back on a good track.

"I know you want to help him, Claire, and he's a very nice young man. I enjoyed having dinner with him last night, I really did," Liza began. "But I'm just not sure. You haven't seen him in a long time. He may have changed. He may be very different from the boy you remember."

"He's grown up. He's more mature, that's for sure. But that's a good thing. I don't think he's changed, not really. I'll make sure he knows what's expected," Claire promised. "I'll treat him just like any other person starting off in this job."

"I'm sure you would supervise him. But if it didn't work out, it could be a problem." Liza's expression became serious. "It could be very difficult if we had to let him go. Especially considering your friendship with him."

Claire knew that was true. But she couldn't help feeling as if there were some unseen hand in this situation; the amazing coincidence of Jamie finding her just when he was out of work and there was a job here, perfectly suited to him. Claire felt very sure she was not the only one who would be watching over Jamie and helping him do well here. She felt sure that the good Lord above had brought him to her doorstep for this very reason.

Liza had finished her breakfast and pushed the dish aside. "You never told me much about Jamie or your relationship with him. I can see now that it was very important to you."

"It was. Still is," Claire added, lifting her gaze to meet Liza's. "Jamie was always special to me. I don't really know why. There were so many children coming in after school every day. The center was just a big drafty warehouse, fixed up inside, painted bright colors, clean and safe. And free to their parents," she explained.

"We gave them meals and helped with homework. We gave them school supplies and coats, or winter boots. But what they really needed most was attention. Someone who cared what sort of day they had. Someone who cared if they understood their homework or did well on a test or got scolded by their teacher. There were so many stories at the end of their day." Claire smiled, remembering. "When my work in the kitchen was done, I would go out to the main rooms and help with the children. My heart went out to all of them, but

Jamie was the one who caught my eye. Always quiet, hanging in the corners. Didn't smile much, or have many friends. His clothes were usually dirty and mismatched or outgrown. I could see he wasn't just shy. He was scared. It took time, but he began to trust me. I was the only one who could help him with his schoolwork. We would memorize multiplication tables or the names of the fifty states."

He never cared how long he had to wait. He only wanted her, Claire recalled.

"As soon as he got to Crosby Street, he would come to the kitchen door and look for me," she added. "I would give him an apron and gloves, and let him do small tasks. Something fun, like making cookies. He took it very seriously. He was very proud when we brought the cookies out to the other kids." Claire could still see him, a skinny little boy carrying a platter piled high with treats.

"I knew that he lived with his grandmother," she went on. "But she had problems of her own. Sometimes his father lived there, too. He drank heavily and disappeared for months at a time. Which was a blessing of sorts . . . because Jamie's father abused him, verbally and physically."

"Oh, dear. That's awful." Liza's tone was sympathetic. "What did you do?"

"I didn't even know at first," Claire admitted. "Jamie was so good at hiding the truth from everyone. Ironically, he adored his father, made some sort of hero out of him in his mind. I was very angry at myself at the time for not seeing the signs. But once I did, I tried to get him out of that terrible household. He was removed once, but sent back," she recalled. "I was applying to foster him myself, and maybe eventually adopt him, when my father needed me here." Claire sighed, remembering one of the saddest days of her life. "My last afternoon at the center, I tried to explain to Jamie why I had to go. But he didn't understand. He was far too young. Later, after my father died, I tried very hard to find him. Now . . . out of the blue . . . here he is." Claire shook her head. "I can hardly believe it."

Liza nodded, taking in the story. "Thank you for telling me all that. I knew that you really cared about him, but I had no idea the situation was so . . . so intense."

"Intense," Claire repeated. "I guess that is a good word to describe it."

"I didn't realize you had such a hard choice to make. An impossible choice," she added. "I didn't really understand why giving him this job seemed so important to you. Now I do."

It had been hard for Claire to share her memories, especially the most painful ones. But it seemed a small price if Liza could be persuaded.

"It is important," Claire admitted. "It would be a great favor to me if you would agree. If your only objection is that it might be hard to let him go—hard for me, especially—please know that I will accept the situation if it comes to that. Though I don't think it ever will."

Liza gazed at Claire and rubbed her cheek with her hand. Claire knew she was putting her employer—and good friend—in a difficult spot, but she felt it was for a very worthy reason. Claire believed with all her heart that Jamie would not disappoint them. Liza would look back on this conversation and wonder why she'd had any objection at all.

"All right. We can offer him the job," Liza said finally. "You seem certain he'll be good at it. You know how much I trust your judgment."

"Thank you, Liza. I think with some training he will do well. I'm sure you won't regret it."

That was all he needed. Just a decent opportunity and some help putting his life on a good track. There was no limit to where he could go with that kind of wind at his back. Claire felt very sure about that, too.

Liza carried her dish to the sink and put it in the dishwasher.

"Why don't you tell him about the job when he comes down? If he's interested, I'll talk to him about the pay and the hours and all that."

Claire thought that was a good plan. Liza left for her office, needing to check e-mails and make some calls this morning before working on the flower beds.

Jamie came down to the kitchen a few minutes later, wearing a clean T-shirt Claire had found for him the night before. His hair was combed back from his shower, and she noticed the red flush of sunburn on his nose and cheekbones. It was probably from their walk on the beach; he hadn't used any sunblock. He would get into the habit once he started working here. That would be one of her rules, for sure.

As he poured himself coffee, she noticed that he had a train schedule tucked in the back pocket of his jeans. "There's a train to Boston in an hour," he said. "Do you think I could make it? The next one after that isn't until eleven."

"That's plenty of time. I'll drive you to the station. No need to call a taxi. There's French toast and bacon on the table. Help yourself."

Jamie sat at a clean place and filled his plate. She could tell he was trying hard to be polite and not take too much at once. Though he looked tempted to simply tip the entire dish of bacon onto his own.

"You're the last one down, so don't be shy."

He fixed his French toast with butter, syrup, and cinnamon before taking a bite. "Mmm, this looks good. I never eat a real breakfast like this . . . unless I go to a diner or someplace like that."

"You should learn to cook. It isn't hard." She was about to remind him of how he had helped her in the kitchen at Crosby Street, but decided this wasn't the right time.

"I can make a few things. Scrambled eggs," he said between mouthfuls. "But not like this. This is really good."

"I'm glad you like it." Claire enjoyed watching him gobble down the breakfast. She couldn't deny that. She waited until he was almost done eating, then said, "Before you go, I'd like to talk to you about something. We need someone to help here at the inn. Liza took an ad in the newspaper yesterday. But I had an idea that you might be interested, and I suggested it to Liza."

"Me? Working here?" He seemed surprised but pleased. "That might be cool . . . What did she say?"

"She said I could offer you the job, and if you wanted to take it, she would talk to you about the salary and hours and all the other details."

"Sure . . . I'd like a job here. What would I have to do?"

"Oh, a little of everything it takes to run an inn. You might help serve meals and clean up the kitchen. We would need you to clean rooms and carry guests' luggage. You might help us do small repairs, like freshen the paint on the picket fence in back or patch a window screen. Daniel Merritt does all the big repairs and painting for us, but he can't run over every minute." She paused. "Do you have a driver's license?"

"Yeah, I drove a cab, remember?"

"Yes, you did tell me that. Well, then you might drive guests back and forth to the station, and do errands in town, like shopping or going to the hardware store. You might also help with the outdoor work. You'd be good with the lawn mower, I just have a feeling. Better than me and Liza."

"It's like, I'd be working all over, wherever you needed me?"

"That right. That's it exactly. It's very important for the person who takes this job to be flexible. Then again, you would be doing something different almost every day. So it wouldn't be boring. And meeting new people all the time is never dull. The guests who come here are very interesting."

Claire waited, giving him time to think things through. He had to make his own decision.

Jamie nodded and bit the fingernail on his thumb, a gesture she suddenly remembered from his childhood. He did that when he was nervous and didn't know what to say.

"I'm sure you can do it. I'll be right here, helping you every day."

He nodded and looked up at her. "Okay. I'd like to try."

"Good. I'm very glad," Claire said honestly. "It's just a summer job," she added, making sure he realized that. "Liza will talk to you about your pay. But you would get free room and board, so you could save some money while you worked here. Until you found something better, that is."

"Room and board is a good deal. You almost don't have to pay me at all after that."

Claire laughed. "I don't think you'll say that after you've worked here a day or two."

"Do you live here year-round, too, Claire?"

"I'm here so much, most people think I do. But no, I have a cottage on the other side of the island. It is a ride late at night or in bad weather, so I have a room here, too. I stay over most nights in the busy season so I can start breakfast on time and all that. I don't mind. It's a lovely place to be in the summer and easier for me, too."

"That makes sense." He nodded. She wondered if he had heard half of her explanation. He seemed to be thinking very hard about the job offer. He suddenly stood up from the table and took his dish to the sink. "Will you tell Liza I said yes?"

"I'll tell her," Claire said, smiling.

Jamie cleared the rest of the dishes off the table and started wiping it off with a sponge. Wasting no time getting started. That was a good sign, Claire thought.

Everything was falling into place. As if it were all meant to be. She truly felt it was and took a moment to offer up another prayer of thanks for Jamie's return to her life.

AVERY and her staff spent most of Tuesday morning doing more setup work in the café. There were still dishes and glassware to unpack, and cartons of nonperishables to be stored in the kitchen and small pantry that doubled as Avery's office.

Avery had bought some of the cookware used, at the same auction where she found the tables and chairs. Her new kitchen helper, Teresa Biggs, did not approve of the careworn pots and pans, and spent most of the morning scrubbing them down in the deep sink.

Like most professionals, Avery had her own special sauté pan and a set of knives that traveled with her wherever she cooked. She had not put those items out in the kitchen yet and wouldn't bring them in until Friday. For one thing, she didn't want Teresa to pounce on her prized, seasoned pan and possibly scrub a hole in it.

Teresa was a small, sturdy woman who wore her brown hair in a knot at the back of her head, and a red bandana tied low across her forehead. She needed a stepstool to take command of the big sink, where she wore long yellow gloves that reached over her elbows. But her bare arms, visible above the gloves, were pure muscle, and she handled the pots—some as big as she was—like a pro.

She told Avery that she worked in the school lunch program during the year and needed a summer job. A cafeteria was not the best recommendation for the fine cuisine Avery planned to serve, but Teresa was so amiable and clearly hard-working that Avery knew instinctively she was tough enough to take the heat in a small, short-handed kitchen.

Avery also felt lucky to find an experienced waitress, Gena Turner, who lived on the island with her husband and three children. Gena's husband, a fisherman, had already given Avery some good contacts for finding fresh seafood at a local market.

Gena was a few years older than Avery, but they had hit it off instantly; Avery felt they were becoming friends.

"I would love to have my own restaurant someday, but it's pretty intimidating," Gena confessed as they worked together, carefully hanging wineglasses on wooden ceiling racks above the bar.

"Yeah, it is," Avery admitted. "But I've gotten this far. It will all be over by Friday. Once the doors open and we're serving customers, it won't feel so scary anymore."

"I think you're right. We just have to get the ball rolling. Are you inviting anyone special, like your family?"

Or a boyfriend, Avery knew Gena wanted to ask. But she was too polite to pry about her new boss's social life—or lack of one.

"I really wanted my mom and sister to come up from Connecticut, but my sister, Christine, can't get the time off and my mother can't drive here on her own. They'll come later in the summer. It might even be better not to have them here for the opening. That way, I won't be distracted."

Avery was trying to look at the upside of the situation, but secretly she was disappointed that her family would not be there to celebrate her big night.

"That's too bad. But I think you're right. Sometimes when you're trying to impress your family, it can drive you crazy. I can give great table service to perfect strangers but totally screw up a holiday dinner."

Avery thought Gena must be exaggerating. She had only known

her for a week or so, but so far Gena seemed capable in every way, with an easy, no-fuss attitude that seemed immune to stress.

"That's the way it is sometimes, in my family, too." Avery didn't bother to mention that her sister was the only person she knew who could make a lemon out of lemonade. It would certainly be easier to face opening night without worrying about one of Christine's critiques.

The café had not received all the scheduled food deliveries yet, especially the perishable items. Avery planned to shop at local markets herself for most of the fruits and vegetables. For that day's lunch, she had picked up some big sandwiches and salads at the General Store, and her staff sorted them out.

First, though, they would try a dish that was pure Café Peregrine. She and Teresa had been experimenting with a recipe for sweet potato chips with a creamy yogurt dipping sauce. The staff was now going to sample their efforts and offer reviews. Jack, the busboy, pushed a few tables into one, and they all sat together. There was something for everyone, and they all seemed satisfied with their choices.

The chips and sauce got raves, and when lunch was done, it was time for some training. Avery was not looking forward to the session, but it had to be done.

At the Tulip Café, Paul had been in charge of the staff. He had a way with the employees, especially pretty waitresses. Avery tried not to dwell on that now. But she did try to remember how he ran the sessions.

"Okay, everyone, I hope you enjoyed your food. I just want to review the type of service we're aiming for. You guys, out on the floor, are as important as the food, the decor . . . even the ocean view. We all know of great meals that were ruined by poor service. The success of Café Peregrine is literally in your hands. So, from the start, I'd like to be clear on what our goals are."

Avery had made a point of saying "our" goals. Not simply "my" goals. She wanted everyone to feel invested in the enterprise and building its success. She so wanted the café to be known for great service—polite but not fawning; courteous but professional; friendly and helpful but not overly chatty. But how to convey all that—and without insulting anyone? Avery knew she was treading a fine line.

She scanned her small audience, wondering how best to reach them. Jack, the busboy, and Serena, a college-age waitress, both seemed bored. Jack was checking his text messages under the table, and Serena was checking her manicure. Gena and Teresa sat together at the other end and were giving her their full attention, which Avery appreciated.

"Let's try this. I'll be a customer, and we'll just act out serving a meal." Avery smiled as if to say, "Hey, kids! Won't that be fun?"

Serena looked at Jack and practically rolled her eyes. Gena slipped Teresa a small, tolerant smile. *Sort of silly, but she's the boss . . .*

A few moments later, the Café Peregrine Follies had begun, Act I, scene I, Avery thought. She stood at the restaurant's entrance, where a large reservation book stood on a high podium. Serena was going to have the first turn seating the customer, and Gena was going to wait on the table.

Avery went outside and walked in, going straight up to Serena, who discreetly removed a wad of gum from her mouth with a tissue. Avery decided to act as if she hadn't seen that. Serena wouldn't dare pull something like that once they opened, would she?

"Can I help you?" Serena said.

Avery nodded. "Yes, I have a reservation. Avery Bishop, at six o'clock."

Serena pretended to look in the book. "Let's see, where are you . . . Just give me a sec."

Avery winced. "Just say, 'Please give me a moment, and I'll check.' "

"Um, okay. I hope I can remember all that."

"I'll write it out for you at the top of each page. All you have to do is read it," Avery told her.

"Okay. Can we keep going? I have to be at my other job by three." Serena had two jobs. She was a very hard-working girl, Avery had to grant her that.

"No problem. Keep going."

Avery put on her customer face again, and Serena continued.

"Let me show you to a table. Right this way. Follow me . . ."

Avery followed her to a table in the middle of the café. The row of French doors stood open and a cool sea breeze whispered through the space, ruffling the edges of the tablecloth.

"Okay, here you go. Have a seat." Serena abruptly pulled out Avery's chair.

"Great . . ." Avery forced a smile and sat down. "But you can just say, 'Here's your table.' "

Serena nodded. "All right. Here's your table," the girl parroted. "Anything else?"

Avery could tell she was getting annoyed. But this was important. She would have a talk with her privately about her attitude.

"One more thing, you need to say, 'I'll get your waitress. She'll be right over.' Otherwise, people feel a little stranded, as if no one knows they're there."

Serena nodded. "Right. You mentioned that before. I forgot."

"That's okay," Avery said. "It takes a while to remember everything. But do smile. You have a very pretty smile. That counts for a lot."

Serena smiled at her compliment, displaying her deep dimples.

She would do fine, Avery decided, if she would take it a little more seriously. Real customers—and real tips—would probably be more inspiring.

It was Gena's turn next. She walked up to the table smoothly, menus under one arm. "Hello, how is everyone here tonight?" she said amiably. "Welcome to Café Peregrine. My name is Gena, and I'll be serving you." She handed Avery a menu. "May I get you something to drink while you're deciding? We do have a few specials tonight that I can tell you about . . ."

Avery breathed a sigh of relief. If only she could clone Gena, she could happily stay in the kitchen all night.

While Avery waited for her fake drink order, Gena returned to the table with a serving of sweet potato chips and dipping sauce.

"A little something from the chef, to start off your meal," Gena said cheerfully.

The chips smelled good and looked even better, Avery thought, sampling one.

Gena returned. "Have you made your choices, or would you like a little more time?"

Perfect. Avery beamed at her. "I have a question about the halibut," she said. "The menu says it's served with a soba noodle cake. What is that exactly?"

She had gone over the menu with Serena and Gena last week, and wondered if Gena would remember.

Gena was holding back a self-conscious laugh. "Wait . . . I've got this . . . Just give me a second . . ."

"Take your time," Avery said. She bit her lower lip. Okay, one slipup. Gena was otherwise batting a thousand.

"Soba noodles are a traditional Japanese noodle, made from buckwheat flour. They're served either cold with sauces or hot, in soups," another voice answered.

Avery spun around. Mike Rossi stood just outside the French doors. When she met his glance, he smiled and walked into the café. As if she had invited him in. Which she definitely had not.

"I've never eaten a cake made from soba noodles," Mike said in a relaxed tone. "But I'd love to try it. Sounds pretty tasty."

Before Avery could answer, she heard Gena say, "Hi, Mike. Thanks for helping out. I was sort of stuck."

"No problem. What is this? A dress rehearsal?"

"Sort of," Avery admitted.

Except that no one was dressed as they should be. She looked particularly awful, she realized. Her baggy cargo shorts and an old black tank top were grounds for arrest by any roaming unit of the fashion police. Working in the hot, sweaty kitchen for the last few hours had not improved her appearance either.

"Cool. Can I watch?"

Avery couldn't tell if he was serious. It was difficult enough to run her staff through this drill without an audience, especially a glib, teasing one. She decided to ignore the question. Luckily, the sweet potato chips distracted him.

"Those chips smell good. Are these little starters?"

He reached across the table to take a chip, and Avery stifled the impulse to slap his hand.

"Hmm. Interesting. Nice seasoning . . ." He chewed thoughtfully. "Did you put some cumin on there?"

"And a touch of garlic powder. A little sea salt, too," Teresa quickly replied.

"It's the amuse-bouche," Avery told him, using the proper terminology.

Mike's eyes widened. "The *what*?"

"The freebie you give out when they sit down. So they don't get too restless waiting to order," Teresa explained.

"Like a dish of coleslaw or pickle spears?" he asked.

"That's right," Gena answered cheerfully. "In French it means amuse the mouth . . . or tickle the palate. Right, Avery?"

Avery had explained the term when the staff went over the menu. "Exactly," she said, forcing a smile.

"Cute. I'll have to remember that." He caught her eye and smiled again.

Could he be any more condescending? Avery thought of a few snappy comebacks but decided they were all beneath her. Amuse-bouche was a real term that people in the restaurant business used all the time. Why did Mike Rossi make her feel like some . . . some pompous prig?

Gena turned to the others. "This is my friend, Mike Rossi," she said introducing him to the rest of the staff. "He owns the Lazy Tuna, down on the corner."

Avery watched Mike greet her crew. Even around a second mouthful of chips, his natural charm shone through. Teresa blushed up to the edge of her bandana when he shook her hand, and Jack, who mostly moved like molasses in January, jumped out from behind the bar to meet him.

"You own the Tuna? Cool. I love that place. I could eat three meals a day there."

Avery restrained herself from sighing out loud. Doubtlessly, a college boy like Jack Malloy would prefer Mike's menu over hers any day. But did her own busboy have to be so unabashedly starstruck by the King of Fried Seafood?

Mike didn't seem to notice her distress. He just stood there, soaking up the adoration.

"Hey, thanks, pal." Mike slapped Jack's shoulder. "Come down to the Tuna sometime and say hello."

Avery stared at him, her arms crossed over her chest. He finally seemed to get the hint that he'd overstayed his welcome.

"Sorry to interrupt your rehearsal. I'm sure everything will go fine on your grand opening. Good luck, everybody!"

Her crew sang out a chorus of thanks-yous. Avery felt obliged to chime in. "Thanks, Mike. See you around."

He met her glance a second and waved, then slipped out through the French doors, into the sunshine.

Once Mike had left, she stared around, unable to remember what course they were up to. Had Gena even taken her order?

Gena stood by the table with her pad and pencil out. "Want to keep practicing?"

Gena was the last person who needed this dry run, Avery thought, and of course, the most willing to comply. The others stood waiting for her to answer.

"That's all right. Let's take a break."

Serena had already taken off her apron and had her handbag slung over her arm. "Okay. But remember you said I could leave at three?"

"That's all right, you can go," Avery replied.

"Should I make more chips?" Teresa picked up the basket and peered inside where a few crumbs clung to the white parchment paper. "Boy, these went over big. Somebody liked 'em."

They both knew that somebody was Mike. He had more than sampled the prop; he had made a meal of it when she wasn't looking.

"I think Mike stuck a few in his pocket," Avery joked. "I guess he doesn't serve many dishes like this at the Lazy Tuna."

Teresa glanced toward the Tuna with a dreamy smile. "I don't know about his cooking, but he's a very nice guy and kind of cute."

"I didn't notice," Avery fibbed. "And you're married." *With children and grandchildren,* she could have reminded her. "You shouldn't be noticing these things."

Teresa laughed. "I'm married, honey, not blind. And neither are you."

Avery sighed. She wasn't going to win this debate. Why even try? She picked up the stray menus and busied herself stacking them.

Okay, he's attractive. She would grant him that. But what difference did it make to her? None at all.

She had a fairly low opinion of all men right now. Not to mention being totally focused on getting her business off the ground. She had zero interest in dating at the present and had promised herself that if she ever did start to date again, she would not even consider a guy in the restaurant business.

Which included Mike Rossi. Especially Mike Rossi. So why was she even wasting one millisecond thinking about it? It was definitely time to get back to work.

If only those dark, laughing eyes were not so firmly stuck in her mind. Avery shook her head, trying to dislodge the image. She definitely did not need Mike Rossi in her life. But she knew that if she was honest, she had to admit there was a part of her that wouldn't mind seeing him again.

Chapter Four

CLAIRE met Jamie's train on Friday morning at nine. He had been in Boston since Tuesday, packing his things and doing whatever a young man his age had to do before leaving town for the summer.

He waved when he hopped off the train and walked over to meet her, carrying a large duffel bag and a knapsack over his shoulder.

"Hey, Claire. I made it."

Claire was so happy to see him. She wanted to give him a hug but restrained herself. "Yes, you did. Right on time."

She had honestly been afraid he might oversleep and miss the train, which had left the station in Boston before seven. She was relieved to see he was responsible enough to keep his appointments.

They walked to her Jeep, which was parked in front of the old-fashioned station house. Jamie had on the same pair of jeans and black sneakers she had seen on Monday, but he wore a plaid cotton shirt with short sleeves and a stand-up collar that must have been brand-new. The fabric was still stiff and creases in the front showed where it had been folded in its package.

He had also gotten a haircut. A chunk of dark brown hair still flopped across his eyes, but was not nearly so long. He was trying to make a good impression. That was a good sign.

"I need to make a quick stop at the store, then we have to hurry back. Several guests are checking in this afternoon. The rooms are ready," Claire explained as she started the Jeep and headed toward the village. "But there's still plenty to do."

Jamie nodded. "Okay. Whatever you need me to do, I've got it covered."

She smiled at him briefly. It was so good to see him again, sitting beside her in the car. Once or twice this week, she had wondered if she'd imagined the entire thing—Jamie coming so far to find her and Liza giving him a job at the inn.

But here he was, back on the island, and would remain for the rest of the summer. Enough time for her to make amends for abandoning him so long ago. Enough time to win his trust and be a positive influence in his life.

The drive to the inn passed quickly. Claire pointed out a few local sights on the way.

"Where are those cliffs you used to tell me about?"

"The cliffs are on the other side of the island," she explained. "I'll take you there sometime—maybe next week when the inn empties out again."

They drove up to the inn and found a large shiny SUV parked on the curve of the drive that circled in front of the entrance.

A group of guests had arrived, though it was barely ten. Check-in time was twelve noon, but Liza never had the heart to remind anyone of that. Liza had come out to greet their new guests—two middle-aged couples who were traveling together.

Claire parked on the side of the inn and grabbed the shopping bags as she got out of the car. Jamie reached in back for his duffel and knapsack.

"You'd better leave those for now. Go help the guests with their luggage and see if Liza has anything else to send up to the rooms." There were often requests as soon as guests walked in the door—extra towels and pillows, tea or coffee, hair dryers and ironing boards.

"Oh, right." Jamie dropped his own bags in the backseat again and loped toward the SUV.

One of the men tugged at a large suitcase stuck in the trunk. The bag was large enough for a month's vacation, Claire thought, with a smile.

"Hey, mister, hold up. I'll help you with that." Jamie trotted across the gravel to the car.

Claire winced a bit. "Hey, mister" was not the most cordial address. But the guest looked pleased to have a helping hand. Jamie pulled the suitcase out with ease and grabbed a canvas tote. He soon got all the bags into the inn, and Claire watched the man follow, sifting through the front pocket of his khaki pants for a tip. She had nearly forgotten. There would be some tips with this post as well. Claire never accepted tips, though they were often offered. But she was sure Jamie would and she saw no harm in that. It was definitely a perk to the job.

Claire headed for the kitchen with her grocery bags, but Liza stopped her to introduce the guests.

The Rapps had been at the inn the summer before. They had first come early last summer and liked it so much they returned again in August. This time they had brought their good friends, the Foxes. Both couples appeared to be in their early sixties and very fit. Claire remembered that Mrs. Rapp was a dedicated bird watcher; her binoculars were already strung around her neck.

Mr. Rapp liked Claire's cooking. He was a tall, lanky man whose slim waistline belied his large appetite. He rubbed his hands together, anticipating the meals to come. "What's on the menu for lunch today, Claire? I told the others we couldn't stop and spoil our appetites."

"A few things you might enjoy: Rhode Island chowder and a seafood pasta. And some johnnycake. I recall you like that."

His eyebrows rose into his hat brim. He quickly turned to his friends. "Claire makes the best johnnycake you ever tasted. She makes the best . . . everything."

Claire blushed at the compliment. "Let's not go overboard. I wouldn't want your friends to be disappointed."

"No chance of that," Mrs. Rapp assured her.

Jamie had made another trip to the car and brought up all the Foxes' luggage as well. He came down the stairs looking a bit breathless, his new shirt already wrinkled. But he was smiling, looking pleased to have completed this first official act.

"Thank you, Jamie. I have to save my back for golf," Mr. Fox said. "I can't let that old guy beat me every weekend."

The two couples went upstairs, laughing at their repartee. Liza and Jamie followed Claire into the kitchen.

Liza picked up a pad from the kitchen table. "Good to see you again, Jamie. And I was glad to see you jump right in there."

Jamie shrugged. "No problem. That's what I'm here for."

"One of your jobs, for sure," Liza said. "There will be a lot more bags to carry before the weekend is over. I made a list of chores you can work on today. I put a check mark next to the most important. If you can't get them all done, don't worry. We get interrupted here a lot."

Liza glanced at Claire. "Claire will show you what to do, but you should get settled in now. Your room is on the third floor."

"I put a navy blue spread on the bed," Claire added. "It's at the end of the hall."

"Do you have any bags?" Liza asked him.

Jamie nodded. "Out in Claire's Jeep."

"This is a good time to bring them in. There's a dresser and closet in the room. I think you should find everything you need. Just come down to the kitchen when you've unpacked."

"Thanks. I'll be right back," he promised.

After he left, Liza turned to Claire, who had started to rinse off the clams she was going to use for the chowder.

"Well, so far, so good," Liza said. "He'll be thrown in the deep end this weekend. I had another call this morning, and that fills the second floor."

"Good thing you told me. Sounds like I'll need to stretch this chowder." Claire always bought a little extra and knew she had enough ingredients. Besides, it wasn't the amount of clams necessarily but the quality of the broth that made good soup.

"Oh, you're a magician in here. I'm not worried about that." Liza patted her arm. "Look over that list and let me know if you think it's too daunting for his first day."

"I think the first day at a new job should be daunting. Then it will always seem easier after that," Claire replied.

Liza laughed. "You have a good point. I'm going into the office for a little while. See you at lunch."

CLAIRE was not used to having a helper. It was almost as time-consuming to explain to Jamie what he had to do and how to do it than to do it herself.

She didn't realize that she would feel that way. It was a surprise to her, and she even had to laugh at herself when she was showing

Jamie how to sweep the porch and wash it down without ruining the paint or getting any of the wicker furniture wet. Claire usually took care of this task early in the morning, before most of the guests were up, but there had not been any time today.

Everything had to be moved to one side of the porch, and then everything had to be moved to the other. The trick was to keep the water stream steady and pointed down, so the entire house wasn't dripping all day.

Jamie started off all right but used too much water pressure, and Claire feared he would peel the paint right off the boards.

"Slow down. The water is too hard," she said.

"It's okay. I get it, Claire. I can take it from here."

Jamie didn't mean to spray her, but as he tried to keep hold of the hose and adjust the water, Claire tried to grab hold of it, too. Startled, Jamie dropped the hose and it jumped around on the porch, spraying in all directions, as if it were alive. By the time Jamie got hold of it and turned off the water, the two of them were soaked, head to toe.

"I'm so sorry . . . I didn't mean to spray you."

He did look truly sorry. Claire had to laugh as she wiped her face on her apron. "That's all right. It's a hot day. That was . . . refreshing." Then they both started laughing.

After the porch was cleaned and set to rights again, Claire showed him the power mower and edger. She was relieved to see he knew even more about lawn work than she did. Among his many jobs, he had worked for a landscaping company. The day passed quickly, with Jamie mowing the lawn and cleaning off the bikes in the barn.

Claire gave him a short break in the late afternoon to clean up and rest in his room. Later, he ate his dinner quickly in the kitchen while the guests lingered on the porch with appetizers. Then he helped Liza serve dinner in the big dining room.

After dinner, his last official act was taking out the trash. When he came back inside, Claire had just finished with the kitchen and was making herself a cup of tea.

"Anything else?" he asked. She could tell from his tone he was weary and sorely hoped that she was going to say no. But it was good of him to ask anyway.

"That's it for today. Thanks for all your help."

He nodded, looking relieved. "No problem."

"Would you like some tea?" She filled a teapot with boiling water. There was plenty there for two.

"I'm good . . . What are you going to do now?"

"Sit on the porch and knit."

"Oh, right."

"There are some books in the sitting room. I think you may have left the one you started the other night."

"It was sort of boring . . . Is there a TV around here somewhere?"

Claire checked her tea. "We do have a TV, a very nice one. But we only use it for emergencies. It's down in the cellar, locked up."

She waited and watched his expression. Surprised at first, then disappointed. Then he realized she was teasing him.

"Right, good one."

"It's in the sitting room. Just open that big hutch across from the couch. The remote should be in there, too."

"Great. I just wanted to see how the Sox are doing."

"Help yourself. No problem with that at all."

When Claire walked out to the porch with her knitting and tea, she saw that Jamie already had the TV tuned into the ball game. He sat on the sofa while he talked on his cell phone. All the guests had left the inn soon after dinner, and he had the sitting room all to himself.

He worked hard all day and deserves some relaxation now, Claire thought, glad he was able to find the game he wanted to see.

* * *

It was half past eight on Friday night, prime time for dining out. At least back in Boston it had been. Avery kept telling herself to focus on the cooking, but she couldn't help walking over to the kitchen door every other minute and looking out to see if any more customers had come in.

She had taken three or four reservations during the week and hoped that more customers would walk in during the night. But so far, the dining room had been practically empty.

Embarrassingly empty. *Frighteningly* empty. Avery's dark side couldn't help embellishing it into a full-blown disaster.

Calm down. It's the first night in an out-of-the-way place. It's not like couples are strolling around a busy neighborhood, looking for a place to eat. People have to come out here intentionally in the evening, she reminded herself. *It's not a place for random traffic.*

She was glad now that her mother and sister had not been able to come. She would have been even more anxious and embarrassed at the poor showing on her big opening night.

She just hoped Mike Rossi didn't saunter by again. He would probably have some clever remarks tomorrow about the lack of traffic in the Peregrine. Or maybe not. It pained her to admit it, but the truth was, he was probably too busy to notice what was going on in her restaurant. She had walked outside and looked down the street at his place a few times so far tonight.

The Lazy Tuna was bursting with customers, a noisy, boisterous crowd of adults, kids, and seniors. Every seat seemed to be filled, with pop music blasting from speakers over the wooden picnic tables set up outside.

Inside the Peregrine, you could hear a fork drop despite the mellow jazz standards playing on Avery's sound system. Mike's music was practically drowning out her own.

She would have run down there and asked him to lower it, but that would have meant admitting her café was quiet and empty.

Avery was preparing an order of halibut. The menu listed the fish sautéed with a special glaze, but the customer had asked for it plain broiled.

No fun at all, Avery thought, slipping the fish onto a dinner plate and adding a garnish. But the customer is always right. She had done the best she could with it.

Gena ran into the kitchen as Avery was cleaning off her cutting board. "Do you have anything back here you can throw together for kids? A couple just came in with two children, about five and seven. Chicken nuggets, mac and cheese?"

Mac and cheese? It took Avery a moment to wrap her mind around the idea. Of course, there would be families on vacation out here, but she had never thought of this café as a likely destination for children. Still, she had better rethink things if she didn't want their parents to wind up at the Tuna. It had been a mistake not to list anything for them on the menu.

"That's four covers, Avery," Gena reminded her when she hesitated. "We've only had six other customers so far—"

"All right, all right. I can do mac and cheese, no problem." Avery pressed her fingers to her forehead, a little habit she had when she felt stressed. As if to hold the top of her head on when it felt like it might blow off. In a calmer voice she added, "We have some fresh orecchiette and artisanal—"

Gena had handed in the order for the table to Teresa and was already halfway to the kitchen door. "It's better if I don't know. Just use a lot of butter and make sure the cheese isn't too smelly."

"Coming right up," Avery promised.

Teresa started on the appetizers—steamed mussels with white wine and garlic, and an arugula salad with goat cheese.

Avery set some water to boil for the pasta then stared into the big steel fridge, wondering which of the exotic cheeses she had on hand was the least odoriferous.

"There's a block of cheddar, down on the bottom. Behind the cream," Teresa told her.

Avery eagerly dug out the modest New England staple, good old cheddar cheese. She set in on the work table, sliced off a chunk, and dumped it in the Cuisinart to shred it.

"Is this your secret stash of cheese?"

Teresa laughed. "It's Jack's. Whenever you go out on an errand in the afternoon, he makes himself cheeseburgers."

"Cheeseburgers? Where does he get the burgers?"

"Oh, those are hidden back in the cold box somewhere. You'll have to ask him if you want to borrow a few."

Avery sighed. "It is slow out there . . . but not slow enough to add burgers to the specials."

A short time later, all the dinner orders were filled and no new customers had come in. Avery felt so fidgety back in the kitchen, she put on a clean white jacket, smoothed her hair—which she wore in a tight bun while cooking—put on a dab of lipstick, and walked out in the café. It was half past nine. Customers filled exactly four of the tables. She doubted that many more would come in now, but she walked from table to table with a welcoming smile and asked how everyone had liked the food.

Some reactions were very enthusiastic, some merely polite. While she got more yeas than nays, to Avery, a tepid response felt crushing. A young couple in the corner, holding hands across the table, was the most lavish with their praise. Avery could have stood listening to them compliment her all night.

And almost did. Until Gena gently tugged her away. "Sorry, but you told me to say something if you were hovering."

"Was I hovering? I thought I was just . . . chatting."

Gena gave her a kind but doubtful look. "No one wants to go out for a romantic evening and have the chef sitting in their lap."

"Oh, right." Avery could not argue with that. She was trying to advertise her café as the perfect setting for a romantic dinner. She didn't want word to get around that food was good but the chef stalked the patrons. Not good.

As she headed back to the kitchen, she caught a bit of conversation from an older couple. "—the place is pretty, but the halibut was a little dry," the husband complained.

Dry? Aren't you the guy who asked me to hold all the sauces and broil it to smithereens? Avery wanted to whirl around and counter. But she just bit her tongue, waiting to hear what the wife said. "I liked my dish. You just ordered the wrong thing."

Avery took a breath, feeling vindicated. Until the husband said, "If you ask me, we should have gone down the street to Larry the Tuna."

"The *Lazy* Tuna," his wife corrected him.

The husband waved his hand at her. "Whatever."

Avery stomped into the kitchen, wanting to cry and scream at the same time. She stood at the steel work table, taking deep breaths to calm her nerves.

Teresa came up beside her and rested a hand on her back.

"What happened to you? Did you eat a bad scallop or something?"

"I'm fine, thanks." Avery marched to the cold box. "Tell Gena not to let table three get up from their seats. Tell them the chef is sending out a special dessert."

A few minutes later, Avery watched from the window in the kitchen door as the Lazy Tuna fans practically had a duel with their teaspoons as they devoured their complimentary dessert.

"They loved it," Gena reported gleefully. "They practically licked the dish and left me a huge tip."

"Score one for our side," Avery murmured.

"What did you send out there?" Teresa had been busy at the stove and hadn't seen the final masterpiece.

"The Chocolate Barge, with an extra-heavy cargo of praline ice cream and bittersweet fudge sauce."

An admiring light shone in Teresa's small blue eyes. "Like I always say, when the going gets tough, the tough get cooking."

"Two orders of the Barge," Serena announced coming into the kitchen.

"I got this," Avery told Teresa. It was a small victory, but something.

But at half past ten it seemed apparent that no one else was coming to dine at Café Peregrine. Serena asked if she could go. She had a date in town. The rest of the crew stayed, and by the time they shut the door, Teresa had cleaned the entire kitchen. Jack set to work sweeping and mopping the floor while Gena stored the dishes and glasses that had gone through the dishwasher.

Avery was busy making everyone a late dinner. She had told them to order anything they wanted from the menu. Most restaurants gave their staff an evening meal, but it was usually an inexpensive dish, pulled together by the chef with odds and ends.

Even though the night had not gone as planned, everyone had worked hard. Avery still wanted to celebrate her first night in business; she wouldn't let this rough kickoff bring her down.

She was sure that the tips had not been great for her servers. Some waitresses would complain, but Serena and Gena had not said a word. She hoped business would be better as the weekend went on, for their sake, too.

They gathered at the big steel work table sitting on high stools, and Avery served them each her special dishes. They talked and laughed and finally relaxed, joking again about the couple who gobbled their dessert and the kids who had curious looks for their gourmet mac and cheese.

It was half past eleven, but Avery could still hear music from the Lazy Tuna. She was sure her staff could hear it, too, and felt grateful when no one mentioned it.

CLAIRE was not sure how long she had been out on the porch knitting. She just wanted to finish the sleeve of the sweater she was working on. The murmur of the baseball game floated out through the sitting room window, a pleasant, summer night sound, blending with the dull, distant beat of the ocean waves and the soft hum of insects out in the darkness.

On her way up to bed, she passed the sitting room and peeked in. Jamie was stretched out on the sofa, fast asleep, his head propped on a throw pillow, his long legs dangling to the floor.

His cell phone was on his chest, buzzing and vibrating. She was surprised it didn't wake him.

She didn't mean to breach his privacy, but it was not hard to read the short message that lit up the screen.

Yo dude. Hanging @ Ryans Pub.
Where is $$$ U owe me, man?

Claire took a quiet step back. She shouldn't have looked at the message; it was private. But now that she had, it made her wonder.

Jamie owed someone money. Was that why he'd come out here—seeking help but not being able to say it outright? Either way, it seemed that this job had come at a good time for him for more reasons that one.

If he were in the city tonight, he would be carousing with his friends, not sleeping in front of the TV at half past ten. She wondered if he would get bored out here. That could be a problem. Claire caught herself. She couldn't fret over every little possibility. He was an adult and could figure things out for himself.

She leaned over and roused him. "Come on, Jamie. You ought to go up to bed."

He nodded sleepily, then slowly sat up, grabbing his phone before it fell on the floor. He rubbed his face and yawned. "I can't believe I fell asleep . . . I'm beat." He rose to his feet, then signalled good night with a dazed wave. "See you tomorrow," he said, walking wearily out of the room.

Claire said good night, then shut off the television and snapped off the lamp. She wondered if Jamie had second thoughts now about the job. Maybe he had not expected it to be so much work.

She hoped he would give it a chance. Life at the inn had its own distinct rhythm, like the tides and the sea. An ebb and flow of activity, hectic and slow times. It was never hectic forever, nor did the quiet last very long.

When she passed his room, no light came from under the door and she heard soft snoring. She would have to see how he acted tomorrow. It was his decision to stay or go. If this didn't work out, it would be hard for her, but either way, Claire knew she would have to accept it.

Chapter Five

CLAIRE barely caught sight of Avery over the weekend. She was a slim, fleeting shadow, first one out in the morning and the last one back at night. But on Monday morning, Claire noticed it was almost ten and Avery still had not come down from her room.

Liza was in the kitchen, pouring herself coffee. The guests were starting to check out, and she had to get the bills prepared.

Once the guests were gone, Liza had some errands to take care of in Boston with Daniel and would be gone the rest of the day.

"Do you think Avery is all right? She's usually up by now. Maybe she's not feeling well," Claire said.

"She must be tired. Even if the café didn't do a huge business, opening weekends are very stressful." Liza spoke from experience. It wasn't too long ago she had suffered from those same jitters.

"I guess you're right. I won't bother her. I was just concerned. I'll save her some breakfast," Claire added.

Avery had not given them too many details, but from the little she did say, Liza and Claire gathered that the café, had not been mobbed with customers. They offered words of encouragement, but Claire could sense Avery's disappointment and even her doubts about choosing the island.

Claire was sure the young chef was tougher than she looked. After a second breath, Avery would dust herself off, put her apron back on, and head back into the ring.

Sometimes it seemed to Claire that the art of getting along in life was a series of adjustments. Like steering a sailboat. You could never reach your destination in a straight line, but only by tacking this way and that, adjusting to the wind and current and whatever else God, in His wisdom, saw fit to toss at you.

Jamie was outside, preparing a stretch of fencing for a fresh coat of paint. Claire watched his progress from the window. He was scrubbing the old paint off with a wire brush and seemed to be doing an able job.

Jamie had given his best effort at all the tasks asked of him over the weekend and had also been very helpful with the guests, seeming eager to keep them comfortable, running in and out of the dining room, or up and down the stairs, for their many requests.

Claire was pleased to see him making such a sincere effort. Liza seemed pleased so far, too, which was a relief. Claire felt so responsible for Jamie doing well. She knew she had put Liza in a difficult spot by asking her to hire him.

"I can't believe I slept so late. You must be serving lunch by now." Claire turned from the window as Avery walked into the kitchen. Though she was dressed in brown cargo pants and a pale blue tank top, she still looked half asleep.

"Not quite. You've been working hard. You needed the rest. Your body will tell you what you need if you listen to it."

"I think it's telling me now I need some coffee. Lots of coffee."

Avery met Claire's glance with a small smile as she lifted her mug for her first sip of the day.

"I hope it said you need some food, too. There's some scrambled eggs and bacon in that covered dish. And banana muffins on the table, too."

Avery took a seat at the kitchen table and helped herself. "This looks good, thanks. I didn't eat much last night. When I'm cooking I smell the food so much, I lose my appetite."

"Really? I can't say that's ever happened to me. With all my taste tests, I must be eating my full share in the kitchen. Then I sit at the table and have even more," Claire confessed.

"That is the danger of being a professional cook, too much tasting. Though we get plenty of exercise." Avery took a bite of muffin, closing her eyes a bit to savor the flavor. "I hope I get a chance to watch you in action sometime, Claire, and learn some of your recipes. I've heard you're a real genius with shellfish."

Claire laughed at the compliment. "Oh, my. I don't know about that. My cooking is pretty basic New England fare. But I would be happy to have you in my kitchen anytime, Avery. That would be my pleasure."

Avery had been at the inn for a full week. She hadn't had time to search for a rental on the island. Liza had generously offered a long-term rate for the next few weeks, so Avery wouldn't have to worry about her housing situation on top of getting the café off the ground.

Avery rose and brought her dishes to the sink. "That hit the spot. I'll see you later." She picked up her big handbag and slipped on her sunglasses. Claire wished her a good day and continued cleaning the kitchen.

By eleven, the inn had emptied out. The Rapps and Foxes were the last group to go, and Mr. Rapp stopped by the kitchen to say good-bye to Claire.

"You let me know when that cookbook is ready. I have friends in the publishing business."

He had teased her about this before. Claire smiled and nodded. "Yes, Mr. Rapp. I haven't forgotten about your connections. I'll let you know when I get to work on it."

She was sure he wasn't serious, though it was a very nice compliment. She had no idea how she would ever go about writing a cookbook, even if she wanted to. Practically all her recipes were in her head and the few that were written down were so stained by kitchen spills and annotated with changes over the years, they were all but illegible. It would be a real winter project, she decided, one that could take a few winters.

She had just finished mopping the floor when Liza appeared in the doorway. She looked very pretty in a floral-print cotton dress and sandals with heels, her long hair gathered at the back of her neck. Her city outfit, Claire called it.

"Well, I'm off. I guess we won't be back until late. Don't worry about dinner for me," she added.

"All right. If anything changes, just call."

"I will. Jamie can help you clean the rooms upstairs," Liza added. "Where is he?"

"He's out back, working on the fence behind the barn. He's been scraping all morning."

"Oh, right." Liza looked as if she had forgotten about telling him to paint the fence. "He can leave that to help you inside. It will be too hot to paint out there in a little while anyway."

"Right." Claire had thought of that, too. Besides, he couldn't go much further with the job. They needed to buy some primer and paint.

After Liza left, Claire headed outside to check on his progress. A blue, cloudless sky arched above and the sun beat down mightily, though it wasn't even noon, searing the back of her neck as she walked across the property.

She found Jamie scratching at the pickets with the brush in one hand, the other hand holding his cell phone to his ear. He was laughing at something and didn't notice her standing there. Suddenly he turned. He clicked off the call and stuck the phone in his pocket.

"A friend of mine has a problem. I had to talk to him a minute."

"All right." She looked over the pickets. He had missed a few spots. More than a few. But the new paint would cover it, she reasoned.

"I couldn't get it all. I did the best I could."

He looked at her, wondering if she was going to tell him to do the work over, she guessed. He wasn't even a third of the way done. She thought he would have gotten further by now.

"As long as you get most of it off. The primer will help. But you need to press the brush harder," she added, doing a patch herself to demonstrate. "Maybe some steel wool would help. We can get some when we run into town later for the paint. Liza went into the city today. You and I will clean the rooms. You can get back to this later."

"Fine with me. It's getting hot." Jamie put his hat back on, then followed her back to the house.

Cleaning the guest rooms was not the most appealing job, she thought, but it was easier than scraping paint off a fence.

It was past one o'clock by the time they'd cleaned all the bedrooms and baths. They had decided not to stop for lunch until they were completely finished. The beds were left without sheets but Claire liked to make them up right before the room was occupied, so the linens smelled fresh.

While Claire fixed lunch—ham and cheddar sandwiches with fresh coleslaw on the side—Jamie carried several baskets of laundry down to the laundry room in the basement.

Claire sliced a juicy tomato to top the sandwiches. It seemed like such a luxury to have a young man around doing the heavy work. That alone was worth an extra salary.

Jamie gobbled his sandwich then made himself another.

Claire realized he must have been hungry awhile and had agreed to put off lunch to be a good sport. She would think twice before suggesting that idea again. She was nibbling the last of her own sandwich while he ate dessert, chocolate cream pie left over from Sunday night's dinner.

"This pie is awesome. It's the best thing I ever ate in my life."

Claire laughed at the extravagant compliment. "You said the same thing about the coconut cake on Saturday," she reminded him.

"Right. I did. But if I had to live on a desert island, I'd take the pie," he said decisively.

Claire had never considered that scenario, eating pie on a desert island. "That would be more like a dessert island," she quipped. "Given the choice, I'd take the pie, too," she added. "And I'd also take some utensils, so I could cook with the local ingredients."

Jamie smiled at her reply. "When are we going to town? I need to pick up some stuff at the drugstore. If we can make a stop," he added.

"I suppose we could." Claire sipped her iced tea. She had been thinking of skipping the trip to town today. She really wanted to get started on the laundry. She didn't like to leave it piled up down there, even for a day.

But what would Jamie do all afternoon? He had finished the jobs on Liza's list, and Claire didn't know what else needed fixing. She could ask him to clean the porch and water the flowers, but that was really busywork and the flowers shouldn't be watered until late afternoon when it cooled down.

"I can go myself if you're tired," he suggested. "I could get the paint and my stuff and stop at the grocery store for you."

He had misread her delay in answering. But that wasn't a bad idea. He could go by himself. Why not? If she stayed here, she could have all the wash done by suppertime.

"I think that would be all right, if you promise to drive safely. The Jeep can get a little finicky in the heat. But it's a short trip. It shouldn't bother you."

Jamie listened attentively. She could tell he was hiding a smile. He was feeling a bit cooped up, she guessed, and eager to be on his own awhile. He had been here since Friday and hadn't even had time for a swim.

While he washed up and changed his T-shirt, she made a list of items they needed at the hardware store and a few at the supermarket. Then she drew a map of Cape Light's Main Street on the back. She handed it to him along with the car keys and a fifty-dollar bill. "If you get lost or can't find something, just call me."

"Okay, see you later."

Claire watched out the window as he started up the Jeep and turned onto the main road. She suddenly had second thoughts about letting him take her vehicle. Just nerves, she told herself. She hoped he was a careful driver. She hadn't even stopped to ask him about that. But what would his answer have been? Of course he would say he was a good driver.

Well, this was bound to happen sooner or later. Running errands was part of his job. Claire reminded herself that so far, at least, he had done nothing to suggest he wouldn't be trustworthy and responsible.

AVERY worked alone at the café on Monday. Her staff did not arrive until four, and they wouldn't open for dinner until five. She busied herself with small jobs, checking how much food they had used up over the weekend and tallying up the receipts.

The guest checks from the grand opening weekend added up to a number that was anything but grand. Avery knew she had to do better if she was going to stay in business. She put the accounts aside, poured herself a big glass of iced water, and went outside to get some fresh air.

She sat at an umbrella table and watched the ocean awhile. The beachfront was quiet today, almost deserted compared to the weekend. Not that the beach crowds had helped her much. She really had to figure out a way to take advantage of that.

She leafed through a pile of local newspapers and circulars, trying to see where she could place more advertisements. Maybe people were just reluctant to try a new place that hadn't been reviewed. She had to work on bringing reviewers in, too.

What's Happening in Cape Light? seemed like a good place to start. It was a large-format tabloid. A scenic shot of Cape Light Harbor was featured on its glossy magazine-type cover. The magazine was published every week and was mainly advertisements—ads for everything from B&Bs to renting Jet Skis—with a few articles about local attractions and lists of things to do in the area.

Avery cut out a few ads from other restaurants that caught her eye. She was so intent on cutting neatly, she didn't notice Mike walk up to the table until he was peering over her shoulder.

"Looking for a place to eat out? There's a cute café that just opened on Ferry Street."

She turned and forced a smile. It would have been funny if the café had done better business over the weekend. As it was, his gentle joke felt like a jibe.

"Hi, Mike. What's up?"

"Nothing much. How are you? Recovered from the weekend?"

She glanced at him, then back at the magazine. "I was surprisingly tired, considering how little business we did."

I might as well say it before he does, she reasoned.

He looked at her a long moment. She hoped he wouldn't gloat. "It's the stress. No question," he said finally.

He sat down at the table without waiting for an invitation. He looked very attractive today, in a white polo shirt and sunglasses. A light breeze ruffled his dark hair. He looked tan and fit, without a care in the world. She wondered what he did for a living when he wasn't running the Tuna. Maybe he was one of those restaurant owners who did so well during the summer, they took the fall and winter off and wandered around the Caribbean or Hawaii.

She decided not to ask him. If that was true, it would be too depressing to think about right now.

"Hey, I know your place was slow this weekend. But don't panic." His quiet tone drew her attention.

She put down her scissors and looked up at him. "Slow is not the word. Torpid. Deserted . . . Forlorn?"

"Hey, what did I say? Don't panic." He said it again, even slower. He had slipped off his glasses and stared at her. She suddenly noticed he was touching her shoulder. "It takes time to build a following, Avery. We're not exactly on the middle of Main Street. People have to find you out here. Then it becomes a fun place to visit for dinner. A destination."

She knew that but felt better hearing him say it.

"And you can't compare this place with the Tuna," he added. "We've been here nearly thirty years. People who went to the Tuna as kids are bringing their own families now."

Avery sighed. "I hope it doesn't take that long for the Peregrine to catch on."

She couldn't last the summer, serving only four or five tables a night. But she didn't admit that to Mike. For one thing, she already knew what he would say: "Don't panic."

The words did calm her, she had to admit. Especially when he said them.

He looked at his watch. She hoped he was getting ready to go. She enjoyed talking to him, but she just felt too awful right now about her failed grand opening, and the only way she would feel better was to take some positive action. Like calling up the advertising department at *What's Happening in Cape Light?* Not hanging out with her biggest—albeit, very attractive—competitor.

"What time does your crew come in?" he asked.

"About four." It was already three. Avery hoped she had enough time to make her phone calls.

"Want to take a walk on the beach?"

His invitation surprised her. When she hesitated he said, "I bet you haven't even been out on the beach once since you got here, have you?"

She wanted to deny it, but it was impossible to lie looking into those big brown eyes. "I wanted to, but I haven't had a chance. I don't really have time now either," she added.

"Just what I thought. At least come out and walk the boardwalk? Have you seen Mrs. McNulty's tube collection? I'd love to show you the highlights. I think she even has the Loch Ness Monster. Do you think kids really like that, or are they scared to death?"

She couldn't answer the question but couldn't help laughing at it, either. He was referring to Sunshine Sundries, right next to the café, and the vast collection of water toys and tubes displayed out front. The Loch Ness Monster was not much of an exaggeration. From where she sat, Avery could clearly make out a shark, a whale, and even some kind of giant squid thing with tentacles.

"That is a tempting invitation." She was teasing him back now, and he seemed to enjoy it. "But I have to take a rain check. I have too much to do."

He looked disappointed, and she wondered if she should change her mind. Then he shrugged his big shoulders. "It is getting late. I probably ought to get back to the Tuna. I have to get things rolling for the dinner rush."

Dinner rush? Did he have to use that exact term?

Any qualms she'd had about refusing his invitation vanished. It was Monday night, for goodness sake. Who had a crowd on a Monday? But Avery didn't doubt that if anyplace did, it was the Lazy Tuna.

She felt even more resolved to stay at the café. She was too worried about her business to enjoy the beach right now anyway.

"See you around," Mike said as he started to go. "Don't forget what I told you," he added.

"I won't," she promised. Was it his simple but sound advice that had calmed her down—or just his natural charm? Either way, she couldn't help smiling as he turned and strolled away.

Avery opened up the magazine then snuck another look at Mike. He had slipped on his sunglasses and walked down the street as if he owned it. As if he owned the whole boardwalk . . . the whole island, for that matter.

She hoped she hadn't hurt his feelings when she'd turned down his invitation. She certainly hadn't meant to; it just all happened so fast. But he seemed pretty sure of himself. He had probably forgotten about it already.

Mike Rossi was quite a character. He was nothing like the men she was used to meeting. In fact, he was the complete opposite of the type she was usually attracted to. She remembered when she had first fallen for Paul; he had seemed so sophisticated with his fine clothing and his knack for always being ahead of the latest trend. Whereas Mike was running a restaurant that hadn't changed since 1960. But she did like him. She couldn't deny it. Not to herself, at least. She enjoyed talking with him and even liked his corny jokes, and the way he teased her.

But she didn't have time for a relationship right now, and she had definitely learned her lesson about men in the restaurant business. And besides all that, wouldn't it be a dumb idea to get involved with her only competition on the entire island?

Sorry, Mike, I guess you're ruled out on a few counts.

And I hope I can remember that, next time you come around with your charming smiles and helpful advice.

CLAIRE folded a crisp, clean sheet, but her mind was not on her task. Jamie had left at two o'clock and should have been back around half past three or even four. But she had not heard from him and only got his voicemail when she called his cell phone.

If the car had broken down or he'd been in an accident, wouldn't he have called? Even if his own phone didn't work for some reason, wouldn't he have found a phone and called her?

The phone rang then. It was half past five. Claire picked it up, trying to make her voice sound normal when she saw the caller ID. "Hello, Liza," she said smoothly.

"Just checking in. How is everything going?"

"Fine . . . just fine." Claire felt bad lying to Liza, but she didn't want to worry her, either. Especially when there might be some perfectly reasonable explanation for Jamie's lateness. Though what that might be, she couldn't begin to guess.

"Claire . . . are you there?" Liza's voice broke into her thoughts. She wondered again if she should tell Liza what was going on. "We're staying in town for dinner, so I probably won't be back until ten or so. You must be tired from cleaning all day. Did Jamie help?"

"Yes, he did every well. We were done quickly." That much was true. He had worked hard at that job.

"Oh, good. Glad to hear it. Where is he now?"

Claire took a breath, preparing to explain what was going on. What was the use of withholding the information? If something bad had happened to Jamie, or the Jeep, it would only look worse later.

"He took the Jeep and went into town. To get some paint for the fence, mainly . . . The thing is . . ."

"Claire? I'm sorry . . . I can't hear you that well. My connection is breaking up. I'll try you back later, okay?"

"That's fine," Claire nearly shouted. But the connection had already been lost.

Claire wasn't sure if she felt relieved or frustrated. She knew she felt torn between her loyalty to Liza—their deep friendship and her respect for Liza as her employer—and her feelings for Jamie, her vow to help him all she could, given this extraordinary second chance.

For not the first time that day, Claire considered taking Liza's SUV to go out looking for him. But that would be too extreme, and how likely would she be to find him? He would probably come back while she was out. That was the kind of luck she had been running today.

She returned to the dining room, where she was ironing and folding the clean linens, then setting them in piles on the long table to be put away. At least the work gave her some outlet for her stress and some distraction.

Finally she heard the front door of the inn open.

"Claire? I'm back," she heard him call out.

She walked to the foyer to meet him, practically shaking with anger and worry.

Jamie gave her a quick, nervous grin. She could tell he knew that he had done wrong, that he had deliberately taken advantage of the situation. But he was going to see what she would say first before he explained himself.

Did he think she would just let this go without saying anything? That she was afraid to confront him? Well, she wasn't.

"Where have you been? You left here more than four hours ago. You should have been back by three thirty, or maybe four o'clock. It's past six now."

He nodded. "I know. I lost track of time. I got a little lost finding the stores on the list, and I needed a few more things than I thought—"

"What happened to your phone? I called several times and it went straight to the messages. Did you turn it off?"

"My phone? Gee, I didn't see any messages." He took his phone out and stared at it. "Maybe it needs a charge. It's one of those cheap phones, pay as you go? Doesn't work so good," he added.

Claire didn't believe that. "Are you sure you just went to Cape Light, Jamie? Or did you drive into Boston to see your friends?"

"Of course not. I went to the stores, like you told me. I stopped to have some ice cream . . . Hey, what's the big deal? Did you think I stole your car or something?" he flared back at her, losing his contrite manner.

Claire felt shocked and hurt by his angry tone. Was he trying to scare her with this outburst? She would not be shouted down or cowed. He hadn't even said he was sorry or given any logical explanation for his disappearance.

"You have no right to use that tone. So far, I've heard a lot of excuses and no real explanation for why you disappeared all day on a simple errand into town. What is the real story, Jamie? I'll find out sooner or later."

He took a breath and stared at her. When he finally replied, he seemed to have his temper under control. "There aren't any guests around, so I thought I could chill awhile. All I did was drive around a little and get a look at the town . . . I should have called you. I'm sorry."

His tone was forced and annoyed, but at least he had apologized. Halfheartedly, but it was something.

"If you're sent to town on an errand, you need to come right back. You need to make sure your phone is charged and stay in touch." Her tone was controlled but stern. "Liza and I will work out a schedule, so you'll know when you have time off. I suppose that might have been unclear," she added, giving him a slim out.

He nodded, his expression blank, an unreadable mask. She had seen that face before—when he was a boy and wanted to detach, to go off by himself into a dark, angry world.

"Okay. I didn't know. I guess it's better to know the rules straight off," he added somewhat reluctantly.

"I can see we need to be clearer with you." She was still angry with him but didn't see the point of belaboring this. They both had to cool down before they could talk about it in a reasonable manner. "If you want to wash up, I've made dinner."

"No thanks. I'm not hungry. I'll just empty the Jeep and go up to my room. Unless you have more work for me to do?"

"No, that's all right. There's nothing more to do today."

Claire was annoyed that he had gone off with her Jeep all afternoon and hadn't called, leaving her to imagine the worst.

Then he tried to convince her it was all a miscommunication, that he didn't know he was expected to come back right away. Clearly, he was testing her, trying to see how much he could get away with here. And with her. Claire couldn't help feeling a deep disappointment. She thought Jamie knew better than that. She had trusted him, and he had let her down.

She remembered now how she questioned so many of his stories when he was younger. When he would "find" fistfuls of money or take the "wrong" jacket home "by mistake." They were forgivable transgressions for a little boy fighting for his survival, but not for a young man. Claire thought he had outgrown those testing behaviors. But maybe not.

She remembered when he was young, how he would disappear for days at a time. A week, sometimes two. She would be frantic with worry, but even a call to his grandmother's house would yield little information or honesty. "Jamie is down with a bug," his grandmother might say, or, "He has a case of the sniffles." But Claire sensed his grandmother didn't know where he was either.

When he returned to the center, there would often be bruises or a black eye. Jamie always had a ready explanation. "Some kid tripped me." "I fell down the stairs at school." Or, "I got into a fight. No big deal," he would assure her if she questioned him.

Claire knew those stories weren't true either. He had run because he was scared or angry or both. But her attempts to press the issue, to get him help, were fended off by his grandmother. And even by Jamie. She had walked a fine line back then and realized she was walking it again, right now.

She felt caught. She didn't want to come down too hard and alienate him or see him quit. He would disappear into thin air again, and her chance to help him would slip through her fingers.

It seemed that fond memories had brought him here, but that was not nearly enough to move forward. Their old relationship was a leaky boat that would not get them very far across these rough waters. They would have to build something new, based on mutual respect. No matter how much good she wished to do for him, she couldn't let him take advantage of her or Liza.

Claire had never known the joys of motherhood. She had wanted a child so very much at one point in her life, but that blessing was not to be. *This situation with Jamie today is just a taste of that awesome responsibility,* she realized. He had come to her, looking for maternal care and nurturing, she was sure, even if he didn't realize that consciously. But a good mother teaches limits and self-control. Which is not always easy, not easy at all.

She heard Jamie go up to his room after he unloaded the Jeep. He did not appear again until much later that night. She was on the porch knitting when she heard him come down the stairs and then rattle around the kitchen.

She was tempted to go inside and fix him something then decided to let him fend for himself. *He's survived a long time without me taking care of him,* she reminded herself.

After a few minutes, he opened the screen door and stuck his head out. She stopped knitting and looked up at him.

"I wanted to say good night," he said simply. "I'm sorry about what happened . . . about staying out too long."

"Thank you for the apology. I appreciate it," she said sincerely. "We'll talk about this more some other time, okay?"

He nodded then went inside.

Well, that was something, she thought. She sat with her knitting in her lap and tipped her head back to look up at the stars.

It was a moonless night, and the sky looked like a blue-black scrap of silk, unfurled across the universe, covered with clouds of sparkling white. Millions upon millions of stars. Were there enough numbers in the language to count them all?

She felt so small and insignificant but at the same time part of something so great and magnificent.

If God could make all those stars and distant planets, and this perfect, blue jewel of a world, surely he can help me. Surely he can show me the right way to help Jamie.

This is going to be hard, God. Much harder than I thought.

She bowed her head a moment and prayed, sending her intentions off into the heavens, hoping with all her heart they would be heard.

Chapter Six

LIZA returned late on Monday night. Claire had already gone up to bed and had no chance to tell her about Jamie's disappearance with the Jeep. On Tuesday there was more catching up and cleaning up from the weekend, and the two women didn't have a minute alone together.

The longer Claire waited to tell Liza what had happened, the harder it got. She hadn't really lied to Liza, but she had withheld the whole story, which was actually the same thing in her book—and in the Lord's book as well, she had no doubt.

She noticed the way Jamie glanced at her from time to time. She knew he was wondering if she had told on him. Or wondering if she was going to bring the topic up again. Though she had told him they would talk about it more, she hadn't been able to initiate that conversation either.

She didn't like the feeling of keeping a secret, especially where Liza was concerned. She didn't like it at all.

I'm too protective of him, that's the problem. I don't want Liza to think she's made the wrong decision hiring him.

You can't control what other people think, Claire. Or what they do, she reminded herself. *And you can't cover up for Jamie and be anything less than truthful with Liza. That will not do,* she scolded herself.

Claire promised herself she would talk to Liza that night. But Liza went out right after dinner with Daniel. It wasn't until Wednesday night that they finally had a quiet moment.

Liza came to sit out on the porch with her. She carried a book she had been reading but didn't open it. "I think Jamie is doing well so far, don't you?"

Jamie was in the sitting room, watching a police drama that was very noisy, the sounds of sirens and screeching cars carried through the open windows. The volume was up, and Claire felt certain he couldn't hear them talk.

"He puts a good effort into his work and seems to be getting into a routine with his daily chores." Claire paused and put down her knitting. "But something did come up on Monday while you were in the city. I had to be very stern with him . . . I've been meaning to talk to you about it. I just couldn't find a time these last few days when Jamie wasn't around."

"What is it, Claire? What happened?"

"He suggested that I let him take the Jeep to town on his own, to do a few errands. I think he had . . . oh, three stops to make. The hardware store, the drugstore, and the market. I thought it would be all right. Doing errands in town or picking up guests at the station should be part of his job. I think we talked about that."

"Yes, we did . . . Go on."

"He left at two and I expected him back in an hour and a half, maybe two. But when he didn't return by half past four, I started to worry," she confessed. "I called his cell phone a few times. It went straight to voicemail. I couldn't imagine what had happened to him—"

"You started to worry. I understand." So far Liza didn't seem upset or disturbed by the story. She was such a reasonable person; Claire was thankful for that. "What time did he finally get back?"

"After you called. Around six o'clock. I asked where he had been, why he'd taken so long. He didn't have much of an explanation. He said he thought with the inn empty, it was all right to take some time off and look around the town, have an ice cream . . . Oh, it was a lot of trumped-up excuses."

"I see." Liza pressed her hands on the book that she held in her lap. "Did you two have words?"

"I suppose you could say that . . ." Claire paused. She wanted to tell Liza the whole story, including the fact that Jamie shouted at her. But the words wouldn't come out of her mouth. "He got mad at me for asking so many questions. He thought it was all 'no big deal.' He lost his temper. And I did, too," she added quickly.

Liza looked surprised. "My, my . . . I would have liked to have seen that. I've never even seen your feathers ruffled, Claire."

"I was quite ruffled. But I did my best to speak in a reasonable tone with him."

"I'm sure you did. What did you say?"

"That when we send him out on an errand, we expect him to come right back, not go gallivanting around . . . Well, I didn't say it quite like that." She paused and took a breath. "I told him that he would, of course, get some time off and you would talk to him about his schedule."

Liza nodded. "I think you handled it very well. I will talk to him. I told him he would have one day off a week, but I never told him when that would be. Maybe he just . . . misunderstood me."

Liza was letting Jamie off easily, Claire thought. But then again, she hadn't been the one waiting and waiting for him. Or the one at whom he'd shouted.

She had tried to tell the story as objectively and completely as she could, but maybe she had downplayed it? Or maybe it was not that egregious a situation and she had overreacted.

"I'll talk to him tomorrow about this. He's bound to need some feedback from us. Nobody's perfect." Liza leaned back and opened her book.

Claire took up her knitting once more, trying to remember what stitch she'd been up to in the pattern. "Thank you for being so reasonable about this, Liza."

Liza just smiled and shook her head. She had started reading and seemed to think enough had been said.

Claire felt relieved. She had been carrying this for two days and now felt a load had been lifted. To think how she had dreaded telling Liza the story. Wasn't that usually the way? *Anticipation of the things we fear most is so often far worse than simply facing them.* It was lesson one learned again and again.

When the right moment arrived, she would have another conversation with Jamie. It would be uncomfortable. *But if you really want to help him,* she reminded herself, *it doesn't help at all to sweep this sort of thing under the rug.*

AVERY felt lucky to get a new advertisement into the local newspapers by Wednesday. It appeared again on Friday, in time for the weekend. She had worked with a graphic designer at *What's Happening in Cape Light?* and thought the new ad looked bold and eye-catching.

Once the new ad appeared, Avery watched anxiously. A few customers wandered into the café each weeknight. Avery felt disappointed, but it was still early in the summer and during the week. People weren't on vacation yet, she reminded herself.

Her reasoning seemed logical, though it didn't explain why the Tuna was crowded every single night. She and her staff watched the crowds come and go. Her crew never complained and carried on bravely, giving their best service to their few customers. But Avery knew it had to be frustrating for them, and demoralizing.

The real test is the weekend, she reminded herself. *Maybe we'll give the Tuna a run for its money.*

On Friday and Saturday nights Avery saw some improvement. The café was at least half full from eight o'clock to ten, and she prepared many more entrees than she had during the grand opening nights. But if this was as good as it would get, it still wasn't enough to keep the doors open all summer. She didn't need to spend hours with her calculator to figure that out.

On Saturday night, as the staff cleaned up, Serena approached Avery. "I'm sorry, Avery. I think this place is really cute and your food is awesome, but I need to earn a certain amount of money this summer. I really want to buy a car and . . . Well, I found another job. I need better tips. I'm sorry," she apologized.

Avery felt sorry, too. Sorry and embarrassed.

"That's all right, Serena. I understand. I know it's been slow here. Good luck with your new job. Come back and see us sometime, okay?"

If we're still open, she silently added.

Serena smiled, looking relieved. "I will, honest. Thanks a bunch . . . and good luck to you, too." She leaned over and gave Avery a quick hug then said good-bye to her coworkers.

After Serena left, a quiet, glum mood fell over the group.

They hadn't been working together long, but somehow they had bonded, Avery realized. Probably more than usual because they were taking part in building something totally new.

Avery sat at a table, sorting out the menus, removing any that looked worn or had food stains. Gena rested a hand on her shoulder. "I'm sure you feel bad about Serena, but don't take it personally. I'm not sure this café was really her style."

Avery had actually felt the same thing, but Serena had been a good waitress. It would be hard to find a replacement now. On the other hand, maybe she didn't even need to hire another waitress right now. She could save on that salary, and Gena could get more tips.

"She could have waited a little while longer. To see if that new advertising worked," Teresa said.

Avery looked up at them. "Oh, I don't know. It's probably best that she left if she really wanted to. I don't know about those ads either. If they were going to bring in more business, I think we would have seen it by now."

"Don't be such a sad sack," Teresa scolded her. "So you ran a few ads. So they didn't get us customers. So what? Run some more."

Her moxie and tough love made Avery smile. "I guess I have to try something. But ads cost money. How much advertising can I do?"

"My sister-in-law works for the local radio station. Maybe she can get you a break on some radio spots," Gena suggested. "That might reach more people than these local papers and magazines."

Avery liked that idea. "I never thought of radio."

"They have someone there who gives reviews, too. Maybe he would come over here. That would be free advertising."

"If he likes the food," Avery added.

"Oh, he'll like the food, don't worry. But a lot of places don't even have good food or good reviews, and they're packed. Like, that Lazy Tuna. Why is that place jumping every night and this place is like a graveyard?" Teresa asked bluntly.

Gena glanced at Teresa and then at Avery. "All those theme nights? People around here love that kind of thing."

Avery rolled her eyes. "Are you seriously suggesting we do Two-for-One Tacos here? Did I spend years slaving away at an elite culinary institute to serve my finely prepared dishes as if this were a drive-through window on the turnpike?"

Avery had not meant to sound so cranky. But she was tired and stressed and all these suggestions were starting to drive her over the edge.

"Calm down, Avery," Gena said gently. "We're just trying to help." She looked at Teresa over Avery's head. "She's a chef. She gets a little emotional."

Teresa waved her hand. "Oh, bunk. Give me a break. We don't have to do tacos. But we have to do something." Teresa sat down next to Avery, and leaned forward, until they were almost nose-to-nose. "Let's take on that Tuna, Avery. We can't sit here and watch the world go by. We'll beat that big fish at their own game."

Before Avery could reply, Gena waved her hands and hopped up and down. "I've got it! I've got it! Remember that special appetizer you made last week? How about using it for an entree theme night—Lobster sliders, with different kinds of sauces and those sweet potato fries as the side dish?"

"Brilliant! This woman is a freaking genius!" Teresa declared before Avery had barely considered the suggestion.

"That's not a bad idea," Avery said slowly. "Actually, it's a good idea, a very good one. How about 'Lobster Sliders Saturday'? It says relaxed, fun, but still gourmet."

"If you sell them two-for-one, it says, 'Come in and get a gourmet meal at a bargain price!'" Teresa chimed in.

Before Avery could object, Gena said, "It wouldn't have to be forever. Just to bring people in, to taste the food and start talking about the place. To get some buzz going, Avery."

"Word of mouth works wonders around here," Teresa added.

Avery hoped that was true. People certainly weren't responding to her ads. The café did need some buzz.

"Good point. We don't have to be all gimmicky forever. Like some people," Avery mumbled under her breath. "Okay, let's try it." She turned over a soiled menu and pulled out a pen. "What else should we do? This could be fun."

"So you're ready to take on the mighty Tuna?" Teresa asked.

"If that's what it takes to make this place a success, yes, I am."

Avery felt a pang making the vow, even though it was partly in jest. Mike had been so encouraging, almost a friend. Avery still wasn't sure why he went out of his way to boost the morale of a competitor. He was a genuinely nice guy, she decided, a rare specimen indeed.

But all's fair in business and war. And Teresa was right. Unless they declared an all-out war on the Lazy Tuna, they might not survive the summer. There was no denying that in this business it was survival of the fittest. Every tuna for themselves.

JAMIE picked up a small ceramic sugar bowl and the delicate spoon that went with it. "Mr. Rapp says he only uses raw cane turbine sugar in his coffee," he told Claire. "I said, it was no problem."

"That's raw cane *turbinado* sugar," she corrected him with a smile. "It's supposed to be healthier than white sugar."

Jamie shrugged good-naturedly. "If you say so." He looked around the kitchen. "Anything else I should bring out?"

Claire gazed over the stove and kitchen table, checking off a mental list: spinach and cheese frittata, cinnamon scones, fresh whole grain bread, fruit salad, yogurt, and cereals. Coffee, tea and all the fixings. "No, I think that's about it."

She untied the strings and slipped her apron on a hook near the kitchen door as Jamie returned to the dining room. The inn was just as busy this weekend as it had been last weekend, maybe more so. But Claire didn't like to miss church too often, even in the summer. With some planning and preparation and Jamie's help, she managed to have the breakfast all cooked and set out in a buffet in the dining room by eight. Liza was happy to take it from there.

Jamie reappeared in the kitchen. "Everyone's eating," he reported. "No more special requests, at least for now."

"Good. I appreciate your help, Jamie," she said. "Would you like to come to church with me?"

She glanced at him, wondering what he would say. She wasn't sure where that question had come from. It had no sooner popped into her head then she found herself speaking it aloud.

He shrugged again and stuck his hands in the front pockets of his jeans. "Okay. I guess I'll go . . . Is it in town?"

The hopeful note in his voice could not be ignored. He hadn't left the island since Monday, after the incident with her Jeep.

"Yes, it's in Cape Light. The old stone church near the harbor."

"What time do we need to be there?"

"The service starts at ten o'clock. We should leave here about nine thirty. I'm going upstairs to change." She glanced at him. "You might want to clean up a bit, too."

She didn't want to seem critical, but she thought he could do a little better than the worn jeans and faded T-shirt, even considering his limited wardrobe. And he needed a shave. After all, dressing appropriately and showing respect for sacred places was part of being an adult.

When she came down at half past nine, Jamie was waiting for her on the porch. He wore the plaid cotton shirt he had worn on his first day of work and a pair of khaki trousers she had never seen before. He had also shaved, she noticed, and combed his hair.

As they approached the Jeep, she offered him the keys. "Would you like to drive? I'm a little tired from rushing this morning."

He looked surprised but pleased. "Sure, I'll drive. No problem."

They got in the car and slipped on their seatbelts. Liza had spoken to him on Wednesday about disappearing with the Jeep and also about a schedule for time off. Claire had not brought the subject up again. It was not really a question of rules, but one of trust and respect. That's what she was concerned about, and that was much harder to discuss.

They didn't talk much on the way to town. Claire directed him down Main Street to the church, and he found a spot easily in the lot.

"Wow, this place is old." He stared up at the building as they approached the big arched wooden doors. "How long has it been here?"

"Well, the first church in Cape Light was built by the colonists, sometime around the year 1600," Claire explained. "That one burned down, though, and this one was built in the early 1800s. The typical church for our denomination is the classic white clapboard with a high steeple. But by the 1800s, the people in Cape Light knew the storms off the sea could be fierce. Since they wanted their church to be near the water, they built it from stone, low and sturdy. It's stood firm ever since."

Jamie touched one of the big gray stones near the entrance as they passed. "Looks pretty solid to me."

Claire smiled, pleased that he was impressed. To her the stone church was a beautiful symbol of God's love, a solid, unwavering structure, a shelter from the storms of life. A safe haven where she could always find peace, stillness, tranquility, a sense of belonging, and even a touch of mystery.

The wooden doors stood open and they entered the narthex. Tucker Tully, the head deacon, came to greet them and handed them each a program. He wore a white carnation in his lapel and a button that read, *Best Dad in the World.*

"Happy Father's Day, Tucker," Claire said. "I hope you have a good day."

"I can guarantee that already," he said as he showed them to two seats at the back of the sanctuary.

Claire had not forgotten about Father's Day. Though her own father had passed on eight years ago, she still recognized the day in her own way. Every year she brought a bouquet to his grave, in the cemetery on the other side of the island. But more important, she looked over photos that reminded her of the happy, loving times they had shared, especially when her mother was alive as well. And reminding her of his full and productive life. She had been blessed to have such a gentle, loving, intelligent father. He had taught her so much. She still missed him.

Many people were not as fortunate. Jamie, for instance. She guessed he had mixed feelings about this day and all the tributes to fathers. She knew it had to be a hard day and her heart went out to him. But she wasn't quite sure how to help him with that, or even how to try.

The choir soon entered, singing the opening hymn. Reverend Ben followed slowly and stood to one side of the altar, waiting for them to finish.

"Good morning, everyone," he greeted the congregation. "I especially welcome all the fathers here this morning and wish you all a happy day."

Soon after the opening prayers and introit, Reverend Ben announced the scripture readings. Claire liked to follow along in the Bible, and opened to the chapter and verse. The second reading was one of her favorites, the parable of the mustard seed, from the Gospel of Mark.

Reverend Ben still read in a strong, clear voice that rang through the sanctuary with authority, and he still led the church with his quiet, gentle strength. He was in his mid-sixties now, Claire knew, and had even tried to retire once, after a heart attack. But the congregation wouldn't let him, and once he regained his strength, he realized he wasn't quite ready to leave his post. Claire was glad of that. She knew he had to retire one day, but she couldn't imagine this congregation without him.

"'. . . Then He said, "To what shall we liken the kingdom of God? Or with what parable shall we picture it?"'" Reverend Ben paused a moment to let his listeners absorb the echoing words. "'"It is like a mustard seed which, when it is sown on the ground, is smaller than all the seeds on earth;"'" he continued, "'"but when it is sown, it grows up and becomes greater than all herbs, and shoots out large branches, so that the birds of the air may nest under its shade."'

"This is the word of the Lord. Thanks be to God," Reverend Ben concluded.

Claire closed the red Bible and glanced at Jamie. She couldn't tell if he was enjoying the service or just sitting there to appease her. Maybe he was just so bored and church was at least some place to go and something to do.

She recalled taking Jamie to a church near Crosby Street when he was younger. But they had only gone together a few times—on Christmas and Easter, maybe?

She did recall he sat quietly and had not fidgeted, like some children. She remembered that he liked the candles and the stained glass windows there. But she couldn't recall much more than that. She wondered now if that was the last time he attended a service. She had a feeling that church was not part of his life now.

Reverend Ben stepped to the wooden pulpit and settled himself, preparing to begin his sermon.

"Father. A simple word that can have so many different meanings. For each of us, a particular image comes to mind, of our own father, living or deceased, present or absent. A figure in our childhood and often, all through the years since. The word stirs our memories and our hearts.

"Today is the day we honor fathers everywhere. Fathers that raised us, and for some of us, the men who stood in that place. Our grandfathers, too."

Claire was concentrating on Reverend Ben's words and didn't immediately realize that Jamie was restless, shifting in his seat, unable to get comfortable. He took a deep breath and turned his head, looking back over his shoulder at the door.

She leaned toward him. "Are you all right?" she whispered.

"Yeah, I'm okay . . . It's a little stuffy in here."

Claire didn't think so. It wasn't a very hot day, and the doors and windows were all open. Large overhead fans spun in quiet, slow circles, creating a pleasant breeze.

But Jamie did look drained and pasty under his tan.

". . . But there is one Father we all know and love. The same Father to all of us, showing each of his children the same magnificent love and understanding. The same forgiveness . . ."

Jamie bowed his head a second and pressed a hand to his forehead. Claire touched his shoulder, wondering if he was going to faint. "Jamie, put your head between your knees and take a few deep breaths," she said quietly.

He turned his head sharply and stared at her, practically wild eyed. Or had he started crying? "I have to get out of here. Sorry."

He stood up abruptly. A hymnal that had been on the seat next to him fell to the floor with a dull thud.

He stumbled out of the pew and down the aisle, then out the sanctuary doors.

He was suddenly gone and she wasn't sure what to do. To stay in her seat—or chase after him?

Chapter Seven

TUCKER caught Claire's eye, then mouthed the words, "I'll go check on him."

Claire breathed a sigh of relief. She had a feeling Jamie needed space right now, some privacy. But she still wanted to know he was all right.

Tucker returned a few minutes later. Reverend Ben had finished the sermon and the choir was singing a hymn. Tucker walked up to Claire and touched her arm. "He's fine," he whispered. "Just needed some air. He's out in the park, waiting for you."

Claire felt relieved. "Thank you, Tucker," she whispered back.

She was tempted to go out to him a few times as the service continued. Then she decided it was best to leave him with his thoughts awhile. A few minutes in the park, watching the harbor, might do Jamie good.

When the service ended, Reverend Ben stood in the narthex, near the center doors to the sanctuary, and greeted the congregation.

Claire usually liked to get in line to say hello and thank him for his thoughtful sermons. But now she slipped out the side door and headed along the path to the green, checking the benches for Jamie.

She walked down to the harbor. The benches, which stood in a long row, were all filled, but there was no sign of Jamie. She turned and walked around the small park, past the big gazebo where community concerts were held all summer and past the path to the shady playground on the far side of the green.

He might be waiting for me at the car, she realized. Claire then followed a path that led back to the church. She could see the Jeep in the lot, practically the only vehicle left. But Jamie was not in it or anywhere around.

She settled herself on a bench in the shade, wondering if she should call his cell phone. She decided to wait. There's no reason to panic, she told herself. He must have just taken a walk in the village.

Claire sighed and looked out at the water. The bay was filled with boats, many crowded against the public dock, and more moored out on the water. The green was filling up now, families and old people, couples holding hands. She scanned the faces walking near the water but still didn't see Jamie.

When she looked back at the church she noticed Reverend Ben coming out a side door near his office. When he saw Claire, he waved and walked toward her.

"Hello, Claire. Everything okay? You don't have car trouble, do you?"

Claire realized she was a curious sight, sitting in the park alone at this hour on a Sunday. If she made it to church at all during the summer, she usually bustled right back to the inn.

"Oh, no. I'm fine. Just waiting for somebody. Happy Father's Day," she added, trying to change the subject. "Any special plans?"

Reverend Ben had two adult children and grandchildren. Was it three or four by now? Claire couldn't recall.

"Rachel and Jack are having us over for a barbeque," he said, mentioning his daughter and son-in-law, who lived in town. "And I might do a little surfcasting later. I have a feeling my special gift today is another new rod and reel set," he added with a laugh.

Ben was an avid fisherman and one of his favorite pastimes was surfcasting. Claire had often seen him on the beach near the inn in the early morning or late afternoon, out in every season.

"I'm looking forward to seeing my grandchildren," he added. He took out a hanky and cleaned his glasses. It was warming up outside, even though they sat in the shade of the tall, old trees. "How's everything at the inn? Are you busy up there yet?"

"We have been. A full house, two weekends in a row. Liza is very pleased. We even hired a helper. His name is Jamie Carter. He came to church with me this morning. Maybe you noticed him?"

Ben nodded. "I did. I noticed he left early. Was he feeling all right?"

"He needed some fresh air. He felt a little queasy. But I suspect it was something more. I think he was upset by the sermon," she admitted. She wondered if she should tell Reverend Ben the whole story. She didn't want to keep him if he was trying to get home to his family.

"My sermon? What did I say?" Reverend Ben seemed concerned.

"It wasn't anything you said exactly . . . just the topic, I think. Fathers," she added quietly. "Jamie has had a very troubled past, a bad family life. I met him when he was nine years old. I haven't seen him in over ten years. But somehow, he found me and came out to the island two weeks ago. Just appeared one morning when I was weeding the vegetable patch."

"Really? What a surprise for you . . . How did you know you each other? Where did you meet?"

"Oh, it's a long story. I'm not sure you have the time right now to hear it."

"I'm not in any rush." As if to prove his words, he sat on the bench beside her and slipped off his suit jacket.

"I'm not sure if you remember, but about ten years ago, you had a guest preacher here from Boston, and I was very moved by his sermon about the work he did in the Crosby Street Center."

"I do remember," Ben assured her. "You moved to Boston to work there. Is that where you met Jamie?"

"Yes, he came there almost every day, after school. Or wherever he'd been instead of going to school," she added. "There were a lot of volunteers there and a lot of children who needed attention. But Jamie and I had a special bond. Of course, he was looking for a mother figure. He never really knew his mother. She left the family when he was only two years old. His father was a troubled man who left him with his grandmother. Jamie barely knew him, either, though Mr. Carter would come and go from the family home, visiting every few months."

"How sad. It's hard to see how some children are neglected and emotionally abused."

"It was more than emotional abuse. Jamie's father was an alcoholic who physically abused him. I tried to help him, to intervene, but even though he was taken out of the house, he was eventually sent back." Claire sighed. "It was very . . . complicated."

"These situations always are."

"Despite everything, Jamie loved his father. At that time, anyway. He talked about his father a lot and got very excited about his visits. He even begged his father to take him along whenever he left. I could see that he yearned for his father's love. Jamie would tell me how he was leaving soon, to live with his dad. He always sounded very sure of that. But when the day came, his father always left without him, sometimes slipping out of the house without even saying good-bye. To avoid a painful scene, I suppose. Though no matter how he did it, those partings always left Jamie brokenhearted and deeply upset. I could see his face across a room, and I would know instantly that it had happened again. It would take him weeks to come back to himself. He's never really gotten over any of it, if you ask me. Now, I would guess that even the word 'father' brings up such a toxic mixture of disappointment and pain, it's no wonder he felt sick this morning."

Reverend Ben nodded thoughtfully. Claire could see the sympathy in his blues eyes.

"What a sad story. So you tried to help him back then, and you're trying to help him now with the job at the inn. Is that it?"

"I'm trying," Claire said. "I was so happy when he found me, Reverend. You can't imagine. Back then, I considered adopting Jamie, or being his foster parent. But when my father got sick I had to come back home, and I lost touch with the boy. So when he appeared at the inn like that, it seemed as if God had finally answered my prayers and reunited us. But it isn't as easy as I thought it would be."

"Of course it isn't. Life is seldom that simple or easy," he said knowingly. "Your reunion with him after all this time, that is remarkable."

"Isn't it? There was an article about the inn in the *Boston Globe* a few weeks ago, and he said he saw me in the photo. It made me think he had come back into my life for a reason. That God was giving me a second chance to help him."

She glanced at Reverend Ben to see if he agreed. "Quite possibly," he said, "though God works in mysterious ways. His will is rarely as simple or straightforward as we would like it to be."

Claire knew that was true. "I've asked God for guidance, to help Jamie. Aside from giving him a job, I'm not sure I've made any difference in his life so far. It isn't nearly as easy to talk to Jamie these days as it was years ago. I think he's happy to have the job and earn some money. But he hides so much of himself these days. He thinks I don't even realize it, but I do. It's hard to connect, to build trust again."

"I'm surprised to hear you say that, Claire. I know you're a patient person, one of the most patient I've ever met. And it doesn't sound as if Jamie has been at the inn very long,"

"I am patient, Reverend. And he hasn't even been at the inn two weeks," she added. "But every night I wonder if I'll wake up and find he's gone without a word of warning. Just the way he arrived. I feel as if I'm working against the clock. And I'm not allowed to show it and possibly scare him off."

She glanced over her shoulder, suddenly realizing Jamie might be near and listening. She scanned the faces of people walking or sitting nearby but still didn't see him.

Reverend Ben nodded. "I understand. It sounds as if he's had a difficult time and it's hard for him to trust anyone—even a nurturing presence from his childhood, like you. I'm sure he doesn't realize it, but all these years you've been in his mind as an idealized figure, a safe haven. He probably expected you to just take care of him, like you did when he was a child. He doesn't expect—or want—you to ask anything of him. To expect him to change or improve himself."

Claire hadn't seen the situation quite that way, though she did realize that Jamie looked to her for comfort and care and even a kind of unconditional love.

"All you can do is be there for him," Reverend Ben continued, "and show him you are still the same consistent, loving presence you were ten years ago. There's a reason he came all the way here to see you, Claire. Don't forget that—or discount it."

Claire knew this deep inside, but it helped to hear Reverend Ben say it aloud.

"He did come a long way to find me. He didn't need the newspaper article. He could have come years ago. He always knew where I lived. But for some reason, the spirit moved him to find me at this point in his life. And I still care about him deeply," she added. "He wasn't wrong about that."

"You've already helped him by being that person, Claire. Don't doubt it."

"Thank you for saying that. It helps me feel a little less frustrated and confused. It's just that I want to do so much more for him . . ." Claire's voice trailed off as she caught sight of Jamie walking by the benches that faced the water and heading toward the church. "There he is now." She stood up and waved. Jamie waved back. "I'd like to introduce you if you have a minute."

"Certainly, I'd like to say hello."

Jamie walked up to the bench and then stood with his hands stuck in the front pockets of his jeans. "Hey, Claire. Waiting long?"

"Not that long. I haven't seen Reverend Ben in a few weeks. We had a good chat."

"Hello, Jamie. Good to meet you." Reverend Ben rose and shook hands with him.

"Nice to meet you," Jamie said, sounding a little shy. He was probably wondering if they'd been talking about him, Claire realized.

"I was telling Jamie how the church was rebuilt after the fire, but I couldn't remember the exact year."

"Eighteen-oh-four," Reverend Ben said, glancing at the church now. "I have to confess, it could be more comfortable and convenient, with all-new plumbing and whatnot. But we like it. We try to take good care of it." He turned to Jamie with a smile. "Claire tells me that you're working at the inn. How do you like it?"

"It's fine for a summer job. There's always something different to do and new people around."

He's not doing cartwheels but at least he's honest, Claire thought.

A few moments later, Reverend Ben said good-bye. Claire and Jamie got into the Jeep, and Claire let Jamie drive again. He seemed to enjoy it so much.

"Back to the inn?" he asked as he fastened his seatbelt.

"I guess so." Claire glanced at her watch. They didn't serve lunch on Sundays, just a big early dinner. "Are you hungry? Do you want to stop for a bite in town?"

"I'm okay. I picked up something in town when I was walking around." He turned to her. "I didn't mean to leave you waiting there. I wasn't sure what time church got out."

"No problem. It was good to talk to Reverend Ben." Claire had been watching out her window and turned to him. "I hope you're feeling better. Did the sermon upset you?"

"It was just stuffy in there. I couldn't get any air. I'm not used to sitting still that long."

Claire nodded but didn't reply. She glanced out the side window again. They were crossing the land bridge that connected Cape Light to the island. It was a clear day and the water was relatively calm, small waves lapping against the rocks that were piled up against each side of the two-lane roadway.

"I have a good idea. We should take a ride out to see the cliffs. You've been here almost two weeks and you still haven't seen them. That's unforgivable."

He looked surprised. "Don't you have to get back and cook something?"

"We have some time. Just go left when you come off the bridge, the same way you would go to get to the inn. But go straight through the village center and then turn left again at the crossroads."

Jamie was a good driver, she thought. He didn't drive too fast, at least not with her in the passenger's seat. He slowed down even more as they drove through the island's small village, where the General Store, the medical clinic, and Daisy Winkler's tearoom and library circled a cobblestone square.

A group of cyclists were gathered on the porch of the store, and a few more stood nearby at a scenic overlook. They took turns taking pictures of each other with the ocean in the background.

It looked as if Daisy's shop was open, too. The small, enchanted-looking cottage was set on a postage-stamp bit of property and circled by a rickety picket fence.

"What a weird little place," Jamie said as they passed the cottage. "It looks like Snow White and the Seven Dwarves live there."

Claire laughed. "I don't think there would be room for all seven in there, but I know what you mean."

They finally left the square and were on the smooth blacktop road again. Jamie picked up speed. "Is it much farther?"

"A ways," she answered. "It's worth it once you get there."

They followed the road past more cottages and gracious old houses, some in good condition and some sadly run down. Then past empty areas filled with woods and meadows or stretches of tall marsh grass. They passed places where the view of the coastline would suddenly open up then disappear just as quickly.

Claire had lived on the island all her life, except for those two years in Boston. She never tired of the island or failed to be amazed at the variety of landscape compressed into such a small parcel of earth. She never failed to be awed by the island's beauty. She felt blessed to live in this place, still so natural and untamed.

She glanced over at Jamie and wondered if he was affected at all by the stunning views. He stared straight ahead, concentrating on the road, but seemed more relaxed than she had seen him all day.

They rounded a bend and the cliffs suddenly came into view straight ahead of them—jagged, golden, at least ten stories high.

"Wow," Jamie said quietly.

Claire felt pleased to see him so impressed. "You can park anywhere on this road. We can walk the rest of the way."

They got out of the car and began walking toward the cliffs. She was so happy to be in this place with Jamie, to finally show him the sight she had described so many times when he was young.

They walked along the sandy shoulder of the road, getting closer for a better view. Jamie walked ahead, seeming mesmerized. He pulled out his phone and took pictures.

The outline of the cliffs stood in stark contrast to a backdrop of clear blue sky. The legendary wing shape could be seen clearly from this angle, a golden crescent, with a point flaring out at the bottom, like a long feather.

Finally, Jamie put the phone back in his pocket. "Well, what do you think?" she asked.

"Pretty awesome. They look just like you told me. But even bigger."

It was just past noon and the sun shone brilliantly, making Claire squint as she smiled at him. A breeze blew off the water, chasing away the heat. Claire felt the wind catch at her hair and pull loose a few strands from the pins that held her bun.

"What is that story about this place again? There were some sick people on the island and angels came to help them?"

"That's right, more or less . . . When the first settlers came to Cape Light there was a terrible illness during their second winter. They brought all the sick ones to this island, to quarantine them, and the poor people were stuck here all winter without any help. Do you remember the rest?"

"Yeah, I think I do. The villagers left all the sick people here and expected them to die. There was so much snow and stuff, no one could get out to help them. But in the spring, the sick people came back on boats by themselves and were, like, totally cured. They told the villagers that these mysterious strangers came to the island and helped them get healthy again."

"That's right." Claire nodded. He had remembered. She glanced at the cliffs again. "Many believed that the visitors must have been angels and pointed to the cliffs as a sign that the island was a sacred place, a place of help and healing."

"I remembered that part, too. About the angels." Jamie nodded. "Do you believe that?"

She had a feeling he would ask her that. "Let's just say I don't disbelieve it. I've seen amazing things in my lifetime, things that seemed totally improbable. The fact that you found me after all these years, I'd call that a miracle."

Jamie slowly smiled. "I saw your name in a newspaper article. It's not like an angel whispered in my ear or something."

"Really? How do you know? Maybe an angel pushed that paper in front of you." Her tone was light and teasing, but she half meant it.

They walked a little farther. Jamie stopped to pick up a shell and stuck it in his pocket. A few steps later, he stopped again and showed Claire what he had found.

"Look at this . . . beach glass. I've never seen that color before. Have you?"

He held the piece out on his palm for Claire to see. About an inch long or slightly less, almost a triangle but smooth along the edges, it was golden yellow in hue, almost an amber color.

"Yes, it is very rare," Claire agreed. "I've hardly ever seen one that color. You ought to save it." Claire collected beach glass. She kept her finds in a big glass bowl near the window in the kitchen, where it caught the light at different times of the day.

Jamie stared at the treasure a moment. "Here, you take it."

Claire was surprised. He had seemed pleased at first to find it. "You should save it. To remember this place," she added.

He seemed to consider that a moment, then offered it to her again. "I'll just lose it somewhere. You save it for me."

Claire didn't know what to do. She didn't want to refuse this gift, honestly offered. Small as it was, she knew she would cherish it. "Thank you. I will save it. In my collection, in the kitchen."

He nodded. "I knew you'd have a good place for it."

They kept walking. Claire saw a man with two small boys standing at the edge of the water, all of them wearing swimming trunks. Their suits were wet, their hair plastered to their heads. The man was in the middle holding the boys' hands very tightly and walking slowly into the surf. As the bigger waves rolled in, the man showed the boys how to duck and turn to the side, and let the water roll over their shoulders.

"He's teaching them how to get into the waves, so they won't be knocked over," Claire said.

"Good thing to know. My dad never even took me to the beach." Jamie laughed, but Claire could hear the hurt in his voice.

"When was the last time you saw your father? Are you still in touch with him?" she asked quietly.

"My dad died. About two years ago." His voice was flat. He glanced at Claire and then back at the water. "He came back to my grandmother's house right before. He was pretty sick. I hadn't seen him for years. He'd been in jail but they let him out. My grandmother kept saying I needed to come see him. To say good-bye.

I didn't really want to but I finally did. I'm not sure he even knew I was there but . . . I saw him that one time."

Claire felt a bit stunned. Jamie had been through so much in his young life. It didn't seem fair.

"I'm sorry," she said finally. "That must have been very hard for you."

Jamie shrugged. "What's the difference? I just did it for my grandmother. She cared . . . He wasn't much, my dad. He was sort of a useless bum. I could barely stand to be around him at the end."

Claire was silent, not knowing what to say. She had wanted to get Jamie away from his father, and yet now, it seemed terribly sad that Jamie had so little love for him. Finally, she said, "I think you did the right thing by visiting him. You may think it doesn't matter, but someday, you'll look back and you won't have any regrets."

He glanced at her and smirked. She knew he didn't believe her. She glanced at her watch. It was getting late. "Ready to go back?"

He nodded and turned to follow her.

Poor Jamie. He felt such scorn for his father. Claire suspected it was also turned inward. *He's afraid,* she realized. *Afraid that he'll turn out like his father, and there's nothing he can do about it.*

But Jamie was better than that. She was absolutely sure of it. His past did not have to determine his future.

Just before they got in the car, they both glanced back at the cliffs for one last look.

"There's another explanation for those cliffs, you know," she said, "the reason for their shape."

"What's that?"

"Well, the water and wind, the tides and rain, slowly wearing them down, shaping them," she explained. "Just like God's love shapes our lives. Working so gradually, we hardly know it."

He met her glance but didn't reply. The smile he offered was humoring her, at best.

Claire was fine with that. She got into her side of the Jeep and fastened her seatbelt.

It was true, what she just told him. It happened all the time and could happen to him, too, if he allowed it. That was as great a miracle as any story about angels.

If there was only one thing she could do while Jamie was with her, it would be to convince him that he was essentially a good person, who could rise above his past. To make him believe that he could be a success in life, that he didn't have to end up a broken man, like his father. The question was: *How* could she do this? How could she make him believe what she knew to be true?

It will take a lot of patience, love, and understanding, and help of the Heavenly Father above, Claire thought. *And maybe an angel or two.*

Chapter Eight

Avery was saving the Lobster Sliders idea for next Saturday. In the meantime, the plan for Monday night was "Pizza and a Movie." Avery and Teresa had worked out a special menu of individual-sized pizzas with a choice of gourmet toppings—grilled mushrooms, artichokes, roasted asparagus, prosciutto, black olives, caramelized onions, barbequed chicken, and goat cheese. There were a lot of interesting things you could do with a lump of pizza dough. Avery did not feel she was lowering her standards in the least by devising these tasty, creative combinations.

Gena had generously offered the loan of a large, flat-screen TV and a DVD player. They were going to set it up on one side of the dining area, in full view of most tables, and run a classic movie.

Avery arrived at the café around noon on Monday, after a quick stop at the Gilroy Goat Farm, next to the inn, where she bought several kinds of goat cheese and some lavender for the vases.

On Sunday afternoon, she and Teresa had made pounds and

pounds of pizza dough, and formed it into large balls. It was now stored on flat pans in the fridge. They would take out what they needed at about three o'clock, so it could rest at room temperature awhile, then separate each ball into smaller chunks and stretch out the individual pizzas.

She put the cheese away and set about moving the tables. It was really a job for Jack, she knew, but she was excited and needed to burn off some energy. There had been no time for advertising, but she and Gena had a made an eye-catching sign to post outside the café. Gena, who was the most artistic and had the best handwriting, was going to write out the special menu on a chalkboard, once she came in.

Avery had also made some handbills on Liza's computer and printed piles of them. She hoped that some extra pay would persuade Jack to go out on the beach and boardwalk this afternoon and hand them out.

She wasn't sure what else she could do. It was too late to hire a little private plane to drag a sign across the sky at the beach. Maybe next time, she joked with herself.

The crew had haggled a bit about which film to show. Suggestions ran the gamut from *Gone With the Wind* to *Jaws*—Jack's suggestion, which actually made some sense.

They had finally agreed on *Casablanca,* mainly because Teresa wore the rest of them down. "Who doesn't like *Casablanca*? You have to be dead to not like that movie. I've seen it a million times and I could see it a million more. 'Here's lookin' at—' "

"Okay, done," Avery cut in. She hurried to settle the matter before Teresa could quote any more dialogue "I think there's a copy at the inn. I'm sure I can borrow it." Avery made a note to ask Liza.

"Save that list of movies. We'll need it for other Mondays," Gena said.

Avery glanced at her. *If* the idea worked. If it didn't, they would end up with a fridge full of pizza dough, a mountain of fresh mozzarella, and a long list of random ingredients. But she held her tongue and didn't undermine the enthusiasm.

By the time they had left the café on Saturday night, Avery had a week's worth of customer-attracting ideas: "Two-for-One Tuesday," "Pasta Party!" on Wednesday and "Fish-Kabob Friday."

On the weekend, the most important time to pack in the customers, they had high hopes for "Lobster Sliders Saturday," and would follow up with a good old-fashioned Sunday brunch.

Had she ever expected to be marketing her café this way?

Never in a million years. *But when life hands you a piece of Stilton, you can't just stand there and hold your nose. You have to make a little fondue out of it,* Avery reasoned. *Or even a gourmet pizza.*

"Hey, what are you up to in here? Redecorating already?"

Mike walked in through the French doors, which stood open to let in the morning air. It was so sunny outside and so dark in the café, Avery hadn't noticed him. She had also been pushing around the tables and chairs at a furious pace.

"Just . . . reorganizing a bit," she said vaguely.

She glanced at him, wondering if he could guess that something was up today at her café. *He's been in the business so long, he can probably smell it,* she thought.

Avery felt torn. Part of her wanted to share her new plans with him, to see what he thought of her strategy . . . and just because . . . well, because she liked him and liked confiding in him. Another part of her needed to show him she could do it on her own. Without his coaching or advice. He had been very kind, but for some reason she felt that she needed to show him that she could do anything he could do. And better, too.

And yet another part of her warned that all these warm, mushy feelings for Mike were not a good idea. He was in the business, which meant it just couldn't go anywhere, no matter how happy she felt when he cast one of those megawatt smiles her way.

"Here, let me help you with that." While her thoughts rambled, Mike stepped over to help her move a particularly stubborn table.

He stood very close, hip to hip, shoulder to shoulder. Her bare arm rubbed against his muscular biceps. She suddenly felt so nervous that when they pushed together, the heavy wood table nearly flew across the room.

"Whoa, you're stronger than you look, Avery." He was trying to tease her, as usual. But a slight blush showed under his tan. Avery could tell he felt flustered by their nearness, too. She didn't know what to say and took a step away from him.

"Yes, I am. Can I take that as a compliment?" she teased him back. Before he could answer, she added, "Would you like some iced coffee? I was just going to make one for myself."

A cold drink would be a good distraction, she thought. She knew from the warmth in her cheeks that she was blushing. She hoped he didn't notice.

She hoped he didn't stay long, either. Gena and her husband would arrive soon with the big TV. Then she would be obliged to tell him about their plans, and that didn't feel right.

"Iced coffee sounds good." He followed her into the kitchen, where she grabbed the pitcher of cold coffee out of the fridge and slammed it shut again. She scanned the kitchen, looking for telltale signs of pizza dough prep, and was relieved to see there were none.

"So, what's going on here tonight? Looks like you're clearing a space. Are you going to have music?"

"Music? . . . Not tonight . . . but I've been thinking about it," she said honestly.

They had been so busy working on menu gimmicks, she hadn't

even gotten around to something obvious, like hiring a trio of some kind. Though Teresa said her grandson and his friends had a very good group that played jazz and popular songs at parties in the area, and he was going to stop by this week to meet Avery.

Mike poured a dollop of milk and two sugars in his coffee.

"I have a few cards from musicians that are pretty reasonable," he offered. "How did you do this weekend? Any improvement?"

"Not much better than my very ungrand Grand Opening." She shrugged and sipped her coffee. "I don't think the new ads worked very well."

"Too bad," he commiserated. "But—"

"I know, don't panic," she cut in, beating him to his favorite line. "I'm not. Honestly."

He smiled at her, his bright expression and the warmth in his brown eyes made her feel . . . all melty, she thought. Like a marshmallow under the broiler.

"You're a quick study, Avery."

"I try to be." Her phone buzzed with an incoming text. "Excuse me a minute, I think it's Gena." She picked up the phone and checked the message, careful not to let Mike see the screen.

> TV is packed. Sorry it took us longer than I thought. But will be there in a few minutes.—G.

Avery took a sharp breath and put the phone down. Gena would be here any second with the huge TV, and then Mike would be full of questions . . . and comments and advice.

He'll find out soon enough when you put the sign up and Jack goes around with the flyers.

But by then it will be so late in the day, he'll be too busy at his own place to bother with me much. Avery imagined how good it would feel to have him see the Peregrine with a full house, all her own doing. Besides, she reasoned, it wasn't as if she was under any obligation to tell him everything about the café. He would never expect that.

"Anything wrong?" Mike had just about finished his coffee and tipped it back to the last drops and the bit of sugar that always settled at the bottom. Avery couldn't help looking at his strong tan neck and the patch of dark hair at the top of his open polo shirt.

"Nothing," she said, clearing her throat a bit. "Gena's running a little late." She put down her glass and smiled at him. "Hey, you know what? I still haven't gotten out on the beach. Isn't that unbelievable?"

"Sure is. I have to get out there at least once a day. I take a walk early in the morning, or around sunset, when it's empty and quiet. Clears my head and makes me feel all energized again."

"That sounds great. I could really use a break like that." She glanced at her watch. Gena would be pulling up in five minutes or less. "Maybe I should head out right now. Nobody's here yet and pretty soon I'll be so busy, I won't have a spare minute."

"Good idea." Mike rose as well and put his glass in the sink. "Want some company? I could use a little exercise."

Avery hadn't expected that. She was just trying to get him out of the café. Hadn't he said he took his walks early or late in the day? It was already close to eleven.

But she liked the idea of going with him. "That would be great. I'm going to send Gena a quick text," she added, closing the French doors and leaving the main door in front unlocked.

Park in the alley. Kitchen door is unlocked. See you later.

Avery grabbed her sunglasses and they set out down Ferry Street, walking side by side. She suddenly realized that she had never seen

Mike outside of her café. It was a slightly odd feeling to be out in the world with him, but at the same time, not odd at all. She felt relaxed in his company, as if they were already familiar in some way, though the truth was they hardly knew each other.

As they passed Sunshine Sundries, the owner, Mrs. McNulty, was setting up some new beach chairs in front of her shop. Mike paused to greet her. Avery had met her neighbor once or twice so far and also said hello.

"How's business this summer, Nancy?"

"Very good, Mike. People always forget something when they go to the beach. And I've always got just the thing they're missing," she said with a laugh. "How is the café doing, Avery? Are you open every night?"

An innocent question but it made Avery wince. Did her place look so empty that people thought it was closed? Well, that could be part of the problem right there.

"Yes, every night," she said in what she hoped was an upbeat tone. "And we're going to start serving brunch on Sunday."

"Everybody loves a nice brunch. Good for you," Nancy said approvingly.

"Good idea, Avery. I think you'll bring in a lot of business with that one," Mike agreed.

"I hope so," she said lightly. She hadn't meant to tell him that either, but now that he knew, she appreciated his encouraging words.

They walked a bit farther and then crossed the street and climbed a few steps up to the new wooden boardwalk that bordered the beachfront.

The boardwalk was very wide, fringed with beach grass on one side and equipped with long wooden benches that were sheltered from the sun. There was a large building at one end, near the ferry station, that housed showers and changing rooms with lockers. Visitors could rent umbrellas, beach strollers, and other beach equipment there.

"Would you like to walk on the boardwalk or the shore?" Mike asked.

Normally, Avery preferred being as close as possible to the water, but she wasn't dressed for it this morning. "The boardwalk is fine today. I just wanted to get some air. I don't want to get back into the kitchen all sandy," she added.

And risk getting sand in the pizza.

"Good point," he agreed. "You get a great view of the ocean from here. They really thought that through. I know a lot of people on the island didn't want to see anything built here, but I think the county did a nice job with the changes."

Avery had read about it in the first article she found about Angel Island and then heard more from Liza and Claire. Many people on the island had opposed the development of the ferry station area and, for a while, it didn't seem as though the plan would go through.

"There was a lot of debate," Mike recalled. "I felt sort of caught in the middle. I knew it would be a boon to my restaurant, but I do love the island and felt protective of this place."

"How do you feel now?" she asked curiously. "Do you think the changes have ruined it?"

"Not at all. I think the county did a good job respecting the environment and the area's natural beauty. And I'm sure a lot more people can come here now and enjoy this part of island without feeling as if they're trekking into uncharted territory."

Avery was sure the island wasn't quite that rugged or isolated back in the day, but she knew what Mike meant. There were a lot of conveniences for families here, and she saw many seniors on the boardwalk, too, even some in wheelchairs. People who might have once found it very challenging to enjoy the beach could now come here easily.

They stopped walking and stood together, leaning against the railing and looking out at the beach and the wide blue sea. There was a light breeze today, catching the waves and creating whitecaps all along the shoreline. The surf was a little rough for swimming, but the swimmers did not seem daunted, and screams of delight echoed up and down the beach.

"It's a good thing," she agreed.

"And more business for us," he pointed out.

"Undoubtedly. At least for one of us, that is." She glanced at him. Her tone had been teasing, even though it was the truth.

But maybe not for long, she reminded herself.

Mike laughed. "Don't worry, Avery, you're going to surprise me one of these days. I just have that feeling."

Avery returned his smile and took a deep breath of the salty ocean air. "I think I will surprise you," she admitted. She met his glance and suddenly felt as if she couldn't look away. She decided to tell him. She was being silly. It was just a little promotional idea, not an international security secret.

At just that moment Mike reached out to brush aside a strand of her hair that had blown across her cheek. His hand lingered there for a moment and she felt mesmerized. She could hardly breathe, much less talk or even think.

"You're awfully pretty . . . for a chef, I mean," he said quietly.

"Um . . . thanks," she managed. His compliment took her totally by surprise. "I look like a mess most of the time you see me."

He laughed. "If this is a mess, I'd really be in trouble if we ever went out on the town . . . though I'm willing to risk it," he added.

"Out on the town—like a date?" Avery suddenly felt very conscious of his nearness. She felt their gazes meet and lock. The wide smile slowly faded from Mike's handsome face, replaced by a different expression, something she couldn't quite interpret—a wondering, bemused look.

"Yeah. That's what I mean. A date." His voice was low and soft. Even a little nervous, she thought. Though she imagined that he must ask women out all the time. And they must ask him, too, she suddenly realized.

But when would they go? she wondered. They were both so busy with their restaurants. Neither of them ever took a day off, and they would only get busier as the season picked up. How could anyone in this business ever have a relationship?

Does that even matter? Get a grip. You can't go out with him. No more guys in the restaurant business. And you have work to do this summer. Your entire future—and your mother's retirement savings—are riding on this, Avery. You can't let yourself get distracted. No matter how appealing he is.

Her heart thudded in her chest so loudly she was sure he could hear it, even above the crash of the waves.

He was incredibly attractive. And funny and thoughtful and smart, though not in an annoying, pompous way.

"So . . . what do you think?" he asked again. His anxious look melted her heart.

Avery stared at him wide-eyed, not knowing what to say. Before she could answer, a boy on a skateboard suddenly sped toward them. He veered so dangerously close, Avery gasped. Mike reached out and put his arm around her shoulders, pulling her back against him so she wouldn't be hit. The boy passed by, but Mike still held her.

"Are you all right?"

She nodded. "I think so."

She looked up at him, feeling breathless. Before she could say another word, he leaned down and kissed her. Avery was shocked for a moment. Then she closed her eyes and kissed him back. She stood on tiptoe, her hands holding on to his broad shoulders. His arms were wrapped around her waist. She felt totally lost in the sensations of his nearness, drowning in it, as if hit by a giant ocean wave. She wasn't sure how long they stood there. But the sound of her cell phone buzzing suddenly washed her up on dry land again. As they slowly broke apart, Avery felt dazed. Mike looked a bit dazed, too.

"Do you need to get that?" he asked politely.

She glanced quickly at her phone. "It's just Gena. I'll look at it later." She could already imagine what it said. "I'd better get back to the café. People are looking for me."

They turned to walk back the way they had come. He was uncharacteristically quiet for a few moments, and she wondered what he was thinking.

She could only think about one thing: that impromptu, impulsive, wildly exciting kiss. Where had that come from? What did it mean? And where was this relationship going? She didn't know the answer to any of those questions.

"I'd better get to work, too. It is Monday," Mike said finally. "Someday we'll have to come out here for a real beach break. We can each bring some specialties from our kitchens and have a taste-off."

Avery laughed. "Are you asking me on a date—or challenging me to a throw down?"

He smiled at her sassy comeback. "Maybe a bit of both. Competition isn't a bad thing, Avery. It makes life more interesting, shakes things up a little."

"Shakes things up?" She wasn't quite sure what he meant by that. Wasn't her situation shaky enough? And that kiss—it had shaken her to her bones.

"That's right. You need to be bold, fearless. Go out on a limb. That's where all the fruit is."

Was he talking about her restaurant or whatever it was that was growing between them? The guy could win a contest for double entendres, Avery decided. Still, she couldn't help but enjoy his charming smile and the affectionate light in his warm dark eyes. Then again, there was something smug in his pep talk. He was once again giving her advice, and the tiny twinge of guilt she felt about keeping her marketing plans secret dissolved.

She knew he was just trying to be helpful, but she wanted him to respect her, to consider her an equal, not just the floundering newbie on the block.

They walked down a few steps that led off the boardwalk then crossed to Ferry Street. Mike's restaurant stood a few storefronts to the right. Café Peregrine was to the left. A ferry had just landed, and the street was filled with beachgoers, carrying their tote bags, chairs, and umbrellas.

Mike looked down at her, squinting in the sunlight. "Looks like a good crowd out here today. Hope you have a lot of customers tonight."

"Thanks. Same to you," she replied.

They stared at each other a moment. Avery wondered again about that kiss. What was going to happen now? Was he going to kiss her again? She wasn't sure she could survive that. She would most likely melt into a puddle, right there on the sidewalk.

But finally he just smiled and lightly touched her shoulder.

"Catch you later, okay?"

"Sure, see you later." She nodded, feeling awkward and suddenly self-conscious. Was she blushing again? Geez, she hoped he thought it was just the sun.

She turned and waved as she walked away, knowing he stood watching her a moment or two.

She had the funniest feeling, as if she could have hung out with him all day. Not just goofing off at the beach, but doing what they had to do: working in a kitchen, running a restaurant. Together. The image was . . . startling.

Yes, she had sworn off men in the business but . . . Mike was totally different from Paul. Was she being foolish to ignore the possibilities here? There was no ignoring the way he had kissed her. That was for sure.

Avery had walked all the way to the café, and before she could sort out her thoughts about Mike any further, Gena and Teresa both came running to her.

"We've got the TV set up. It looks great," Gena reported.

"I brought in a framed poster from the movie and hung it by the reservations desk. The perfect touch," Teresa added.

Of course, Teresa would have the movie poster. I should have known, Avery realized, smiling ruefully. The women led her into the café to show off their helpful touches, and Avery put her worries and wonders about Mike Rossi aside.

But Mike was not very far from her thoughts for the rest of the day, even when the café was filled with diners and the gourmet pizzas were flying out of the oven, one after the next.

In the midst of their rush, she heard someone knocking on the kitchen door. Teresa ran over to open it.

"Hey, Mike. What are you doing here? Why aren't you at the Tuna?" Teresa asked bluntly. Obviously, she was surprised to see Mike away from his kitchen during prime cooking time.

Avery was, too. "Hi, Mike. What's up?" She wiped her hands on a cloth and walked over to greet him.

Mike stared down at her and just squinted a moment. Avery suddenly realized she had never seen him in his cooking whites. He looked even cuter, she thought. But that wasn't the only difference in his appearance tonight. She suddenly realized he was not smiling.

"Nothing's up with me. What's up with you?" He glanced over at the steel table, where Teresa had gone back to work, stretching out circles of dough to dinner-plate portions. "Why didn't you tell me you were planning a pizza night? We were hanging out, walking on the boardwalk . . . I was helping you move your furniture!" He shook his head. "Did you really think you had to keep it a secret?"

Avery sighed. "I was going to tell you, but the crew made me promise I would keep it under wraps."

"Really? And I thought you were the boss."

"I am," Avery said in a definite tone. "But we all came up with this idea together. They earned a say in how we pull it off."

"I just don't get it." Mike sounded confused and a little exasperated. "One minute we're all friendly and . . . fine. The next, you're acting like you're afraid I'll steal your idea. You really don't trust me at all, do you?"

Avery felt her face redden as he recalled their time together and came close to mentioning that kiss. That was one thing she definitely was *not* going to discuss.

"It's not that I don't trust you," she said, mustering the calmest tone she could. "It's that I wanted to put something together on my own. Without any advice or suggestions from anyone else. It's important to me that *I* figure out how to make the Peregrine a success."

He tilted his head to one side and crossed his arms over his chest. "So all that time, I was giving you advice, trying to pump up your morale . . . you were planning Operation Pizza?"

"Just since Saturday night," she admitted.

He shook his head, and she wondered if she had just made everything worse.

"Look," she said, "you're the one who told me to be bold and fearless. To climb a tree and grab some fruit . . . or something like that. I was just taking your advice."

His mouth twisted to one side. "Maybe I've been giving you too much advice. My place is practically empty. Then I noticed that you had all the customers," he admitted.

Avery was surprised but definitely pleased at that report. She quickly tried to hide her reaction. She didn't want to gloat. *Maybe now he'll think of me as more of an equal,* she thought. That realization was almost more pleasing than the profit she knew the café was taking in tonight.

Mike just stood there. He didn't look quite like his jaunty, confident self. It was obviously easier for a guy like him to give advice and be in charge. He looked a little lost in this role.

"I think you must be exaggerating," Avery said, trying to help him save face. "I bet we didn't even make a dent in your traffic tonight." She carefully spooned some sauce over the circles of dough. "But thanks for the compliment—and for your advice. Seriously, I do appreciate all the encouragement. It's made a huge difference."

"Well, I'm glad it's working out for you." He straightened his cap and headed for the door. "Just to let you know—because *I* don't treat the Tuna like a state secret—we're doing a theme night tomorrow, Tex-Mex Tuesday. We even have a piñata."

"Tomorrow, we might have dancing girls," she countered. And when he looked at her darkly, she added, "Kidding."

He gave her a reluctant smile then left the kitchen as quickly as he had come.

As she slipped another batch of pizzas in the oven and Gena

arrived with another fistful of orders, Avery hummed with satisfaction. This was how a kitchen was supposed to be, hectic and pressured, a complicated dance that had to be performed with meticulous precision as the music got faster and faster. That was the rhythm she thrived on, what she had trained for years to do. When she was cooking in the zone, like tonight, she didn't even have to peek out into the dining area. She felt all was well in her café—and in the entire universe.

But her contentment was tainted when she recalled the look on Mike's face tonight and the lovely time they'd spent together, strolling along the boardwalk that morning. And the way he'd kissed her. Was that really why he was upset? They'd had that amazing kiss, and then it seemed as if she didn't trust him.

Was he right? She was definitely attracted to him—madly attracted—but did she trust him?

Avery wasn't sure. All she knew was that her restaurant had to come first, even if Mike Rossi seemed to be finding a way into her heart.

LIZA and Jamie had agreed that he would get paid every other Tuesday, and Tuesdays would also be his day off. On Tuesday morning, Jamie arrived in the kitchen just as Claire was loading the breakfast dishes into the dishwasher.

"Guess I missed breakfast. I'll just grab some cereal," he said as he poured himself a mug of coffee.

"I saved you some pancakes, though they may have gotten tough sitting in the oven." Claire took a dish from the oven and placed it on the table.

Jamie suddenly looked awake. "Thanks, Claire. These look

good." He nimbly slipped a few of the flapjacks onto his own plate and coated them with butter and syrup.

Claire poured herself more coffee and sat across the table.

She knew that Liza had paid him last night. Now he had a pocket full of money and a whole day free of duties from the inn. She hoped that wasn't a recipe for trouble.

"So, your first day off. Do you have any plans?" Claire didn't want to seem nosy or anxious, but she was genuinely worried. She wondered if he would take the money he had earned so far—almost two weeks' salary, which had to seem like a small fortune to him—and disappear.

"I'm not sure what I'm going to do. I was thinking of going up to Newburyport. Or maybe into Boston. Or I could just hang out at the beach here."

"I don't think you've seen the new beachfront on the north side of the island yet, where Avery opened her restaurant," Claire said. "There's a new boardwalk and a ferry that crosses to Newburyport."

"I thought of that. But I sort of miss the city. I miss my friends."

He did get a lot of calls and text messages. Claire could see he had not lost touch with his buddies back in Boston. She didn't know if that was a good or bad thing. If he wanted to go into the city and see his friends, that was his decision.

"Let me know what you decide. I have to do some shopping in town today. I can give you a lift to the station."

"Cool. I'll go check the train schedule."

So that was that. He would go to Boston. And she would say a prayer that he wouldn't get into any trouble there.

A short time later, Claire pulled into the train station in Cape Light. She parked near the ticket house. "Give me a call later and tell me what train you're taking back. I'll pick you up. No need to waste money on a taxi."

"That's okay. I'll be fine. I don't want to bother you. I might be late. I might go down to Fenway with my friends and try to scalp some tickets to a ball game."

That plan didn't sound too bad, she thought. Better than standing around a bar, drinking beer.

"All right. If you change your mind, let me know."

Claire pulled away from the station, she couldn't help wondering if she had said good-bye to him for good. She had always worried about Jamie. There was always so much uncertainty in his life,

Neither fret nor worry, she scolded herself with a scrap of scripture. *He's a young man, practically still a teenager, and he needs to see his friends, to blow off some steam, have a little fun.* The inn was a haven to her, but it must seem like living in a stuffy museum to Jamie, she realized. At least some of the time.

She vowed to put Jamie out of her mind for the rest of the day and not to trouble herself with what he might be doing in Boston. That wouldn't help either one of them.

God, please help me to put this aside today, she silently prayed on her drive back to the island. *I know that what Jamie does on his day off—where he goes and who he sees—is none of my business. But please guide and protect him. Please help him make good choices.*

Keeping her mind off Jamie was hard but not impossible. She and Liza had gotten used to having Jamie around and now, with their extra worker gone, Claire found herself busy throughout the day, hardly having a moment to fret about Jamie's whereabouts.

When it was time to serve dinner, Claire thought he might call at the last minute, saying he was at the station. But she and Liza ate together in the kitchen at the usual time.

"I guess Jamie must be enjoying his day off," Liza said as she helped herself to some salad. "He's been working so hard, he really deserved it. Have you heard from him?"

"No, I haven't." Claire spread some butter on a roll. "I told him to call if he needed a lift from the station, but he said he'd didn't want to bother us. I have a feeling he might be late."

"There are cabs at the station all night. But I hope he doesn't get in too late. He'll be dragging tomorrow, and we have a lot of guests coming in Thursday. We'll need him to help us clean and bring down a few cots."

Among the many other jobs he was needed for, Claire added silently. Jamie had been doing a good job. Well, most of the time. She did occasionally find him texting or talking on his phone when he should have been giving his full attention to some chore. But he was young, and friends were important.

Was he entirely responsible? No, not exactly. But she didn't have any reason to think he would not act responsibly on his day off. No concrete reason. Just a niggling little doubt.

"Claire? You're so quiet. Is something wrong?"

Claire shook her head. "Not at all. You're right. Jamie's worked hard. I hope he was able to get into the ball park. He really loves baseball."

"So I noticed." Liza smiled then took a bite of her dinner: broiled cod with lemon butter and a toasted pine nut, herb, and cracker-crumb topping. "This fish is good."

Liza was tired and went up to her room soon after dinner. Claire took her knitting out to the porch as she usually did. She sat out for a few hours, until it was nearly eleven. She told herself that she wasn't waiting for Jamie, but in her heart she knew that wasn't true.

When she was too tired to knit anymore or even sit without feeling her eyes close, she got up and went inside. She went into the sitting room to turn out the light but turned on the TV instead, to check the ball game. Perhaps it had gone into extra innings, and Jamie couldn't stand to leave before the game ended. But when she found the official channel of the Red Sox, she learned that the team wasn't even in town today. They were in Texas and had already lost to the Rangers.

He probably didn't realize that this morning. He was so excited to get to go down to Fenway. He didn't mean to purposely mislead me.

Claire wondered then if she should call him, to see if he had caught the last train. If he hadn't caught the train at eleven thirty, he would have to wait until one A.M., or even later.

But I'm not his mother, she reminded herself. Even most mothers wouldn't call a young man that age to check on him. That was going too far.

She wondered if it would seem too obvious if she was out on the porch knitting when he returned. It might look as if she had been waiting up for him.

But you sit there every night. That's your habit. You don't have to worry so much what he thinks, she reminded herself. *Go out and knit if you feel like it.*

So she did and sat in the wicker chair and knit until her eyes closed. She had no idea of how much time had passed when she felt someone gently shake her awake.

"Claire? You must be cold out here. It's late."

She opened her eyes to find Avery smiling down at her. "Oh . . . Avery . . . I fell asleep. What time is it?"

Avery glanced at her watch. "It's almost one."

"Just getting home from the café? Did you have a good night?" Claire picked up her knitting from her lap and slipped it into her tote bag.

"Yes, we did. Much better than last Tuesday. We did sort of a theme thing to bring more customers in. Two entrees for the price of one. Not that original, but people seemed to like it. And it won't be forever—just until our name gets around a little."

"That sounds very smart. I'm sure Café Peregrine will be the talk of the town in no time." Claire stood and smoothed her dress. Could Jamie have returned and not woken her? As much as she hoped that had happened, she was pretty sure it was not the case.

Avery and Claire went inside together. Claire locked the door. Jamie had a key. Well, he was given one. She hoped he hadn't forgotten it.

They walked up the stairs together and said good night. Avery went into her room on the second floor, and Claire started up the next flight to the third.

Avery felt so tired, she was tempted to sleep in her clothes. But of course, she would never do that. She needed a shower to wash away the cooking smells and hot water to relax her sore muscles. Her back hurt and so did her biceps, from stretching out all the pizzas the night before. But she was satisfied so far with their new marketing ideas. Business was definitely picking up.

Before heading for the shower, she checked her e-mail. There was a note from her sister and she quickly read it:

Hi, Avery, Hope all is going well at the café. So sorry we haven't been able to get up to Massachusetts for a visit. I've been crazy busy at work. But am definitely taking off a few days around the Fourth of July. Mom and I will come to your island the Friday before the holiday and stay for the weekend. Can you speak to the woman who runs the inn where you're staying and get a room for us? Can't wait to see the café. Mom is excited, too. Call when you have a chance—we'll iron out the plans.

Love, Christine

Avery glanced at her calendar. June 29? That wasn't that long from now, she thought dismally. Yes, business had picked up the last two nights, but she had no guarantee that her other theme nights would work as well. She wanted her sister and mother to see a thriving, jumping restaurant. Not a struggling little enterprise, run on a shoestring . . . and forced to run theme nights.

Avery felt so bad she wanted to cry. And she did weep a little, alone in the shower. But once she came out and dried herself off, she realized she was mainly just very tired.

What was it her mother always used to say? *Things will look different in the morning.*

She certainly hoped so. She shut off her light and crawled into bed, too exhausted to worry about another thing.

CLAIRE normally fell asleep after reading the Bible for a few minutes and shutting off the light. But she felt wide awake tonight, her eyes flying open and peering into the darkness at every sound outside, listening for Jamie to come home.

She wasn't sure what time it was when she finally drifted off. Her sleep was deep and dreamless. But she woke up at her usual time, half past six, feeling rested and alert.

She quickly dressed and walked down to Jamie's room. The door stood open. The bed was neatly made and the room looked just as it had after he left yesterday, his big sneakers side-by-side near the closet and a T-shirt hanging over a chair.

He had not come home last night.

Claire felt a cold ache in her chest. She hoped that nothing bad had happened to him. An accident or maybe he'd gotten sick. He could be in a hospital somewhere right now . . .

She stopped herself. *He's probably fine. He's managed to take care of himself all these years.* She was letting her imagination run wild. Making excuses for him, mostly. He was probably stretched out on some friend's couch, sleeping off a late night. He would wander back in his own good time.

Claire went down to the kitchen and turned on the coffeemaker. She began to assemble the ingredients for breakfast but felt too upset to continue, her hands shaking as she cracked an egg.

She decided to take a walk on the beach. Liza wouldn't be up for at least an hour. There was no reason to wake her with this news. Maybe Jamie would be back soon, in time for work this morning.

Claire went out the back door and crossed the street. She took her time making her way down the long flight of wooden stairs that led to the beach. The wooden steps were still damp and a little slippery. The sun was low and wisps of fog lay low on the landscape, like long white veils, floating on the meadow of the Gilroys' farm next door and along the shoreline.

She left her shoes at the bottom of the stairs and walked over the sand to the water. She hadn't thought to bring a jacket or sweater. The air was still cool and damp, the sky a little overcast. She felt the mist on her face, felt it dampening her hair.

Liza would be upset if Jamie didn't come back soon. She might even fire him, Claire realized. Not that she could blame her. Unless he had a very good reason for this.

What did they say in the judicial system—innocent until proven guilty? Her faith advised the same perspective. Well, she would try to think of Jamie that way, though her heart felt heavy with dread.

She had not gone very far when a figure emerged from the mist, a man dressed for fishing, in a canvas hat with a floppy brim, a khaki green vest covered with pockets, and hip-high rubber waders. He was tugging back the line from his fishing pole, concentrating on reeling it in smoothly. Claire stepped around him.

Then he turned and glanced over his shoulder. "Claire, is that you?" Reverend Ben asked. "You're out early this morning."

"I might say the same about you, Reverend. Early bird gets the halibut?"

He laughed. "I'm trying for striped bass, but that's the basic theory."

He finished reeling in his line and grabbed the hook that was dangling at the end. "It's a wonderful time out here. Not a soul around . . . except for a few other crazy fishermen."

"I don't get out on the beach much in the morning. I'm usually too busy. But the inn is almost empty this morning, and I . . . I needed the exercise."

Reverend Ben gave her a skeptical look. "With your schedule, I doubt that. But walking along the ocean is a wonderful way to calm the soul. I've even heard about walking meditation, though I never tried it."

"That sounds interesting. I just try to focus on all the beauty down here. That's enough to meditate upon for me."

Ben laughed. "Very true . . . How is Jamie doing?" he asked. "Is the job going well?"

That was just like Reverend Ben. Even if you didn't want to unburden yourself, he had an uncanny knack for asking the one question that would make it impossible to avoid a troubling subject.

Claire stared down at the wet sand; her bare feet were now buried up to her ankles. She felt stuck, in more ways than one.

"Jamie has been doing a good job. Liza and I both agree on that.

But yesterday was his first day off. He went into the city and hasn't come back yet." She looked up at the minister. "He may have a perfectly good excuse. But probably not," she said simply. "I'm very upset about it, Reverend. I think when Liza wakes up and finds out, she might fire him. And I feel so . . . responsible. I talked her into hiring him. She wouldn't have taken the chance otherwise."

Reverend Ben sighed and scratched his forehead, his hat slipping backward. "'God grant me the serenity to accept the things I cannot change; courage to change the things I can—'"

"'—and wisdom to know the difference," she finished for him. "The Serenity Prayer. I recited it last night to help me get to sleep."

He reached out and touched her arm. "I feel for your dilemma, Claire. I truly do. When my son, Mark, was wandering all over the country, squandering his youth and his health, and so angry at me and Carolyn he would barely speak to us, I was practically tearing my hair out. I'm not saying it's easy. It's the hardest thing in the world to see someone you love wasting their life, going down the wrong path. But you can't help someone who doesn't want to be helped. You can't save Jamie. He has to save himself. He has to want to make something of his life. It won't be easy for him. He'll need something deep inside to draw on, something more than your support. Even more than your love," he added quietly.

Claire nodded. "I know that's true. But it makes me feel sad and defeated. And hopeless," she admitted. "I had such high hopes when I found him standing there in the garden. It seemed he had stepped out of a dream. But I shouldn't feel entirely hopeless," she corrected herself. "Wherever there's faith, there's hope."

"That is true, Claire. Don't ever doubt it. Don't stop praying for Jamie. Don't stop loving him. But stop blaming yourself. Stop holding yourself responsible for his behavior. Jamie has to see that he's responsible for his own choices and the consequences, good or bad."

Claire knew that was true. The consequences for this choice were going to be dire. He would lose his job. It made her so sad. As if some rare treasure had slipped through her hands. Wasn't there some way she could hold on to him? Hold on to this opportunity to help him?

Jamie, why do you do things like this? Why do you have to ruin your chances?

Reverend Ben's light touch on her arm pulled Claire from her thoughts. "Claire, are you all right? What were you thinking just now? Can you tell me?"

Claire sighed, then nodded. If there was one person in the world that she could confide in, it was Reverend Ben.

"I'm afraid, Reverend Ben. I'm just so afraid for him."

Chapter Nine

When Claire returned to the inn, Liza was sitting in the kitchen, sipping coffee and checking her laptop. "Were you out on the beach, Claire?"

Claire nodded and smoothed her hair back into place. "It was misty, but the fog seems to be burning off. I met Reverend Ben. He was fly casting, going after striped bass. I don't think he caught anything . . ."

Her voice trailed off as she slipped on her apron and tied the strings. She knew she was just putting off the inevitable question about Jamie, but couldn't help it.

"Jamie must have come home late," Liza said. "I'll go up and wake him. We have a lot to do today."

Claire took a deep breath. "Jamie didn't come back last night. His room is empty, just the way he left it."

Liza looked surprised. "Did he leave a message?"

Claire shook her head. "Unless he called while I was out walking . . . no, I haven't heard from him."

"There are no new messages. I just checked." Liza's tone was edged with concern. "Something could have happened to him. There might be a reason why he's delayed." She looked back at Claire. "Do you know where he went, what his plans were?"

"He said something about going to see a baseball game. But the Red Sox aren't in town right now. I think he must have gone to see his friends, at the apartment where he was living, in South Boston. He must have stayed over with them."

"Partying," Liza said bluntly. "He's probably sleeping off a hangover somewhere while we're sitting here, worried that he's in a hospital."

"I know." Claire had already gone through this chain of thought, about a hundred times. "I did try his cell phone this morning, but he didn't pick up."

Liza stood up and closed her computer. "I'll call him again then. I have the number in my office." She sighed and gazed at Claire across the table. "I'm sorry, Claire. But if he doesn't have a good reason for this, I have to let him go. You know that, don't you?"

"I understand." It was hard for Claire to say the words, but she knew she had to. "You don't have to apologize. I'm sorry now that I persuaded you to hire him."

"That was my decision. For the most part, he's done a good job," Liza said. "It's just this unpredictable . . . goofing off. I don't feel as if I can trust him. He's unreliable, not mature enough or something. It's as if he has two personalities. Do you think when he acts so amiable and hard-working that he's putting on an act for us? I honestly can't figure it out."

"I don't know. He was always that way a bit when he was a boy," Claire admitted. "Moody. Helping out in the kitchen one minute, disappearing the next. But he was so young and had such a difficult life back then. I always thought it was just his way of surviving."

Claire didn't know what else to say. She couldn't explain or defend him. Liza's description was accurate, but it was painful to hear it laid out so plainly. Claire knew Jamie wasn't perfect, but who was? There was also so much good there, so much courage and resilience. And love. He had wanted to love his father. He had wanted to love her. She couldn't stop hoping that the good in him would grow and someday overcome the flaws.

Liza glanced at Claire and tucked the laptop under her arm. "I'll go call him. I hope he picks up," she added. "Then we have to get to work around here. We have a lot to do by tomorrow."

And without any extra help, Claire added silently.

She felt so sorry for putting Liza in this situation. Liza had a good heart. It would be hard for her to fire Jamie, even though it was the right thing to do.

And she felt so sorry for Jamie, even after this bad behavior. She couldn't help it. As irresponsible as he was at times, this job was his lifeline. He was just too immature to realize it.

But she had to remember Reverend Ben's advice. She couldn't help Jamie until he was committed to helping himself. Maybe once he suffered the consequences of acting out like this, he would wake up and smell the coffee. She surely hoped so.

CLAIRE worked with Liza the rest of the day, getting the inn in shape for a big wave of weekend guests. The two women worked like a well-oiled machine, instinctively knowing what needed to be done without much need to speak.

Which was just as well, Claire reflected. Liza's concern and confusion about Jamie seemed to have crystallized into anger. Claire dreaded his return, as much as she waited for it. She listened all day for him to come through the front door, or even call. Then she would catch herself and try to take a step back from the drama, silently reciting the Serenity Prayer. She could not control this situation or protect Jamie from the outcome of his actions.

She and Liza were eating supper in the kitchen when she heard the front door of the inn open and quietly close again. Liza had heard it, too. Claire watched her sit back and put her fork down, her lips pursed.

"Jamie, is that you?" Liza called out.

"Yeah . . . it's me . . . I'm back." He soon appeared in the kitchen doorway. Claire glanced at him then down at her plate. She felt a cold weight in the pit of her stomach, as if a stone had lodged there.

Jamie sought her out with his gaze. *Looking for the weak link,* Claire realized. She met his glance and looked away. She would let Liza handle this. They both knew it was her territory.

He took a glass from the drain board and filled it with water. He looked rough, as if he hadn't shaved or showered, still wearing the clothes he had left in.

"I'm really sorry I'm so late getting back . . . I was hanging with my friends and I must have eaten some bad food. A bad hot dog, or something . . . We went to Fenway and I got so sick, I couldn't even move . . ."

Claire felt almost sick with disbelief. *How could he lie like that? Did he think so little of her, of both of them?*

"The Red Sox didn't play in Boston last night, Jamie. They're in Texas this week," she said quietly.

She saw surprise flash across his features, shock at being caught. He didn't think two women would have known that.

"Yeah, that's right . . . They weren't in town. We got screwed up with the schedule. We went over there, though, and bought some food on the street."

"Bad food?" Liza stared at him. "That's why you're a day late getting back here?"

Jamie looked at Liza. He held a hand up, as if testifying in a court of law. "Honest, I swear, I was sick as a dog. My friends could barely drag me back to their place. I was puking my guts out for, like, hours . . . I thought I was dying or something. They were saying maybe I had appendicitis and I should go to the hospital. But I knew it was the food. After I got sick, I was wiped. All I could do was sleep. I kept telling them to call you and tell you what happened. But those idiots didn't listen to me. They didn't even wake me up. I told them I had to get back this morning for work, and they just let me sleep all day . . . I was way too messed up to take the train last night, honest."

He sounded so annoyed at his friends. As if it was all their fault that he was a day late returning.

Liza came to her feet and faced him. "You were given one day off, Jamie, not two. If you were really unable to return, you should have called us."

"Yeah, I know I should have called you guys. Totally. I'm so sorry. But my phone went dead and I told my friends the number and thought they were going to let you know what happened and—"

"I don't believe you," Liza said before he could go on again.

Jamie shrugged and tossed up his hands. "I don't know what to say . . . I don't know how I can prove it. I don't have a note from a doctor or anything . . . But I was really sick," he insisted. "I'll work double tomorrow. I'll work extra hours. It's not like there are any guests here right now—"

"We needed you here today, not tomorrow," Liza cut in. "More than that, you should have called. That was completely irresponsible. And disrespectful," she added. "Not that it would have made things much better. But that would have been the right thing to do, the responsible thing. I've already talked to you about taking off time without permission," she reminded him.

Jamie nodded, looking serious. "I know. I remember . . . But it was like a sick day. I mean, if I was here and I got sick, I wouldn't have been able to work anyway. So what's the difference? I just thought, like, what can I do? I can't work, so I'd better just hang here until I feel normal, you know?"

Claire felt so sad listening to his excuses, so disappointed in him. Did he think they could be so easily manipulated?

"That's enough, Jamie," Liza said abruptly. "This isn't working out. I have to let you go."

His face went pale with shock. He stared at Liza, then at Claire. Claire felt a piercing jolt in her heart. She didn't want to watch this scene unfold, but she had to support Liza. She could hardly get up and leave now.

"You're letting me go . . . like . . . firing me?" He leaned closer, then suddenly stepped back, touching his forehead with his hand. His eyes grew wide and glassy. "I can't believe it . . . I was really sick. I mean it. Ask my friends if you don't believe me . . ."

"Jamie, just stop. I know you're lying. Yes, I am firing you. Is that clear enough?" Liza was angry now. Claire could see it was hard enough for her to tell Jamie to go. She didn't want to argue with him.

"What do you mean? I've been working really hard, breaking my back around here. Doing everything you say . . ." He sounded angry now, too, and frustrated with them. "How can you just say, like, out of the blue, 'Hey, you're fired, man.' When it was, like, one little stupid thing I did wrong."

Liza faced him squarely. "Don't you dare shout at me. If you think that was a minor issue, it just goes to show how wrong you are for this job. And you were warned."

He pressed his hand to his mouth a moment. Claire watched the anger drain from him, his body growing slack.

"I'm sorry. I'm sorry . . . please don't fire me. I really need this job. Just give me one more chance? Please? . . . I'll do whatever you say. You don't even have to give me any days off at all. For the rest of the summer, I swear. And I'll take less pay," he added, trying to catch Liza's eye again. "I won't screw up again . . . I really promise."

"No. I'm sorry," Liza said. "That's my decision."

Claire felt so bad for Liza. *She wouldn't be going through this now if it wasn't for me,* Claire thought. But it was so hard to watch Jamie struggle. To hear him beg to hang on to his job.

He suddenly turned to Claire. "Is that what you think, too, Claire? Do you think I'm lying? Do you think I should get fired? For doing one little thing wrong?"

"Oh, Jamie . . ." Claire shook her head. "You've done this to yourself. Can't you see that?"

He stared at her a moment, surprised that she wasn't sticking up for him. "Okay. I get it. You're on her side. You say you want to help me, but not that much, I guess."

Claire felt stung by his words. She couldn't take a breath for a moment. Her heart was bursting. She felt like she might cry.

Liza stepped between them. "That's enough, Jamie. Go up and pack your things. I'll take you to the station tomorrow morning. First thing," she added emphatically.

He let out a long breath then turned and left the kitchen. Claire heard him go up to his room with slow, heavy steps.

"Well, that's over with. I didn't think he'd argue with me nearly as much. But I've never fired anyone before," Liza admitted. She sat down again, nearly collapsing into the chair. Claire could see how hard the confrontation had been for her.

"I'm sorry, Liza. I'm so sorry it came to this."

"I know, Claire. It isn't your fault."

Claire sighed. "I bear responsibility here. I do," she insisted. "I wish I had been tougher from the start."

"How tough do we have to be?" Liza asked, sounding a bit exasperated.

Claire met her glance but didn't answer. *Jamie is . . . Jamie,* she wanted to say. She should have known there would be some acting out. Some testing. She should have warned Liza. She should have seen it herself from the start. Maybe it wouldn't have come to this.

Claire rose and began clearing the table, though neither of them had eaten much dinner. They had both lost their appetites now. She hung over the sink, dawdling with the dishes. She thought she might cry and didn't want Liza to see.

"Claire? Are you all right? I'm sorry, Claire but . . ."

Claire shook her head, her back to Liza as she stacked the dishes into the dishwasher. "I understand, I do. I'm sure it wasn't easy for you. But . . . oh, nothing. Never mind."

"But what? What were you going to say?"

"It doesn't matter. I don't want to interfere. I've interfered enough already."

"Claire, please . . . Do you really think he deserves another chance?" Liza asked, guessing what Claire wanted to say. "After coming back an entire day later than he should have? Not even a phone call, to let us know. And then he comes in here and just makes up a bunch of inane excuses. With a totally straight face. As if anyone would believe that story."

"I know." Claire couldn't defend any of it. "But if we send him away from here, what will become of him? He'll have no job, no money, no place to live . . . Where will he go? Back to that group of low-down friends who made him lose this job in the first place, I'll bet."

"No one *made* him lose this job, Claire. He did that completely on his own."

Liza's tone was sharp. *She's angry but not at me,* Claire reminded herself. *At Jamie.* But it felt like the same thing.

"I'm not trying to defend him," Claire insisted.

"You sound as if you are," Liza countered. "You're making excuses for him."

Claire sighed. That was true. She didn't mean to but . . . she couldn't help it. "Maybe I can call around and help him find something else on the island. Or in Cape Light. Maybe Daniel or Reverend Ben will know of something."

She sounded desperate. As plaintive as Jamie had, begging Liza not to fire him. But she suddenly felt as if Jamie's entire future was on the line. Once he left the inn, he would surely disappear from her life again.

Liza shook her head. "Claire, please. Don't put me in this position. How can I recommend Jamie to anyone? I just couldn't, not in good conscience."

That was true, too, Claire realized. *Even if I could find a spot for him through someone around here, the next person would surely ask Liza what she thought of Jamie's work and why she was letting him go.*

Claire suddenly felt as if she were in a boat and Jamie was out in the water, grasping for her hand. She was trying to pull him back in, but her hold on him was slippery and he was slowly letting go, sliding under, and there was no way for her to help him. No way to pull him back to safety.

"Please, Liza . . . I know he's done wrong and taken advantage of you. Of us both. But . . ." Claire felt so full of emotion, she could barely find the words. "I'm so afraid that his life is going downhill. So quickly. He has no direction, and no one to put him on a good path. No one," she repeated. "Except for you and me."

Liza's voice was low and solemn. "What are you trying to say, Claire? Are you asking me to let him stay?"

Claire slowly nodded. "Yes, I guess I am. I know I shouldn't, but I can't help it. It seems like there's a bigger picture here. There's so much more at stake than him just flaunting our rules and coming back late from his day off. Even lying to us about why . . . I wouldn't ask you to do this, Liza, if it didn't mean so much to me. You know I wouldn't."

Liza's voice softened. "I do know that, Claire. But try to be realistic. Do you think it will be any different if we let him stay longer? We'll just go through this agony all over again—a few days from now or maybe in a week or two. And where will that leave us? We'll be stuck shorthanded at the height of the season. Isn't that just what I didn't want to happen?"

Claire knew it was not the right moment to answer her. They both needed a moment to cool off. Beyond that, Claire knew she should just back down and accept this situation. But something in her resisted and instead held fast to defending Jamie, to arguing for a reprieve.

Liza paused and lowered her voice again. "I just don't trust him anymore, Claire. I don't believe a word he tells me."

Claire bit her bottom lip. "It's hard for me to hear you speak so harshly about him. Even though he deserves it. He's been coasting so far, seeing what he can get away with, how far he can bend the rules. But I'll talk to him. I'll lay down the law and make him understand he can't stay unless he's committed a hundred and ten percent. No more chances after this. If he crosses the line, he's out. And I won't ever ask you again," she promised.

Liza let out a long breath but didn't answer.

Claire said a silent prayer. *Dear God, please let Liza give Jamie another chance. Please give me the words to change her mind.*

"Liza, I know he's done wrong. But please find it in your heart to forgive him. I know it's a lot to ask. I know he doesn't deserve it. But please forgive him and forgive me for asking you. Give him one more chance, and give me one more chance to help him . . ." Claire's plea trailed off. She didn't know if her words had reached Liza's heart, but she didn't know what else to say.

Liza sighed. "I'm sorry. I'm not sure," she said finally. "I hate to refuse you, Claire, I really do. You know how much I care about you . . . and how much I owe you. But I need to make the right decision here. I don't know what to say. I guess I need to sleep on this."

Claire nodded. "All right. That's fair."

"I will tell you this . . . If Jamie wants to continue here, he has to start from square one. He has to be totally truthful with me. With both of us. I need to be convinced that he knows what he did today was wrong—and why it was wrong. He can't just say things he thinks I want to hear."

"I understand. He's gotten by so long doing just that. It's a bad habit," Claire replied. Even when she first met him, when he was just a boy, Jamie had a knack for getting out of a tight spot by saying exactly what someone else wanted to hear, whether or not he meant it. Claire wondered if he even realized what he was doing—and if he could ever stop maneuvering through life that way.

"It's more than a bad habit, Claire." Liza's tone was sharp. Claire could see her measuring her words, not permitting herself to say all she was thinking. "I know it seems harsh to hold the line on this. I know I owe you the world. But part of me objects to letting him stay because I see the way he manipulates you. He hasn't been here very long and he's already betrayed your trust. More than once," Liza reminded her. "I love you, Claire. I hate to see you hurt that way," she said honestly. Before Claire could answer, Liza sighed. "All right . . . talk to him. See if you can get anywhere. I'm going up now. We'll figure this out in the morning."

Claire nodded. "I'll do my best."

Liza touched Claire's shoulder a moment. "I know you will. I'm sorry we had words. This isn't easy to sort out."

"No, it isn't. Not for either of us," Claire said. Part of her wondered if letting Jamie stay was the best thing to do. Maybe he really had to sink to some desperate depth in order to take hold of his life.

But she couldn't do that to him. Not yet.

Once Liza left the kitchen, Claire finished clearing the table and cleared her head, too. Ever since Jamie had arrived, she felt responsible. She had persuaded Liza to hire him. Now here she was pleading with Liza again on his behalf, when there seemed no good reason at all to let him stay.

Liza was not just her employer, but her good friend. Claire felt an abiding loyalty to her and to this inn. But she could not ignore her feelings for Jamie, a deep need to make good on the promise that she had broken ten years ago. Claire felt torn in two, as if a war were raging inside her and she had no idea which side was winning.

She did know that if Jamie had any chance of staying on, he had to speak up for himself tomorrow and convince Liza that he was ready to mend his ways and stop testing them at every opportunity.

Could he do that? Sincerely? Claire was not sure.

UPSTAIRS on the third floor, Claire walked down the hall to Jamie's room. The door stood halfway open. She glanced inside and saw him lying on top of the bed, fully dressed, his hands folded behind his head as he stared up at the ceiling.

She knocked on the door to draw his attention, and he quickly turned to her.

"Oh . . . hey, Claire. What's up?" He sat up and looked at her curiously.

"May I come in? I'd like to talk to you."

"All right . . . I was just going to pack up. I didn't feel so good again and needed to lie down." He rubbed his stomach and made a face. Trying to elicit her sympathy. Or still clinging to his silly story.

There was a small desk in the room, near the window. Claire turned the chair around and sat down. Jamie's duffel bag was on the floor near the chest of drawers. It was open and a few pieces of clothing had been tossed inside. It hurt her heart to see how little he had.

She sat back and met his gaze. She wasn't sure how to begin.

"Did you come to say good-bye?"

Claire looked down at her hands. "I hope not. I'm trying to persuade Liza to give you another chance. But she's not convinced you deserve one. Mostly, she says you're too unreliable . . . and she's very angry that you lied to her. To both of us."

A flush rose on his fair skin. "Yeah. Well. I'm sorry. I got confused. We were talking about going to a game but—"

"Never mind that," Claire cut in quickly. "Are you willing to make a sincere apology—and really commit yourself to this job? That's the question now."

He started to answer but she held up her hand.

"Don't talk yet. I'm not done." He looked surprised by her firm tone, but sat back, giving her his full attention. "I just want you to listen. As hard as you can. I'm afraid for you, Jamie. Of all the things I could say to you now, that's the most important one. I'm afraid what might happen if you leave here. Your entire future may depend on this conversation."

She saw his mouth twist to one side, as if hiding a nervous grin. He didn't believe her. He crossed his arms over his chest.

Dear God, please give me the right words to reach him. To reach his reasoning mind and his heart.

"Liza and I trusted you. We believed that you were going to do what you said you would do, come back on Tuesday night. But you didn't live up to our trust. You didn't keep your promise. So now you have to lose this job. Which is a pity because this place is a good stepping stone for you. Please try to think about your future, beyond your next paycheck or party with your friends. Do you want to be stuck in some minimum-wage job your whole life? Don't you want to have a good trade? A path to improving your life? If you saved your pay, you might be able to start college again, or attend some trade school in the fall. Even if it's only part-time, that would be something. It would be a very good start in the right direction."

"Right. I didn't even finish high school. How am I going to do that?"

Claire felt stung. "You told me that you did," she reminded him. "You said you finished high school and even took a few courses at a community college."

Jamie's face turned red. He'd obviously forgotten that conversation. "I did? I must have said something else that made you think that."

"No, Jamie. That's what you said." Claire forced herself to remain calm, to keep her voice steady. They weren't going to get anywhere if she lost her patience. "So you never graduated. When did you leave school?"

"Junior year. I just got sick of it . . . I'm sorry I said that, Claire. I just . . . I just didn't want you to think I was such a loser. I wanted you to think I'd done a little better."

"I understand," she said quietly. "I think you can do better. I know you can," she insisted. "I believe it in my heart," she added, tapping the spot above her breastbone. "I wish you could believe it, too. I want to help you so much, Jamie. I couldn't care about you more if you were my own child."

She knew that was true. Jamie was the closest she'd ever come to having a child, and all the worry, hope, and prayers that came with that blessing. She felt tears fill her eyes. She took a steadying breath. She didn't want to start crying now. Her feelings about all this—her anger, frustration, even her love for him—were not the point.

Jamie didn't answer. He stared at her a moment, then looked away. She wasn't sure what he was feeling. He seemed a bit confused, even ashamed.

"Please don't cry, Claire," he said finally. "I'm sorry I screwed up . . . I really am," he added quietly.

She met his glance and thought he was telling the truth this time.

"Did I get you in trouble, too?"

She shook her head. "Don't worry about me. This is about you. I know this job isn't very glamorous. But it could be the first step on a path for you, a path to a better future. Something to build on . . . if you can commit to it wholeheartedly. Not just when you feel like it. Do you understand what I'm trying to say?"

Jamie was leaning forward now, his hands clasped together. He glanced at her and then down at the floor. "Sure. I know what you mean," he said quietly.

Claire stared at him. "I'm not sure you do. I'm really not sure I'm getting through to you."

Finally, he said, "I don't understand. Is Liza going to let me have my job back? I hope she doesn't fire me. I need to keep working . . . I-I owe this guy some money and I've got to pay him back. Or it's going to get pretty ugly."

He stared straight ahead as he made this confession. Claire could see he was worried. And scared. Was that why he had come here a few weeks ago? And why he had come back tonight? She couldn't even stop to try to figure that out now.

"I don't know what Liza is going to say," Claire replied honestly. "That depends on you. Totally on you. Not me. Not your friends. Not anybody else in the world. She told me that tomorrow she'll have a talk with you and see if you're willing to make a sincere commitment to this job. Not just coast along, seeing what you can get away with. She wants to hear you apologize and really mean it. And no playacting, Jamie. She'll see right through it."

He nodded, looking a bit relieved but nervous now, too.

"She wants to know if you're willing to make something of yourself. I want to know, too," Claire added. "Becoming a better person is a slow process. It doesn't happen overnight or even over a summer." She paused and reached in her pocket then showed him what she had in her palm. "This is the piece of beach glass you gave me, remember?" She tilted it slightly so the amber fragment caught the light. "Do you see the way the ocean wore down the sharp edges, little by little? You wouldn't have noticed any change at all day to day, until one day you would see that it was smooth and polished, like a jewel."

His mouth was pressed in a tight line. It was hard to guess what he was thinking. Did he understand her?

She set the bit of beach glass on his bedside table, hoping he would see it there after she left and think about it.

"I know what you're trying to say, Claire. I want to do better. But I'm not sure I can do it. I've been too long . . . the other way. I'll screw up and disappoint you."

"It's not about me. It's about you. I think, deep inside, you know you can do it. That's why you came here to find me, and why you came back tonight. Even though you knew Liza and I would be upset with you. Part of you knows you can do better, Jamie. And I do, too."

Before Jamie could reply, Claire said, "I think I've said enough. More than enough for now. It's time for you to think about these things we've been talking about. I will, too. I need you to know that if Liza lets you stay, this is your last chance. I won't be able to stand up for you again. Do you understand me?"

She hated to put it in such a final way. She wasn't even sure that if he crossed the line again, she could turn her back on him completely.

Jamie nodded, his expression solemn. "I do . . . And thanks, Claire. Thanks for helping me."

"Don't thank me yet. We still have to see what we can work out in the morning." She paused by his bedside. "Jamie, do you remember when I taught you to pray?"

"Yeah, I guess. That was a long time ago."

"Yes, it was," Claire agreed. She had taught him some simple prayers: grace before meals and a prayer of thanks to say at bedtime and the Lord's Prayer, of course. "It doesn't matter if you remember the exact words but do you remember how I told you you could talk to God, to ask for His help any time you needed it?"

He glanced at her and then away. "Yeah, I remember."

"Do you ever?" she asked quietly.

He shrugged. "Sometimes . . . Not lately."

"God is a friend we can call on for help, even if we've been out of touch a long time. He wants to help you," she assured him. "I can try to help you, but I can only do so much. You might make a decision to help yourself now. I hope you do. But when all is said and done, it's the one above who will help you make the right choice—and help you talk to Liza tomorrow. He'll help you stick to your promises and commitments, too. Because it won't always be easy," she added. "But with God, all things are possible. Tell Him all your worries, everything that's in your heart, and I know He will help you figure this out."

She wished him good night and closed the door behind her. Back in her own room, she couldn't fall asleep long after her bedside light was shut. She said prayers for Liza and Jamie, and for herself, too. Asking for Jamie to make the decision to stay and for Liza to give him one more chance. And the wisdom and faith to accept whatever happened.

I know you can't change someone who doesn't want to be changed, Lord, she said finally. *But please work on Jamie's heart so that I can have one more chance to help him.*

Chapter Ten

BEFORE Claire headed down to the kitchen to start breakfast on Thursday morning, she glanced up the hallway to Jamie's room. The door stood open and the linen from his bed had been stuffed into a pillowcase and left in the hallway, the same way she had taught him when they cleaned out a guest room.

She took a few steps toward his door and looked inside. It seemed—empty. No clothes draped on chairs or doorknobs. No big shoes on the floor. She didn't see his duffel bag either.

Had he left already? Without saying good-bye to anyone?

He must have been unable to face her. He knew how disappointed she would be when he gave his answer. *No, I can't commit to do the work it will take to change and move forward with my life.*

Staring at the empty room, Claire felt stunned and sad. *I thought he'd at least try. He sounded so sincere about wanting to keep this job.*

She couldn't believe that he hadn't at least left a note.

She looked around the room, on the dresser and night table. But there was no note. She noticed the bit of beach glass near the lamp stand and put it in her pocket.

Downstairs, she checked the mail table in the hallway and then the kitchen. No notes there either. Claire felt another wave of loss wash over her but knew she had no say in this matter. If this was what he wanted, nothing she could do or say could keep him here. *Or should keep him here,* she reminded herself.

Liza would be relieved. That was some consolation.

Still, she wondered, *How can I help him now? Even if I call his cell phone, he probably won't stay in touch with me. He'll be too angry—and ashamed.*

Why did God bring us together? I thought it was so I could help him. Now there's just sadness and disappointment. It's almost worse than the first time, when he was a boy.

Claire sat at the table with a cup of coffee, thankful for a few minutes alone to gather her thoughts and get control of her emotions before Liza came down. They faced a busy day shorthanded, a full house of guests checking in, and lots to do. She couldn't wallow in sad thoughts about Jamie. She had let Liza down enough lately.

Still, she couldn't help a tear or two that squeezed out the corners of her eyes. She sighed and dabbed them with a paper napkin.

A noise out in the yard drew her attention. Metal clattering on metal. She stood up and looked out the back window, expecting to see Daniel there early to fix something.

But it was Jamie. His long, lean body staggered across the yard, paint cans dangling from both hands, and a few brushes and rags tucked under one arm.

Jamie? Jamie was still here?

She didn't understand at first, though her heart filled with happiness. She opened the door and called out to him. "Jamie . . . what are you doing?"

He turned and set some of the cans down on the grass. "I thought I would work on the fence awhile. Unless you need me to do something else this morning. There's not much left to paint. I can be done in an hour or so . . . It shouldn't have taken so long," he admitted.

That was true. He had dragged out a task that should have taken a day, but at least he admitted it.

"All right, that's fine. But I thought you were gone. Your room looks empty and the linen was out in the hallway."

He looked confused for a moment. "I picked up my stuff a little, put things away. You always tell me to change the sheets on Thursday."

"Oh, right." She did tell him that. So he was just trying to be neater. To clean up his act, Claire quipped to herself.

"I thought about what you said. You called me out. You and Liza gave me a chance, and I shouldn't have paid you back like that. Like, being a total slacker. If Liza lets me stay, I'm going to work hard, and mind what you say. I want to do better, Claire. I think I can this time."

"I'm happy to hear that, Jamie. Happier than you can possibly understand." She smiled at him, the edges of her eyes still wet from her tears. "Liza isn't up yet, but she will be soon. You still need to talk to her," she reminded him.

Jamie walked to the back of the property to start the fence, and Claire headed back to the kitchen. Her heart felt light, like a balloon that might float up out of her chest and sail into the sky.

She found Liza in the kitchen, pouring herself some coffee.

She turned from the counter as Claire came in. "What's going on out there? Did you tell Jamie he could stay?"

Liza sounded angry. Claire knew why. This wasn't the plan they had agreed on. Liza was supposed to have the final say.

"He decided that on his own. He was up so early, I thought he had left without telling anyone. He cleaned his room so well, it looks empty," Claire admitted.

"Really?" Liza leaned back. She looked doubtful. "Is that supposed to make everything all right again?"

Claire sighed and shook her head. "Not entirely. I know that. But he says he's ready to change, to try hard here. Liza, I didn't say he could stay. But I didn't think you would turn him away. Will you at least talk to him?"

Last night, Liza had promised that she would. But Claire thought it was possible that she was so annoyed this morning, about Jamie just jumping back into the work, that she might change her mind.

Liza didn't answer right away. "All right, Claire. I'll go out in a few minutes," she said finally. She took a sip of coffee, her expression growing more serious. "You know I'm more doubtful about him than you are. No matter what he says. But I can't refuse you this favor. I guess I can forgive him and we can try again."

"Thank you," Claire said simply. She felt so grateful and relieved. But there was even more pressure now for Jamie to keep his word and more pressure on her to see that he did.

That's all right, she decided. *Some battles are worth fighting.* They had more time together now. That was the main thing. She would somehow persuade him to start studying for his graduate equivalency diploma. He couldn't get anywhere in life without a GED. Claire tried not to think too far ahead. She watched Liza walk out to Jamie and sent up a small prayer.

Thank you, God, for giving us both another chance. Please help Jamie to keep his promises to me and Liza . . . and please show me the way to keep the promise I made to him.

Then she took the bit of beach glass from her pocket and put it back where it belonged, in the glass bowl on the kitchen windowsill, with the rest of her collection.

* * *

GUESTS began to arrive at noon. Claire was thankful to have Jamie there, helping with the luggage and the many other demands of the day. As the inn filled up, they had no time for any more debates or soul searching. It was time to see if Jamie was going to follow through on his promise to work hard. Or if once again, he had just been stringing them along.

But he did work hard, Claire was relieved to see. On Sunday morning she wondered if she could slip away for church and perhaps leave Jamie to help Liza serve breakfast.

Outside the kitchen window, the sky hung heavy and low with banks of dark gray clouds. Claire flipped on the radio and tuned to the all-news station. The newscasters were all talking about one thing—the big storm that was moving into the area.

"Batten down those hatches, folks, whatever that means," a weathercaster warned with false cheer. "This system is blowing in with some high winds and heavy-duty precipitation. You folks on the coast might think we're being hit by an early hurricane. The worst of it should strike right at the peak of high tide. It's going to be windy and wet out there for a while. But with any luck, this mess will blow past quickly . . ."

A storm? Why hadn't they heard of this? They had been so busy this weekend and the weather so fair, she and Liza hadn't paid much attention to the forecast.

They had to pay attention now. Claire decided to wake Liza. They needed to prepare—take out flashlights and maybe even board up some windows. And wake up the guests and get them off the island quickly before the land bridge was flooded.

As Claire was heading upstairs to wake Liza, she passed Avery coming down. The poor girl was working such long hours she had circles on top of circles under her eyes. But she did seem much more upbeat this week. She had told them business was picking up a bit, and she felt she was on the right track.

"Avery, have you heard the weather report? We're in for a big storm today. You should probably close the café and put boards on the windows. Maybe I can find some wood in the barn for you."

Avery stared at her curiously. "I thought there weren't any bad storms around here until September."

"We can get a sudden summer squall that tears the shutters right off the building," Claire assured her. "It doesn't have to be hurricane season. The radio is on in the kitchen," she added. "You can hear the reports. I'm going up to wake Liza. I'll be down in a minute."

Avery went into the kitchen and looked for the radio. She turned up the sound and listened as she helped herself to coffee and a muffin.

It looked like Claire was just about to make pancakes and bacon for the guests. If all she had said about the weather was true, their breakfast would not be the usual, leisurely affair. Thankfully, she would be at the Peregrine by the time the crowd of guests were rushing out of here.

She listened closely as the storm alert came on. It did sound bad. Thunder, lightning, heavy rains, and high winds. The possibility of hail?

Claire had not been exaggerating. But what should she do?

She didn't have the tools or supplies to board up her building. Even if Claire gave her some wood, she couldn't put it up herself. She could barely hang a picture on a hook. But she could stop at the General Store and at least buy some tape for the windows. That would help.

Avery took an extra cup of coffee and headed out to her SUV. As she drove toward the island's village center, her cell phone rang with a call from Gena.

She just wanted to make sure Avery had heard about the forecast and wasn't thinking of trying to stay open during the storm. Avery assured her that she wasn't. They decided that Gena would call Teresa and Jack and make sure that they didn't head over to work.

"You're going to need some help closing up. I have to help Gerry get his boat secure," Gena said, mentioning her husband. "We might need to take it out of the water. But we'll try to come over right after we're done at the dock."

If the storm doesn't start by then, Avery thought. She didn't know how long it took to pull a fishing boat out of the water, but felt sure it wasn't a small job.

"That's all right. Don't worry. I'll figure it out."

"I'll ask Teresa or Jack if they can come help you," Gena said. "Or maybe you could ask the McNultys . . . or Mike Rossi?"

Avery didn't find either of those choices appealing, each for different reasons.

"Don't worry," she said. "Weather forecasters always exaggerate. I'm sure it won't be half as bad as they say."

"Are you taking this seriously?" Gena sounded concerned.

"I just pulled up at the General Store, about to buy tape and batteries and all kinds of stuff. That's serious, right? Don't worry, I'll be fine."

"All right. I'll call you later," Gena promised.

The small store was so crowded, Avery had to park on the opposite side of the square. She glanced at the overlook as she walked across the cobblestones. Banks of grayish-blue clouds hovered over the horizon. The ocean looked dark and deep, a mysterious blue-green hue today. Even the air felt heavy and thick. Avery could barely get a good breath. Some rain would be a relief from this.

The brightly lit General Store was a sharp contrast to the desolate square. The small space was crowded with customers, their arms full of groceries and household needs—bread, milk, water, eggs, batteries, and flashlights.

Avery headed for the aisle that held hardware supplies and had to wait her turn to squeeze in and check the shelves. Which she found were practically bare.

She had a hammer somewhere around the café, she recalled, but couldn't find a pack of nails. *I don't have any wood, so what's the difference?*

She grabbed a few rolls of wide tape and decided that would have to do. She also found a box of large white candles and what looked like the last pack of D batteries for her flashlight, which felt like a small victory.

"Got everything you need, miss?" the woman at the register asked.

Avery had been in the store a few times so far and knew that the cashier and her husband, who worked behind the deli counter, were also the store owners. Marion and Walter Doyle were their names.

"I think so . . . Do you really think this storm is going to be that bad?"

Marion shrugged. "Hope for the best, prepare for the worst. That's what I always say."

Avery nodded. Who could argue with that?

Avery parked her SUV in front of her café. She saw the neighboring store owners scurrying around to secure their shops. Down at the end of the street, the Lazy Tuna was already sealed up tight with wooden flaps that came down over the windows; the big open front of the restaurant was covered with a pull-down metal gate. Avery had seen the restaurant closed up that way during the winter when she first came looking at real estate.

It looked as though Mike was taking the weather forecast seriously. The realization ramped up her concern. Her building didn't have any protection like that, and now the lovely trio of French doors facing the ocean seemed like an awfully bad idea.

And they'll cost a fortune to repair if the wind blows them in.

Avery didn't want to waste time thinking about that now. *Hope for the best, prepare for the worst.* Marion's motto rang in her head. She set to work doing just that.

The sky was growing darker and the wind picked up, blowing bits of trash around the empty boardwalk. Avery began to carry in the outdoor tables and chairs that stood under the open awning. Although they were made of wood, they were mostly light enough for her to handle. But there were plenty of them and she wished that she had some help.

Neither Jack nor Teresa had called her to say they could come. They were probably busy with their own homes and belongings. Avery didn't want anyone driving in the storm anyway. It was just as well.

I can do this. It's not that much, she told herself.

She cleared the patio then looked up at the awning. Yikes, that had to come down. But she could never manage it. She didn't even have a ladder. *The best I can do is close it up as far as it will go,* she decided.

It was an old-fashioned mechanism, and Avery hooked the long metal bar to the winding piece on one end. The awning moved a few inches then wouldn't budge.

"Come on . . . just roll up, would you please?" The custom-made canvas had cost her a small fortune, imprinted with hand-designed lettering and the restaurant insignia. She hated to see it torn to shreds. But time was passing and she had to cover the glass doors before the storm hit—or at least put tape on them.

Avery left the metal winding handle dangling and ran inside to look for something to cover the glass. Hadn't the carpenters left some extra paneling somewhere or some plywood? She was almost sure of it.

She frantically searched through a storage closet and found a thin piece of beadboard. It didn't seem very substantial, but it would do for at least one door. She hunted around and found scraps for the other two, and the hammer.

But no nails. She suddenly remembered she didn't have any.

Maybe they had some at the inn? It was too late to drive there and back. The McNultys . . . maybe they had some nails. They had nailed down their entire shop.

She ran to their shop but realized instantly that the older couple was gone, undoubtedly sitting out the storm someplace inland. Where anyone with any brains would be right now.

She carried her armful of wood scraps and the hammer into the dining area and set the burden on a table. Could she tape the wood up?

That idea is so stupid, I'm going to pretend you didn't even consider it . . .

"Avery? Are you in there?"

Avery heard someone call her name. She looked outside and saw Mike. He stood near the dangling awning handle then grabbed it and began to wind, before she could even answer.

"Wait . . . I'll be right out."

Avery ran outside, happier to see Mike than she could have ever imagined. Since the scene in her kitchen Monday night, they hadn't exchanged a word. She had only seen him once or twice, walking down the street toward his restaurant, his eyes straight ahead, his step quick and determined. He no longer seemed interested in stopping off for more friendly chitchat or unsolicited advice. But here he was for some reason, checking to see if the café was ready for the storm.

"You've got to close this up all the way. It will blow right off the building."

"I tried but it was stuck. How did you get it going again?"

He tipped his head down to look at her with a *you've got to be kidding me* expression.

"I untied it at the corners, Avery," he said simply, pointing to the laces at each far corner of the frame.

"Oh, right. I knew that," she insisted. "I was just rushing so much, I guess I forgot." Got blinded by sheer panic, was closer to the truth, but she didn't bother to explain. "Well, thanks," she said sincerely.

"No problem. Tables and chairs are inside, that's good. What about these doors? Do you have some wood or something to cover them?"

"I have a little wood—but no nails," she admitted.

"I've got plenty. And a hammer."

Avery carried out the wood she had found, and they worked together covering the doors. She held each piece in place while Mike quickly and smoothly tapped in the nails. She felt a little self-conscious, working so close together, their arms practically entwined. Rain had started to fall and the wind was howling.

Avery felt her hair and clothes getting wet.

Mike didn't seem to notice, not the rain or her nearness, his entire attention focused on the wood and nails. A few minutes later, the doors were covered.

"Just in time. It's starting to come down." Mike had to raise his voice to be heard over the wind.

Avery went inside and Mike followed. It was dark in the café with only the light of a few small windows on the side of the building.

"I guess I'll cover the other windows with tape." Avery picked up a roll and started the job. Mike sat in a chair and wiped off his face with a dinner napkin, then smoothed his wet hair back with his hand. He looked even more handsome than usual with his hair that way, she thought. But she forced herself to focus on her taping task.

"I hope you have a flashlight and batteries. Or some candles," he said. "You can't drive till this blows over, and the electricity might go out . . . What about a generator?"

"A generator?" That seemed a bit extreme.

"For the cold box. If we lose power for more than an hour, you'll have to throw everything out," he reminded her.

Avery sighed. That was true. "I did think about buying one, but I haven't gotten around to it yet."

Generators were expensive. She had already spent more on the renovations than she should have.

Avery had no sooner said the words when she heard an ominous rumble of thunder, followed by a loud crack of lightning. The lights flickered and she held her breath.

Seconds later, the lights went out and Avery stared into pitch-black darkness.

"Uh-oh," she said quietly.

"Uh-oh is right . . . Where's your flashlight?"

"In the kitchen. Don't trip on anything," she added as she heard Mike slowly walk toward her.

With the doors in front boarded and tape covering the windows, it was quite dark in the café. It took a few minutes for Avery's eyes to adjust. She managed to make her way into the kitchen and found the big yellow flashlight right where she had left it on the worktable. She grabbed it and switched it on.

"Geez . . . get that thing out of my eyes. Are you trying to blind me?" Mike was encompassed by a circle of light, one arm raised over his eyes to shield himself from the beam.

"Sorry," Avery said sincerely. "I didn't see you there."

She heard him laugh lightly in the dark. "Right."

She turned the flashlight toward the wall and put it on the worktable. Mike sat on the opposite side.

They heard the rain pounding the roof and battering the kitchen window, as if someone were standing outside with a hose, turned on full force.

"It's really coming down now," Mike said.

"We got in just in time. Thanks for coming over here and helping me." She suddenly realized she hadn't even said that yet.

Mike shrugged. "That's all right." An awkward silence fell. "How did your theme nights go last week? It seemed pretty lively here," he conceded.

"Pretty well. Better than I expected. The Lobster Slider night worked the best, but that was a Saturday."

"Any time is the right time for a Lobster Slider," he said. "Any leftovers? All that hammering made me hungry."

They had done a lot of work outside, and it was just about lunchtime, Avery realized. Still, she felt a little intimidated feeding Mike. The only food of hers he'd had so far was a handful of sweet potato chips. What if he didn't like her cooking?

"Never mind," he said quickly. "I don't want to bother you. I can wait. I'll grab something down at my place later."

He had misread her hesitation. "No, please. It's fine. I'm hungry, too."

Avery took out the box of candles, lit two, and set them on the worktable. Then she took the flashlight and headed for the cold box. "I'll be right back."

"Don't worry, I'm not going anywhere. I forgot my boat." Mike watched her from his perch on a stool, his arms folded over his broad chest. With his hair slicked back from the rain and the candlelight shadows, he looked very handsome.

She felt nervous again about serving him lunch. Nervous about . . . something, she realized.

Get a grip, Avery, she told herself as she walked into the room-sized refrigerator. *So what if he doesn't like your cooking? It's not like you're interviewing for a job—or dating him.*

But he had said that he wanted a date with her. And they'd had that impromptu, amazing kiss. She'd had some vague notion that would mark the start of a new phase in their relationship. And he would ask her out after that.

But so far, nothing. Maybe he really was put off when she had concealed the great pizza night plan—or when she hinted that he had given her enough advice?

Or perhaps he also had second thoughts about getting romantically involved with someone in the same business, someone who was his only competition on this entire island.

And even if he did ask me out, I'm not even sure what I would say, Avery reminded herself.

Yeah, right. I'm going to pretend that you didn't even think that.

Avery finally emerged with some tasty offerings and brought them out to the kitchen. While she prepared their meal, Mike set two places on the worktable with mats and china. He filled the water glasses and adjusted the candles just so then folded the napkins with professional flare. Avery glanced over her shoulder and watched him working.

"Very nice," she commented.

"Glad you approve of the . . . ambience." He was teasing her, of course. But she didn't mind it.

She brought over two plated salads, cold poached salmon on mixed greens with walnuts and grapes. There was some dill sauce on the side.

Mike looked impressed as he glanced down at his place, and she felt quietly proud . . . and relieved.

"My, my. This looks lovely. I was thinking more of a turkey and Swiss on rye."

"It wasn't any trouble. I had everything prepped for the brunch."

"Oh, right." He glanced at his watch. "If the lights don't come back by the time we finish eating, we'll take your perishables to my place. I do have a generator."

"Oh . . . that would be great, thanks." Avery had forgotten all about that problem. She was grateful for his offer. But as they sat together in the cozy glow of the candlelight, the rain coming down steadily outside, she actually didn't want the lights to come back on too quickly.

He took a few bites of his salad. "This is great. And fun," he added, glancing at her. "Probably the only break I'll get for the rest of the summer. Next Sunday is July first. That's when it really hits. Fourth of July is in the middle of the week this year. The island will be full of people all week long," he predicted.

"Hey, I'm ready. I just have to hire another waitress," she added. "Serena quit."

"Really? That's too bad. I hope you can find someone. It's getting late."

"Jack's girlfriend needs a summer job. She's coming in tomorrow for an interview."

"That was lucky," he said around a mouthful of salad. "Maybe your luck is starting to turn, Avery."

"Maybe," she said, crossing her fingers under the table. One fairly good week wasn't going to save her. But it was a start, she thought. "I can hardly believe it's the Fourth already. The summer is going so fast."

Mike paused to spoon a dab of dill sauce on the side of his dish. "I know. It passes faster and faster each year. I can't figure it out." He tasted a drop of the sauce with his fork tine. "What's the base on this—sour cream?"

"Greek yogurt," she replied, pleased to have stumped him. "I think it's lighter and has a little more tanginess."

He nodded. "Good idea. I like it . . . I'm going to steal it from you," he added with a grin.

She laughed. "All right. I owe you one, I guess." She took a sip of water and sat back. "So what do you do for the rest of the year, Mike, when you're not running the Tuna?"

"I work at the high school in Cape Light," he replied.

"Really?" It was hard for Avery to hide her surprise. She could see from his expression she hadn't done a very good job. "You're a teacher?" He was fit enough to be a physical education instructor, that was for sure.

"Not quite. I'm a counselor, in the guidance department. I like working with kids. I have two of my own."

"Wow, that's great." She hadn't expected him to have children for some reason. But now that he had said it, she could see it. He was probably a great dad. "How old are they?"

"Noah is eight and Emily is six."

She was still stunned but managed to say, "You should bring them by. I'd love to meet them sometime."

"Oh, you will. They spend a lot of time at the beach down here during the summer. But they're both in camp right now." He paused and smiled at her. "You seem surprised to hear I'm a dad. Don't I seem responsible enough?"

She was surprised but tried to hide it. They had finished their salads and she took the plates away. "Now that you mention it, no, you don't seem responsible enough," she teased back. "You just never mentioned them, that's all . . ."

What else had he never mentioned, she wondered. Was he married?

Single men can have children, she told herself. *He's probably divorced. He'd better be divorced if he kissed me that way.*

She brought over their desserts and served him first. Slices of key lime pie, the plates garnished with whipped cream and mixed berries.

"Hmm, this looks good . . . Nice presentation." He turned the dish and looked it over approvingly. "The kids like to help me at the restaurant sometimes, too," he added smiling. "I've got to keep an eye on them, though. Too easy to get into mischief at that age. My mother helps me out, but she can't have them every day," he said as he finished up his salad.

Avery listened carefully to his child care issues. "What about their mother? Does she live far from here?" she asked, carefully wording her question.

Mike paused and put his fork down. "You might say that . . . She's . . . up in heaven." His tone was calm and matter-of-fact. "But I'm certain she has her eye on them twenty-four/seven."

Avery was mortified. "I'm so sorry . . . I just assumed that you were divorced . . .That was so stupid of me . . ."

"I should have said something. It was my fault." He reached across the table and touched her hand a moment.

"No, it was mine," she insisted. "I'm very sorry for your loss. That must be so hard for your children," she said sincerely. "How long has it been?"

"About three years. She had cancer. She went very quickly. Maybe that was a blessing. I don't know." There was no trace of cockiness or irreverence in his manner or tone now. Avery felt as if she was suddenly with a whole different person.

"We met in college," he explained, "and got married right after graduation. She was a teacher, too. English literature," he added. "She was very good. All her students loved her."

"I'm sure they did," Avery said quietly. "What was her name?"

"Kara. My daughter, Emily, looks just like her. She loves books, too. She already says that she wants to be a writer when she grows up. But I'm sure she'll change her mind a thousand times before then."

Avery smiled, but didn't say anything, though her mind spun with questions about his home life. It couldn't be easy raising two children on your own, even if you had family nearby to help. Mike always seemed such a happy-go-lucky type. Now she knew he had problems, too, just like everyone else. He had been through a terrible loss, but he never seemed bitter or angry at the world. He always seemed so positive and full of energy.

Maybe because he had faith? He clearly believed his wife was in a better place, watching over all the people she loved. Avery thought it must be nice to have that kind of faith. Her mother took her to church as a child, but she hadn't been in a long time.

"What about you, Avery? Did you always want to be a chef, or did you change your mind a thousand times?"

Mike's question caught her off guard. "Oh, I always wanted to, in my heart. But I didn't always have the courage to admit it. I thought about safer careers, like becoming a lawyer or something. That seems incredible now. I can't imagine doing anything else."

She looked up at him. "How about you? It sounds like you enjoy being a counselor. Would you like to run a restaurant all year round if you had the chance?"

He shook his head. "Three months running a restaurant is just right. And six months in a high school is more than enough," he added with a pleasant laugh. "It's a good balance. I have nothing to complain about. My life is good. I wouldn't change a thing," he added. "Well, maybe one thing . . ."

He met her gaze across the table. She had the feeling he was going to say he would like to have someone special in his life, a special relationship . . . the kind he had with his wife.

She wished she had that, too, though she truly had her doubts about whether she would ever find a man who would put up with her hours and her craziness about the café.

"What's that one thing?" she asked him.

"Nothing. I'm fine. No complaints. And this lunch was awesome. I won't need dinner tonight."

"Me either," she agreed. She looked out at the rain. It was still falling, though not nearly as hard now. "I guess it won't hurt to lose the business for one day, but I hope we can open by tomorrow night. The lights will be on by then, don't you think?"

"Oh sure. Don't worry. Next week is the big one. The Fourth of July makes up for a lot. Every place around here is packed on that holiday and then again on Labor Day."

From her experience at other restaurants, Avery already knew that would happen. But being so close to the beach would multiply the phenomenon many times over, she expected. She certainly hoped so.

"My mother and sister are coming for a visit then. They want to see the café. I'm glad it will look busy."

"They haven't been here yet? Where do they live?"

"Not far. In Connecticut. But my sister doesn't get much time off from her job and my mother can't drive here on her own. She's getting older." Avery paused, wondering how much she should confide. But the low lights and his warm smile encouraged her to say more. He had told her about his wife. She felt safe to share a few of her own secrets.

"My mother helped me when I got turned down by some banks. She gave me a big loan from her savings to start the business," Avery confided. "It was money she had set aside for her retirement. I hope I can repay her."

He listened thoughtfully. "Your mom gave you all the start-up money?"

"Most of it. I had some money from selling a piece of jewelry . . .

a diamond ring someone gave me," she said vaguely. She met his glance then looked away.

His head tilted back a bit. "You mean, like, an engagement ring." It wasn't a question. It was more his wanting her to clarify this disclosure.

"That's right. We ran a restaurant together. We were planning to get married but . . . it didn't work out."

"Oh, that's rough," he said sympathetically.

"It was. For a long time. But I'm okay now," she insisted, though she wasn't sure she was entirely. "I've turned a page and I'm starting over, all on my own," she added, which was true.

"Yes, you are. And I get it now," he added.

She wasn't quite sure what he meant by that. But she wanted to get off the subject of her failed romance. She had told him the whole story. Practically. They had been having such a pleasant time, sitting here talking. She didn't even want to think about Paul.

"So, getting back to your mother, she loaned you a load of dough. That's a lot of pressure."

"It is," Avery agreed flatly. "I didn't realize it at the time. I probably wouldn't have even asked her if I knew."

His dark eyes were soft and sympathetic. "You'll be all right. Don't worry. Things are picking up here. If you have good food, people will find you. And you do have good food," he added with a smile.

"Thanks. You're not just saying that because you have to, are you?"

Mike laughed. "Of course not. This food is great, top-notch. Have more confidence in yourself, Avery. That's all you really need."

She smiled at him. Mike had an abundance of that ingredient. If only he could bottle it, she would definitely buy some.

"I'll tell you the truth: Starting with that pizza night of yours, my numbers have been down. I think I actually have to take this place seriously," he confessed.

Avery's eyes widened. "You mean, you weren't taking me seriously before?"

He laughed, realizing how much he had admitted. "Well . . . our menus are so different . . ." He paused. "So not really, no. But I am now," he added quickly.

"That's sort of a backhanded compliment, but I'll take it. So we're giving the Mighty Tuna a run for the money?"

"Hey, I wouldn't go that far," he teased her. "And I just want to warn you, next Tuesday, Taco Night? I'm bringing in a mariachi band."

He sat back with a *How do you like that?* smile on his handsome face.

Avery rose and picked up a few of the dirty dishes. "Do what you have to do." She shrugged. "I have a few more surprises planned, too."

"Like what? More fancy-schmancy sliders?" Mike got up and began to help her.

"Like . . . none of your business. That's what."

He looked surprised but amused by her tart reply. He set some dishes in the sink and stood facing her. "Hey, that's not fair. I told you about the mariachi band."

Avery shrugged. "That was your choice. I don't have to give away all my secrets if I don't want to. You'll just have to wait and see."

He laughed again. "Well, I guess I don't have to make room in my cold box for all your melting food, either. You'll just have to wait and see if the electricity comes back on." He made a big show of checking his watch. "Let's see . . . we're getting perilously close to the spoilage deadline."

Avery just stared at him. "You're blackmailing me?"

He looked shocked by the word. "Avery, please . . . No need to get nasty about this."

"You are too much. Do you really want to know my plans that

badly? I think you're scared," she said, suddenly realizing what was really going on.

"Are you kidding?" He laughed at her but the sound was a little hollow. "No way. This café is pretty cute and you're doing better. But you're no threat to the Tuna. Sorry to disappoint you."

"And you're a terrible liar. But that's an admirable quality."

Among many he possessed, which she was just beginning to recognize.

He looked surprised. "Wait. Did you just give me a compliment?"

Avery glanced down, feeling embarrassed. "Yes, I did. I can think of a few more, too. Like you're generous and kind. And very funny . . . and smart," she added. "And I do appreciate how much you've helped me. Even though I don't always show it . . . and I have no idea why you've been so nice to me," she admitted.

He looked surprised but pleased by her compliments. His smile was full of affection. "I don't know. Maybe because you try so hard?" He shrugged and took a step toward her. "I just . . . I just . . . oh boy . . ."

Before he could finish his sentence, he put his hands on her waist and pulled her closer and she found herself in his arms. She met his dark gaze for one instant and then felt his lips on her own, warm and soft, the taste of the tartly sweet pie lingering.

She twined her arms around him and felt lost in his embrace, his warmth and rock-hard strength. She wasn't sure what had prompted her outpouring of compliments, but she had meant every word of it.

She hadn't thought much of Mike when they first met. He was definitely an acquired taste, one that she had come to appreciate more with every passing day. He had become an advisor and a friend. But Avery knew their relationship could be so much more. And that was the part that truly surprised her. And scared her. Right down to her toes.

She heard a dull humming sound. Then the lights flickered and came back on. They stepped apart. She felt dazed and suddenly shy. She glanced up at him, wishing her heart would stop racing.

"Your food is saved," he said quietly.

Avery had to laugh. Of all things to think about right now. "Yes, I guess so. Just in the nick of time."

"Divine intervention. Someone is looking out for you, Avery."

"No question."

It had to be her father, she thought. If there was a heaven, she was sure her dad was there, playing bridge and watching baseball games. Her father would have liked Mike Rossi. She was certain of that.

With the lights on, the kitchen suddenly looked different. Like a kitchen again, nothing romantic about it.

"Looks like the rain slowed down," Mike said peering out the window. "I guess I'll get going," he added, pulling on his cap. "Thanks again for lunch. It was four stars, all the way."

"You're very welcome. Thanks for the review," she added, getting her bearings back. "Maybe you can send it to a newspaper, or post it for us on the Internet?"

He laughed. "Right. I'll think about it."

They stood together at the kitchen door. Mike had his hand on the doorknob but made no move to open it.

He's close enough to lean down and kiss me again, Avery realized. She had a feeling he was thinking the same thing and was about to do just that. She met his glance, suddenly wanting him to—then recoiled at this errant thought.

You can't get involved with Mike Rossi. He's kind and attractive and smart. He's all those things you told him he is. But it would never work. Never in a million years, a little voice warned her.

"Well, this was nice. See you around." He leaned forward and dropped a quick kiss on her cheek. Then he darted out the door and splashed through the puddles in the alley behind the shops, dodging raindrops all the way.

Avery leaned out the doorway a minute and watched him until he was out of sight. She closed the door, suddenly feeling very odd. She felt . . . lonely. Which made no sense. She hadn't felt that way when she and Paul split. But something about Mike just filled a room with energy and laughter. Whenever he was around, she felt so alive and so safe.

She was falling for him. Falling really hard.

Avery couldn't believe it. She shook off the thought like a dog coming in from the rain. It was just the quiet, cozy lunch and all the confidences that they shared. It was just another of those hit-and-run kisses of his . . . *I shouldn't put too much stock in the feelings I have right now.*

She sat down on a stool and took a sip of cold water.

Splash some on your face while you're at it, a chiding little voice advised. *And snap out of it!*

Wasn't that a quote from a famous movie? Oh, right. *Moonstruck.* When Nicolas Cage tells Cher he loves her, and she slaps him across the face.

Moonstruck would be a good choice for tomorrow night, one of her all-time favorites. She started to clean up the dishes from lunch again, wondering if Mike liked that movie, too.

Chapter Eleven

"We'll need to have two seatings for dinner, one at six and one at eight. Even if we put more tables on the patio and the porch, it will still be tight," Liza said, thinking aloud. "And we'll have to worry about the weather."

Liza stared at her computer, which stood open on the kitchen table. For the past half hour, she had been mulling over strategies to handle the crowd of guests that would check in over the Fourth of July week. With so many people to accommodate, it was important to keep everything running smoothly.

"We're always crazy busy on the Fourth, but the holiday falls on a Wednesday this year, just one week from today," Liza said to Jamie. "Some people are taking vacations before, and some people are taking the time after. So we'll be booked up from this coming Friday right through to next weekend."

"That's good, isn't it?" he asked.

"Absolutely." She paused to smile at him. "I don't mean to sound like I'm complaining. But it's hard to maintain a certain level of service when there are so many guests here. We want everyone to leave feeling one hundred percent satisfied. As if this is a place they would return to, and recommend to a friend."

"And it's just the three of us to handle everything," Claire put in. "That's why it's so important to stay calm and focused on what you're doing—and do that one job thoroughly, without worrying about the next. Whether you're making a bed, or setting a table, or sweeping sand off the porch. *'Whatsoever you do, do it heartily, as to the Lord and not to men,'*" Claire advised, adding one of her favorite quotes from Colossians.

"Win them over, one bowl of chowder at a time?" Jamie teased her.

"Exactly. God is in the details," Claire reminded them. "Even in the chowder. If you want to get silly about it."

"That's very true, Claire," Liza agreed, her gaze fixed on the computer screen as she typed a few notes to herself. "Speaking of chowder, let's work on the menus."

"I thought you'd never ask." Claire sat back, happy that Liza had come to her favorite planning task at last. She glanced at Jamie, wondering if he was bored and wanted to go.

He still seemed interested and focused on the conversation, making suggestions of his own here and there. Like an extra table with coffee and tea out on the porch in the morning when the inn was at full capacity. He had noticed how guests crowded around the single urn in the dining room. "Like sea gulls fighting over a French fry," he told them.

The image made Claire laugh; it was a very apt description.

She was glad Liza had included him in their planning session. Claire hoped Jamie felt more involved in the inn, having a say in how things were done. It was important to show him they respected his opinion, and he wasn't just taking orders all the time.

He had worked hard since their talk and Liza's decision to let him stay. Claire hadn't caught him on his cell phone, talking or texting, even once during work hours. Even Liza had noticed these changes, though she told Claire privately it would take more than a week of good behavior to dispel all her doubts.

Claire understood her caution. She prayed each night for God to help him stay firm in his commitment to change his life and keep him from falling back into old ways again.

"I'll just close this file and get the menu charts up." Liza clicked the mouse a few times then sat back and expelled an impatient sigh. "It froze again. I can't believe it. I just had this stupid machine fixed!"

"Oh my, I can't help you there," Claire said. "I'd have better luck fixing a washing machine or the lawn mower." Claire rose and looked around for a pad and pen. "Why don't we just resort to the old-fashioned way . . . writing things down?"

"Can I take a look? Maybe I can fix it." Jamie had also gotten up from his chair and now peered over Liza's shoulder.

She glanced back at him skeptically. "Do you know a lot about computers?"

He shrugged. "A little. I'm not bad, fooling around with them."

Liza hit a few more keys on the keyboard. Claire could tell by her expression that she wasn't making any progress.

"I guess you could have a try," Liza said to Jamie finally. "You won't mess it up worse than it is, will you?"

"I don't think so. If I do, you can take it out of my pay."

"Oh, I won't do that. I'm the one who froze it . . . Here, give it a go. I have all the reservations on there and the billing and everything. I always tell myself to back things up but I rarely do," she admitted.

Jamie sat down next to her and she turned the laptop toward him. Claire went to the sink and filled the kettle. Jamie coming to the rescue with Liza's computer was a surprising turn. She felt a bit nervous about it, though, and couldn't bear to watch him. She hoped he knew what he was doing, and it wasn't just that high-tech bravado men had around these sorts of gadgets.

Claire asked if they wanted tea, but they both declined, not even looking at her. They sat shoulder to shoulder, their heads bent over the computer screen.

"Oh . . . how did you do that?" Liza asked, sounding pleased and surprised. "I can never find that screen."

"You just turn it off and then on again and hit this key combination." Jamie showed her his trick.

"Wait, I'm going to write that down." This time Liza did take the pen and pad Claire had found and eagerly made a note.

By the time her tea was brewed, the computer crisis was solved. Jamie had even changed some setting that would save the day if this were ever to happen again. Which was unfortunately very likely, as far as Claire could see.

She still wasn't sure what was wrong with good old paper and pencils. She had never had any problems with that method.

"Where did you learn how to do all that?" Liza asked Jamie as she happily took over the computer again and set up her menu planner.

"I had a job once in the stock room of this company, and the IT guy was stuck back there, too. In a little cubicle. We hung out and he showed me things." Jamie leaned back in his chair. "Most of my friends have computers and I fix stuff for them. Nothing too complicated. They're usually just playing video games."

Claire didn't doubt that was true. Jamie would need a computer if he was going to get back to school, even to study for his GED. Perhaps Liza would let him use hers for that purpose, now that she knew he wasn't going to harm it. But she was getting ahead of herself. Jamie hadn't even agreed to study for the diploma equivalency test.

Claire had picked up some information at the library and talked to her friend Vera Plante about it. Vera had taught history at the high school for many years and earned extra income now tutoring. The test covered five subject areas and it was not easy, Vera had told her. But not impossible. Nothing was impossible with God's help, Claire knew.

But she didn't want to overwhelm Jamie. He was trying to be a better worker at the inn right now, to prove he was serious about this job. That was enough on his plate.

But summer was quickly passing, another voice reminded her. *He wouldn't be here for long, in reach of her help and influence.* That was a reality that couldn't be denied or avoided.

AVERY had a lot to do to prepare for the Fourth of July rush. The stream of visitors coming onto the island had begun steadily building on Thursday, each ferry from Newburyport more crowded than the last. On Friday morning she waited at the inn for her mother and sister to arrive.

She sat on the porch, working on another flyer she wanted Jack to hand out at the beach and at the ferry station. She also had to tend to some bookkeeping and the payroll.

The staff had been limping along with only one official waitress, Gena. The rest of them had been filling in and somehow managing without alienating every customer they had. Luckily, Jack's girlfriend, Courtney, was going to start today. Just in the nick of time, Avery thought.

Liza came outside with a tray and began picking up stray coffee mugs and dishes that guests had left after breakfast. "On the lookout for your mother and sister?"

Avery nodded. "They left Connecticut very early. My sister always loves to beat the traffic. Even if she has to leave in the middle of the night."

Liza laughed. "Probably a good strategy this weekend." She balanced the tray on her hip and stood by Avery's chair.

"My sister can be a bit intense. It's just her personality." Avery stood up to stretch. "She sounds like she can use a vacation."

"This is the perfect spot to unwind. I hear there'll be beautiful weather right through next week."

"That's good news." Avery was thinking of business at her café. Good weather brought more people out to the beach and the boardwalk—and to the Peregrine.

"I'm almost afraid to ask this, but . . . have you been to the beach at all yet, Avery?" Liza gave her a humorous, quizzical look.

Avery felt a little self-conscious, almost guilty. She thought about the pleasant stroll she had taken down the boardwalk with Mike. That had been the highlight of her outings.

"I do go out for some air for a few minutes in the afternoon. Before we start serving dinner. Some days," she qualified.

Those brief visits to the beach were precious to her and amazingly refreshing to her state of mind. But unfortunately, they were few and far between.

"I can't say that I've sat on the beach with an umbrella and all that," she added honestly. "I think I will have to wait until September to unfold my beach chair."

"I hope not," Liza replied with a kind smile. "Everyone deserves a little time off, even in the busy season. Maybe you'll have a minute to get out to the ocean with your mother and sister."

"Maybe," Avery said doubtfully.

Even if she had the time, she wasn't sure she really wanted to spend hours trapped on a blanket with her sister, Christine. They would be bound to get into a heavy conversation about the café and its prospects.

Christine was an accountant and thought she knew everything about business. Even the restaurant business, which she did not.

Avery was sure her older sister was making this trip mainly to check out the café's prospects and decide if it was a safe investment for their mom.

Avery knew very well that so far it didn't appear to be a safe bet for anyone. Fortunately, their mother wasn't one to listen too closely to reason when her heart got involved in a decision. Even a financial one.

Helen Bishop had pursued motherhood relatively late in life, after trying hard to succeed in show business as a singer and dancer. She had spent many years performing on local stages and had even made a record while Avery was growing up. But eventually, she gave up her aspirations to make it to Broadway and focused instead on teaching music and raising her two daughters.

Avery knew that her mother's failed hopes had made her very sympathetic to Avery's struggles and she was unerringly encouraging. Which more than made up for Christine's skepticism. But Christine meant well. She was only trying to be the voice of reason, Avery reminded herself. One surrounded by irrational dreamers . . . who were all bad at bookkeeping.

Avery leaned on the porch rail, gazing out at the vast swath of dark blue ocean and clear sky.

"Families are . . . funny," she said finally.

Liza had put down the tray and was picking off a few wilting flowers from the hanging pots of pink geraniums. "Yes, they are," she agreed.

A small blue hatchback with Connecticut plates pulled up to the inn, and Avery recognized her sister's car—a model voted the most economical and best on mileage by a consumer watchdog group.

Avery waved and hopped down the steps to meet them.

Her sister had dressed in comfortable clothes for driving, khaki shorts and a dark blue T-shirt. But her mother, always particular about her appearance, appeared ready for a garden party, wearing a flowered sundress and high-heeled sandals, her hair swept up and her lipstick fresh. She emerged from the car and quickly whisked on a stylish sun hat with a floppy brim.

Always ready for the spotlight, Avery thought with a secret smile. *Even this morning, after a drive of several hours. That's my mom.*

"What a lovely place. What a breathtaking view," her mother said as she gave Avery a hug.

She stood back, admiring the inn, which did look picturesque and welcoming on this perfect summer morning. Avery had been here so long, she didn't even see it anymore.

"Look at those flower boxes. I can never get mine to look so abundant and colorful. I can't wait to go inside."

"Very pretty," Christine agreed. "A little pricey," she added quietly, "but the customer reviews on the Internet say the food is good."

"It's very good," Avery promised. She walked to the back of the car to help with the bags, but Jamie quickly appeared.

"Welcome. I can grab your bags. I'll take everything up to your rooms. No worries," he said.

Christine seemed surprised but pleased by the service and took her purse from the front seat.

They found Liza in the foyer, standing alongside Claire. She introduced herself and the housekeeper, and welcomed Avery's family.

"What a gorgeous place you have here, Liza," Helen Bishop said. "I'm so happy you found a room for us."

"It helps to know important people around here," Liza joked and glanced at Avery. "I've put you in a suite, right next to Avery's room," she added as she led them to the staircase.

Avery walked next to her mother, who eagerly peered through the doorways at the sitting rooms near the foyer and back to the big dining room near the kitchen. "This is so lovely, like something out of a movie." She smiled and squeezed Avery's arm. "And I can't wait to see the café. Can we come over this afternoon?"

"That would be great. Claire has made lunch for you here, so why don't you and Christine come right after lunch? The café will be empty, and I'll have a little time to show you around."

Avery partly dreaded her sister and mother seeing the Peregrine. Not because she was ashamed of how it looked, but because business was still erratic. Some of her theme nights—pizza and a movie and Lobster Sliders—were going well. Other nights, the café was far too quiet. Traffic had picked up, but it was still slower than she wanted. The Peregrine was not yet what anyone would call a success.

But they don't know that. You aren't open for lunch so it's fine if the café is empty, she reminded herself.

Still, she felt as if she was only putting off the inevitable. Embarrassment and disappointment on her part and her sister's long-suffering looks.

She only hoped that the crowds of Fourth of July visitors would save her. Even if they didn't rush into her café and fill every table, she hoped the place would look lively enough.

After one of Claire's delicious lunches, Avery took her sister and mother to the north side of the island, explaining that it was an up-and-coming area, a perfect opportunity for new businesses.

"Oh, isn't this charming?" her mother said as they drove past the ferry station. "I bet that ferry ride is fun. Why don't we try it, Christine? I read about the town on the other side, Newburyport. We could go shopping."

"How many times a day does the ferry run?" Christine asked, ignoring their mother's suggestion. "Is the fare expensive?"

Avery didn't want to admit that she didn't know. "It runs very frequently. Even more on the weekends and holidays," she added, thinking that must be true.

The dock did look very busy with people coming and going off the island. A ferry had just arrived, and a throng of island visitors was crossing the street to the boardwalk.

Dressed in shorts and T-shirts, or sundresses over bathing suits, they carried umbrellas, beach chairs, and bulging tote bags, marching along like the invasion of a small, disorganized army. Small children, toting plastic pails and sand toys, brought up the rear. A few families had even brought dogs. Avery could practically smell the sunblock in the air.

"Well, it seems like you have a lot of potential customers around. For such an out of the way place," Christine observed. "Of course, it is the Fourth of July. Every place is crowded."

Avery didn't answer, steering her SUV into a space near the Peregrine.

"My, look at that view. Can you see the water from your restaurant, honey?" her mom asked.

"We have a great view. I opened up the front with big glass doors and made a patio," Avery replied.

"How romantic . . . I can't wait to see it."

A few moments later Avery was unlocking the front entrance as her mother admired the French doors she had just described.

"How lovely. It reminds me of a wonderful old restaurant your father and I liked to visit in New Orleans. I sang there once," she added, smiling wistfully.

"Maybe you could sing here sometime, Mom," Avery said, thinking that would be a nice idea. She had been looking for some live music.

"Oh, no, I couldn't," her mother demurred. "I haven't performed for years . . . Well, maybe if I got my voice back in shape. We'll see."

When Avery got engaged to Paul, her mother had promised to sing at their wedding. Avery wondered if she remembered. If she did, she never mentioned it. Avery was grateful for that.

Once inside, her mother and sister were full of compliments for the decorating and atmosphere. Though her sister was not without a few needling comments and questions. "How many people can you seat in here at one time?" she asked as she began counting the chairs. "I read that the rate of turning tables over is really critical to a restaurant's bottom line. I think they say you can't let people take more than forty minutes for a meal."

Avery knew that some people made a science out of figuring how to maximize profit in a restaurant. Though she wanted to be efficient, asking her waitresses to carry a stopwatch wasn't her style.

"That's very true. There are more seats outside, Chris," Avery added, directing her through the glass doors.

While Christine went outside to survey the patio, Avery stayed inside with her mother. Helen watched her older daughter a moment and shook her head. "She likes to count things. She's always been that way, since she was a little girl." Helen shrugged and turned back to Avery. "You've done a wonderful job, Avery. It's a beautiful restaurant. Everything is so stylish and still relaxed. Beachy," she added, smiling. "And look at that view. Anybody would love to have a meal here. You found a perfect place, honey."

"I hope so, Mom." Avery felt very pleased that her mother "got it." It was good to have her here. It meant a lot to hear her mother's words of praise, more than she had even expected.

"I can't wait to try the food. Should we come tonight?"

Avery wasn't sure the café would be crowded tonight and tried to steer them toward Saturday.

"I guess you could," she said vaguely. "But Claire had a lobster bake planned at the inn tonight, to welcome Fourth of July guests. I thought you and Chris might want to do that, and come to the café tomorrow night. There might be some fireworks on the beach tomorrow night, too."

Christine had come back inside and heard the last part of their conversation. "I think we should have the lobster dinner at the inn, Mom. I mean, meals are included and we're paying for it," she reminded her.

Saved by Christine's calculator, Avery thought.

"Oh, all right. That sounds nice, too," Helen said agreeably. "I love lobster. But you won't be there, honey?"

"Sorry. I have to stay here until at least midnight. But maybe we can go to the beach tomorrow morning. I think you should take my car back and drive around to see the cliffs," she advised. "Someone will give me a ride home later."

"Good idea. We ought to get in some beach time, Mom. We can go see those cliffs, and I think there's a lighthouse somewhere, too." Christine had a guidebook in her purse and pulled it out.

"Sorry you can't come with us, honey." Helen gave Avery a kiss good-bye on her cheek. "Don't work too hard. I just love this place," she added. "I'm going to take a lot of pictures to show my friends. Maybe we'll come back for a girls' weekend sometime."

"Good idea, Mom." Avery was glad to see her mother enjoying herself. But her mother was the type of person who rarely complained and seemed delighted wherever she went. It was, Avery reflected, a very rare talent.

* * *

THE brief visit with her family had been fun but exhausting. Avery was eager to get to work. Gena, Teresa, and Jack arrived, and they began to set up the café and prep food for dinner.

"Sorry, Avery. Courtney couldn't start tonight. She had to drive her folks to the airport. It's a long story—" Jack began.

"That's all right. You don't have to explain." Avery didn't have the time for a long story right now. "Does she still want the job?"

"Oh, yeah. She wants it. She'll be in tomorrow, I promise."

"Okay. Tomorrow then. In the meantime, we'll all have to help Gena. That's all we can do."

The dinner hour was busy but not completely unmanageable.

Avery thought it was just the right amount of customers, especially shorthanded. She now regretted that she had not told her sister and mother to come. She would have felt some relief getting their visit over with.

But tomorrow night should be even busier and make the café look more successful, she reasoned. That was the main thing.

BE careful what you wish for. Avery recalled the old saying as she peeked out at the dining room on Saturday night. It was only six o'clock, and the tables both inside and out were filled, and more people stood in line, waiting to be seated. She felt her heartbeat quicken. This could be their biggest night yet. Perfect timing for her mother and Christine, who would be coming in soon for dinner.

"Wow, what a crowd! People are coming down to see the fireworks," Gena said as she swooped through the kitchen. "Did Jack's girlfriend get here yet? I thought she was going to be here by five."

"I don't know what happened to her. Teresa went to ask him." Avery had no sooner mentioned her name than Teresa marched into the kitchen.

"Bad news, no Courtney. The lovebirds broke up."

"What do you mean, no Courtney?" Gena demanded. "I can't handle all those tables on my own."

Gena was usually so cool and levelheaded, the sane one of the group who often calmed Avery down. Avery felt a prickle of alarm as she realized her ace waitress was in a panic. But something in this scenario wasn't making sense.

"What's the difference if they aren't dating?" Avery asked. "Courtney accepted the job."

Teresa threw her hands up. "You know kids. I spoke to her myself. She says she's sorry but, 'It would, like, be, like, too weird.' Then she hung up."

Avery took a deep breath. "Okay, let's just calm down a minute and figure this out. We'll all just have to pitch in, like we've been doing since Serena left. We'll be fine," she told the others, though she hardly believed it.

"That was barely working when we had no customers," Gena moaned. "How will it ever work tonight? The customers are going to freak out. We might as well give up now and claim there was a kitchen fire or something."

For a single desperate moment, Avery considered the idea.

Teresa, bless her soul, was undaunted. "Get a grip, Gena. I know how to waitress. It's not exactly rocket science." The feisty little woman pulled off her white apron and pulled out a black one with the café's logo, the silhouette of a peregrine falcon, on the front pocket. "I'll take the patio and the bottom half of the dining room, up to the photo of the lighthouse. You've got the rest."

"Okay, you're on. Want some lipstick?" Gena offered up a tube, and Teresa looked at it doubtfully. "Take some, you need it."

"Oh, all right." Teresa swiped on some glossy pink lipstick and suddenly looked about ten years younger. She forced a fake smile. "Welcome to Café Peregrine. My name is Teresa. I'll be your server tonight," she recited.

"That was pretty good. I didn't even know you were paying attention at those rehearsals," Avery said.

"There's not a lot that gets by me. You two ought to remember that." Teresa pushed through the kitchen doors and headed for her customers.

"Good luck in here," Gena called over her shoulder as she followed. "And don't worry, I won't let Jack mope. He can bus and run food. It's all hands on deck."

Avery smiled but didn't have time to reply. She was already busily attacking the orders, making up four arugula and goat cheese salads and a crab cake appetizer, working as if she had six arms instead of two. With Teresa out of the kitchen, she would need a few extra tonight.

Though the waitstaff shortage was patched over, there were more speed bumps to come. They were serving so many more customers than usual, Avery ran out of two of the specials before her sister and mother even arrived.

When they did arrive, Avery wasn't even able to go out and say hello. The kitchen was backed up with orders, and both Gena and Teresa were desperate to keep the food flowing.

Despite everyone's sympathy and pep talks, Jack was dragging around, looking heartbroken. Which made Avery even doubly mad at the mysterious Courtney. Couldn't she have waited until July fifth to dump him?

"Jack, clear table nine and serve these desserts at seven," Gena barked at him. He nodded and floated off like a sleepwalker.

"Just what we needed tonight. A heartbroken, zombie bus boy," Gena said, grabbing two orders of lobster bisque off the serving counter. She checked the rest of the order. "How's that striped bass coming?" They had been substituting striped bass for the halibut since seven.

Avery had just emerged from the cold box. "Small problem . . . We're out of bass. I'm out of . . . everything. Where did all the food go? I thought I bought more than enough for the entire weekend." She stared at Gena feeling an acid taste of panic rise in the back of her throat.

Gena put down the dishes she was holding. "Take a deep breath, Avery. Just calm down. This happens at places. It's not the end of the world . . . Don't we have anything in the freezer? Like some shrimp or chicken wings?"

"Chicken wings?" Avery stared at her. Just what she wanted to serve her sister tonight. Christine would take an hour choosing an entree and then end up with chicken wings?

"Oh, you know what I mean." Gena caught herself, realizing how ridiculous the question actually was. "A spare tire in the trunk, that's what I'm asking . . . Frozen ravioli?" she asked hopefully.

Avery sighed and shook her head. "We haven't been in business long enough to have any extra supplies like that. That's something bigger restaurants do."

"Bigger restaurants . . . like the Tuna?" Gena asked. Before Avery could reply she added, "Maybe Mike can give you some food. Why don't you call him?"

Avery felt her heart clutch at that suggestion. Mike was the logical choice here, and she was sure he'd help her. But she felt too embarrassed to ask him. "I can't," she said simply.

"Sure you can. He'll be happy to help. He likes you, Avery. I know he does," Gena answered quickly.

Avery felt herself blush and hoped Gena thought it was just working over the hot stove that made her cheeks fiery red. "What would I say? 'I'm running out of food. Can you loan me some?'"

Teresa nodded. "I think that would work."

Jack walked into the kitchen. He still looked glum, his chin hanging down to the edge of his apron bib, but he was doing his job. Avery's heart went out to him. She knew how it felt to be dumped and try to keep up the pace in a busy job.

"Jack, I have a special mission for you," Gena said pulling him aside. She was scribbling something on her order pad. She tore off the check, folded it in half, and handed it to him. "I want you to take this note down to the Lazy Tuna and give it to Mike Rossi. Only Mike, okay?"

Avery was running up and down in front of the burners and broilers, trying to turn out five more entrees.

"Gena, what are you doing? What did you write on that note?" Gena shrugged. "Just what you told me to say. What's the worst thing that can happen? He'll say he's sorry but he doesn't have any extra food, right?"

Avery glanced over her shoulder but didn't answer. She wasn't afraid of that at all. She was more afraid that Mike would come to her rescue and make her like him even more.

A short time later, Jack returned to the kitchen toting several giant bags of frozen shrimp, a box of beef patties, and two giant bags of wings. Nothing that was on her menu, Avery noted, but she was good at improvising. In culinary school, she had always done well with assignments where students were given random ingredients to combine and cook together.

Along with the bags of frozen food, she found a little note:

Don't think, just cook. Hang in there.—Mike

Short and sweet. But the advice gave her more of a boost than she would ever admit. She wasn't sure why, but she tucked it into her apron pocket, storing it in a safe place.

As the night wore on, the dining area became even more hectic. And the customers became surly. Some had waited too long to be seated only to discover that the dishes they wanted were no longer available. Others waited too long to be served or flat-out hated the menu changes. Nearly all of them were rude to Teresa and Gena. Some walked out. One table was so angry, they didn't pay their bill.

A bit after nine, the fireworks show started out on the beach. Some customers got up from their tables to go outside and watch, their dinners left half eaten. It was impossible for Gena and Teresa to tell if they were coming back again. Meanwhile, another wave of customers, who didn't care about fireworks, were waiting impatiently to sit down.

Avery popped out of the kitchen to help. But she couldn't bear to watch the chaotic scene for very long—or catch sight of the stunned looks on the faces of her mother and sister. Besides, if she stayed out of the kitchen too long, the food suffered and there would be even more complaints.

Back in the kitchen, she heard the fireworks explode. She felt as if she were cooking in a battlefield. She kept her head down and worked furiously. "Don't think, just cook," she kept repeating to herself.

She smelled smoke and thought a little grease had splattered in the broiler. When she finally turned to check, tall flames were shooting out of the grill. A large piece of meat had fallen through the grate and caught fire.

Avery tried to smother it with a big pot cover then threw a wet towel on top, which only made it worse. She finally grabbed a ten-pound box of salt and managed to douse it.

Gena walked into the kitchen, waving her hands in the thick clouds of smoke. "What in the world is going on in here? Did you have a fire?"

"Just a bit of meat. But it didn't go quietly."

"I'm surprised the alarms didn't go off."

"Yikes, they still might." Avery turned the exhaust fan on full blast and pulled open the back door. All she needed now was a fire alarm, causing the diners to stampede out of the restaurant. And a fire truck to come racing along.

"It's all right. I'd better get back to cooking," she told Gena. Avery got back to the stove, wondering if her mother and sister were still out there. What were they thinking, dining in this disaster area? She couldn't even imagine.

Actually, she could imagine. That was the problem. She could already hear her sister insist that Avery do the right thing and try to salvage some of their mother's investment. Avery just hoped her mother wasn't swayed. But Christine always spoke with such an air of authority; she could be very persuasive.

Can't worry about that now. Don't think, just cook, she kept telling herself.

Finally, she dolloped the last swirl of cream on the last dessert order, and handed the order to Teresa.

"You don't look so hot . . . I mean, you look too hot. Oh, you know what I mean. Just sit down or something," Teresa advised.

Avery did feel hot and exhausted. Her curly hair had practically come completely undone from its bun and was falling all round her face and shoulders. She staggered out to the dining area and stared around at the empty tables, finally catching sight of her mother and sister, who were practically cowering in a corner. She couldn't believe they were still here.

"Hi, honey! We were waiting for you!" her mother called out gaily.

Christine just turned and stared at Avery. She looked too overwhelmed to speak.

Avery struggled to summon one last spark of energy, a drop or two of gas left in her tank. She forced a smile and walked toward them.

"So how was your dinner? I don't even know what you ordered," Avery admitted. She had meant to take careful note of their meals, but had been in too much of a rush to keep track.

"I had the shrimp and pasta," Christine reported. "It was . . . interesting."

A slapdash concoction of ingredients pulled out of the cold box and off the seasoning shelf—some exotic mushrooms and sundried tomatoes and the frozen shrimp Mike sent over. All things considered, Avery didn't think it had turned out half bad. Most people had said they liked it. Christine, of course, was a master at backhanded compliments.

"My dish was very tasty," her mother insisted. "I think it was pheasant, or something like that. The sauce was sublime," she told Avery. "Was there wine in there?"

"Yes, Mom. Some white wine . . . and lots of butter . . . and some chicken wings," she finally admitted.

Of all people, her poor mom had to get the chicken wings?

"Really?" her mother looked surprised but even more pleased by the admission.

"I knew that. I was just wondering if you would admit it." Christine looked smugly satisfied.

"No wonder you spent years studying cooking. I could never make wings taste like that," her mother countered.

"Glad you liked it. We ran out of our usual specials and had to improvise. We were a little crazy in here tonight, with the holiday crowd."

And we're down a waitress and had a small kitchen fire, she added silently.

"I thought it was a lovely dinner. We could see the ocean and the fireworks," her mother said. "Quite a show, wasn't it, Christine?"

Christine stared at Avery. "I've never seen anything like it," she said dryly.

That was not a compliment, Avery knew by now, and there was more to come.

But her mother saved the day with a huge yawn. "I'm sorry, girls. All the fun and sun today just wore me out. I think we had better head back to the inn. Avery still has work to do here, don't you, dear?"

"Yes, Mom, I do," Avery replied, grateful to her mother for whisking Christine away before her sister could critique the evening.

Christine rose but gave Avery a *this isn't over yet* look.

Avery watched them go then and finally collapsed in a chair. Teresa, Gena, and Jack had started cleaning up, but they all looked so exhausted, Avery didn't have the heart to make them stay.

"We'll get the rest of this tomorrow. I think we should just all go home and get some sleep. The weekend isn't over yet," she reminded them.

Her crew groaned in unison, and everyone thanked her for letting them leave. Gena lingered, following Avery into the kitchen as she gathered her purse and shoes.

"Want me to wait until you lock up?" Gena asked.

"Thanks but I'm fine. I'm just going to check the broiler one more time, make sure that fire is totally out."

"Good idea." Gena nodded. "Okay, see you tomorrow."

Avery poked around the bottom of the broiler and extracted the charred bits of meat with a pair of long tongs. Then she managed to clean out the ashes with some rags and a spatula.

She heard a knock and thought it was one of her crew. Jack was always leaving his phone and car keys somewhere. But when she pulled the door open she found Mike.

Another survivor of the kitchen wars, she thought. His chef's whites were covered with food stains, his baseball cap was on backward, and his strong jaw showed more than a shadow of dark beard.

Unfortunately, these signs of wear and tear looked pretty good on him, Avery thought. *Too good.*

On the other hand, she was sure that she looked like an unholy mess and instinctively reached up to do something with her hair, which was apparently shooting out in all directions around her head.

"I just stopped by to see how you're doing," he greeted her. "Looks like the Peregrine was hopping tonight."

"We had the customers, just like you predicted, but . . . it was sort of a disaster. I don't think anyone will come back. Even my own mother . . ."

Mike stared down at her, his expression confused but warmly sympathetic. "What do you mean? What happened?"

Avery took a deep breath and tried to describe the night's horrors as calmly as possible. From Courtney's no-show to diners walking out on checks to her mother getting the chicken wing special.

Mike listened with a serious expression, though she spotted a mirthful spark in his dark eyes. "Sounds like a rough night," he said finally.

"It was more than rough . . . it was horrible. Everyone who ate here is going to think this place is the worst restaurant in the entire universe. Some people asked for their money back. I'm surprised all of them didn't . . ."

"Come on, Avery. We've all had bad nights. I'm sure you've had a bad night like this before . . . somewhere?"

"Not like this," she insisted. "Not in my very own restaurant. While I'm trying to build a good reputation so I can get more business . . ."

She had her head down as she rambled, embarrassed that he had caught her at such a weak moment. She didn't want to cry, but once she started she couldn't seem to stop.

"Aw, come on now, don't cry." Mike took hold of her shoulders.

"I had all these fantasies about running my own café . . . how great it was going to be . . . But it's not great. It's not even good." She was wailing now, and Mike pulled her closer and patted her back.

"It is good. It's very good," he insisted.

"No, it's not," she argued with him through her sobs. "Whatever made me think for one stupid minute I could do this? I'm going to lose my mom's entire investment . . . and the poor woman insisted that her chicken wings tasted like pheasant . . ." She pulled back for a minute and met his confused gaze. "She had to know it wasn't. She was just saying that to be nice to me."

Mike didn't seem to know what she was babbling about but nodded thoughtfully. "I've had pheasant. It's no big deal. Give me a good old honest chicken any day. I bet your mom feels the same way."

"Oh, Mike, I'm such a failure," she said as another wave of sobs overcame her.

"Avery, don't even say that. You're very brave. You're a trouper. You're a hero," he insisted. "But you're just tired and upset right now."

Avery took deep, heaving breaths, trying to collect herself. She sat on a stool near the worktable and wiped her eyes and nose on some tissues. When had she ever been such a blubbering mess before? She couldn't remember. But somehow, she was glad Mike was there. She would have felt embarrassed acting so loony with anyone else. Even her mom. Somehow it felt fine to let Mike see all her sadness and insecurities. She felt so—so safe with him. It was really quite remarkable.

"I still have my sister to deal with. She doesn't think I'm such a hero. Believe me."

"Who cares what she thinks? Is she Jacques Pépin or something? Even if she was, I thought you said this was your dream, opening your own café. Are you going to give up just because you have an annoying sister? And you didn't buy enough halibut? And you hit a few nasty bumps in the road?"

"More like potholes . . . the size of swimming pools."

"All right, potholes the size of swimming pools. Things aren't working out the way you hoped they would. You have to keep at it. Pick yourself up, brush yourself off. There's an old saying that I tell my students when they get discouraged, Avery. 'Knocked down seven times, get up eight.'" He paused, letting the words sink in. "You want to win the fight? There's no magic to it. You just have to get up off the floor one more time than the other guy."

Avery nodded. The metaphor seemed a little macho to her, but he made a good point. She wasn't a quitter, even though she sounded like one tonight. Even though she was terribly tempted to be one and stay on the floor, just this one time in her life.

"Have a little faith in yourself," Mike added, cutting into her rambling thoughts. "You're a great cook. Honestly. I wouldn't tell you that if it wasn't true," he insisted. "Other people will figure that out, too, trust me."

Avery sighed. He was staring down at her, and she managed a

very small smile. "Thanks, Mike. Thanks for the frozen shrimp and the wings . . . and the pep talk. Again," she acknowledged.

"You're welcome again. Anytime," he said quietly. "I'm sorry, but that part about your mom saying she thought she was eating pheasant was pretty funny."

She laughed with him. "My mom's really sweet. You ought to meet her. She would like you." Avery felt embarrassed blurting that out, though in her heart she knew it was true. Her mother would find Mike absolutely charming.

Mike looked pleased by the suggestion. "I'd love to meet your mom. Anytime."

Avery met his gaze for a moment then slipped off the stool. "It's getting late. I'd better get back to the inn. They'll be wondering what happened to me."

"I'll wait for you," he said.

"Okay." Avery quickly checked the stove burners, oven, and grill. Then she pulled off her cooking jacket and grabbed her bag from a closet.

Mike opened the door and held it for her. Avery smiled as she passed and paused to shut the lights.

Suddenly, they were alone in the dark, standing very close. Avery saw him take a tiny step toward her. Or maybe he had merely shifted his weight, or turned his body her way.

She didn't want to look up at him but couldn't help herself. She met his gaze, and felt he was going to kiss her. She wouldn't have minded that at all . . . though she still didn't understand what this relationship was. Or could be. It seemed they had slowly but surely moved from a friendship and a joking rivalry to something else. A budding romance? Or could it possibly be even more?

But when he put his arms around her in a warm, strong hug,

Avery stopped wondering and worrying. All she could do was hug him back, pressing her cheek to his chest, drawing comfort and strength from his strength and affection. Yes, his jacket smelled like onion rings. But they were his onion rings and that was comforting, too.

"Feel any better?" he asked quietly.

She tipped her head back and smiled at him. "I do. Thank you," she replied, though she knew the words didn't do her feelings justice. Not at all.

He smiled and dropped a quick kiss on her forehead. "Good, I'm glad."

"Thanks again for listening to me. And for your words of wisdom."

"Are you sure you mean words of wisdom . . . not just that I'm a wise guy?"

"That, too," she assured him. He laughed and stepped aside, letting her walk through the door before him. Avery locked up and walked beside him down the alley. Her SUV was parked in the space between her café and Sunshine Sundries. She got in and started the engine, then said good night to Mike again.

"Good night, Avery. And remember, just take it one kitchen fire at a time, okay?" He was back in wise-guy mode again but she didn't mind.

She waved and drove down Ferry Street. He stood watching her, his white jacket catching a beam of light from a street lamp.

She still wasn't sure what she meant to him . . . or what he meant to her. And she wasn't sure why this kiss had only been on her forehead. All she knew was that she was grateful to have Mike in her life, grateful that he was the one who had appeared at the kitchen door, offering words of encouragement and advice—and a strong shoulder to cry on. Right now, she couldn't think of anyone else in the world she could have been so open with, so much herself. Was she actually falling for the Tuna Guy? It sure looked that way.

But what was she supposed to do with that? Avery knew she didn't have time for a real relationship right now, and even if she did, she probably still wasn't ready.

But when the summer was over—if her café survived that long—she and Mike would have time to really get to know each other and figure out if there was something real between them. Something as real—and rare—as she suddenly suspected.

WHEN Avery returned to the inn, she was surprised to find Christine was still up, reading on the porch. "Chris, you didn't have to wait for me," Avery said as she came up the porch steps. "It's so late, and I know you have a big drive tomorrow."

"I went to bed but I couldn't fall asleep. I think I got regular coffee instead of decaf."

Your waitress screwed up, she really meant to say.

"Well, I'm beat."

"I'm sure you are. You work so hard. But could we talk just a minute or two? We hardly get together, and Mom and I have to leave early tomorrow."

Avery would have much rather gone straight up to bed, but she didn't want to hurt her sister's feelings. It was true that they saw each other rarely these days, and Avery had been so busy during their visit, she hadn't spent much time with them at all.

"Sure, I can sit a minute. How's your job going? Still like the firm?"

Christine was an accountant and worked at a big firm in Hartford. She was smart and ambitious and definitely corner office material, Avery thought.

"It's going well. I'm up for a promotion. I'll hear about it soon, probably September. Not much happens in the summer in a big company."

"Unlike my business. Everything happens in the summer," Avery quipped, trying to keep the talk light.

Christine didn't answer right away. She closed her book and put it aside. "I think the café is very pretty, Avery. It couldn't be nicer, that way," she began. "But I have to be honest. Do you think you're really cut out to run your own place? I can see that you're trying hard. But the café didn't seem to be very well managed or . . . organized."

Avery felt her stomach drop. She had known this conversation was coming and wasn't at all surprised. She just didn't want to lose her temper or have an emotional meltdown, the way she had a little while ago. She was sure her sister wouldn't be half as sympathetic or encouraging as Mike.

"I know it seemed chaotic there tonight," she said carefully. "But we're just starting out. Everyone hits a few bumps in the road."

"Maybe that's it." Christine shrugged. "I hate to sound negative. You know I'm not that kind of person."

Avery forced a smile. Her sister was exactly that kind of person and always had been. But this was not the time to get into that.

"All I'm saying is, maybe you should rethink this situation a little. Are you making much of a profit?"

She wasn't making any profit. She was actually dipping into her reserve most of the time.

"I'm not really sure," Avery murmured. She gave a big theatrical yawn. "I have to check the books. And I will, right after the holiday."

"Too bad I have to leave. I'd love to work on them for you. Maybe you should e-mail me the files?"

"I know how busy you are, Chris. I can handle it."

"You're a fabulous cook, Avery. No one would deny that. But you could get a job doing cooking anywhere, if this business doesn't work out. It wouldn't be the worst thing. And you might still have some of Mom's investment left," she added. "I think you need to think about that."

"I do think about it, Chris. Believe me, I do." *Night and day,* Avery nearly confessed. But she didn't want her sister to know she was quite that worried about succeeding.

Christine picked up her book and rose from her chair. "All right, enough said. I'm just concerned. Mom and I are very proud of you." She patted Avery's shoulder as she walked by. "We'll see you tomorrow, I hope, before we go?"

Avery nodded. "Sure, I don't have to go back to the café until the afternoon. We can at least have breakfast together."

"Great. Sleep well." Christine said good night and went inside.

Avery stayed out on the porch and gazed out at the ocean, a dark blue ribbon under the night sky. There was a bright half moon; the silver light glimmered on the rolling water. It was so quiet she could hear each wave hit the shore.

Her sister's words made her worry and doubt herself. But she suddenly heard a stronger voice prevail—Mike's voice, urging her to shake off the naysayers and hang on to her dream. To have faith in herself. *Fall down seven times, get up eight,* she reminded herself as she headed upstairs and literally, fell into her bed.

In a few months, Christine will see that she's totally wrong about the café, Avery promised herself. *I'll make her a special dessert—a nice deep-dish Humble Pie.*

SUNDAY morning, Avery woke with a start, eager to get back to work. She hadn't slept very long but realized that adrenaline was still pumping through her body. She just hoped it would last until the holiday rush was done.

She had to help the crew clean up the café today before they could reopen. She also had to run over to the restaurant supply warehouse in Beverly to pick up more food, including a few bags of frozen items to replenish Mike's walk-in freezer.

But she did want to spend more time with her family. She doubted she would see them again before September.

She met her mother and sister in the dining room as they were enjoying Claire's delicious breakfast buffet—baked French toast with mixed berry compote, fluffy scrambled eggs with cheddar cheese and chives, crispy bacon, and cinnamon scones. Avery had been so busy the night before, she hadn't stopped to eat a bite. Now, she more than made up for the missed meal.

While Christine finished her packing, Avery and her mother took their coffee mugs out to the porch. "You've found such a beautiful place to live, honey. Are you happy here?"

Avery smiled, surprised at the question. "I've been too busy the last few weeks to even wonder about that, Mom," she said honestly. "It's been hard at times. But I do love it."

"That's good. That's what I wanted to hear. You have a special talent, a gift from God. It's important to use that gift and express yourself with it. You give a lot of people pleasure with your cooking."

"Thanks, Mom. That's sweet of you to say."

"I didn't mean it to be sweet, dear. It's true. I'm glad to see you've gotten over Paul," she added. "He wasn't good enough for you."

Avery smiled wistfully. "I am over him. Well, just about." If she could make the café succeed, she knew she would shed the last bit of sadness over his rejection. She wasn't sure why; it was just tied up somehow with her feelings about their failed relationship. "I think it all worked out for the best. I'm starting to think now that in the long run we wouldn't have been happy together."

Maybe it was time, or distance, or a combination of both, but Avery saw her broken engagement very differently now. It seemed more like a lucky break than a heartbreak.

She hated to admit it, but meeting a really good guy, like Mike, who wasn't all wrapped up in himself, definitely helped her turn a corner. She felt an impulse to tell her mom about Mike, then decided it was too soon, too new and uncertain.

"I know the café isn't exactly the way you want it to be. Yet," her mother said, turning the conversation back to Avery's business. "But be patient. Give it time. Everything's a process, dear."

That was very true. Words that could apply to her relationship with Mike as well. She had to be patient to see what would come of that as well.

"The café can use improvements, Mom. I'm working on it all the time. I'm just worried sometimes though—about how long this will take. And worried about your investment," she admitted.

"Nonsense. Let's not even go there." Her mother waved her hand as if swatting away a pesky insect. "Did your sister start in on that with you? I asked her not to."

"Well, she's concerned. I understand," Avery said honestly.

"Avery, please. I gave you that money with no strings attached. You have to go forward, wholeheartedly, or it won't work. My money is on you, dear, literally and figuratively. Give it your all. I know you can do it."

"Thanks, Mom." Avery felt a lump in her throat. She leaned over and squeezed her mother's hand. "I just don't want to disappoint you."

"The only way you could disappoint me, honey, is to give up

before the finish line. I gave up on my career much too soon. I don't want to see you make the same mistake. If the café doesn't work out—and I know it will," she quickly added, "you can come back home, and we'll both move in with your sister. She's doing quite well now. She can afford to take care of us."

Her mother smiled, her blue eyes twinkling with their usual mischievous spark.

Avery laughed. "All right, I'll remember that. But you're the one who has to tell her."

"Tell me what? Are you two talking about me again?" Christine came out to the porch, carrying her purse and laptop in its black padded case. She had managed to squeeze some work in this weekend, Avery had no doubt.

"Nothing, dear. Ready to go?" Helen asked as she stood up.

A few moments later, Jamie came out with the rest of Christine's and Helen's bags, then stowed them in the trunk of Christine's car. There were hugs and kisses all around as Avery bid her family a safe drive back to Connecticut.

She waved as Christine drove out to the main road. Avery felt an unexpected wave of sadness as she waved good-bye. Part of her wished they had stayed longer. But another part yearned to get back to work and prove to Christine, and any of the café's critics, that they were all wrong.

Chapter Twelve

"HERE we are. This won't take long," Claire told Jamie. She had driven them into the town of Cape Light on Tuesday morning and parked in front of the bank on Main Street.

It was Jamie's day off, but he didn't have any plans except to go out to the beach in the afternoon, he told Claire at breakfast. Claire was grateful that he didn't want to go into Boston to see his friends. It had been three weeks, practically to the day, since he had disappeared and nearly lost his job. He hadn't been to the city since.

Claire wasn't sure if he thought he would be too tempted to get in trouble if he went. But she didn't feel comfortable asking him that question. She was satisfied that he had agreed to go into Cape Light with her. Liza had asked her to bring a deposit from the inn to the bank, and Claire suggested to Jamie that he come along and open an account, a safe place to save his pay each week.

"I had a bank account for a while when I was working steady.

Then I didn't have anything to put in it, so I didn't bother," he admitted at the breakfast table.

"Well, now you do have something. It will encourage you to save for some good purpose," she added, hoping that purpose would be continuing his education.

The bank on Main Street looked remarkably old-fashioned for these modern times, Claire realized as she led Jamie toward it. Marble columns flanked the heavy glass and brass-trimmed revolving door. The interior was cool and quiet, with tellers posted behind windows to one side and a few bank executives seated at heavy wooden desks on the other.

Claire led Jamie to the first desk, where they were greeted by a helpful assistant manager. "I need to visit the hardware store. I'll wait for you outside," Claire said once she was sure Jamie would be taken care of.

He looked doubtful for a moment, like a small child being left at school, she thought. Then a look of resolve and maturity replaced that expression.

When Claire met him on the street a short time later, he seemed cheerful.

"How did it go?" she asked him.

"The woman kept calling me Mr. Carter. That was sort of weird," he admitted with a grin. "I got a checking account, too. It was free." He patted his shirt pocket. Claire saw the edge of a checkbook peeking out.

"Well done. Are you hungry? I think we should have some lunch." *To celebrate,* she wanted to add. But she didn't want him to feel too self-conscious about it.

They decided on the Clam Box Diner, a short walk down the street. "Is this place good?" Jamie asked as the sign came into view.

"Depends on what you mean by *good.* A lot of people must like the food. It's been in business a long time."

Claire didn't really care for the food at the Clam Box, but she did like the casual atmosphere and speedy service and thought Jamie might like it.

They found an empty booth near the window and Trudy, a waitress who had worked there for years now, greeted them and handed down two menus.

Jamie looked at his menu then back at Claire. "I don't know, Claire. There's something really weird about you sitting in a restaurant. It's like unnatural or something."

Claire laughed. "Everyone likes to have a meal out once in a while. By the way, watch out for the chowder . . . You might be disappointed," she practically whispered.

Jamie ordered a clam roll and fries, and Claire asked for a grilled cheese and tomato sandwich, which she believed was one of the better choices. *Not too much could go wrong with good old grilled cheese,* she thought.

Jamie took a few bites of his clam roll then wiped his mouth on a napkin. "Not bad, but not even close to your cooking."

"Thanks. Just for that compliment, it's my treat," she promised, making him smile.

She had planned on buying him lunch anyway. Though she saw him every day, from sunup to sundown, they rarely had time to spend together just talking and having fun.

"Why didn't you go into the city today? I thought for sure you would have," Claire said honestly.

He shrugged. "I can go another time. Maybe next week."

Claire nodded, hoping he wouldn't go next week either. The problem was, he didn't have anything to do around here on his days off. But she had an idea about that, too.

"Now that you have a steady job and can save some money, it's a good time to think about the future. Do you have any thoughts about what you want to do when you leave the inn?"

She hated to say it out loud, but they were halfway through the summer, and they both knew his job wouldn't last forever.

Jamie just shrugged. "I haven't thought about it much. I'll find another job, I guess, back in Boston."

Another dead-end job. The only kind he could get without a high school diploma.

"But what if you could do anything at all with your life, be anything you wanted to be, what would you do?"

He seemed surprised by the question, then smiled. "Oh, I'd be some rich guy with a Porsche and a big apartment on the Charles. I'd, like, be so rich I didn't have to work at all. One of those Internet millionaires, you know? Just go out to clubs and see sports every night—a skybox at the Garden and Fenway . . ."

Claire nodded and smiled. Of course, he would say something like that. What twenty-year-old male wouldn't? But she had hoped he would voice some secret dream or goal he could pursue as his life's work.

"That all sounds very . . . glamorous," she replied. "Like an after-shave commercial. But I think it might get awfully boring after a while."

"Why would it get boring? I don't think so." Jamie popped a French fry in his mouth and grinned.

"Maybe not, maybe not," she compromised. "I guess what I'm really asking is if there is anything you would really like to do, as a trade or a profession. Just until you're a millionaire," she teased him. "I'm sure you can find another job, after the inn. But you don't have to jump from job to job your whole life, Jamie. You could learn some useful trade—become a carpenter or an electrician. A professional cook, maybe?"

He had not shown much interest in anything like that at the inn, Claire knew. But she hoped her suggestions would spur some response in him.

Jamie just shrugged and examined a packet of sweetener.

"I believe that God gives everyone some talent," Claire went on, not about to give up. "Some special spark they can develop and use to express themselves, and do some good in the world. It might be some rare ability, like being a rocket scientist. Or as simple as being a good cook, like me. There are no better or worse gifts in the eyes of God. Everyone is important in the role they play in the world. The main thing is to put your heart in something, to take pride in what you do. 'Whatsoever you do, do it with all your heart,'" she said, recalling a favorite psalm. "I believe that you have some talent, too," she added. "I'm sure of it."

Jamie looked up at her. "Me? Sure. I've got a talent, for getting in trouble."

"That's not what I meant," Claire said, biting back a smile. "I'm sure you have a real talent. You just haven't found it yet. You seem pretty handy with computers," she added. "I've seen you fix Liza's computer a few times now."

Jamie pushed a shock of dark hair out of his eyes. "That was no big deal. Everybody knows how to do stuff like that."

"What was that thing you set up for Liza—a wire system? Is that what you call it? Well, everybody doesn't know how to do that. Liza said if you hadn't done it, she would have had to hire a technician."

Claire had no clue as to what Jamie had actually done. All she knew was that Liza was so pleased, she had given him a bonus in his paycheck.

He shrugged again, but at least he smiled this time. "All I did was set up wireless Internet access for the guests. It was pretty simple . . . and you call it Wi-Fi."

"Wi-Fi, right." Claire nodded, feeling they were getting somewhere. "I think you have a knack for it. If you like that sort of work, I'm sure there are classes you can take to learn more. Maybe in a trade school or at a junior college." She shook her head, feeling out of her depth. "Listen to me," she said ruefully. "I don't know the first thing about computers, and here I am, trying to tell you how to start a career with them. But all I mean to say is, wasn't it fun to do work you liked and found easy—and get paid for it?"

Jamie nodded. "Sure it was. But I didn't really think of it as work."

"That's just my point. When you find something you have talent for and enjoy doing, it doesn't seem like work. Not all the time," she added honestly. "That's how I feel about cooking."

Jamie sighed and stared at her. "I guess I could see myself fixing computers. It would be pretty cool if I could. And I bet the pay is good, better than what I earn. But how would I get jobs like that? Who would hire me?"

"Oh, I'm sure you could get a job in that field. I think there must be plenty. It seems everything involves computers nowadays. But first you have to look at the big picture. And have some patience. Getting your GED would be the first step. Then you need to take some courses. We could look into it together. I'll help you figure it out," she added. "I'll help you with the tuition, too."

"You would? I don't know . . . I don't think I could let you do that."

"I want to. It would make me happy to see you headed on a good career track. It would make me very happy," she assured him.

Jamie let out a long sigh. "I'll pay you back. I have to." He was silent for a moment, then said, "Claire, I don't know if I can do this. I'm not a very good student. I just get too bored sitting still too long and trying to memorize stuff."

"I know studying is not your cup of tea," she admitted. "But you are very intelligent. Everyone says so. You just haven't found that special thing to apply your smarts to. If you have a real goal, a real destination in sight, you'll be a much better student that you used to be. It won't be like sitting in class and memorizing how many angles in an octagon or when the pyramids were built."

Jamie laughed. "Do you remember how you used to help me study for those tests?"

"I do," she replied. "I knew it didn't make much sense to you. You used to always ask me, 'Why do I need to learn this stuff?' and I couldn't always give you a good answer. But now it's all your choice. You can learn things that do make sense to you, that add up to something in your real life. Do you understand what I'm trying to say?"

Jamie rubbed his jaw a moment. "What about the GED? I heard it was hard."

"Oh, it's not so bad. I asked a friend of mine about it. She used to teach history in the high school. She said there are books we can buy, and there's all kinds of help on the Internet, too. Vera, my friend, tutors students who are preparing for the test. I'm sure she could help you," Claire added.

Jamie looked a bit overwhelmed by the suggestion.

Claire didn't want to scare him. "You just think about it. You don't have to figure it all out right now. I have to return some books to the library. I'm sure we can find some material there about the GED, and about places where you can learn to work with computers."

"All right, we can look around at the library. I guess I'm sort of curious now."

Claire breathed a silent sigh of relief. She had him interested in the idea of education—that was the first step. "Would you like some dessert?" she asked.

"Nah. I was thinking of ordering some blueberry pie, but I know it won't be half as good as what I'm used to at the inn. You spoil me, Claire."

Claire laughed and asked for the check. She had never enjoyed a meal at the Clam Box more and doubted she ever would again.

Avery wasn't really superstitious, but Friday the thirteenth still made her wary. She hoped the café would have a lot of customers this weekend. The big wave of business over the holiday had helped her bottom line some. But a week or so later, the flow of customers had dwindled again. Some of the special theme nights filled the café, and others didn't work quite as well. Avery felt the business was just bumping along and still worried every day if she would make it to the end of the summer.

She had hired a new waitress, Teresa's granddaughter, Brittany, who was a hardworking young woman, attending college in Rhode Island and home for the summer. Teresa had taken charge of training and supervising her and was far tougher at that than Avery ever would have been.

Though Jack was still licking his wounds from his breakup, Brittany's arrival had added a spark to his day. He definitely seemed more cheerful and energetic lately, and Avery thought it was cute to see this little romance start to blossom.

Heaven knows, I have no social life anymore.

Even if she had a spare moment from the café, she was either exhausted or doing some extra job to save a little on overhead. Like washing and ironing the linens herself, instead of sending them out to a laundry.

Sometimes Gena came in and helped her. Avery was standing at the ironing board around noon, working on a pile of tablecloths while Gena folded, when she noticed a peculiar sight—an army of seniors were marching up the boardwalk.

Dressed in bright summer clothes, sun hats, and sunglasses that wrapped around their heads like welder's goggles, they were led by a tour guide who carried a little yellow flag with a smiley face on a plastic pole.

"Did you see that?" Gena asked. "Looks like we're being invaded by the silver-haired set. I bet they're going down to the Tuna." Gena stepped to the open doors and looked outside.

"He's bringing in tour groups now?" Avery sighed. "What next?"

"It's a good idea. Why didn't we think of it?" Gena said as she set to work again on the linens.

"Why, indeed," Avery muttered. "I'm going to look into it. Unless he has it all locked up."

Which was possible, knowing Mike. His laid-back manner belied his sharp business sense.

They worked a few minutes more in silence. Avery heard the phone and eagerly picked it up, hoping it was a reservation.

"Café Peregrine, may I help you?"

"I hope you can," a familiar voice replied. "Want some easy business? I have a big group of hungry tourists here and not enough table space. They all have to go back on the three o'clock ferry, otherwise I'd do two seatings," Mike explained.

The senior invasion. He wanted to send the overflow her way.

"But I don't do lunch," Avery reminded him.

There was a short but distinct silence. "Are you kidding me? You keep telling me you need more business. I'm sending you a boatload of customers. What is the problem, Avery? You're not open? Get open," he advised.

Avery was taken aback a bit by his tone. But she could hear the noise in the background. He was under pressure, and he had helped her when she was in a crisis, with all that emergency food. She did owe him one.

"All right. Send them over. I'll see what I can do."

"I knew you'd come to your senses sooner or later. You don't have much time to get ready. They move quicker than you'd think."

Avery hung up and turned to Gena. "You know that parade that just passed by? They were going to the Tuna . . . and we're getting the overflow."

"The overflow? You mean we're opening for lunch?"

"That's what I mean." Avery hastily gathered up the linens and cleared up the dining area. Then she ran back to the kitchen. "Call around and see if anyone can get over here to help. I'm thinking a short, blackboard menu. We have lots of pizza dough left over from Monday. I'll add the two specials I was planning for tonight and get more food for dinner later."

There would be an hour or two to get more supplies for dinner entrees. It would be close, but she did need the business.

An unexpected shopping trip should be the least of my problems, she reminded herself.

The tour group soon marched up to the Peregrine and filed in. Avery invited everyone to find their own tables.

"What a pretty little place," she heard a lady say as she passed by.

"It looks a lot nicer than that fish shack," another lady agreed. "That one's a little too funky for my taste."

Funky, huh? She would have to tell Mike about that review. Then again . . . maybe not, she decided.

Avery ran back to the kitchen, leaving Gena in charge of getting everyone settled. Brittany and Jack walked through the back door. Luckily, they had been nearby, just down at the beach when Gena called. Avery quickly explained the situation, and everyone got to work.

The pizzas were a popular choice and easy to turn out quickly. Teresa showed up just as Avery was getting the first wave of orders in the oven. Her seasoned helper didn't ask too many questions and jumped right into the work.

"They keep telling me they need to make the three o'clock ferry," Gena said each time she came into the kitchen. "I hope we make it."

"Tell them to eat faster," Teresa groused. "We can always pack a few things to go."

Avery didn't want that to happen. They would never come back again. She cooked like a demon, consoled by the knowledge that there was a time limit to this madness.

She happened to be in the dining room, helping serve dessert, when an attractive woman, about her own age, appeared at one of the open French doors. Avery recognized her, the tour guide who had been holding the little flag.

"How's everyone doing here? Having a good time?" she asked the group cheerfully.

Avery was relieved to hear a chorus of positive replies.

"The food was very good," one woman shouted out.

"And I loved my dessert," her husband chimed in.

Would you please post those reviews on the Internet? Avery nearly asked. But she didn't want to beg for good comments, and she wondered if the couple even used a computer. Though many seniors did, she reminded herself.

"Well, this was a nice surprise. Sorry we didn't have a reservation," the tour guide said to Avery. "I'm Cindy, by the way. I'm with Pilgrim Tours." She offered her hand and Avery shook it.

Cindy was an attractive blonde, about Avery's age, with long bangs and layer-cut hair that swooped to her shoulders. Her outfit, a French blue blouse and short white skirt, complemented her summery looks perfectly. She looked very calm and collected, even in the midst of her demanding customers, the total opposite of how Avery felt. Even Cindy's hair seemed calm, totally defying the humidity, Avery noticed. Unlike her own, which curled so wildly today, she looked as if she had stuck her finger in a light socket.

"I was pretty worried for a minute there that half the group wasn't going to get lunch. Now that would have caused a small riot. These lovely folks can turn on you quickly," she confided.

Avery laughed, though she suspected it wasn't entirely a joke. "I'm glad we were able to accommodate you."

"I am, too. Let me give you my card. I bring tours here all the time. Maybe I can bring another group here for lunch one day?"

"Please do." Avery had to get a hold of herself to keep from hugging the woman out of sheer gratitude. "I mean, I'd be happy to work something out with you."

Cindy reached into her handbag and handed Avery a business card. Avery handed her one of the café's cards, too. "That's me, Avery Bishop," she noted, pointing to her name on the bottom. "Give me a call or e-mail anytime."

"Will do," Cindy nodded, and stuck the card in her wallet.

"Mike said you would be a good sport." Her tone of voice and the way she smiled gave Avery the impression that she knew Mike well. "He's such a character, isn't he?" Cindy asked with another indulgent smile.

Avery smiled back, her teeth gritting together. "He sure is," she agreed. A charming, attractive character who must flirt with a lot of women—and maybe even impulsively kiss a few, too? She couldn't help but wonder.

Cindy had turned away from Avery and missed her flustered expression. She took out her yellow flag from somewhere, then clapped her hands. "Listen up, everybody. Time to settle your checks and head down the boardwalk. We don't want to miss the ferry."

The announcement inspired a flurry of activity. Bills were paid, leftovers wrapped, and the group marched out as quickly as they had come in.

Avery and her crew soon collapsed into empty chairs.

"They came, they ate, they talked about cholesterol," Gena observed dryly.

Avery had to laugh. "How true. I'm not sure if we did lunch, or it did us. But the important thing is, we survived."

"Every table was filled, and they didn't bat an eye at those overpriced gourmet pizza pies," Teresa observed. "This lunchtime crowd could be a good thing."

"I've thought about it, but I didn't think we'd be able to handle another meal," Avery confessed. The truth was, they had barely mastered serving dinner. "But today went very well and with no advance notice. Would you all be willing to do a lunch shift—maybe two or three days a week?"

Gena, Jack, Teresa, and Brittany answered with an affirmative chorus. Gena reached into her apron pockets and began sorting out her tips. "I wouldn't mind doubling my pay. I did better just now than I do on some weeknights."

It was soon decided by a majority vote that Café Peregrine would open for lunch Thursday through Saturday. On Sunday they already served brunch. Avery thought it was reasonable to start with a few days and take it from there.

Am I going out on a limb now to get the fruit? Avery wondered, remembering Mike's advice. She wasn't sure. But she did know that if today was any measure, the extra profits might save the café.

She had one person to thank for this stroke of insight—and for forcing this lunch group down her throat. Mike Rossi. Who else? She wanted to laugh when she recalled what she had said to him over the phone. "But we don't serve lunch."

Well . . . duh . . . it's a good time to start.

As her staff cleared up the dining room and began to set up for dinner, Avery wondered what Mike was doing right now at the Tuna. She half expected him to pop in the back door any minute and ask how they had survived the tsunami of seniors.

But he didn't come. *He must still be busy,* she thought. *I could go see him . . . or I could call. Maybe that would be better.*

Considering that I look like a total wreck.

She glanced in the mirror, despairing over her hair, a mass of dirty brown curls, piled on her head and haphazardly secured with a handful of hairpins. It was her hair versus the humidity every day down here and so far, the humidity was clearly winning. She would get one hunk of hair in place with a pin and moments later, another wave would spring out from some other spot. And she was tired and sticky from cooking as well.

No, it's not the time to surprise Mike, she decided. Then she had to catch herself, worrying so much about her appearance. Hadn't he seen her at her very worst, at her very lowest moment on the Fourth of July weekend? What was the difference now?

Avery wasn't ready to examine that question too closely. *It's just . . . different,* she snapped at the little voice in her head. *I don't have to look like someone used me to wipe down the kitchen floor every time I see him, do I?*

She wouldn't visit. She would call. And thank him for *encouraging* her to serve lunch—and sending her all those customers. It was the decent thing to do, she decided.

But when Avery called the rival restaurant, a polite, unfamiliar voice answered. Mike was not around, and no one knew when he would be back. "Do you want to leave a message?"

"Um, no. No, thank you," Avery replied.

She hung up, feeling deflated. She would catch up with him soon and tell him in person. She realized that in all this time, she had never even been inside the Lazy Tuna. She had only seen it from the outside, full of customers.

It was high time to visit him on his own turf, Avery decided. But even though it was fun to think of Café Peregrine and the Tuna as rivals, Avery was finding it impossible to think of Mike that way anymore.

It took Avery a few days to work out a lunch menu. She consulted her cooking files, online recipes, and food websites, and even got help from Claire North at the inn. Little by little, she was starting to realize that she wanted the café's offerings to compliment the setting, the natural beauty of the island and the relaxed, fun atmosphere of the beach and boardwalk.

When she had first formulated her ideas for the café, maybe she had been a bit of a food snob. She could admit that now. Perhaps living out here these past few weeks had changed her. She wasn't quite sure how it had happened, but she was willing to try dishes she would have once called too simple. But simple, well-prepared, high-quality ingredients could be very elegant. Like Claire's cooking, for example. People raved about her fried oysters with homemade tartar sauce and her grilled scallops with citrus marinade. Even her fresh corn pancakes were delicious. Any cook could learn a lot from Claire. Of this, Avery had no doubt.

She worked on the lunch menu a full week, though her staff was chomping at the bit to work the extra hours. Finally, the last

Monday in July, she went to the café early and tested out the recipes, preparing each one, so her staff could sample them and give their opinion.

She hadn't seen Mike or heard from him for over a week, since the senior invasion. And she hadn't had the courage to walk up to the Tuna and say hello. It never seemed the right time for that.

But she kept a vigilant eye out, waiting for him to pass, and as she assembled the sample lunches, she was rewarded. She caught a glimpse of Mike walking down the street toward the Tuna, and she called out to him from inside the café.

He turned and peered inside, then walked to one of the open French doors. "Hey, Avery. Catching up on the ironing today?"

Avery shook her head. "I'm thinking of sending the linens back to the laundry service. I should be able to afford it, once I start serving lunch."

He looked very handsome, she thought, in a burgundy polo shirt and khaki pants. *And I don't look so bad either,* she reminded herself. She had hoped to see him and was wearing a nicer-than-usual outfit, a periwinkle blue tank top and a long skirt with a pale blue paisley print.

"So, you're opening for lunch. What in the world ever gave you that idea?" His amused expression more than made up for his sarcastic tone.

"It's a funny story. Some crazy guy sent a busload of seniors over here the other day, around noon. So what could I do? I had to feed them . . . They came, they ate. They talked about cholesterol . . . Amazingly enough, it worked out fine."

She was pleased to see him laugh. "I hope that crazy guy learned his lesson. Now you'll really put him out of business."

"No chance of that. His restaurant has an equally crazy but loyal following. I'm just hoping I can carve out a nice niche for myself down here."

He smiled at her. "So when does this lunch service start?"

"Possibly tomorrow or Wednesday." She waited and watched his expression. "What are you thinking?" she asked quietly.

"Nothing much. Just wondering if that mariachi band books daytime gigs." He flashed her a mischievous grin. "Only kidding. I thought you might be starting today. It smells so good in here. What's cooking?"

"I made sample dishes of the menu so my staff could taste test. I want them to be able to answer the customer's questions and make honest recommendations."

"How about the competition? Do they get to taste test?"

Avery had already considered inviting him back to the kitchen. "Why not? I'm always interested in your opinion," she said in a half-teasing tone.

He laughed at her. "I'm not sure that's true, but you know I'll always give you my opinion anyway."

A few moments later they were standing side by side at the worktable. Mike surveyed the dishes Avery had prepared then started on the fried oysters. His eyes widened with surprise and delight as he savored the cool sauce and the warm, crunchy bite of oyster that had been dredged in a special mixture of panko and cornmeal crumbs Claire had recommended to her.

"So what do you think?" she asked eagerly.

"Is this what they teach in those fancy cooking schools?" He stared at her, trying to keep a straight face. There was a drop of sauce on the corner of his finger and he licked it off, smiling again at the taste. "I don't know . . . I think I need to have a few more of those to tell you what you're doing wrong."

It took her a full five seconds to realize he was teasing.

"That bad, huh? Well, maybe I should just chuck this whole platter and start over." She lifted the platter of seafood and held it over the garbage pail.

Mike leaped out of his seat to rescue the food. "Are you crazy?" He grabbed back the platter with both hands and carefully set it back on the table. "I was only joking. For goodness' sake, if the rest of the food tastes that *bad*, you're really going to put me out of business."

"I doubt that, but my mom always says it's important to have goals," she teased him back. "Try the other dishes. See what you think."

Mike eagerly helped himself to samples from the other platters, giving a thumbs-up all the way and offering a few insightful suggestions for fine-tuning spices or sauces.

When he was done, he patted his mouth with a napkin. "Since you're not serving lunch today, maybe you're free this afternoon? I was thinking of taking my boat out. I have it moored at the dock near the ferry, but I've hardly been on it all summer. It's the perfect afternoon for a sail."

The invitation took Avery by surprise. She needed a moment to think about it. Had he just asked her to go sailing . . . like on a real . . . date?

She was so surprised, she didn't know what to say. She walked over to the sink, suddenly needing to wash her hands and get her bearings.

She had been secretly hoping their relationship would take some sort of step forward, even though neither of them really had time to date. Well, Mike seemed to think that they did. Like today. This afternoon. Right now.

She turned to him, drying her hands on a towel. "Gee, a sail sounds great. But I'm not really dressed for it."

I didn't just hear an excuse, did I? a little voice screamed at her. *What are you making excuses for?*

Because . . . I'm scared? she said to herself.

Mike looked surprised by her reply about her clothes. His gaze swept over her, from head to toe. "You look great to me. If you feel cold on the water, I'll give you a sweatshirt."

You look great to me? She liked the way he'd said that.

But was she really ready to take this step?

Ready, schmedy, a little voice said. *If you don't say "yes" you're going to regret it.* Avery knew that was true.

She bit her bottom lip and impulsively pulled off her apron. "Well then, I'll just put this food away and meet you down at the dock."

Mike looked pleased by her answer, but before he could reply, his cell phone buzzed. He pulled it from his pocket and checked the number. He looked concerned and then amused as he spoke to the caller.

"All right, Mom. I get it. No, you don't have to come all the way over here. I'll come get them and drop Noah at his practice . . . It's not a problem. I'm not even at the Tuna yet. Okay, see you in a minute."

He hung up and shook his head. "My mom," he explained, looking a little embarrassed. "She needs me to pick up the kids. She has to go to the library for her book club meeting or something, and Noah has a swim team practice. And they're acting up on her today . . . but they're really good, normally," he quickly added.

"I'm sure they are," she said. She sighed, not sure if she was disappointed or relieved by the sudden change of plans. Maybe a bit of both.

"Sorry the date didn't work out. How about a rain check?"

"Sure, absolutely," she said lightly. "Though we're both so busy, I hope we don't have to wait until after Labor Day."

"I hope not, too. I go back to work in September. I only keep the Tuna open on weekends after that."

She had forgotten that. "Oh, right. The summer sometimes seems like it will never end."

"That is true, but it always does, Avery. Sooner or later." He smiled briefly and pocketed his phone. "See you around. Good luck with the lunch shift. You've got a killer menu going there."

Avery smiled and watched him go. She felt as if something very subtle had shifted between them. But she wasn't sure what.

They almost had a date. He would ask her again. Or she could ask him. Avery wasn't quite sure if she had the courage to make that move. Not quite yet. But she told herself to be patient. Just the fact that he'd asked her was a good sign, wasn't it?

As Mike walked out, Gena came in. They waved and greeted each other. Avery hoped Gena hadn't caught the wistful way she had been watching Mike's exit. But as usual, little escaped the notice of her astute head waitress and friend.

"I haven't seen Mike around here lately. Were you two having lunch together or something?"

It did look like that, Avery realized. Mike's place setting was still on the worktable and all the platters of food were out.

"Not exactly. He was taste testing the new lunch menu. I wanted to give him fair warning. He's been so helpful to—to the café," she said quickly, though she almost said *helpful to me*.

Gena was changing her shoes and putting up her hair. "Uh-huh," she replied, in an *I am so not buying any of that* tone. "So, what's going on with the Tuna King? You guys dating yet?"

"Don't be silly. Mike's a great guy. And I really like him." More than she ever thought possible when they first met. "But I have to focus on this business right now, Gena. You know that. Do I seem like someone who has time for a relationship?"

Gena smiled but still looked skeptical. She took out a fresh apron and tied the strings around her waist. "You're the boss. Whatever you say. But you might want to make time for a guy like Mike. These things don't always come along at our convenience."

Avery glanced at her friend and sighed. Before she could reply, the kitchen door swung open again. Jack and Brittany walked in, holding hands, which was not the easiest way to make it through the kitchen doorway.

They were officially going out. They had both changed their relationship status on Facebook, Brittany explained, a ritual Avery knew little about. It had not taken them very long to figure it out, either. Why was *she* so slow at these things?

Jack was drawn to the platters of food on the worktable. "Hey, that smells good. What is all that stuff?"

"The new lunch menu. Help yourself," she invited them. "I want to know what you all think. I'll tell you the ingredients so you can answer questions."

"Wow, this stuff looks awesome." Brittany lifted the lid on a platter of crab cakes and pulled up a seat between Jack and Gena. Teresa had arrived and quickly joined the others. She didn't want to miss the party.

At least her new dishes were a hit, and the café would soon be doing more business. A bright spot to focus on, Avery reminded herself, on this otherwise confusing day.

Chapter Thirteen

"LET'S be thankful it's only a rehearsal dinner and not an actual wedding. There's still a long guest list, the bride still wants a ton of flowers on the tables and in the guest rooms, and all kinds of special foods . . ." Liza had opened a thick binder on the kitchen table, the kind she used to keep track of big parties. She pulled out one of the sheets and looked over a list. "Oh, and a certain brand of organic soap and bath gel in all the rooms. I'll put out our usual lavender goat's milk soap, too," she murmured. "I bet everyone likes ours better."

Claire was making iced tea, large glasses with slices of lemon and orange. One for herself, one for Liza, and one for Jamie. He was still cleaning off the porch. If he didn't come in soon, she would bring it out to him, she decided.

"Isn't this the couple getting married in the village this weekend? I saw something about it in the bulletin." Claire rolled an orange on the cutting board, to make the juices flow before she sliced it. "I think Reverend Ben is performing the ceremony."

"Yes, they mentioned Reverend Ben. The groom, Jim Hatcher, grew up in Cape Light. Mari O'Hara, the bride, grew up in New York," Liza clarified. "The O'Haras and most of the bridesmaids will be staying here the whole weekend. So we'll be helping when they get dressed for the wedding . . . which reminds me, I need to buy a few new blow-dryers and another ironing board."

The inn often hosted weddings. Everyone looked so glamorous when the curtain finally went up, but Claire knew that behind the scenes, the nuts and bolts weren't nearly as pretty. But she did love to take part in a wedding, even if the ceremony wasn't taking place at the inn this time.

Wednesday was often a slow day, even in high season. And they were having a little break in occupancy this week, since the entire inn had been booked by a bride and her family. Claire was relieved that Liza had given them two full days to get the place ready. She not only had to help ready the rooms but also do all the cooking.

"I think I'll send Jamie out for a few things this afternoon. Where is he?" Liza asked, looking up again at Claire.

"Still weeding. He should be in any minute."

Liza rose and went to the back door. "Thank goodness we have Jamie around. I'm not sure how we ever did these big parties without him."

Claire was pleased to hear Liza say that. She thought Jamie had been a great help these past few weeks. More than just a helper, part of a team. While she knew that she and Liza could handle just about any challenge thrown their way, it was just easier to have another able worker around, someone they could depend on. And over the past few weeks, Jamie was proving himself to be just that. If the only thing she had done for him this summer was teach him a good work ethic, Claire thought she could be thankful. That was something he would take with him, long after this job had run its course.

THE next two days passed in a blur of preparation, and some anxiety, Claire had to admit. Though they had prepared for large parties and family reunions like this one many times, it was always stressful and there were always unexpected challenges and emergencies.

Fortunately, the shipment of expensive soap and bath gel the bride requested did show up on time. As did the special brand of protein powder for the fruit smoothies the bridal party needed at breakfast.

But on Friday morning, Claire was in the hallway, polishing the wooden side table when she heard her usually cool and collected employer go into a panic. Liza was on the phone with a florist in Boston, and it didn't sound like good news.

"What do you mean, you can't make the delivery until tomorrow? I was told that the flowers would be here already, by ten A.M." She paused and listened a moment. "Why didn't anyone call and tell me that? I would have made other arrangements," she added emphatically.

A few minutes later, Liza walked into the hallway, looking pale and frustrated. She carried a sheaf of papers in her hand. The flower order from the florist probably, Claire thought.

"Where's Jamie? I need him to go into Boston right away. Someone has to pick up the flowers. If he leaves now and doesn't hit much traffic," she added, glancing at her watch, "he could make it back by two thirty or three. The O'Haras will be checking in about the same time. I wanted the flowers in place by then. But what can you do? As long as we have them for the dinner tonight."

It was half past ten. It was possible, counting two hours each way, if there were no traffic tie-ups and no extra stops.

"He'll have to bring cash," Liza added, checking the bill. "It's a few hundred dollars." She looked up at Claire. "We can trust him to do this, don't you think, Claire?"

Claire felt caught for a moment, wondering if they could trust Jamie. Yes, he had been reliable and hard-working for almost a month now. He had spent a good part of each Tuesday, his day off, sitting in the library, studying for the GED and being tutored by Vera Plante. He had been saving his money and looking at school catalogs.

Could they trust him to drive into Boston with a large sum of cash? A few weeks ago, she would have said, "It has all the ingredients for a complete disaster." Had he mended his ways since then? Claire felt guilty doubting him. But she had to be honest with herself. And with Liza. The temptation to visit his friends and goof off a bit might prove too much.

Oh, Lord, I hope not. Claire said a silent prayer. *He's been doing so well. Please don't let him fall back. And please help me to trust him. If I can't trust him completely, who will?*

"I think he'll do fine," she said finally. "As long as you're clear. As long as you tell him he has to come right back. No side trips."

Before Liza could answer, Jamie came in through the back door. Claire followed Liza into the kitchen to meet him. He had been working in the garden, and his face was streaked with sweat and dirt, as were his clothes. But he looked happy, Claire thought. Practically victorious, stretching out his T-shirt, which he had used as a basket and filled with ripe vegetables from the garden.

"Look at all these tomatoes. They're awesome. And I found some lettuce and string beans. I think that new patch of fence is keeping the rabbits out, finally. But I have to check it every morning."

"My, what a harvest. Here, put them on the counter by the sink. I'll take care of it."

Claire stepped aside so Jamie could dump out the contents of his shirt. Liza laughed. "I think we need to buy you a real basket, Jamie."

"There's a wooden bushel in the barn. But I didn't expect to find so much stuff ripe today. It's amazing how it just grows overnight."

"A garden is amazing," Claire agreed. She hadn't been in the vegetable patch much this year. Jamie had taken over practically all of her work out there. But she already knew the pleasure that came from working in the earth and helping things grow. It was wonderful to share this with Jamie.

He had worked hard out there these past weeks. It was good to see him take pride in the fruits—well, actually the vegetables, Claire silently amended—of his labor.

He poured himself a glass of water and gulped it down at the sink. "I guess I'll clean up and change my clothes."

"Before you go up, I need to ask you something," Liza began.

She quickly explained the problem with the flower delivery and showed him the florist's order. "The shop is not far from Quincy Market. You can jump right off the highway and back on."

Claire saw Jamie's expression brighten as Liza described the quest. She hoped that was a good sign, his pleasure at being trusted with this important mission.

"And you need to come right back. No side trips," Liza added. "The bride will check in around two. She was expecting the flowers to be delivered. We can't have them any later than that."

"I'll be back before she notices anything's missing," Jamie promised.

He met Claire's gaze, and she smiled. "I'll pack you some lunch. This way you won't have to stop."

She sent up a quick prayer. *Please let him carry out this errand promptly and properly.* It seemed such a small thing to ask, but so much was hanging in the balance.

For the next few hours, Claire had little time to worry about Jamie as she helped put the finishing touches on the guest rooms and began preparing for the many meals she needed to cook over the weekend.

The bride and her family arrived promptly at two o'clock. Liza seemed tense as she showed Mari around the inn, carrying the list of all her requests and showing how she had followed them down to the letter.

"There's been a small delay with the flower arrangements, but I've sent a special messenger to pick them up. He should be back any minute," Liza added, glancing at her watch.

Mari looked a bit distressed. "I did want the orchid plants in the guest rooms when everyone arrived. But as long as he returns before the dinner, I suppose that will be all right."

"He'll be back long before then," Liza assured her.

Claire forced a smile. "I have some refreshments ready—iced tea, lemonade, fresh chocolate chip cookies," she announced, hoping to distract from Liza's single slipup. "It will all be out on the porch when you're ready."

The bridesmaids arrived in two full cars at three. There was a great deal of chatter and giggling as the young women gathered in the bride's suite and helped her figure out which dress to wear for the rehearsal. Claire thought it sounded like a group of middle-school girls having a pajama party. At least the bride was no longer standing anxiously on the porch, watching for Jamie's return.

Liza was, though. She called Jamie on his cell phone, but he didn't answer.

Claire returned to the kitchen and started working on dinner again. She felt so anxious, she overworked the pie crust and had to start a new batch of dough.

Mari came down, dressed for the rehearsal in a bold, tropical-print dress and high-heeled sandals, her long glossy hair pulled back and dangling down her back in a long ponytail. She looked like a model walking down a runway, Claire thought.

"Are the flowers here yet?" she asked. "I ordered some for tonight, for the bridesmaids to put in their hair."

"I don't think so," Claire said, glancing at the clock. "But you should ask Liza. She's out back."

Liza had gone out back to check the setup for the cocktail hour. Perhaps Jamie had called her cell phone by now to say he was on the way. Claire certainly hoped so.

Mari left and Claire glanced at the clock. Three twenty-five. It was possible that he had hit traffic. It was a Friday afternoon and the height of the summer. Her heart felt full of dread. Jamie had not answered his phone. That was a bad sign.

Claire went outside to get a handful of mint. She heard Liza and Mari talking, their voices tense and brittle. It was about the flowers. She felt so helpless. Had Jamie really gone off the rails now that they had finally put their trust in him again?

Then the crunch of gravel in the drive announced the arrival of a car. Claire could barely make herself turn to see who was coming. More relatives or bridesmaids? The groom and his family?

No, they were meeting up with the bride's family at the church.

She squinted into the sun, relieved to see her old green Jeep pull up to the back of the house.

It was Jamie, back with the flowers. Just as he had promised.

She could see the trunk loaded with blooms and more on the seat beside him. He jumped out and called to Liza. She had come around the back of the house and was practically running toward him.

"Sorry I'm late. There was a ton of traffic and the battery on my phone died. I was going to call you but I didn't want to stop. I got all the flowers," he said. He pulled open the back of the Jeep and began to take out boxes filled with flowers. "The florist didn't have the white roses," he added.

"He didn't?" Liza let out a long sigh. "No wonder he said he couldn't bring the order until tomorrow. I hope he took that off the bill."

"Don't worry. I made sure he didn't charge you. I had to park the Jeep a few blocks away, at a lot, and I was just walking back and I saw some white roses in another flower shop. So I got those for you at a different place. I guess that took a little extra time. I hope that was okay."

"Okay? That was brilliant!" Liza gave Jamie a quick hug. "Thank you, Jamie. You did a great job. The bride will be very happy. So we'll all be happy," she said quietly.

Claire saw Jamie laugh, looking tired but pleased. He carefully pulled out a box that held a huge, intricate arrangement. Claire walked closer and took another box of small purple orchids in individual pots.

As she carried the flowers inside, she said a silent prayer. *Thank you, Lord, for watching over Jamie and helping him do such a good job today. Please forgive me for ever doubting him.*

AT four o'clock all the guests scurried out of the inn, heading to Cape Light and the church on the green for the wedding rehearsal. Liza came into the kitchen where Claire was still cooking and Jamie was eating a sandwich.

"They've left for town. We have about two hours," Liza said, glancing at her watch.

"Is there anything I should do?" Jamie asked

"Not right now. You must be tired from all the driving," Liza said.

Jamie shrugged. "I'm all right. It was sort of fun, having a deadline. Though I don't think I want to drive a delivery truck, or anything like that."

Liza laughed and headed off to check the place cards. "Don't worry, I think you're meant for better things."

"You did a good job finding those white roses. The bride wanted those flowers most particularly," Claire said, glancing at him. "I will say we got a little worried when we didn't hear from you and it was past three."

"Yeah, I thought you might. But I couldn't stop to call and waste more time. I know you must have been thinking I stopped to see my friends and hang out."

Claire felt her body grow tense, but she didn't turn around.

"I didn't mean that," she said.

"You're a bad liar, Claire. It's all right. I sort of deserve that. I hope you and Liza can trust me now; that's all I'm trying to say."

"We do trust you, Jamie," Claire said sincerely. "You've earned it. You've come a long way in the last few weeks—working hard and studying." She turned to look at him. "I'm very proud of you."

She could see he was embarrassed by the praise and maybe didn't quite believe it.

"Well . . . thanks. I'm trying. I don't know that I've done anything that spectacular. Except to keep the rabbits and deer out of the vegetables."

Claire smiled. "That, too, but I mean it. Liza feels the same. But I hope that you're proud of yourself. That's the most important thing."

He shrugged and leaned back in his chair. "I'll be proud if I pass that test. But it's going to be hard. I'm not sure I can do it, and I hate to waste your money."

"Vera says you're doing very well. You have several more weeks to study. Besides, you can take it again and again. The important thing is that you're trying. You'll get there. Don't worry."

Jamie looked down at the table, fiddling with the crust from his sandwich. "If I do pass, it's because you helped me so much. I just want to thank you, Claire—you and Liza—for giving me a second chance here, and pushing me to get my diploma."

"Oh, Jamie, I'm happy to help you. The test is just a small part. No matter what happens, no matter where your life takes you, there will always be a place for you with me. If not at this inn, then at my cottage. I want you to know that."

Claire suddenly felt very emotional. It had been a trying day, a test for all of them. But they had come through it, and she felt as if a weight had been lifted.

Jamie glanced up at her. He looked confused. "Why are you so nice to me, Claire? I never understood. Why did you pick me out? There were so many kids at the shelter."

Claire was surprised by the question. "Oh, I don't know. I always thought you picked me out," she said, with a small smile. She paused and waited until he looked at her again. "It was because God put love in my heart for you," she added in a more serious tone. "I love you and have faith in you. And I know that God loves you even more and wants you to thrive, to work hard and do right, and use the talents and smarts He's given you. I'm just a helper. A messenger, you might say."

Jamie slowly smiled. "I'm not a big churchgoer or believer, like you. But I'm starting to think maybe there really is a God up there who tries to help people. I can't see any other way I could have been lucky enough to meet up twice with someone like you . . . I love you, Claire. You're the only one who's ever really helped me."

Claire was deeply touched by his admission. She didn't know whether to laugh or cry and ended up doing a bit of both. He smiled at her and rose from his chair, then gave her a hug as he walked by.

"I guess I'll go up and change for dinner. Liza likes me looking smart when I serve these big parties."

Claire nodded and wiped her eyes. "Yes, you do that. We have to get the hors d'oeuvres set up by half past five. I think the hardest part is over," she said quietly.

The hardest part of this gala bridal weekend . . . and for Jamie and his struggles, she really meant.

AVERY arrived at the café around ten o'clock on Wednesday morning.

A reporter from the *Cape Light Messenger* had finally visited the café and given it a great review. Avery had immediately bought a frame and was trying to decide where to hang it. Somewhere near the front door, visible to the outside—but somewhere where people waiting inside could see it, too?

She checked a few spots, walking inside and outside the restaurant. The problem was, she actually needed more than one copy of the article. Or more than one good review. But it was a very good sign. And she was very proud.

She propped it up in a spot near the front door and stepped back to check.

A small child in a pink helmet whizzed by, so close behind her she felt a draft of cool air. Avery spun around just in time to see a little girl on a pink scooter fly past the restaurant, then slip to one side and crash into a pile of Mrs. McNulty's blow-up water toys.

Avery ran to help her. "Are you all right?"

The little girl pushed herself up on her hands. She was sitting on the head of an inflatable dolphin. She looked a bit dazed but unharmed. Avery crouched down to talk to her. Her helmet had fallen forward and Avery pushed it back from her eyes.

Big dark eyes and dark brown hair. She was very cute. And looked very familiar somehow.

"Are you okay?" Avery asked quietly. "Does it hurt anywhere?"

The girl shook her head but still didn't answer. Mrs. McNulty ran out of her store and hurried over to them. "Emily, are you all right? You shouldn't be riding that thing so fast. I'm going to call your father."

"I'm all right. I am," Emily insisted, standing up on thin wobbly legs that stuck out from a pair of pink shorts. "I can go back on my own. Please don't call him."

Mrs. McNulty's phone rang. "Well, as long as you're not hurt. Oh dear, I have to answer that." And she headed back into her store.

Avery was left to comfort the little daredevil. "Don't cry, honey. It's okay. Where do you have to go?"

Emily looked down at her sneakers. "To the Tuna, just down the street."

Avery stared down at her. She was Mike's little girl. That's why she looked so familiar.

"Do you want me to walk you? Are you sure you aren't hurt?" She had taken quite a tumble. Maybe she was hurt and didn't want to admit it.

"I'm not supposed to go anywhere with strangers," she told Avery in a serious voice. "I shouldn't even talk to you."

"That's right. But I know your dad. I can call him for you."

But before she could say more, Emily picked up her scooter and ran down the sidewalk, heading back to the Tuna. She jumped on and pushed with one foot, then disappeared quickly from view.

Avery practically started laughing. Then she saw that Emily had forgotten her helmet. She picked it up and followed.

Halfway down the street, it hit her again, the thought that she had never been inside the Lazy Tuna. Open for two months just a few yards away from her main competitor and never set foot in the door. She had meant to go, dozens of times. But once she met Mike, she had felt intimidated—or possibly too stubborn and proud.

But here she was, hat in hand. Helmet in hand, actually.

It was the perfect excuse to visit, and she did want to make sure Emily was really all right.

The first thing she noticed was the pink scooter, tossed by the entrance. The restaurant was open to the street and the big gate had already been pulled up, though all the tables and chairs were stacked against a wall. A busboy was busily mopping the dark green linoleum floor with strong-smelling cleaner. He stopped to let her pass.

"Is Mr. Rossi here?" Avery asked.

"Mike? Yeah, he's in the kitchen. Just go on back."

Avery nodded and carefully proceeded on the wet floor. It was hard to watch her step. There was so much to look at.

She had imagined the inside of Mike's restaurant would be colorful, but the reality was beyond her wildest guess. The theme seemed to be "Under the Sea." The walls and even the ceiling were covered with murals of undersea life. Smiling starfish, cross-eyed crabs, leaping lobsters and grinning sharks, an octopus wearing saddle shoes and horn-rimmed glasses. Mermaids and Poseidon with his trident . . . spearing a fish sandwich. And in the very middle of the sea life community, the Lazy Tuna himself, lounging in sunglasses and a Hawaiian shirt.

But there was more. Lobster traps and colorful striped buoys, tarnished lanterns and fake palm trees. Fish nets that hung from the ceiling with beach balls and plastic fish inside. Tiny lights were strung throughout, and Avery could just imagine what the place looked like at night. The tables were plain wood, painted blue and white. The chairs were standard, too. A few beach chairs sat near the door, in the waiting area, next to a real lifeguard's stand. She wondered if Mike ever sat up there with a whistle, keeping the crowd of diners under control.

All in all, very cute, she thought. Very fishy-kitschy.

She had just reached the kitchen when Mike came through the door, holding Emily by the hand. She looked up at Avery and pointed.

"There she is, the lady who helped me."

Mike met Avery's surprised gaze. "I thought she was talking about you. I'm sorry she nearly ran you over."

"Oh, I'm okay. I was worried that she hurt herself and didn't want to tell me. Here, she left her helmet."

Emily grabbed it before Mike could. "Thanks." She smiled, showing a gap where a tooth had fallen out. "I'm glad you helped me and not Mrs. McNutty."

"McNulty," Mike corrected her. He shook his head. "You know her name by now."

Avery hid a smile. McNutty did fit fairly well, though she knew Mike was right not to encourage the nickname.

Emily glanced at her father and continued, "She gets very crabby. She doesn't like anyone touching her toys."

"Can you blame her?" Mike asked. "She needs to sell that stuff. You can't use it like some big trampoline. I better go up there and make sure you didn't break anything."

"I don't think she did," Avery reported, winning another smile from Emily. "Though it was some landing. She's really fearless, isn't she?"

Mike tried to make a serious face at his daughter but wasn't quite able. "She needs to slow down and be careful."

"I am, Daddy. Can I go out and ride again?"

Mike paused a moment, then nodded. "Don't go too far. Nana's coming to take you and Noah to the beach."

He had a lot to juggle, didn't he? Running this place, his job at school, and raising his children alone. Any woman who got involved with him had to accept the whole enchilada.

Could I do that? Avery wondered. *I've always wanted kids, but I keep putting it off in my mind to someday. When I get a business going. When I meet the right man . . .*

Could Mike be the right man? It wouldn't take too much more to convince her, she realized.

"Sorry about that. I told her not to go that far," Mike said, breaking into her thoughts.

"Oh, that's all right. I'm glad she's not hurt."

"So you finally made it down the block to the Tuna. I was wondering if you would ever stick a toe in here."

His tone was half teasing, but half serious, too. Avery suddenly felt a little embarrassed that she hadn't visited sooner. She had only seen him once or twice in the past week, she realized, strolling by the Peregrine.

"Sorry, I should have come sooner. But it's always so crowded, I never think I'll make it past the door."

"So, what do you think? Is it everything you dreamed it would be?"

"Oh, it is. And more. Much more," she assured him with a laugh. "Honestly, I love the mural. Was that your idea?"

"My dad's. He was a bit of an artist. We've all added a few embellishments over the years."

There was a lot of history here, a lot of character, Avery realized. That's what made it so charming and unique. And so very popular. It didn't really matter what kind of food Mike served. People came here for the experience. For Mike, she realized. And she could finally understand that.

"What are you thinking, Avery? I've seen that look before," he said in a wary tone. "Are you wondering how you can copy this magical . . . ambience?"

That word again. He never tired of teasing her about it, did he?

"Oh, I could never even try," she said truthfully. "You've got the funky fish house beat totally wrapped up."

He laughed. "Hope so. It's been my life's work . . . So how's the lunch shift going?"

"Pretty good. Business is up," she reported. "And . . . we got a very nice review in the *Cape Light Messenger* last week. In case you didn't see it, I have a few hundred copies lying around. I could give you one. And there will be a good review coming on the radio this weekend. WCLR. So set your dial."

"Sounds like the Peregrine is taking off. I'll have to step up my game," he said with a smile.

Avery smiled back. He knew the Peregrine was still no threat to the Tuna, but it was nice of him to act as if it might be.

Before she could reply, a little boy walked out of the kitchen. He was eating half a peanut butter sandwich and wore a thoughtful expression. A few years older than Emily, he looked like a miniature Mike. He wore a nylon surf shirt, swimming trunks, nose plugs dangling around his neck, and carried a boogie board. "Is Nana here yet?"

"She'll be here any minute. I want you to meet a friend of mine. This is Avery. She owns the café down the street. Avery, this is my son, Noah." Mike gently held Noah's shoulder, just in case he bolted, Avery thought.

"Hello, Noah, nice to meet you." Avery smiled and extended her hand. Noah reciprocated, hesitating to meet her eyes.

"Hi," he said simply. "Can I go outside and wait?" he asked his father.

"Did you drink your milk?" Mike pinned him with a stern gaze.

Noah nodded.

"All right. But wash your hands when you finish that sandwich. And try to find your sister. She's riding her scooter to California." Mike rolled his eyes as Noah ran away. "He has his choice of thirty entrees, and all he really wants is peanut butter. I try not to take it personally."

Avery laughed. "Maybe it's just a phase."

"I hope so. He didn't inherit my appetite, that's for sure. Not yet anyway."

"He looks like you. So does Emily," she added.

"Thanks. They can drive me crazy, but I couldn't live without them. They're my whole life."

Noah appeared again at the front of the restaurant, this time leading an older woman by the hand. Her short white hair framed her face in a stylish cut. She wore a beach cover-up over a bathing suit and carried a big canvas beach bag. She was probably in her mid-sixties, Avery guessed, but looked very fit and youthful, more than able to handle the two children.

"Michael? We're going now. I have Emily's suit," she added. "Oh, hello . . . I'm sorry to interrupt," she added, suddenly noticing Avery.

"Mom, this is Avery Bishop. She owns the Café Peregrine, down the street. Avery, this is my mother, Victoria Rossi."

Avery waved. "Nice to meet you. Great day for the beach," she added, trying to make conversation.

"A perfect day. Too bad the two of you can't join us. You restaurant owners are a pale-looking group. I'm sure that you're both low on Vitamin D. But I do love your restaurant, Avery. I've peeked inside a few times. It's very pretty. I'm going to eat there very soon."

"Anytime," Avery offered.

"Good, don't tell Mike," she added, though he was standing right there.

"It's all right, Mother. You'll like the food. Better than mine."

Victoria laughed. "Have a good day. Time to get buried in the sand. If you don't hear from me in a few hours, come down with a shovel," she told her son as Noah led her away.

"They don't really bury her. My mom likes to joke around . . . Well, maybe just her feet. Up to her knees or so."

Now he was joking with Avery.

"Seems like it's a family trait. Joking around, I mean."

"My dad was the all-time champ. I've inherited it from both sides."

"Not a bad thing," she said, thinking his humor was one of the qualities she liked best about him.

"Some people might disagree, but I'm glad to hear you like my jokes," he added.

He smiled and met her gaze. It suddenly seemed as if time stopped and everything around them just melted away. Avery felt . . . mesmerized.

Then his phone rang, breaking the spell. "Sorry, got to grab this," he murmured. "I have another tour group coming in tomorrow. If there's any overflow, I'll send them your way."

"Thanks, I appreciate that. This time I'll be ready."

She waved and left Mike to take care of his business.

As she headed back to the café, she felt light and happy.

Venturing down to the Tuna had been a big step. She had to admit now that she had felt anxious about it. Intimidated, really. But she was glad that she finally had visited and glad she had seen Mike and met his family.

Maybe today had been the right time to go there. Maybe going there earlier, when she had been so unsure about the Peregrine succeeding, would have been too daunting. But today she had been ready to see and appreciate Mike's restaurant for what it was—a one-of-a-kind and totally fun classic. No wonder it had such a loyal following. There was certainly room for more than one restaurant on Ferry Street. She was ready to see that, too. Maybe she was even more ready for a relationship than she had thought.

Avery was soon busy with the lunch rush. She realized she didn't even need the overflow from the Tuna anymore. Her café had plenty of customers of their own. Finally.

Afterward, as she helped Gena and Brittany clean up the dining room, Gena gently poked her. She didn't say anything but urged Avery to follow her glance out to the street.

Avery did and saw Mike passing by with Cindy, the friendly woman from the Pilgrim Tours. They were too busy talking to take notice of Avery. Mike laughed and Cindy slipped her arm through his as they walked by, perfectly in step with each other.

Avery felt the blood rush to her face but couldn't say a word. Had Mike's interest suddenly turned to the Pilgrim Tour guide? *Has he just been flirting with me all this time, when it didn't mean anything to him?*

Avery turned to Gena, struggling to hide her dismay. "That's the woman from the tour company. They're just friends," she said quickly.

Gena shrugged. "Whatever you say. He sure has a lot of friends." Avery heard the words Gena didn't say. *Don't say I didn't warn you.*

Avery felt a dull ache in her chest. She had assumed Mike was sending his children to the beach with their grandmother so he could work. Was it really so he was free to see Cindy?

Maybe it's a business meeting, to talk about the tour groups that come to the Tuna, she told herself.

Right. There was so much to talk about. Fries or baked potatoes with the entree? Coleslaw or pickle chips? Avery wasn't sure what had come over her, but she was suddenly and totally insanely jealous. Why did Cindy from Pilgrim Tours get to spend the afternoon with Mike, strolling around the boardwalk, talking and laughing and doing who knows what else . . . and she did not?

Maybe I should have reminded him about my rain check on that sailing date, she thought suddenly. *Maybe he thinks I'm not really interested in him that way.* She could hardly blame him. She'd been practically radiating N*ot ready, need to work on my business* vibes ever since they met.

Have I fallen for the Lazy Tuna guy? And I waited so long he's given up?

Avery didn't like the idea of that at all. The good reviews, the uptick in business, and the sense that the café was finally catching on—that was all long-awaited good news. But it suddenly seemed cold comfort if it had come at the cost of missing her chance for a real relationship with Mike.

By the time the weekend rolled around, more great reviews for the Café Peregrine rolled in with it. A review on the local radio station was repeated almost hourly and another that Avery didn't expect popped up in the weekend issue of *What's Happening in Cape Light?*

Teresa was the first to spot it and read the article aloud to the staff as they sat together on Friday afternoon, enjoying Avery's seafood bisque. "'If you're looking for innovative cuisine, reasonable prices, and ocean-side ambience, try the Café Peregrine on Angel Island. A newcomer to Ferry Street this season . . .'"

"Wait . . . did you just say 'ambience'?" Avery asked.

"Right. Ambience. It means . . ."

"Oh, I know what it means. It's just a little joke."

While the rest of the staff clapped loudly and even gave a few catcalls of approval, Avery thought of Mike and their silly joke. She would take real pleasure showing him this one, maybe even highlighting the word in contention—that is, *if* he wasn't otherwise occupied with Cindy.

"Let's frame this and put it up near the other. We'll have a whole wall full before the summer is over," Gena predicted.

A while later, sitting at the tiny desk that was crammed in a kitchen corner, Avery decided to call her family to share the good news. She tried her sister first and found her still working at her office.

"I haven't heard from you for a while. Is everything all right?" Christine asked.

Avery hated to think it, but had a feeling Christine expected her to say, "Everything is terrible. I'm going to take your advice and give up."

Instead she was able to report all the good news. ". . . And this weekend we had a rave on the radio and another one in print. I'm going to send you a copy."

"That's terrific. It was a good idea to serve lunch. I just hope it's not too hectic for you. I hope you're not exhausted by the end of the summer."

Avery thought back to the night her family had dined at the café, and cringed. Christine must think the place looked like a sitcom every night, but there was no convincing her things were under control.

"I hired a great new waitress and everything's going very smoothly. There are just three more weekends until Labor Day," Avery noticed, glancing at the calendar. "We're going to coast into the finish line." It wasn't just hopeful optimism either. She knew this was true.

"That's great news, Avery. I can't wait to tell Mom. It's really strange that you called today to tell me this. I ran into Paul just this morning. He told me that the Tulip Café closed. He's very broken up about it."

Avery was surprised at the news and at her reaction. It was like hearing about the passing of an old friend. Though she was sure Paul was more broken up about the restaurant failing than he had been about their broken engagement.

"The Tulip closed? It was doing so well when I left. Did Paul tell you why?"

"He didn't say much. Personally, I think the food went way downhill after you left the kitchen. I would have liked to hear him admit that, considering what he put you through. I told him about your new place . . . and how well you were doing," she added. "I guess I did embellish a little. But now it seems your café has lived up to my description."

At least her sister was honest.

"I guess so," Avery said vaguely. News about her ex-fiancé was distracting. Once she would have been secretly pleased to hear that he was getting his comeuppance for dumping her. But she didn't feel that way at all now. She felt sorry for him, in a distant, unattached way.

"It's hard to say why a restaurant fails. There are any number of reasons," Avery offered, trying to be fair. "I don't think about Paul much anymore," she said honestly, "but I'm not happy to hear he's lost his business."

"He's the type who always bounces back. Don't worry, he'll talk someone else into putting him in business again," Christine predicted.

Avery thought that was probably true. Paul was a smooth talker, who could be very persuasive when he wanted to be.

They talked for a few minutes more, and Avery promised to send the new review promptly.

"I'm really happy things are going well for you, Avery," her sister said. "I know I sounded a bit negative when we were visiting. I'm sorry about that. I was just worried about Mom. But it seems like everything is working out."

"It is," Avery said. It felt good to hear her sister say that. Christine's approval meant more to her than she wanted to admit.

THE inn was too crowded on Sunday morning for Claire to slip off to church. Reverend Ben was on vacation this week, and one of the deacons was running the service. She enjoyed these guest speakers, but their sermons rarely came close to the reverend's.

She had been up since half past six, along with Liza and Jamie, who worked together to set out the breakfast buffet and set the tables out on the porch and patio, along with the long table in the dining room.

Guests began to come down around seven and took coffee back to their rooms or out on the porch, where Liza had several copies of the Sunday newspapers available. The food was not served until eight sharp. Then they all appeared and swarmed around the buffet tables, like humming bees drawn to sweet flowers in the garden.

Claire stayed at the stove while Jamie and Liza ran from one end of the inn to the other, refilling the platters and coffee urns and clearing the used place settings away.

Most of the guests began checking out at eleven. Claire looked forward to a quiet day after that. She hoped to take a walk on the beach or show Jamie the stone labyrinth that sat in a high flat meadow a short distance from the cliffs. She hadn't been there for a long time and thought he might enjoy walking it, considering all the big questions he faced in his life right now.

She had just gotten the kitchen under control and was wiping down the countertops, when she heard rising voices in the hallway. It was mainly a man's voice, sounding very upset. She stepped outside the kitchen to see what was going on.

She recognized Mr. Rapp, one of her favorite guests, who was back with his wife for the second time this summer. Their bags were neatly piled by the door, and Mrs. Rapp stood nearby, dressed for the car ride and wearing a worried expression.

"Please don't tell me to calm down. It was a Cartier chronograph, worth a small fortune. My wife gave it to me for our fiftieth anniversary . . . It was right on my bedside table last night when I went to sleep. And now it's gone."

"I'm very sorry for your distress," Liza said sincerely. "But I think we can find it. If you'll let me go up and look around the room, I'll pull it apart from top to bottom. Jamie will help me move the furniture."

Liza looked around for Jamie. He was just coming down the stairs, loaded down with suitcases.

"*He's* going to help? He's the one who stole it," Mr. Rapp nearly shouted. He pointed at Jamie, his pale face turned a frightening shade of red.

Chapter Fourteen

JAMIE stared at everyone in confusion. "Stole what? . . . What are you talking about?"

Liza looked alarmed and upset. "I don't think it's right to accuse someone on my staff of stealing your property, Mr. Rapp. Maybe you misplaced it. Or maybe it was left somewhere you haven't looked yet—in a pocket or caught between the bed linens. Believe me, it happens all the time," she assured him.

"It's not under the bed. Or in any of my pockets." Mr. Rapp stood with his arms crossed, staring at Jamie. Jamie had set the load of bags down at the foot of the stairs, but remained there, looking afraid to go any closer.

Claire walked out of the kitchen and stood beside him, though she wasn't sure he even noticed her there.

"We'll check the room again. I'm sure we can find it," Liza said in a calmer tone.

Mr. Rapp looked reluctant but finally nodded. "All right, see for yourself. But I tell you I've already looked high and low. He was the only person who went into the room this morning, besides me and my wife," he added, looking straight at Jamie. "We were going down to breakfast. He came to the door and said he needed to fix the ceiling fan. I know the watch was in the room when he came in. I just realized a few minutes ago I didn't have it on. I looked on the nightstand—and now it's gone."

Claire saw Liza take a deep breath. "We'll look again. It will only take a few minutes. Claire, can you get the Rapps some more coffee while they wait?"

"I've had enough coffee, thank you." Mr. Rapp's tone was sharp. "I've had enough of everything around here."

His wife walked up to him and said something quietly then led him out to the porch where they sat down at the very end of the row of wicker chairs.

Claire felt bad for everyone. It was understandable that he was so upset, losing such a valuable piece of jewelry. But it wasn't right of him to accuse Jamie the way he had. She did believe the watch was misplaced and they would soon find it.

She went upstairs to see if she could help in the search. Liza and Jamie had already pulled the night table and bed away from the wall. Liza was on her hands and knees, looking under the bed with a flashlight.

"Do you need any help?" Claire asked from the doorway.

Jamie turned to look at her. She couldn't tell what he was feeling. If anything, he looked a little angry. Of course he would be. No one liked to be so unfairly accused.

"That's all right, Claire. We can handle this. You should stay downstairs and take care of anyone who wants to check out."

"I'll do that. Don't worry." Claire took a few steps then turned in the doorway. "I'm sure you'll find the watch. I'm sure Mr. Rapp just misplaced it."

Jamie was pushing a heavy six-drawer chest aside, his expression grim as he put his back into the task. He paused and looked over at her. "Thanks, Claire. I don't get it. He seemed like such a nice guy. But now he's like . . . wacky."

Claire nodded. Not the way she would have described the situation, but he did have a point.

DOWNSTAIRS, Claire took care of the guests who remained while silently saying a prayer that the watch would be found. At least twenty minutes passed before Liza and Jamie returned from their search. Claire could tell from their expressions that they had not found the watch.

"Where are the Rapps?" Liza whispered to Claire.

"Out on the porch," Claire answered. "Mrs. Rapp is reading the newspaper, and Mr. Rapp is just pacing back and forth."

Liza went outside while Jamie stayed with Claire in the foyer. "We didn't find it," he reported. "I bet it's in one of his pockets. Or his suitcase or something."

"Perhaps," Claire agreed. She had noticed the Rapps going through their suitcases, backpack, and even Mrs. Rapp's purse while they waited for Liza to return. But maybe the watch had not been on the nightstand as Mr. Rapp recalled. If so, it could be anywhere. It could have fallen off while he was out yesterday on the beach or bird-watching. They might never find it.

Claire felt a sense of dread, pulling at her like weight. She wondered what would happen next.

More guests came down, and Jamie carried more luggage out to their cars. Claire followed, curious.

"I'd be happy to reimburse you, Mr. Rapp," she heard Liza offer. "But I need to file a claim with my insurance company first. It will take a little time. Do you have a receipt for the watch at home? That will probably be needed."

"I'm sure I saved it," Mrs. Rapp said.

"Yes, you'll need a receipt, and a police report would probably help, too." Mr. Rapp's tone was far less conciliatory than his wife's.

"A police report? I don't think that's necessary." Liza sounded alarmed, and Claire felt the same way.

"Too late then. I've already called. I would tell you what time that was, but I don't have a watch," he added sharply.

Mrs. Rapp sighed. "About ten minutes ago," she said quietly. "I didn't think it was necessary either."

"Let them come. When a uniformed officer asks that boy a few questions, I'm sure my watch will magically appear. At least he's had no time to get rid of it."

Claire felt her heart pound in her chest. The police were coming? To question Jamie? That sounded so unfair. So extreme.

She was about to speak up in Jamie's defense when Liza glanced her way and gently shook her head, sending a *Don't worry, I'll handle this* message.

"I think it's unfair to single Jamie out with no proof, Mr. Rapp," Liza said firmly. "But if the police want to ask him questions, I'm sure he'll cooperate. He has nothing to hide."

Claire breathed a sigh of relief. At least Liza believed Jamie was innocent. That was something.

"We'll see . . . Here they are now. Sooner than I thought."

A white-and-blue police car pulled up the drive to the inn.

Claire recognized Tucker Tully at the wheel, familiar in his uniform.

He got out and came up onto the porch steps. "Liza, Claire." He nodded quickly in greeting. "Someone here reported missing property?"

"Stolen property," Mr. Rapp quickly corrected him. "A very expensive watch, stolen out of our room this morning."

Tucker took a pad out of his back pocket. "All right, let me take down some information, sir. Your name, please . . ."

Tucker talked with the Rapps a few minutes at the end of the porch and made notes. Jamie had finished loading the suitcases and came up onto the porch.

"The police are here?" He looked nervous and scared, Claire thought. But that was only natural if you were being accused of such a thing.

Liza rested her hand on his shoulder. "Don't worry, Jamie. The officer is just trying to sort this out. He's going to ask you a few questions. He's going to ask me questions, too. And even Claire."

That was true, Claire realized. The explanation should have made Jamie feel better, but he didn't look much calmer. He just stared down at his shoes.

Tucker soon walked over to them, Mr. Rapp trailing him.

"Mr. Rapp says the room has been searched twice, and he's looked through all his baggage for it and in his car," he said to Liza. "Have you looked around the rest of the inn?"

Liza shook her head. "We haven't had the time yet. But we definitely should," she added. "You never know."

"That's right. Something is lost because it's not where you thought it should be, so you have to look in unlikely places for it," Claire said. She had a feeling her circuitous reasoning was not very convincing, but it was true. You rarely find something you've lost in a place you expected it to be. Or it wouldn't be lost.

Tucker turned to Jamie. "You're Jamie, right?"

Jamie nodded. "That's me."

"This guest says you came into his room this morning to fix the ceiling fan. Did you see a watch on the nightstand?"

Jamie thought a moment. "I don't know . . . I wasn't really looking around the room. I was just there for the fan, wondering if I'd be able to figure out why it wasn't working."

"He's lying." Mr. Rapp suddenly stepped forward. "I know he liked the watch. He had his eye on it. He complimented me when we were here in June, and I was showing him all the gadgets and features. He was quite impressed."

"I'm not lying. I didn't lift your watch," Jamie shouted back. "Maybe you dropped it down at the beach or running around in the woods, chasing birds," he added angrily. "Now you're trying to find someone to blame it on."

"Now, now, simmer down, pal." Tucker pressed a hand to Jamie's shoulder. "We're not going to get anywhere arguing over this. Liza, I think you should keep searching the inn. The Rapps can come down to the police station if they want and file a report."

"That's all? That's all you can do is file a report? The thief is standing right here, right under your nose, Officer," Mr. Rapp insisted.

Claire swallowed hard. Now she really had to speak up. "You can't call Jamie a thief. That's not right. You have absolutely no proof."

"Claire has a point," Tucker said before anyone else could speak. "You need some physical evidence or a witness to bring charges against somebody. Once we file a report, we can figure out if there's sufficient evidence to follow up with legal action."

Mrs. Rapp tugged on her husband's sleeve. "Let's just go home. I'll call the insurance company from the car. I'm sure we have coverage for this."

"That's not the point. I want to make a report, Officer. I want you to ask that young man more questions."

"You can follow me to the station. It's on your way out of town," Tucker replied, ignoring Mr. Rapp's final demand. "I'll send you a copy of the report, Liza. I might have more questions. I'll be in touch." He looked directly at Jamie. Claire felt a chill.

The Rapps followed the police car out of the drive and disappeared down the road.

Liza, Claire, and Jamie went back inside. Most of the guests had checked out. Others had gone out to enjoy the beautiful weather—off to the beach or bike riding.

Jamie looked at Claire and Liza. "What should I do now? Do you want to look around more?"

Liza nodded. "I think we should. At least we can tell the Rapps—and the insurance company—that we did a thorough search." She reached out and touched Jamie's arm. "Don't worry, Jamie. Even if we don't find it, it was very wrong of Mr. Rapp to accuse you that way without any proof."

"Tucker knows that, too," Claire assured him. "Come on, let's look around the first floor. Let's each take a room," she proposed. "We might find it."

The three split up. Liza took the front parlor, Jamie took the sitting room, and Claire took the dining room and patio. She already knew the watch wasn't in the kitchen, though she planned to check again, just in case.

Her thoughts wandered wildly while she searched. She didn't want to think of what might happen if somehow Mr. Rapp convinced Tucker, or some other law officer, to pursue this. What if he made something up? He seemed so determined to find Jamie guilty; he might resort to such a thing.

If Jamie was found guilty of stealing the watch, he would probably have to spend time in jail. She knew that he'd been in trouble with the law before, as a kid. But he had been so young, he had always gotten off fairly easily.

It wouldn't be so simple this time, now that he was an adult. Even a few months in jail would be dreadful, a black mark on his life that he might never recover from. Just when he was getting some momentum in a positive direction. It didn't seem fair.

BRUNCH at the Peregrine—especially the Baked Apple French Toast, one of Avery's recent creations—was the highlight of a rave review that had appeared in a Newburyport newspaper the past week. So many customers showed up at noon on Sunday that a line formed out the door. While Gena took pictures with her cell phone, Avery wondered how to keep her potential patrons from losing patience and walking off. But Teresa calmly sent Brittany out with a tray of cold drinks and mini-quiches, which kept the customers calm and tantalized.

Later that afternoon, Avery was in an upbeat mood as she prepped for dinner. She thought about sending Mike the photo of the customer line, with a silly caption like, "Miracles happen!" Then dismissed the notion. She wanted him to see that the Peregrine was doing well, but she didn't want him to think she was gloating.

She hadn't seen him much on the boardwalk the last few days and suspected the Tuna was very busy as the summer wound down, even more than her café. The tour group had marched by the other day, as scheduled, but an older gentleman with silver hair and a handlebar mustache had led the parade. The vivacious Cindy was nowhere in sight.

Avery thought that was a good sign. She decided she had read too much into seeing Mike and Cindy together. She had let it scare her off too easily. What she really needed to do was march down to the Tuna herself and take Mike up on her rain check for that sailing date—any kind of date. He probably thought she wasn't interested. She wasn't sure how that had happened, but she felt ready now to make it clear that she was interested in seeing where their relationship could go. Very interested.

As Avery mulled this over, Gena pushed open the door that led to the dining room. "Someone's here to see you, Avery."

Avery looked up from the red pepper she had been chopping. Was it Mike? She hoped so. Maybe her thoughts had summoned him.

But before she could even smooth down her hair, someone peeked over Gena's shoulder and smiled. Her heart fell. It wasn't Mike, not even close.

"There she is, chopping away. Making the magic happen," her visitor called out.

Avery felt a knot in her stomach. She couldn't hide her surprise and didn't even try. "Paul. What are you doing here?"

Her ex-fiancé's dazzling smile grew wider, his blue eyes shining. He stepped past Gena and sailed through the doorway. "You look terrific, Avery. The sea air really agrees with you. And this place is beautiful. It's awesome. Honestly."

Avery quickly wiped her hands on a towel and pushed the chopping block aside. Paul was here. Could that possibly be?

She had been working hard all day and suspected she looked terrible, but suddenly realized she didn't really care.

He walked over to the worktable and smiled down at her. "I know I should have called first, but I just stopped by on a whim.

"I was on my way back to the city from Bar Harbor. I wasn't even sure I would find this place. It's barely on the map," he joked. When Avery didn't answer he added, "Your sister told me you set up shop out here."

"Right. She told me she ran into you. Too bad about the Tulip. I was sorry to hear that," she said sincerely.

"Yeah, we had some good times at the Tulip, didn't we? But what can you do? That's the way this business is, up one minute, down the next. How are you doing out here? It's a little off the beaten track, wouldn't you say?"

His tone was half teasing, half mocking. Or maybe she was just extra-sensitive to his opinion. She always had been . . . for no good reason, she realized now. Paul seemed different to her, diminished somehow. He even looked . . . shorter. Could that be because Mike was so tall? She had always thought so well of Paul, maybe just because he thought so well of himself? He was, as always, perfectly dressed, in a black T-shirt and khaki shorts and expensive sunglasses that gave him the "celeb on vacation" look.

"We're doing very well," she told him. "It took a few weeks, but when you have good food, people find you."

"You're a fabulous cook, no question about that."

"Thanks," she said stiffly. "So, really, why are you here?"

He shrugged. "I just wanted to say hi, make sure you're all right. I've been thinking about you," he added. "Are you doing okay, Avery? Really?"

Avery blinked, unable to believe he had asked that. He certainly hadn't been so concerned about her welfare when he dumped her.

"I'm better than ever, Paul," she said honestly. "What did you think happened to me after we broke up? Did you think I was hiding away in my apartment—alone with a bunch of cats?"

He laughed nervously. "I never thought that. You were always more of a dog person." His thin joke fell flat. "I can see you haven't been pining away over me. I didn't mean that. I just wanted to say that I'm sorry for way things turned out between us. The way you left the business . . . When I heard you started this place . . . well, I just wondered if you were managing all right on your own. It's hard to do it all, Avery. The staff, the books, the permits, the insurance. I think I owe it to you to offer some help, some support. That's all."

Help, from him? Was he serious? He was the last person on earth she would allow to help her. An image of Mike flashed into her mind. She had let Mike help her and didn't regret that for a second—maybe because when Mike offered help it was genuine; he was never trying to manipulate her. Paul and Mike were night and day, and Avery knew now that she preferred the daylight.

"You've always hated bookkeeping," Paul reminded her. "I remember that much," he added in a teasing tone.

Avery suddenly understood Paul was trying to weasel his way into her life again—and into her new business.

Handsome, smooth-talking Paul, who was used to being able to charm anyone, was down on his luck and out of work. Despite the Peregrine's rocky start, she was the one who was doing better now, and he was hoping she would throw him a lifeline—though, of course, he was so arrogant that he tried to sound as if *he* were the one doing *her* a favor.

Avery felt a little sorry for Paul. But that was all she felt. The hurt and even the anger were gone. She had finally gotten over him and was more than ready to turn the page. And that, she suspected, had a lot to do with Mike Rossi.

"I'm sorry, Paul, but I don't need help. The Peregrine is doing just fine." She shrugged. "I think it all worked out for the best."

He looked surprised at her reply, but finally sighed and swept his dark brown hair back from his forehead. She smiled at the familiar gesture, remembering how crazy she had once been about him. Now she didn't feel even a twinge of attraction.

"Well, you can't blame a guy for trying. I must have been crazy when I let you go. But I do wish you the best. I hope we can meet again someday with no hard feelings?"

"No hard feelings," she assured him.

"Thanks, Avery. I'm not sure I deserve that," he admitted. "May I kiss you good-bye?"

Surprised by his request, Avery simply nodded. She expected a quick kiss on the cheek, but he leaned over and rested his hands on her shoulders then gently kissed her lips. Avery closed her eyes, and a bittersweet feeling rushed through her as she remembered the good times and the hopes she once had for their relationship. But she knew now that he was not the one for her, and she was finally able to say good-bye.

They had not quite parted when the kitchen doors swung open. Avery quickly turned to see who was walking in, though she still felt Paul holding her.

She expected Gena or Teresa, returning to the kitchen. Which would have been bad enough.

But it was Mike, his eyes wide with shock, his face turning nearly as white as his cooking jacket.

She jumped away from her ex-fiancé, sure that Mike had the totally wrong idea about what was going on. But she had no idea of what to do or say to correct that.

"Sorry. I didn't mean to interrupt." Mike quickly started to back away.

She took a few steps toward him, practically grabbing his jacket to stop him from leaving.

"Wait, don't go . . . This is my friend, Paul. Let me introduce you . . ." Friend? The term was stretching it a bit, but Avery didn't know what else to call him. "Paul just stopped by to say hello," Avery continued in a rush. "He's on his way back to Boston." She turned to Paul. "Mike owns the Lazy Tuna down the street. He's got an incredible following. The place is packed every night."

"Well, that's an accomplishment. I had a little place with Avery in the city. We were packed every night, too. Then business fell off and I had to close." Paul walked around the table and stood by Avery. For some strange reason, he slipped his arm around her shoulders and gave her a little squeeze. "We were just talking about that place, right, Avery?"

Avery forced a smile then quickly stepped away. "Yeah, we were. Well, you were," she added.

Mike's mouth twisted to one side. "It's a tough business. Survival of the fittest . . . So you guys worked together? Is that the . . . connection?"

"Paul and I were partners at the Tulip Café. I told you about that," Avery reminded him.

"Oh, right." Mike nodded, and looked down a moment. She could tell he was silently fact-checking. Yes, she had told him about her partnership in a café somewhere in Boston that didn't work out. And she had mentioned a diamond engagement ring she sold to raise money for the Peregrine. But she had not told him about Paul. Not really.

He seemed to be adding things up now. And she had a feeling the equation wasn't coming out in her favor.

"Paul was just leaving," she said quickly. "Weren't you, Paul?"

But Mike spoke before Paul could. "That's all right. I'll catch you later, Avery." Before she could reply, Mike turned and walked out the door. This time, Avery didn't chase him. There seemed no point to it.

"Well, he seemed a little uptight," Paul said as soon as Mike was out of earshot. "I noticed that fish shack down the street. Is that the place you were talking up? Looks like a fish and chips."

"It's actually very good. People love it."

It occurred to Avery that she had never tasted Mike's food, but somehow, she couldn't let Paul criticize Mike's restaurant.

"Well, maybe I'll stop there for some take-out. Time to get back on the road, I guess." He cast one more wistful glance her way, as if she might have second thoughts about letting him go this easily. Paul wasn't used to rejection.

"I have to get back to my prep work. It's almost time to reopen," she said, glancing at her watch. "Have a safe drive back to the city."

He stared at her a moment and nodded. "Thanks. Good luck again. I hope this all works out for you."

"Thanks. Good luck to you, too, Paul," she said sincerely. "I'm sure some opportunities will come your way soon."

He smiled and left the kitchen, walking out the way he'd come in.

Avery watched him a moment, then breathed a sigh of relief. Paul Miller was the last person she expected to see today. If only Mike hadn't walked in. Avery worried that he thought Paul was some long-lost love and now they were back together. She would have to find a moment to explain things to him, which would not be easy.

Life was so complicated. That's why she loved cooking. You had a very clear recipe and a list of ingredients, and if you followed the instructions, nine times of ten, everything turned out fine.

She didn't even have the time to figure this out now.

Don't think, just cook, she coached herself, remembering another bit of Mike's useful advice.

Claire, Liza, and Jamie spent the rest of the day searching the entire inn for the watch, without success. Claire realized that hours had slipped by. She had never gone out to the beach. She hadn't even stepped outside, except in the morning, when everyone was arguing on the porch.

There were only six guests left at the inn. Claire began cooking dinner around five while Liza set the dining room table for the guests and the table in the kitchen for herself, Claire, and Jamie. Jamie was still searching, going through the old barn where they kept the bicycles.

"I was so sure the watch would turn up somewhere today," Claire said, thinking out loud. "I keep wondering if there's someplace we still haven't looked."

"I was thinking about that, too," Liza said wearily. "And wondering, well . . . if Jamie is really telling us the truth."

Claire turned quickly to look at her. Her heart fell. "Do you doubt his story now, too, Liza?"

Liza took a breath. "I'm not saying I'm sure he's guilty. But I have to admit, I wonder. I'm just trying to be honest with you, Claire. I want to believe he's innocent, but I think we need to be . . . prepared."

Prepared? Prepared for what? Claire didn't like the sound of that word. She turned back to the stove, frantically stirring a pot of chowder. Liza had a right to her opinion. *But she doesn't know Jamie the way I do,* Claire consoled herself. *I still believe he's entirely blameless and with the help of heaven, everyone will soon see that.*

Liza's cell phone rang and she checked the number. "It's the police station," she said quietly.

Claire felt frozen where she stood and said a silent prayer. *God, please don't let Jamie get in trouble over this. Please have mercy on this boy. Please protect him.*

"Yes, Tucker, I understand. Thanks for letting me know. Yes, I will tell him," she added. She ended the call and glanced at Claire. "The Rapps filed a report, and it will be passed to the district attorney. Tucker says the situation is drawing attention because the Rapps say the watch is so valuable, worth about five thousand dollars."

"Five thousand? My goodness, I didn't realize it was that valuable," Claire said.

"Neither did I. Tucker says if someone was found guilty of stealing it, since the value is over two hundred and fifty dollars, it's grand larceny and the penalty is up to five years in prison."

Claire took in a sharp breath. "I don't even want to think about that. There's no evidence."

"Not that we heard this morning," Liza agreed.

Jamie walked into the kitchen then. Claire hadn't even heard steps in the hallway. "Do you need me in here yet?"

"Not quite," Claire said. "The food won't be ready for about twenty minutes."

"I'm going out to start the recycling," he said to Liza. "I'll be back by then."

One of his many jobs was taking care of the trash that needed to be recycled—newspapers, cardboard boxes, bottles, and cans. The recycled trash was kept out in the barn in different barrels, and Jamie had to get everything ready on Sunday night for the Monday morning collection.

After he'd gone out the back door, Liza glanced at Claire. "Do you think he heard us?" she asked.

"I'm not sure. But when he comes back we need to tell him what Tucker said. He needs to know what's going on."

"Yes, I will. I didn't mean to keep it from him. He just breezed by so quickly."

Claire nodded. She knew Liza had not hid the news intentionally. It would be better to talk about this over dinner anyway, when they could sit down together and have a reasonable discussion.

Though it would be hard to talk about terms like larceny and prison in any reasonable way.

Claire's stomach felt so jumpy as she finished cooking, she had absolutely no appetite. Liza had gone into her office but now returned. "Should I call the guests down to dinner?" she asked.

"I think so. It's all ready. You had better get Jamie in here first. He needs to wash up before he serves and maybe change his clothes."

"All right." Liza turned toward the back door, but Jamie was walking in. He still wore the thick work gloves used for packing the trash and gardening. He was smiling very widely as he strode into the room, waving something in the air.

"Look what I just found . . . Mr. Rapp's watch! I knew it had to be somewhere around."

Liza walked over, wide-eyed, and Jamie handed her the elusive timepiece. "Thank heaven! There it is. Case closed," Liza announced. She stared up at him. "Where in the world did you find it?"

"In a pile of newspapers. It slipped out while I was stacking them."

"I took some newspapers out of the room when we were looking for the watch," Liza said. "I just thought I would start cleaning up a bit. It must have been tucked in there all the while."

Claire nodded, relief and gratitude flooding through her as she realized her prayers had been answered. "It's amazing that you found it. It could have easily ended up in the dump."

"Yeah, I guess it could have," Jamie agreed.

Liza stared down at the watch again. "I'd better call Tucker. He can let the Rapps know."

"Why don't you call the Rapps directly, Liza?" Claire asked.

"Oh, I don't know. I think Tucker should do that, since this whole business has gotten so . . . official." She set the watch down on the table. "Besides, I don't want to deal with Mr. Rapp. I'm sure he'll say that it was found very conveniently, now that he got the police involved."

Claire saw a look of offense flash across Jamie's face. "I just picked up some newspapers and it fell out. I swear it."

"I know that, Jamie. But you heard the way Mr. Rapp went on and on. He may make his own assumptions."

"Liza wasn't accusing you of anything," Claire tried to clarify. But the suggestion had even gotten Claire wondering. Had Jamie found the watch too conveniently? He had been all alone out there. It would have been an ideal time to pull the watch out of hiding . . . if he had stolen it.

"Then why even say it? Why even bring it up?" His tone was sharp, wounded.

Liza seemed confused. "You heard the way Mr. Rapp was talking this morning. I'm just being realistic," she tried to explain. "But now I am starting to wonder why you're so . . . defensive."

"Because you're acting like you don't believe me. I found it in the newspapers. The Rapps were reading stacks of them all weekend."

"We believe you," Claire insisted. Though the more he protested, the more unsure she began to feel about the story.

Liza held her hands up in a gesture of surrender. "It's been a long, stressful day. I don't want to argue about this anymore. I'm going to my office to call Tucker. When I get back, we'll serve dinner." She swept the watch off the table and left the kitchen.

Claire glanced at Jamie. "You ought to change and wash up. Then let the guests know dinner is ready."

He nodded and left the room. She could see from his tight expression, he was still upset. There was nothing she could do about it now. She would try to talk to him later when everyone had cooled down.

At dinner Claire heard the guests in the dining room talking cheerfully, but there was not much conversation at the kitchen table. Liza complimented Claire's dish, an herb-crusted cod fillet served over a warm lentil salad. Then she asked Jamie if he had much more to do in the barn, with the recycling.

"Not too much," he said. "I can get it all out tonight."

"I can help," Liza offered. She was trying to make amends for their tense moment, Claire knew.

But Jamie was still sullen. "That's all right. I can do it. I do it every week, don't I? I'll finish right after dinner."

And so he did, without even waiting for dessert, which Claire thought was unusual. But it had been a difficult day, and maybe the physical work calmed him and helped him sort out his thoughts.

Claire went out to the porch with her knitting after dinner. When Liza came out a little while later, Claire asked if Jamie was done with the trash yet.

"He finished a while ago. He went right up to this room," Liza reported.

Claire was surprised. He usually liked to watch TV at night. It was just as well, she decided. He needed his space right now. It would be better to talk to him about this tomorrow, when he would be calmer and in a better frame of mind.

Chapter Fifteen

When Claire woke up the next morning, she felt a certain heaviness in her heart, a worried feeling, and didn't immediately realize why. She'd had a bad dream, very upsetting, though she couldn't recall what it was about. She remembered the tension of the day before, Jamie being accused of robbing Mr. Rapp. That must have been what had upset her, she realized. Even in her sleep. But it was all resolved now. Mr. Rapp probably knew by now that his watch was safe and sound. They could forget all about it and go on as if the ugly incident had never happened. She certainly would.

She paused before getting out of bed and said a silent prayer, thanking God for resolving the problem so quickly.

Thank you, Lord, for your help in this matter, and please help us get back on track and have a positive, productive day.

Perhaps she shouldn't even bring it up to Jamie today, she thought as she got dressed. Even to apologize for sounding as if she'd doubted him. It was too upsetting, she decided. She wouldn't talk about it unless he brought it up first.

She walked into the kitchen and filled the coffeemaker with water. The beans were already ground, and she poured the coffee into the basket and turned it on. She turned to the table, to fill the milk pitchers that were already set out on a tray. That's when she saw it.

A white sheet of paper folded in half, right there, in the middle of the table where she wouldn't miss it. Her name, written in careful block letters across one folded side.

She could see, even from some distance, that it wasn't Liza's handwriting, a note reminding her that some guest was lactose intolerant or had an allergy to nuts.

No, it was Jamie's writing. She picked up the note and held it in her hand, then stared down at it. She felt that she already knew what was inside.

She drew in a sharp breath. *Dear God, why would Jamie leave me a note so early in the morning? Please let it say he's gone into town early or is just working outside already . . .*

She fumbled for her reading glasses then opened the sheet.

> *Dear Claire,*
>
> *I decided to go. I'm sorry but I couldn't wait to say good-bye. You were nice to give me this job. But I can see now things just won't work out here. I tried hard to do everything you told me. I even studied for that diploma test. But it just didn't seem to matter. Things just don't work out for me.*

Claire had to stop reading a moment and put the letter aside. Her eyes had filled with tears and they spilled down on to the page. She dabbed her eyes with a tissue and continued.

I was wrong to come here and look for you. Maybe if we had been together more when I was a kid that would have helped. But it's too late for me now. Nothing can change me. Not even God. I think it's better if I just go my own way. I have some savings and I'll be all right. Please don't worry. Maybe I'll write you sometime.

Jamie

"Oh, Jamie . . ." Claire dropped into a chair and cried with her head on folded arms.

What had driven him away? Had she doubted him when he so conveniently found the watch? She had also spoken up for him when Mr. Rapp made all those wild accusations.

But it must have been very hard being accused that way, being the center of so much suspicion, even questioned by the police. Especially for someone with such little self-esteem. She should have been more sensitive to that, done something more to reassure him . . .

She felt a soft touch on her shoulder. "Claire, are you all right?" Liza asked. "What's wrong? Are you sick?"

Claire lifted her head and forced herself to sit up. "It's Jamie. He's gone."

Looking shocked, Liza quickly read the note. "Oh dear. It's all my fault. I should never have mentioned what I thought Mr. Rapp would say. But Jamie took it so personally. He totally misunderstood. I was going to talk to him today, to try to explain again."

Claire nodded. They had both planned to reassure him. But it was too late.

"Should we try to find him?" Liza asked. "Maybe he's still at the station, waiting for a train. I can run into town and look for him."

"I think he's long gone by now. Off to the city. Or wherever. He never mentioned exactly where that apartment was that he shared with friends. Just somewhere in South Boston. He had some savings. He may not have even gone back to Boston." Claire felt herself about to cry again. She could hardly believe he was gone. It was such a shock. "I don't think he wants us to look for him," she said honestly. "I don't think he wants to see us again."

Liza sighed and sat down in the chair across from her. She reached out and took Claire's hand. "I'm so sorry, Claire . . . I don't know what to say. You can't blame yourself. You tried so hard to help him. You did everything you possibly could. Maybe he's just upset, and he'll come back once he's had time to think things through."

Claire knew Liza was trying to help, to hold out some slim hope. But Claire doubted Jamie would return. The note sounded so final.

She tried to calm herself and get her feelings under control. She had tried to help Jamie, as best as she knew how. She made a plan to help him, step by step. But God had another one.

CLAIRE felt numb as she moved through the rest of the day—and the rest of the week. It was an effort to get out of bed every morning, no matter how much she asked God for strength and help in understanding what had happened. Her heart was in pain, almost as if she were in mourning. Jamie's departure was a great loss.

She did her work automatically, speaking as little as possible to the guests. Sometimes, she didn't even hear them when they talked to her. She kept expecting to see Jamie out in the garden or running up and down the stairs. Every time she heard the front door open and slam, she would automatically think, *It's just Jamie coming back in from collecting the mail or driving some guests to the station.*

Then she had to catch herself. It wasn't Jamie. It would never be again.

It took about two days before she noticed. But one morning in the kitchen, her gaze fell upon the bowl of sea glass on the window-sill. She looked for the amber piece Jamie had found at the cliffs but it wasn't there. She always left it on top of the other pieces, where it could catch the light. She walked over to the bowl and sifted through with her fingers first, then gently dumped the contents on the table and searched more carefully, almost frantically.

But it was gone. No question. Had he taken it with him? Or had it caught the eye of some unthinking guest, who thought no one would miss a little chip of glass from this big bowl?

That was possible, too, Claire realized. Maybe Jamie didn't take it with him. She felt sad to realize it was gone. It was the only gift he had ever given her. On the other hand, she hoped that he had taken it with him, that the bit of glass did hold some meaning for him—a piece of this place he could look at and reflect on. And remember the safe place he had found for a while, the love and care she tried to give him. Maybe the bit of glass would give him strength when he felt down and needed some encouragement.

On Thursday night, Claire's good friend Vera Plante encouraged her to come to church. There was a meeting of the social justice committee. They hadn't met all summer, but the group wanted to get a jump on the fall. Ever since Claire had returned to Cape Light after working at the Crosby Street Center, she'd been an active member of this group. If she couldn't devote her life to helping those less fortunate, she got some satisfaction giving time as a volunteer or raising money for worthy causes.

The meeting was in the Fellowship Hall. Claire came in late and sat at the back of the room. Emily Warwick, who was also the town's mayor, was the moderator this year. She was doing a very good job, Claire thought. She was the very epitome of the old saying, "If you need something done, ask a busy person." Claire didn't know how Emily managed it all, but somehow she did.

When the meeting was over, coffee and cake were served.

Vera took Claire aside. Vera had come to know Jamie well while tutoring him, and Claire had called her right away to tell her the sad news.

"How are you holding up? Doing any better?" Vera asked kindly.

Claire tried to smile. "I'm coming along, day by day. It's going to take some time."

Vera nodded. "Maybe you'll hear from him once he gets settled somewhere. Maybe he'll keep studying for the GED. You never know."

Claire nodded, though she didn't think either of those things would happen. Vera was just trying to be nice and make her feel better.

Claire left the gathering early. She felt tired and wondered now why she had bothered to come. She had been so distracted, she'd hardly heard a word that anyone said. She walked out of the church but instead of going straight to her car, she sat on a bench in the park and gazed out at the water.

Was this the same place she had been sitting when she took Jamie to church on Father's Day? She looked around. Maybe, she thought. She couldn't remember. The thought made her sad. He wouldn't come loping through the park tonight, looking for her, the way he had that sunny day in June. She doubted she would ever see him again . . . and that made her so sad, she began to cry and couldn't stop herself.

"Claire . . . what's the matter? Are you crying?"

Claire looked up and saw Reverend Ben, standing beside her.

She swallowed hard and wiped her eyes with her hand. "Reverend . . . you surprised me. I didn't even hear you coming."

"I was walking to my car and saw you here." He sat down on the bench and leaned toward her. "What's the matter? What's troubling you? Is it a problem with that young man who's living at the inn?"

Claire nodded. "A big problem. He's gone. He left on Monday morning. He didn't even say good-bye. He did leave a note though."

Reverend Ben was surprised. "Why did he go? Did he say?"

"No, but I think I know. There was a problem at the inn on Sunday. A guest accused Jamie of stealing an expensive watch. We couldn't find it anywhere. The guest even called the police and filed a report at the station. Liza and I didn't think Jamie took it. We both believed him. That night, though, when Jamie was bundling the newspapers for the recycle truck, he found the watch. He said it slipped out from between a stack of papers and just fell at his feet."

Reverend Ben listened with a serious expression. "Did you believe him?"

"I did," Claire insisted. "Though thoughts do cross your mind. It's only human to . . . to wonder. And Jamie has made some missteps in his past. When he was a boy, he had little run-ins with the law—shoplifting small things, painting graffiti. I thought he had gotten past all that, especially these last few weeks. He was working so hard at the inn and studying for his GED. I thought he had really turned a corner."

"It sounds as if he did. But I still don't understand why he left," said the reverend. "The watch was found, the police and owner informed, I assume?"

"Liza took care of all that. But she did say, just before she called Tucker Tully, that she didn't want to speak to the guest directly because he would probably say Jamie found the watch awfully conveniently. Or something like that. Well . . . Jamie misunderstood what she meant and thought she was doubting him. I knew he was very hurt, but in the moment all I could think of was how happy

I was that the watch was found, and Jamie would be all right. I was planning to talk to him the next day, and so was Liza . . . but by the time I got up, he was gone. I never had the chance."

The reverend nodded. "I see. He was hurt. He felt . . . ashamed. Humiliated. Angry. Being unfairly accused is an awful experience. And it sounds as if this young man is rather fragile emotionally, doesn't have much confidence or sense of self to draw on."

"Yes, that's it. That's the trouble. He was just starting to feel better about himself and more hopeful about his future. Reverend Ben, it seems so unfair. Things were going so well. Why did God let this happen? I thought God wanted me to help Jamie. Why else would he have brought us back together again, after all this time?"

"You know," Reverend Ben said, "when people are trying to change their lives for the better, the road to becoming whole isn't always a straight one. People tend to fall off the path now and then, or take wrong turns. Especially if they've been damaged, they can't always make all the right choices."

"I do know that," Claire said heavily. "I suppose I just want a straight, easy road for Jamie."

"Of course you do. But, Claire, you have to remember that it's Jamie who's got to find that road and the way to stay on it. All you can do is love him and remember that we are asked to trust God. No matter what. Even when we don't understand why something like this has happened. Especially then," he added.

"'Trust in the Lord with all your heart. And lean not on your own understanding.'" Claire recited the scripture she knew by heart. "Proverbs, 3:5."

"That's right. God's ways are often mysterious to us, even unfathomable. But try to trust that it's all for a purpose," he advised her. "I still believe that God brought you together with Jamie for a reason, Claire. You did help him. If he's truly grown and learned some lessons here, then perhaps he'll move forward in the right direction, using the tools you've given him so far. Maybe someday, you'll even see him again."

Claire nodded. "I dearly hope so. In the meantime, I can still pray for him. I pray for him all the time."

Reverend Ben nodded and softly smiled. "He needs your prayers now, more than ever. I'll pray for him, too," he promised.

"Thank you, Reverend," Claire said. "That is a comfort to me."

Reverend Ben soon walked her to her car and they said good night. On the way home she considered his words. She did think Jamie had grown and developed some real character. She hoped it would serve him in the world, wherever he wandered, and she clung to the slim hope she would see him again.

She considered herself a person of strong faith, who drew her strength from the lessons of the scripture. But at a moment like this she realized that you just didn't learn it one time, and that was the end. One had to learn these lessons again and again. To be battered and worn down by these spiritual trials, the way the wind and sea carved the angel wing cliffs. The way the waves and sand smoothed bits of sea glass.

Dear God, I don't understand why this has happened, but I must trust you, she prayed. *Please let your grace work in my heart and help me learn how to accept even what I can't understand. I'm trying very hard. And please protect Jamie as he tries to find his way.*

AVERY kept a lookout for Mike, who usually passed the café at the same time each day on his way to the Tuna. She wanted to catch up with him and find some way to clear up any misconceptions he had about her relationship with Paul. But that plan was not easily accomplished. The few times she had spotted him, she was either in the middle of a rush of customers, or he marched past her café at an aerobics-level pace; all he needed was a water bottle and hand weights to blend in with the fitness buffs on the beach. He looked so unapproachable, she practically felt a chill as he swept by. Talk about giving a cold shoulder. Now she knew the true meaning of that expression. She had called him twice on the phone, but each time he politely—but coolly—told her he couldn't talk. He never called back.

One sunny afternoon in late August, Mike's mother, Victoria Rossi, made good on her promise to visit the café. She arrived at lunchtime with Emily, whom Avery was especially delighted to see.

Victoria was on foot, of course, with Emily scooting alongside.

Avery met them at the entrance with a cheerful welcome. "Would you like to sit inside or out?"

"Outside's better. We can park the scooter next to the table . . . if you don't mind," Victoria replied.

"No problem at all." Avery brought them over to the table with the best view.

Emily hopped off her ride and stowed it to one side. "This is perfect, thank you," she replied in a very mature fashion.

Victoria helped Emily open her napkin and spread it on her lap. "Isn't this a lovely place? I love the decor and those photographs of the island. The Tuna has its charms, but it's high time a café with a little more style moved into the neighborhood."

Victoria glanced at her menu with interest. "I bet you gave up on me ever showing up. Sorry it's taken so long to come here."

"I'm just glad you finally did. I'm sure you're very busy with Emily and Noah. When does school start? It must be soon."

Emily made an awful face. "Ugh! Did you have to remind me?"

Avery laughed. "Sorry. You have a little time left, don't you?"

"Ten measly days. We go back the day after Labor Day." Emily's expression was sullen, her chin on her chest. She still wore her pink helmet, and it dipped down over her eyes.

"I've started a countdown," Victoria confessed. She leaned over and helped Emily take the helmet off. "We just did some school shopping. New sneakers and jeans and plenty of pink T-shirts. Now we're out for one last fling."

"Oh, I see. This is a special lunch." Avery finally caught Emily's eye and got her to smile again. "I'll see what I can cook up for you. Maybe a special back-to-school dessert is in order."

The prospect instantly perked up Emily's spirits. She suddenly sat up again, looking quite cheerful.

Avery wasn't able to leave the kitchen again until it was time to serve her special customers their dessert. She hadn't been sure what she would pull together, but she took a wild guess that Emily liked chocolate and obviously loved the color pink. She set up the basic Chocolate Barge—a perennial favorite—and added some strawberry ice cream, sliced berries, and a pink berry-based sauce. Then she surrounded the dessert with pink rose petals, picked off one of the table decorations. Finally, she topped the extravaganza with mounds of whipped cream and sparklers. A little pink Post-it on a toothpick read, "Have a Great Year at School!"

Did it qualify for the cover of *Bon Appétit*? More like the cover of a Dr. Seuss book, Avery thought. The mile-high confection looked like something the Cat in the Hat would cook up for a snack.

She carried the masterpiece to the table personally and was totally rewarded for her efforts by Emily's surprise and delight. The little girl knelt on her chair, clapping her hands as Avery set the dessert down between her and her grandmother.

"Nana, look at the rose petals. It's so pretty!"

"It is that . . . and more." Victoria looked up at Avery with new regard, a fondness in her expression. "Thank you, Avery. You didn't have to make such a fuss, but it's very nice of you."

Avery shrugged. "No big deal. I like to go a little wild from time to time. Cooking outside the lines," she joked.

"You went totally native with that one," a familiar voice agreed.

Avery turned to see Mike standing nearby. How long had he been watching them? She wasn't sure. He was trying hard not to smile, but his cheek muscles were losing the battle.

He finally gave in when Emily called out to him, "Want a bite, Daddy? It's awesome."

Victoria turned to her son. "Come around, don't be shy. There's plenty for the whole family."

Mike reluctantly slipped under the thin rope barrier that marked the café's outdoor seating and came up to the table. "Did you tell Avery it was your birthday or something?" he asked his daughter. "You know it isn't until October."

"It's a back-to-school treat. To cheer her up," Avery explained.

"You should make this at the Tuna, Daddy. It's divine."

"Divine, huh? Where did you learn that word?" He reluctantly took a spoonful, tasting with professional flair. Avery could tell he liked it and hoped the confection would sweeten his gruff mood a bit. "Good job. Nice reduction with the sauce . . . This should hold her until middle school. Are those real rose petals on the plate?"

Avery nodded. "Totally edible."

"I know. I was just asking. They look . . . pretty." He glanced at her, finally meeting her eyes.

His expression changed for just a moment, as if he had been hungry for the sight of her and was now taking in his fill. Then just as quickly, a bland, detached look returned.

"Hard to believe the summer is over," she said, trying to make some harmless conversation so he wouldn't race walk away from them.

"I'm glad it's over. It felt long this year, longer than usual."

For Avery, the summer had flown by, and each and every day had been about the Peregrine. She had not really made time for anything—or anyone—else. How she wished now she could turn the calendar back to July. She would definitely make time for Mike.

Instead she said, "Emily says she isn't looking forward to school starting. Are you?"

"Yeah, I guess so. It's a juggling act the first few weeks. The Tuna is open on weekends until Columbus Day."

"Yes, I remember. You told me that once," she replied. She knew she had to find some moment to clear the air about Paul. He might keep avoiding her until Labor Day, but at least she had a little time after that when the beachfront would slow down and they could talk. She hoped so anyway.

"What are you going to do after the summer? Does the Peregrine turn into a snowbird?"

Avery knew what he meant. Quite a few cooks in the Northeast went down to warmer climates in the winter—Florida and the Caribbean—or they took jobs on cruise lines that roamed sun-filled tourist spots.

"That's not my style. I'm not really sure what I'll do."

She had been wondering what to do once the cold weather set in. The café had to be closed, mid-October at the latest. The area would be deserted by then. But a winter job in Boston felt like a step backward. She had considered spending the winter in Connecticut, near her family. Or in New York City or even in the south of France, where she had studied cooking.

She might need to go that far away just to forget about Mike, she realized now. He seemed so distant and detached today, she didn't feel safe musing over her plans aloud.

Was he acting this way because he thought she still cared for Paul? Or did he have a girlfriend now—Cindy or someone else she didn't even know about? That could have been the reason for this chill as well, she realized. But with Victoria and Emily there, she couldn't get into that conversation.

"Well, good seeing you," Avery said to Mike. She turned to Victoria and Emily, who were finishing the last of their dessert. "I'm glad you enjoyed your lunch. This was on the house. No, my treat—" she insisted, when Victoria seemed about to argue with her. "I have to get back to the kitchen. But come see me again soon. And good luck with school, Emily. I know you'll do great."

Victoria thanked her profusely, and Emily jumped up in her seat and gave Avery a big hug.

Avery said good-bye to Mike, mostly with her eyes. She brushed past him feeling suddenly sad and empty. Back in the kitchen, she covered her face with her hands and nearly cried.

It didn't seem fair. How could she feel so bad about him? As if something had ended between them when it had never really begun?

THE island was filled with visitors the last week of August, everyone trying to squeeze out the last sweet, precious drops of summer.

The Peregrine felt more hectic than ever, with Avery's staff quickly dwindling. Jack and Brittany were both heading back to college just when she needed them for the last big push.

Luckily, Gena had a friend who was an experienced waitress and willing to work through Labor Day. Teresa, bless her heart, hung on to the bitter end, too, though she had to start her regular job for the school district lunch service the very next day after Labor Day.

With Avery doing double duty as both chef and waitress, they managed to make it through the last big weekend and limp to the finish line, exhausted but victorious.

"Well, we made it," Teresa said to Gena and Avery as they locked the doors on Labor Day night. "I know the café will be open a few more weeks, but this feels like the grand finale to me. I have to tell you, ladies, it was a little touch-and-go there."

Avery laughed. "You're telling me. I nearly gave up on this place ten times," she admitted. "But here we are. I couldn't have made it without all of you," she added sincerely.

And Mike, she added silently. *Him most of all.*

The three women shared a hug and a good meal, treating themselves to the best table in the house. They toasted to the Peregrine, to the summer they had shared and the one to come. Avery knew that even though things had not worked out well with Mike, Angel Island had blessed her with some wonderful new friends—Gena and Teresa, Liza and Claire.

She had made a new life for herself and felt like a different person than the woman who had arrived back in May. A wiser, kinder, more tolerant person, she hoped. And that was a certain type of success you couldn't measure with good reviews or big dinner crowds, but one that was even more valuable and satisfying.

THE week after Labor Day, Avery was the only guest left at the inn. She hadn't made any progress finding her own place the last few weeks, mainly because rentals had been scarce and she didn't have the time to look for one. As fall approached, there were lots of cottages for rent on the island and in the town of Cape Light. But now she wasn't sure about staying for the winter.

She finally decided it would be best if she left the island in

October. Otherwise she would spend the next eight months hoping to run into Mike or waiting for him to call her. She hadn't seen him since the day Victoria and Emily stopped by for lunch and, sadly, she did not expect to.

But she still had no idea where she would go or what she would do. She hoped some force in the universe would decide for her.

Everything seemed different in September. Even though summer did not officially end until September twenty-first, the beachfront and boardwalk boldly contradicted the calendar. The ferry service from Newburyport followed the same schedule, but the big boats arrived at the dock eerily empty. A handful of beachgoers and cyclists wandered about during the week, and there were a few more visitors on the weekends. But the days were growing cooler and the sun set a little earlier each night.

When Mrs. McNulty deflated her toy menagerie and told Avery she would send her a postcard from Florida, Avery knew the season was drawing to a close. Even though the Lazy Tuna was still open weekends, she knew Mike was back at school now, back to his other life. She wondered if he even ran the Tuna during this part of the year. Maybe he had a manager watching over things. She wondered if he ever thought about her anymore. The way she still thought about him. Funny how three random kisses—one on her forehead, for goodness' sake—and a lot of wise-guy jokes could make such a lasting impression.

The life he led during the school year—his family, all his students, friends, and connections there—probably filled in his thoughts completely. And his heart. Maybe his summer season was put away and forgotten, like the flamboyant shirts he wore on Tiki Night at the Tuna.

The weeknights were so quiet that Avery was down to a skeleton crew, just herself and one waitress. The night before the first day of fall—Equinox Eve, Avery had privately dubbed it—even Gena called in sick with a cold.

Only one couple came in to dine. Avery cooked and served them then decided to close early. The first of the fierce storms that hit the island each fall was predicted to move into the area late that night. She knew by now not to take the news lightly.

As she stepped out the kitchen door to take out the trash, a gust of wind pushed at her body, like a giant hand pressing her back to the doorway. She managed to make it down the alley but could barely lift the Dumpster cover up and get it down again.

Safely back inside, she recalled the storm in July and how she and Mike had waited it out in her kitchen. Mike wasn't around to keep her company tonight. Nobody was. She had to get back to the inn, as fast as possible.

She quickly closed the café, doing what she could to secure the building. It had grown too chilly for outside seating, so she didn't have to worry about bringing in tables and chairs. The awning was also closed and secure, and long shutters had been installed around the glass doors soon after the last storm. She walked around the building, checking twice to make sure she hadn't forgotten anything.

The wind was blowing bits of paper down the street and turning over trash cans on the boardwalk. Dark clouds gathered over the ocean, and the waves were being whipped to a frenzy. Huge whitecaps crashed ominously on the shore.

She put her head down and ran to her SUV, parked in the space between Sunshine Sundries and the café. Mrs. McNulty's store was closed up tight. Avery was sure an earthquake would not disturb it. But as she backed out onto the street, she wondered about the Tuna.

She drove down and took a look. Mike's restaurant was dark and empty. But the storm shutters were not pulled across the windows yet. Why hadn't Mike come and secured the building? Maybe he was busy with his children tonight, or hadn't paid attention to the forecast? Or maybe he had asked someone else to do it and they hadn't gotten here yet.

Avery wondered if she should try to close the place up safely. As a favor to him. Would he think she was being too nosy or interfering? He had always explained his help to her as, "Neighbors look out for neighbors around here."

As she pondered the question, a trash can flew past her car. It slammed into the Tuna, narrowly missing a window but striking a gutter pipe, which hung down precariously after the basket bounced off.

That did it. She got out and went over to the building. Using all her might, she began to yank down the heavy wooden flaps that went over the entrance and windows. It wasn't easy but she managed to get nearly all the flaps down and latched just as a few raindrops began to fall.

Avery was working on the very last flap, which covered the single kitchen window at the back of the building, when a flash of light within caught her eye.

She had already heard thunder rumbling in the distance and wondered if what she was seeing was lightning reflected in the glass. She had to hold the edge of the window ledge and get up on tiptoe to get a good look. Then she felt herself go cold with horror.

There were flames inside. A thick drift of smoke rose to the ceiling. She couldn't tell where the flames were coming from—maybe one of the cooking burners or an appliance?

Avery dropped down and nearly fell to her knees. She fumbled for her cell phone and quickly dialed nine-one-one.

"I need to report a fire, on Ferry Street, Angel Island," she told the dispatcher. "It's in the Lazy Tuna restaurant."

It was hard to say the words aloud. Everything felt so unreal. As if she were having a horrible nightmare. She had to shout the information twice to be heard over the wind and the crackling phone connection caused by the storm.

The dispatcher told her a fire crew was on its way and instructed her to get away from the building.

Avery wished there was something more she could do. Find a hose and start spraying water back here? But she didn't know where to find a convenient hose, and her fire-fighting skills were pretty pathetic.

The wind pushed against her body as she ran to her car and climbed inside. She pulled out her phone again and called Mike, hoping he would pick up. Would the fire department call him? She had forgotten to ask. But she needed to make sure he knew, as hard as it would be to tell him this news.

His phone rang a few times. Finally he answered. He sounded surprised to hear her voice.

"You have to come down to the Tuna right away, Mike. There's a fire. I just saw it through the window. I called nine-one-one. The fire department is on the way."

"A fire? Are you sure?" he asked quickly.

"It's so dark, I couldn't see much. But there are flames and smoke in the back of the restaurant, in the kitchen," she told him. "I'm parked on Ferry Street, and I can see a glow in the window now and some smoke . . . Oh, it's terrible, Mike. I'm so sorry . . ."

"I'll be there right away. Just stay away from the building, Avery. Promise me."

"All right . . . come quickly."

Avery squeezed her eyes closed, unable to watch the Tuna on fire. This just wasn't right. It was going to break Mike's heart. It was his heritage, his family history, so many childhood memories. She imagined the beautiful, zany, undersea mural being ruined and she couldn't help but cry.

The rain had started to fall, which she hoped would help keep the fire under control. But the wind was strong, too. She knew that wasn't good.

When she saw Mike's truck pull up a few minutes later, she ran out of her car. The fire trucks arrived at about the same time, and firefighters dressed in heavy gear and big hats jumped off and ran to the building.

Avery met Mike in the middle of the street. The lights from the fire trucks cast a strange glow on the scene.

He glanced at her, then back at his beloved restaurant. Smoke flowed out of the back windows, which had exploded, and licks of flame slipped up the back wall almost reaching the roof.

"I can't believe it," he said quietly. "How did you even see it start?"

"The storm was starting. I drove down and saw that no one had pulled down the flaps on the windows here. So I got out to do that and when I reached the kitchen, I saw a light inside that just didn't look right . . ."

He turned to her and held both her shoulders. "As long as you're all right . . . You are, aren't you?"

Avery nodded, moved by his concern. He was losing his beloved restaurant and he was worried about her.

A firefighter walked over and asked them to step back. "This is going to take awhile, folks. I know you're concerned, but it's safer if you don't stand here and watch. Is there someplace around here you can wait?"

Mike turned to her. "You go back to the inn, Avery. You don't have to stay here with me."

Avery didn't know what to say. Was he telling her he didn't want her company? She wasn't sure but decided all she could do was be honest.

"I don't want to leave you here alone, Mike. I'm not going anywhere," she insisted.

He looked surprised at her reaction and ready to argue, then something inside him seemed to give way. He nodded quickly and wiped the rain from her cheek with his hand. "All right. If you want to."

She reached out her hand and took hold of his. He squeezed back in answer. She didn't have to say anything more, she realized. The truth was, she couldn't.

THEY sat in his truck, parked an acceptable distance away, and watched the battle between the firefighters and the fire. The storm had reached its height and the wind roared, pushing the water from the hoses back at the trucks.

"I hate to watch, but it's hard not to," Mike said quietly. "I feel as if I owe it to the Tuna. I can't just leave it here alone, battling for its life."

Avery understood perfectly.

A short time later, a firefighter came to Mike's side of the truck. He wore a special medallion on his hat, and Avery realized he was the chief. Mike quickly rolled down the window to speak to him.

"We have the fire under control, Mr. Rossi. We pretty much contained it in the kitchen. We had to break a hole in the roof to get more water inside. You'll have damage throughout. But I don't think you'll lose the whole building."

"Thanks. Thanks a lot," Mike said.

He turned to Avery as he rolled the window up again. "A ton of damage, but it's not totally destroyed. Thank goodness you saw it early. We could be looking at a pile of ashes by now."

She shrugged. "That was just luck."

"Not really. If you hadn't come over to pull down the shutters, you wouldn't have seen it at all," he pointed out. "Why did you come down here anyway?"

She shrugged. "I wanted to help you." She paused. "I think about you . . . a lot."

"I think about you. All the time . . . I miss you." He shook his head. "And I can't figure out what it is between us, everything always stop and go. I kept feeling that there was really something good going on with you and me, and then it would all just . . . seem to disappear." He looked at her, puzzled. "Why is that?"

"I don't know," Avery admitted. "Maybe because we never took time to talk? We were always too busy working. We never even went out on that sailing date," she reminded him.

"I would have asked you again . . . I didn't think you wanted to. And what about that Paul guy? He broke your heart. But when he was here, it looked like you wanted to go back with him."

"I knew you got the wrong idea about that. I wanted to explain, but you were acting so weird toward me . . . like, you didn't want to even talk to me anymore."

"I was just . . . scared," he admitted.

"Me, too." She sighed. "Just to clear this up: I have no interest at all in Paul. Seeing him again made me realize how lucky I've been to meet you."

"Really?" Mike asked.

Avery nodded, unable to find more words.

They heard a loud crash then, and Mike turned toward the window and winced. "I think that was the back wall."

"I feel so bad about the Tuna," Avery said. "How are you going to tell Emily and Noah? I can tell they love this place."

"They do," Mike said. "It's been their home away from home. It's going to be hard to tell them and my mother." He stared out at the smoking, charred building. "But no one was hurt. I know what a real loss is. The Tuna is just a building."

He turned to her, and Avery reached out and took his hand. It was ice cold. And his dark eyes were filled with sorrow. She wished she could just take him in her arms and make all this unhappiness go away.

He gave a small, humorous shrug. "Well, if I had to watch the Tuna burn down with anyone, I'm glad it was you."

She was touched by his strange compliment. It gave her hope.

"I'm glad I was here with you. I just wish I'd seen it sooner."

"Nothing could have changed it. Some things are meant to be. Like you and me," he added quietly. "Maybe something good can come out of this disaster, Avery. Maybe I can finally be honest with you about my feelings."

She watched him carefully and saw the sorrow give way to determination and something else that she didn't dare put a name to, afraid it couldn't possibly be real.

"I think I've loved you since the day we met." He smiled, remembering. "When that closet fell on you. Right then, I felt it. After I lost my wife, I never thought anyone would get to me that way again, get to my heart. But you surprised me. You weren't at all what I expected. And yeah, I did get scared and maybe even used an excuse to back away from you . . . But I hope you can forgive me for that. I know now, I love you. With all my heart. And always will."

Avery was shocked by his confession. Shocked and speechless. Almost speechless, she realized.

"You aren't like anyone I've ever known," she told him. "You . . . woke me up, made me question the way I thought about things. You taught me to have more faith in myself, to keep trying, even when it seemed impossible. And to laugh at myself," she added. "And appreciate the surprises in life, which can be a million times better than anything I ever wished for. Like falling in love with you."

Mike pulled her close and kissed her. Avery felt all their misunderstandings and missed chances go up in a puff of smoke. Holding Mike in her arms was a dream come true. Whatever else happened to her—even if the Peregrine burned downed tomorrow, too—she knew she would be all right. On this little island, she had found more than the perfect place to start a new business. She'd found a new life . . . and true love.

As the firefighters finally packed up, Mike put his arm around her shoulders and held her close. The worst of the storm was over, and the fire smoldered. "I kept saying I needed a new kitchen in there. I guess this is God's way of making me renovate," he joked. "We can probably rebuild it by the summer . . . Maybe change the name to the Grilled Tuna? Or something clever like that?"

Avery laughed at him. "We'll figure it out. A wise man once told me, 'Fall down seven times, get up eight.'"

He laughed and hugged her even closer. "Good line. I think I know that guy."

Avery just laughed, too, thinking how lucky she was to finally end up with the very wise Tuna Guy.

THE first big storm of autumn had come and gone, but it would not be the last, Claire guessed. It swept in on the final night of summer, as if fall were eager to flex its muscles, to make sure its arrival drew the proper respect and attention.

Claire had meant to sleep in her own cottage that night, but the rain had started early, and she stayed one more evening with Liza. She had fallen asleep to the sound of raindrops beating on the roof and the windows, and the wind off the ocean whistling through the trees.

It was still raining when Claire woke up. Avery was out, and Liza had left early for a day in the city with Daniel. It continued to drizzle all through the morning and early afternoon, and Claire busied herself cleaning and making a pot of chicken soup.

Finally, the spongy gray skies cleared a bit. She pulled on rubber boots and a slicker and went outside to survey the storm's handiwork, even though it was late afternoon. Branches were down and clumps of colorful leaves clung to the wet grass.

How had everything looked so green just days ago and now all the autumn colors—yellow, orange, and dark red—made a painter's palette of the dappled, fallen leaves? How did the seasons change so quickly? It always caught her by surprise.

She walked over to the vegetable patch, where most of the plants were already brown and spent, and had been even before the storm. A few hardy stalks were still standing. The last of the summer bounty peeked out from the overgrown rows—some squash and eggplant. Green cabbage was still growing and so were the pumpkins.

She would have to find the ripe ones later or they would rot on the ground. It was hard to work in the vegetable garden now; it always made her think of Jamie. All the work he had put into weeding and mending the fences this summer. She could almost see him right there, kneeling between the rows of carrots and tomatoes. It made her feel sad, and she scolded herself for indulging her emotions this way.

She leaned over and picked up a sunflower that had fallen to the ground. A majestic sight in its prime but now shriveled and brown. The seeds were worth saving. She would plant even more next year, she promised herself.

She heard someone walking down the gravel drive, toward the back of the inn and turned to see who it could be. Maybe Reverend Ben, she thought. She had a feeling he might look in on her after their meeting in the park the week before.

"Claire? . . . I kept knocking on the door. I guess you didn't hear me."

Claire turned quickly. It was a man's voice, but not the reverend.

It was Jamie . . .Could it really be him? She shaded her eyes with her hand to make sure her emotions weren't playing tricks on her.

He walked closer and she could see him clearly, no question now. Yet he still seemed like a mirage, a vision that had appeared in the dim, shady garden. She couldn't even address him, for fear he would disappear again.

When Claire didn't speak he came a few steps closer. "I know you must be mad at me . . . but I needed to see you. I just want to talk awhile, then I'll go," he said quickly.

Claire just stared at him. His abrupt departure had hurt and confused her, had made her question herself and even doubt her faith at times. Her feelings at that moment were a jumble. But one was coursing through stronger than all the rest.

"Oh, Jamie," she said, blinking back tears. "I am so glad to see you." She pulled off her thick gloves. "Let's go inside. It's chilly and damp out here."

Jamie nodded. He followed her, looking nervous and scared. Did he think she was angry with him? It would be a logical conclusion, Claire had to admit, but all she felt was relief that he seemed well and had come back, that she hadn't lost him forever.

He followed her into the kitchen and she put up the kettle and made two mugs of tea, just to have something to do while she got her self under control and gathered her thoughts.

She sat across from him at the table, stirring a spoonful of honey into her cup. "I never thought I'd see you again. Are you all right?"

"I'm good," he said. "I didn't come here to ask for help again, if that's what you're thinking. I came to . . . to tell you I'm sorry for running out on you and Liza. I guess I left you pretty shorthanded."

Missing his help at the inn was probably the least of it, from her perspective. But what he said was true. They hadn't been able to hire anyone else at that point of the summer and had both taken on a heavy load of extra work.

"You did leave us in a lurch," Claire conceded, "but we got by. I wish you had stayed to talk things over. We both felt you had misunderstood us. We both believed you. We never thought you had stolen that man's watch."

He looked down at his hands, his expression sad and serious. "I know that, Claire. And I know I acted as if I was all bent out of shape about being accused but . . . I knew you believed me. That was the problem. I did take the watch. I really did do it. And you and Liza were both so . . . so good to me. So loyal. I couldn't face you anymore, knowing what I'd done. Even though I gave the watch back. I knew I had lied to you. So I did what I always do. I just ran."

Claire swallowed hard. She couldn't believe it. But it had to be true. He had said so himself. He'd stolen the watch. Now she did feel a surge of anger and betrayal, realizing he had lied to her. Lied with a straight face, again and again.

But here he was, coming back to explain and apologize. She didn't understand.

"You took the watch? You lied to us all that time while we stood up for you? How could you do such a thing . . . and then just stand there, watching us defend you?"

He bit down on his lower lip and slowly nodded. "I know. It was horrible of me to trick you like that . . . but I was in a real jam and I didn't know what to do. I owed this guy in Boston a lot of money. A lot more than I had saved working here. I was able to duck him awhile, living out here. But he finally caught up with me . . . He gave me a warning. I had to pay him back or else. I didn't know what to do. I thought if I took the watch, and sold it somewhere, I'd get him off my back. Then I'd be home free and could go on with all that stuff you'd been helping me with."

Claire let out a long breath. So he did have some reason for deceiving her that way. It was something.

"Why didn't you tell me? I could have helped you. Didn't you realize that?"

The color rose in his cheeks. He shook his head. "I thought about it . . . but I couldn't. You'd helped me so much already. And you were thinking so well of me. Making such a big deal about me getting my act together. And here I was, screwing up again. I didn't want you to know I was still . . . you know, acting stupid, getting into jams."

Claire felt sad. He had hid his problem, trying to keep up a good image in her eyes, afraid to disappoint her. He just couldn't believe that anyone could love him enough to see the good in him all the time. Even when he made mistakes.

"I told you once before, Jamie, that I will always be here to help you. I meant it. No matter what," Claire said finally. She looked at him curiously. "But why even tell me about this now? I never had to know that you lied to me that way."

"Yes, you did . . . I didn't want you to go on thinking it was something you did or said to me that made me go away. The same for Liza."

"I did feel that way. Liza did, too," she admitted.

"It wasn't you at all. It was me. I got pulled back, one last time.

Old voices telling me I was fooling myself trying so hard, trying to do better. So I took the watch, thinking what the heck. I'd cash it in, get that guy off my back, problem solved."

"And this guy you owe money to—is he still after you?" she asked.

Jamie shook his head. "No, the cops picked him up for something else. He's in jail, for a long time. I didn't have anything to do with that, but I really am free of him now."

Claire returned to her real question. "So you returned the watch because you were afraid of getting caught?"

"A little . . . But it was more the way you and Liza stuck up for me that made me turn it in. I never had good people like both of you on my side. People who go the distance for you and watch your back," he added quietly. "It was just like you told me. You believed in me. But I had to believe in myself. I've spent some time on my own working on that. So I came back to say I'm sorry. And to tell you that I think I really have changed now. I have become . . . or am on the way to being a better person. A better man. One you can be proud of."

Claire sat silently for a moment, taking in his words. She felt her anger and confusion suddenly swept aside. His realization was more important than anything that had come before that.

Her heart filled with happiness and gratitude. God truly works in mysterious ways. There was no doubt. Just like the small black seeds planted in the earth change into a bounty of fruit and flowers. Just as the tiny mustard seed grows to the grandest tree of all. Faith, hope, and love planted in a heart can yield an amazing harvest.

She reached out and took his hand. "You make me proud, just saying that . . . Where did you go? Where have you been all this time?"

He let out a long breath, looking relieved that the hardest part of this conversation was over. "I didn't want to go back to Boston and get sucked up into my old gang of friends. I had enough sense to take your advice about that," he said. "I went up to Portland. It's a pretty cool place. I found a job in a little tech shop that does computer repairs. I was a helper mostly but I learned a lot. I took the GED, too. I don't know yet if I passed but I feel pretty good about just getting through it."

Claire felt so happy at this news, she couldn't stop herself from crying. But they were happy tears. She gave up silent thanks to God that the story had ended so well. Jamie could have fallen back to old ways, old friends, bad habits. He could have been lost to her forever.

"Claire . . . please don't cry. You'll make me feel bad."

"I can't help it. I'm just so happy for you, Jamie. I knew you could do it all along."

"I couldn't have done it without you," he said quickly.

"Oh yes. Yes, you could. You've done it even better without me," she replied. "Everyone needs a little help now and then. But we are finally responsible for our own lives, answering only to our maker. You took control and did it all on your own. Don't ever forget it. You had to do it without me. I can see that now."

She had been like a mother bird, reluctant to push a fledgling out of the nest. But he had to take off and leave her for a while to prove he was strong on his own.

Jamie reached into his jacket pocket and pulled out a tissue paper packet, tied with a slim piece of ribbon. "I brought you something. I hope you like it."

Claire looked down at the small package, wondering what it could be. She pulled off the ribbon and paper carefully. Jamie was watching her. Whatever it was, she would act thrilled and delighted. She could tell her reaction was important to him.

Finally she unwrapped it. She could see a silver chain and

realized it was jewelry. A piece of amber on a silver chain. "How beautiful," she said, holding it out in her hands to get a good look. "Oh, my goodness . . . is this the beach glass?" she said suddenly. She glanced at him and he quickly nodded, looking very pleased at her surprise.

"I noticed it was gone. I thought you could have taken it but I wasn't sure—"

"I wanted to have it. To remind me of this place," he admitted. "Then I wanted you to have it. To thank you for helping me."

She stared at the gift again and this time blinked back more tears. "This is so beautiful . . . and thoughtful. I don't think anyone has ever given me anything nicer." She reached across the table and gripped his hand. "I'll treasure this, Jamie. Always."

She fumbled a bit with the clasp, but soon had it fastened and patted the amber charm that rested near her heart. "Wherever you go, I'll have this close by, and think of you."

"I'll think of you," he said quietly.

Claire wiped her eyes and rose from the table. She smiled, trying to collect herself.

"Liza should be back soon from the city. You can stay over if you like," she offered. "The inn is empty, except for Avery."

"I'd like to see Liza and talk with her, too."

She knew he really meant apologize to her. Liza would hear him out and appreciate his honesty. She was sure of that.

"I have to leave really early. I have to get back to work tomorrow."

She liked hearing that, the serious way he said it did her heart good. "Oh we don't want to keep you from your job. Believe me. But Portland isn't so far. I hope you'll come down and visit when you can."

"I will. And you can come visit me," he added.

"I would like that very much." She took a clean apron from the hook by the kitchen door, thinking she should start dinner.

"You can help me by going out to the garden and looking for anything ripe that was pushed down in the storm. The gloves and clippers are on the table, right there. And the bushel is back in the barn, in the usual spot."

He rose and headed to the back door. "I missed the garden. I'd like to see how everything's doing."

Everything was doing fine now, Claire thought. They had come full circle.

She knew now that Reverend Ben had been right. She did help Jamie, in her way. She had set him on a good path, though she couldn't walk all the way beside him.

She stood alone in the kitchen, grateful for all the blessings in her life, but most of all, grateful that Jamie was finally finding his way home.

Avery and Mike found the right recipe for romance, but that didn't stop them from having a (mostly) friendly competition as chefs. Now you can taste and rate a special dish from each of them. Avery's is a new take on a favorite comfort food—French toast. Mike's is the crabcakes that have been wowing the crowd at the Lazy Tuna ever since his dad opened the restaurant. As Avery would say, Bon appétit! *As Mike would say, Dig in!*

Baked Apple French Toast from Café Peregrine

2 tablespoons cinnamon
3 tablespoons brown sugar
3 tablespoons white sugar
1 teaspoon nutmeg
3 large apples, almost any variety
(Macintosh, Braeburn, Empire)
1 tablespoon of fresh lemon juice

8 eggs
1 ½ cups whole milk
1 cup heavy cream
1 teaspoon pure vanilla extract
¼ cup maple syrup
1 large loaf of dense quality white bread, whole grain, or cinnamon
(a day old is good but not necessary)
1–2 tablespoons butter

Heat oven to 350 degrees. Butter a baking pan 9 inches by 13 inches. In a small bowl, mix cinnamon, brown sugar, white sugar and ½ teaspoon of nutmeg and set aside.

Peel apples. Remove core and slice. Place in bowl with a tablespoon of fresh lemon juice and toss to coat slices. Add about half of the cinnamon/sugar mixture. Toss again to coat apple slices and let them sit.

Beat eggs in a large mixing bowl. Add milk, cream, vanilla, maple syrup and ½ teaspoon nutmeg. Tear or slice bread into pieces about 1 inch wide and 2 inches long and add to egg mixture. Coat all sides of bread but try not to break bread pieces. Let bread soak up mixture a few minutes. Fold in apple slice mixture and pour all into the baking pan. Dot top with bits of butter.

Cook at 350 degrees about 40 to 45 minutes. When toast looks golden and puffy, a few minutes before completely done, sprinkle on the rest of the cinnamon/sugar mixture and let it cook another 3 minutes until sugar melts.

Serve with maple syrup and butter. This dish can be made ahead and reheated before serving.

Lazy Crab Cakes from the Lazy Tuna

2 pounds lump jumbo crabmeat
1–2 tablespoons butter
½ yellow onion, finely diced
½ red bell pepper, finely diced
1 large egg, beaten
½ cup mayonnaise
1 tablespoon Dijon mustard
1 teaspoon Worcestershire Sauce
1 teaspoon Old Bay seasoning
3 tablespoons fresh dill, finely diced
½ to 1 cup panko breadcrumbs
¼ cup canola oil

Dill Yogurt Dressing

3 tablespoons chopped dill
½ cup plain Greek yogurt
2–3 tablespoons white vinegar
1 tablespoon fresh lemon juice
1 tablespoon water
lemon wedges
Tabasco sauce

Place crabmeat in a large mixing bowl and pick through to remove any bits of shell. (Handle meat gently, do not shred.) Heat 1–2 tablespoons of butter in a sauté pan and cook onion until clear, then add red pepper bits and cook a short time until soft. Set aside.

Add beaten egg, mayonnaise, mustard, Worcestershire sauce, Old Bay seasoning, dill, and onion and red pepper bits to crabmeat.

Gently mix. Refrigerate mixture about 1 hour so it is easier to handle and cakes don't fall apart. Preheat oven to 400 degrees and line a cookie sheet with parchment paper.

Form mixture into cakes about 1½ inches thick and 3 inches wide. Dredge each side in breadcrumbs. Meanwhile, heat about 2–3 tablespoons oil in wide flat pan and when oil is hot (but not smoking), cook cakes a few at a time in pan until brown on each side. If oil gets brown, discard and start fresh. Place cooked crab cakes on the cookie sheet and heat in the oven until heated through, about 2–3 minutes.

Mix all ingredients of Dill Yogurt Dressing and top with a bit more chopped dill. Refrigerate for approximately 30 minutes and serve with crab cakes, lemon wedges, and Tabasco sauce.